BLOOD STORM

BLOOD STORM

A John Henry Cole Western

BILL BROOKS

Skyhorse Publishing

First Skyhorse Publishing edition published 2015 by arrangement with Golden West Literary Agency

Skyhorse Publishing books may be purchased in bulk at special discounts for sales promotion, corporate gifts, fund-raising, or educational purposes. Special editions can also be created to specifications. For details, contact the Special Sales Department, Skyhorse Publishing, 307 West 36th Street, 11th Floor, New York, NY 10018 or info@skyhorsepublishing.com.

Skyhorse® and Skyhorse Publishing® are registered trademarks of Skyhorse Publishing, Inc.®, a Delaware corporation.

Visit our website at www.skyhorsepublishing.com.

10 9 8 7 6 5 4 3 2 1

Library of Congress Cataloging-in-Publication Data is available on file.

Cover design by Brian Peterson

Print ISBN: 978-1-63220-265-9
Ebook ISBN: 978-1-63220-913-9

Printed in United States of America

Chapter One

Two things happened the day John Henry Cole rode into Cheyenne with Frank Straw draped across the back of a stolen roan horse: it rained so hard it crushed men's hats, and Billy Cook, the only other detective besides him working for Ike Kelly's Detective Agency, was shot and killed while taking a bubble bath with a married woman. Ike was waiting for him in front of Shorty's Diner, a false-fronted restaurant squeezed between the White Elephant Saloon and Jacob's Hardware Store. It was a clapboard, unpainted establishment with a plate-glass window and red-and-white-checked curtains. The food at Shorty's was bad, the coffee worse, but Ike Kelly routinely took his meals there. Shorty Blaine was a busted-down cowboy who couldn't cook an egg with the directions written on it, but he had once pulled Ike's carcass out of the Canadian River while on a trail drive and had kept him from drowning. The truth was, Ike couldn't swim any better than Shorty could cook, but Ike figured the least he owed Shorty was his patronage. Ike was a man who believed in loyalty and friendship.

Cole reined in. Water spilled off him and Frank like they were ducks. Ike looked at Frank and said: "I see you got your man."

"What is left of him, anyway," Cole said, feeling the water sluice down the back of his neck. He stepped in under the overhang of the diner. His boots sloshed and the slicker he was wearing seemed alive with yellow light.

"I was hoping you could have brought him in alive," Ike said. Ike Kelly was as tough a man as Cole had ever met. He had killed his share of blood-letters in twenty years of pursuing the law but possessed the disposition of a Quaker when it came to violence.

"Well, I was hoping I could've, too," Cole said.

"You had to plug him?"

"No, sir. He plugged himself," Cole said. He swept his hat off and slapped it against his leg, trying to knock out as much of the weather as he could. He noticed some faces peering out of the diner window at what he had brought back to their town.

Ike's shaggy brows wormed together and he sucked something out of a tooth, no doubt a piece of Shorty's whang-leather bacon, and laid his disappointed gaze on Cole. His eyes were the color of sea water, a warm wet green that the light seemed to float in. "He plugged himself?" Ike shifted his attention to Frank, who was draped like a rug over the blaze-faced roan. It seemed somehow proper that Frank was still on the same roan he had stolen from Ira Priest before he left town. The roan had Ira's initials welted on its shoulder. Its hide was dark and slick from the rain. "Why's he wearing that dress?" Ike wondered. "I thought when I first seen you, you'd killed a woman and brought her back here for me to see."

"Well, that is what he was wearing when I caught up with him," Cole told Ike. He could understand his curiosity about Frank's unusual appearance.

"You want to tell me about it?" Ike's mouth was still working at whatever had stuck in his tooth. He was a clean-shaven man except for long sandy mustaches. His cheeks and neck had the red rawness of a man who had spent his life facing into the sun and wind. Tiny spokes creased outward from the corners of his eyes. Such a look was common in men who had spent a lifetime squinting into the ceaseless sun and the great distances, scouting for danger. Certain things—like a Cheyenne war party, or a

2

tornado, or a fire sweeping across the prairie—were things a man hoped he wouldn't see but all too often did.

"I caught up with him in Julesburg," Cole said, watching the rain water drip from his slicker and collect into puddles around his boots. "He was staying with a woman named Big Tooth Ginny. You know Frank couldn't go ten feet without finding himself a consort. The first place I looked was in the sporting houses. It didn't take long to learn that Frank was in town. Not many men are as handsome as Frank was. I guess it was the one time that being so handsome did not have its reward."

Ike stood staring at what remained of the notorious "Gentleman Bandit"—a sobriquet given Frank by the dime novelist, Ned Buntline. Frank didn't look like much of a gentleman, or a bandit, dressed in a gingham dress with a sprinkle of lace tatted across the bodice and around the cuffs. Ike noticed the round, puckered spot just in front of Frank's right ear, crusted with the color of rust.

The rain percolated in the muddy street and slanted off the edges of the overhangs and danced atop the tin roofs. It sounded like shucked corn hitting the bottom of a wash basin. "I guess one way or the other, Frank was bound for a bad end," Cole said. "After all, I wasn't the only one looking for him. I heard that there was a Pinkerton man from Denver on his trail, also one or two bounty hunters. I heard that King Fisher and Kip Caine were on his trail, too."

Cole saw Ike's eyes narrow at the mention of the Pinkerton man. Ike had once worked for that agency; now they were competition. He wiped a finger across his sandy mustaches and said: "I am not surprised about Caine or Fisher. They would've made good detectives if it wasn't they enjoyed the violent aspects of the work so much." Both men had reputations as man-killers of the first order.

"Anyway, I found Big Tooth Ginny plying her trade with a broken-nosed miner in a crib on Stillborn Alley. You know how

Frank appreciated a woman that could and would work to support him. Women just fell all over themselves to please Frank. Big Tooth was no exception. The miner wasn't happy about my unexpected appearance, and neither was Big Tooth. The miner was still wearing all his clothes because of how cold it gets up there in that high country. But it didn't keep him from his business with Big Tooth."

Ike Kelly pulled his makings out of his shirt pocket with the weariness of a man who had done it a thousand times before and rolled a cigarette, and then offered the makings over to Cole. "So Big Tooth Ginny gave up Frank just like that?" he said through a cloud of blue smoke.

"Not exactly," Cole said.

Ike squinted at him.

Cole was about to go on when three hard shots shattered the peace. He saw Ike stiffen with the instinct of a man who had heard the sound of gunfire plenty of times in his past.

"It sounds like they came from the Inter-Ocean," Ike said, turning in that direction. Cole hurried alongside him as doors popped open in spite of the hard weather, and the idle and curious fell in behind them.

Cole saw City Marshal Leo Foxx come out of the Blue Star Saloon across the street, where he spent the bulk of his time dealing faro. He wore a plug hat, a brocade vest over a freshly boiled shirt without the paper collar, and a fancy little Policeman's Model Colt stuck inside his waistband. Foxx acted reluctant to cross to the other side of the street. He was no doubt contemplating whether to muddy his shoes and the cuffs of his checked trousers. Leo Foxx was a fastidious man like most of his breed— gamblers hired on as the local law. They wouldn't ride out on a posse until they made sure their hair was combed and neatly parted and smelled of rosewater.

"What is it? What's happening over there?" Foxx bellowed.

"Shots!" someone hooted.

Then one of his cronies came up and handed Foxx an umbrella. He popped it open, then crossed the street, carrying it high over his head, tiptoeing like a debutante going to a quadrille. Cole heard Ike grumble under his breath at the appearance of the lawman. They had kept up a running dislike for each other ever since Ike established his detective agency in Leo Foxx's town.

"Don't need more law around here," Foxx had openly complained as he watched the words Ike Kelly's Detective Agency being painted in gold leaf on the small plate-glass window of Ike's office the day Ike went into business. Ike had ignored Foxx's derision, just as he would any man he lacked respect for.

"Fancy name for an old broken-down drover . . . detective," the lawman had derided Ike in the presence of several cronies.

Then with the casual air of a man who had seen too much and done too much, Ike Kelly had said: "I knew you when Harry Longbaugh put a pistol in your ear in a Denver whorehouse and told you to fight or run and you wilted like a rose in winter. Don't trouble me with your nonsense, Foxx . . . you ain't up to a real fight."

There had been bad air between them ever since. Now Foxx tried crowding in the same front door of the Inter-Ocean along with the rest. He smelled like bay rum and sweat. Frank Finn, the desk man, was cowering at the foot of the stairs.

"Mick Bledso . . . went upstairs . . . with a gun in each hand . . . and I guess he has shot Billy Cook and . . . maybe Missus Bledso as well," Finn stammered. A woman was screaming. Several men had come from the bar and stood holding their drinks and long cigars. One man had a napkin tucked down inside his shirt and a drumstick in his right hand.

Ike's jaw knotted and he took the stairs two at a time with Cole on his heels and Leo Foxx somewhere in the rear. A gauze of blue smoke hung in the hallway outside an open door.

Foxx shouted—"This is my jurisdiction!"—but Ike ignored him and stepped into the room with Cole alongside.

Billy Cook was resting in a copper tub of warm water that was turning pale crimson from the ribbons of blood leaking from three dark holes in his chest. His head lay slumped forward, his chin resting on his chest. A cigar floated in the water. A whiskey bottle lay next to the tub, its contents staining the carpet. Mick Bledso was a wealthy cattleman who owned practically everything a mile out in any direction of Cheyenne. He was considered important, a man to be reckoned with. Now he sat on a red velvet settee, insignificant, a smoking pistol in each hand. The smell of nitrate and sulphur filled the room.

Bledso was a man of bulk; he had a head the size of a bull, and close-set eyes. The pistols seemed small in his large hands. He didn't look half so important sitting there like that. Bledso's wife, whose first name was Anita, was too hysterical even to cover herself. She was naked but some of her beauty seemed faded, standing there, hysterical and exposed. She was a tall, slender woman with milk-white skin and bunches of autumn red hair that hung loosely and unpinned down past her soft white shoulders. She had high cheek bones and a long curved neck and dimples. She had pretty eyes as well, even though they were smudged by her tears. It was common knowledge that Mick Bledso had met Anita at a local bagnio called Madam Lou's, and had taken to her like a horse to oats. Anita had what few of her sisters of the working class had—stunning good looks and the keen ability to make any man feel special. She also had a plan to marry the first rich man that came her way. That had been Mick Bledso, a successful man, it seemed, with everything but women. The wedding had been written up in the Wyoming *Weekly Leader* and was the biggest event to take place in the territory that year. Cole hadn't gone, but he'd heard later that Mick had ordered in several hundred pounds of fresh oysters and fifty cases of champagne, among other delicacies. It was said that if Mick hadn't been so eager to get started on his honeymoon, the party might still be going on.

Ike pulled a spread off the bed and wrapped it around Mrs. Bledso and set her in a chair by the doorway with her back toward the tub full of bloody water and Billy. "What happened here?" Ike asked her. His voice was a gentleman's drawl of smooth calmness but one that commanded attention. She dabbed at her eyes, her perfectly curved lips quivering as she tried to regain herself.

Leo Foxx busied himself by wiping the mud off his shoes with one of the hotel's towels.

"We was just . . ." Then she looked over toward her husband and broke into sobs. Mick Bledso looked as stunned as if he had been kicked by a horse. A spot just below his left eye twitched. "Me and Billy . . ." she began again. "We was just . . ."

"I reckon it's plain what you and Billy were doing," Ike said, without the slightest hint of accusation; it would have served no purpose. Ike turned again to look at Billy's corpse and Cole could tell he was disappointed in equal measures at Billy's poor judgment and the fact he was dead. "Well, Foxx, I guess this is your business now," Ike said. "All that can be done has been done." Then he looked at Mick Bledso, whose nearly crossed eyes were looking at something that none of the others could see. "I am sorry that Billy was involved in this, Bledso. But I've never known a good reason to shoot an unarmed man. The least you should have done was let him get to his gun."

Bledso bobbed his head.

"Of course, Billy would've killed you in a fair fight . . . he was one hell of a gun artist. I guess you didn't know what to do, huh?"

When Mick Bledso didn't answer him, Ike concluded by telling Mick he ought to keep his wife at home or put her on the next stage to Denver, whichever was easier.

Cole followed Ike out of the room and down the carpeted stairway. As they reached the bottom of the stairs, Cole saw a row of porcelain cuspidors lined along the ornate oak bar. Behind the bar there was a long mirror etched with frosted cherubs. The waiters all wore white shirts and the bartenders cravats.

"This is some *bon ton* place," Cole said.

"I reckon if Billy could tell us," said Ike, "he'd have wanted to end it in a place like this. He always was a man who liked to live beyond his means. Now he has died beyond them as well."

They walked back down the street to Ike's office. The rain had slackened to drizzle and the wind had shifted east to west and carried with it a sharp chill. Cole was still wet from his ride and was eager to get into some dry clothing. By the time they reached the front of the diner again, a group of callow youths stood in a circle around Frank Straw and the stolen roan. Their eyes were big, and some of them were laughing. Ike paid one of them—a tall, lanky boy with splayed teeth—50¢ to take Frank over to Klingbill's Funeral Parlor and the horse over to the livery. The two men watched as they marched off in a parade, Frank draped over the back of the roan, his skirts blowing in the wind.

They stepped into Ike's office, a small, spare space containing a scarred desk; a swivel chair that, every time Ike sat in it, screeched like cats being kicked; a rack of shotguns and rifles on the wall; the mounted head of a mule deer Ike had shot on an expedition he had helped guide for Bill Cody and the Grand Duke of Prussia; a wash basin on a commode, and a blue china water pitcher with two glasses. The only other item in the room was a Shaker chair hanging on a peg. Cole took it down and sat on it. Ike sat in his swivel chair.

"Need to oil this thing someday," Ike said. He said it every time he sat in it.

8

Chapter Two

A letter lay spread out upon Ike's desk. He motioned to it.
"What is it?" Cole asked.

"The rest of the bad news," he said. "I got it just before the shooting at the Inter-Ocean. It's from a woman I once knew. Go ahead, read it."

"Looks personal," Cole said, before reaching for it.

"No, it's just more trouble," Ike said.

Cole looked at the name on the return address on the envelope before reading the letter. It was from a woman named Lydia Winslow, although at the bottom of the letter she'd signed it Liddy.

Dear Ike,

I can't explain to you how wonderful it was to hear of you residing in Cheyenne. And to receive the news at such a fortuitous time! Dodge seems so long ago.

I hope this letter finds you well & in good spirits. Now for the tragic news I bear you in this letter.

You see, this past summer, I, and a few young women who work for me, arrived in Deadwood. A business venture, but not entirely what you may think. I won't go into details so much at this time. But if you decide to accept my invitation, offer really, to come to my aid, then I will tell you everything.

I will take the chance that we meant something special to each other once. Enough so that you will hear me out, read this to its conclusion before making up your mind as to whether you are willing to risk your life for me. I won't blame you if you refuse.

I won't belabor this longer. Three of my young women have been murdered since our arrival. At first, it was believed the deaths of two of the girls was accidental. But when the third girl (her name was Flora) was found last week—it was unmistakably murder. Without a great deal of proof at my disposal, I am now of the belief that the other two girls were also murdered and made to look like accidents.

I know that it must seem insensitive of me to come to you with my problems after all this time of separation. But when I found you again, I had to take the chance you would hear me out.

However, I've taken the precaution to advertise for someone of experience in this line with the territorial newspapers on the chance that you might not be able to help me.

I hope this letter finds you well and I hope that I hear from you, even if you choose not to come. I understand. Take care, dear Ike. You will always have a place in my heart.

Yrs. affectionately,
Liddy Winslow
No. 24 Front St.
Deadwood, D.T.

Cole placed the letter back on Ike's desk.

"Who is she, Ike?"

"The only woman I ever loved, other than Hester," he said. Cole saw in his stare the pain a man can have in remembering a woman he's loved and lost. He saw it because he'd had the same pain come and go ever since Zee Cole.

"She was young, Irish, beautiful," Ike said as though he'd been asked to describe her. The pain melted into wistfulness. "It was in Dodge City, the last herd I took up there," he continued. Cole listened as Ike let the words flow out, carrying his thoughts, his memories of her. He looked up, his blue-gray eyes watery, hurt. "You know I lost Hester in 'Sixty-Eight, then three years later I lost Wayne . . . you remember Wayne, don't you?"

Cole did. Wayne had been a handsome boy, good-natured, russet hair like his mother, sea-green eyes like hers. He had been killed in Wichita, Kansas on a hot summer afternoon by a deputy city marshal who had said the boy was drunk and firing his pistol off in a dangerous fashion. A coroner's inquest was held and the shooting was termed justifiable. The deputy had quit and left town right after and just before Ike had arrived.

Ike picked up the tintype that was sitting on the corner of his desk and stared at it for a time; the pewter frame shone dully in the low light. Cole of course had seen the picture before; it'd been taken in a Denver photographer's gallery: Wayne sitting against a painted background, wearing a pair of Angora chaps and a wide-brim hat, a cigar in one hand, a Colt Peacemaker in the other— photographer's props. A sly grin on the boy's face revealed just how innocent he had been. He had been a sweet and gentle boy who the prairie came to claim long before it had a right to him.

"Anyway, I went a little crazy after that," Ike said. "After Wayne's killing, I turned to whiskey, and I went looking for the lawman that killed him, only I couldn't find the man. So I found other men instead and took it out on them. Didn't matter who. I just needed to take it out on somebody."

Cole knew that, but he didn't say anything, just listened.

"I took one last herd up to Dodge, that's when I met Liddy. She was working out of one of the houses, you know the ones I'm talking about. I had my pay and my saddle and a bottle, and it was all I figured I needed. Then I met her." He set the tin-type back down carefully from where he'd taken it. His eyes still held onto it long after his fingers set it free. "She was different, Liddy was. For one thing, she was smarter than most. She had dreams and ambition. Dreams was something I'd long forgotten about. But she had something else, too. She had a special way about her, a tenderness I couldn't touch with my anger. And that broke me down." He finally looked away from Wayne's image and down to his own hands. "You know what it's like, a woman that can do that to you? That can be all the things you need, that can see into places so dark in your soul you're afraid to look at them yourself?"

There had been one for Cole, too, his late wife, Zee. "Yeah," he said. "I know what it's like to be with a woman like that."

"Then you know why I fell so damn' in love with her?"

Cole nodded, pulled the makings from his shirt, rolled a shuck, and smoked it there in the dimness of his office, the quiet sucking at their bones for a little while.

"I asked her to marry me," Ike said, his lips curving slightly. "You know what she said?"

"No."

"She said she wouldn't marry a cowboy if a cowboy was the last living man on earth. I asked her why not, and she laughed till she cried. She said she loved me. She said I was the first man to come along that took her heart, but she wouldn't marry me. I asked her why not, and she said . . . 'Don't ask me that if you don't already know.' Well, I already *did* know. I mean, hell, what'd I have to show for my life? What'd any cowboy have to show?" Ile was staring at something in the room only he could see. "The truth was, John Henry, she had brains and ambition and wasn't about to settle for anything less in life than what she wanted, and I couldn't hold that against her. How can you fault a person for knowing what they want? She changed me. Changed me in ways I didn't expect. And by the time we parted, I had lost my hate and taste for getting drunk and mean. I did it because I couldn't touch a person like her with all my force and will, and I knew then and there that there was no point for me trying to go on like I had been. It was time to get up and get moving. Do something worth a damn in my life. It's when I decided to become something, make something of myself, just like she wanted to do for herself. I couldn't fight that. Hell, I admired her."

Then he reached in a drawer and took out a bottle, wiped the dust off with his hand, and handed it to John Henry Cole.

He took it and looked at Ike Kelly.

"I quit drinking for the wrong reasons," Ike said. "This one's for her."

They each took a pull, and then he corked it and placed it back in the drawer.

"You still love her?" Cole asked.

He looked at Cole for a long, full moment, thinking about what he'd just said. Then he smiled and answered: "I'd be lying if I said I didn't, but I can't say I love her in the same way. Too many years have passed."

"Are you going to go and help her with her problem?"

"I want to, but the thing is, I've got several commitments I need to attend to right here. I've given my word to men, and my word is my bond. I've agreed to handle certain matters for them. I can't just drop everything and go to Deadwood, not just yet."

Cole could feel it coming. "You want me to go?"

His look said it all.

Cole thought about the last part of her letter, the part that talked about how she would advertise in the papers. Then Cole thought about the type of men an advertisement like that would attract. He looked at the postmark on the envelope. "This was mailed nearly a month ago," he said.

Ike nodded gravely. "I know."

"I was thinking about men like Fisher and Kip Caine," Cole said.

"Just to name a few," Ike responded. "If Liddy has advertised in the territories, that's the sort of men that will show up. That's another reason why I'd like you to get up there as soon as you can."

"I was thinking mostly of Fisher," Cole said. "He swore he'd kill me the next time we clashed."

"Then I guess, if you run into him, you better shoot him first," Ike said.

"I was hoping I'd left that sort of business behind me in Del Río," Cole said.

Ike smiled politely and said: "You don't ever leave it behind you, John Henry. Not entirely."

Cole knew he was right, of course. A man does what he needs to do, and along the way he makes enemies. King Fisher was one Cole had made in Caldwell, Kansas several years back when Fisher was the law and Cole was a cowboy. It was their first run-in. Then, a year later in Tascosa, Cole was the law and Fisher was the cowboy, and that time Cole had returned the favor by busting him over the skull with a self-cocker for being drunk and disorderly. Fisher hadn't said it to Cole directly, but word spread around later that the next time they met, Fisher would finish him. The last Cole had heard, King Fisher was doing stock detective work up in the Montana Territory, shooting rustlers in the back with a long-range rifle. It was the sort of work that fit him, shooting men in the back.

"Maybe if you could just go and buy me some time," Ike suggested. "Until I can break free here and come up myself."

Cole knew Ike Kelly wasn't a man to ask favors lightly. "I suppose you want me leaving on the next stage out?" he said, half as a joke.

He smiled. "The ticket will be waiting for you."

His handshake was enough to let Cole know Ike appreciated the decision. But something also told Cole they might not see each other again.

Chapter Three

"The Cheyenne and Black Hills stage leaves in the morning. I'd like you to be on it," Ike Kelly said as Cole turned to leave.

Cole thought that the thought of two-hundred and forty-six miles riding in a Concord had all the appeal of being bludgeoned with a Walker Colt, but he knew Ike wouldn't have asked if he'd seen any way around it. "I'll send a wire when I get there," he said.

"Keep a low profile, John Henry. Anyone that would murder women is a man lacking charity. I can't afford to lose another detective. I'm down to my last one." It was a weak effort at humor, dark as it was. "I'll have to leave for Laramie and tell Patterson we brought Frank back," Ike added glumly. "I don't think it's exactly what he was hoping for, buying a dead man."

Phil Patterson had hired the agency to find Frank Straw and return him to Laramie—it had to do with Phil's daughter, Mary, who Frank'd left with an unwanted gift. Mary wasn't the best-looking woman in the territory, or the youngest. Phil had figured the least Frank was going to do was to marry Mary and make an honest woman of her and be a father to the child she was carrying. The way Cole had got the story was that after Mary gave Frank the bad news about her condition, he stole Ira Priest's roan Quarter Horse to make his escape. He also robbed the First Bank & Trust but only got $75 dollars for his effort. But robbing a bank was enough to have a Reward poster for him throughout the territories. That reward was what attracted men like King Fisher and Kip Caine.

As Cole opened the door to step outside, Ike said: "You'll have to tell me the rest of that story about Frank when you get back."

It had stopped raining. The miners, gamblers, prospectors, and teamsters that earlier had been driven indoors by the weather were now drifting back outside again and the town was beginning to get its rhythm back—the rhythm like a defective heartbeat. Cole made his way to the room he kept at Sun Lee's. Sun ran a laundry and let out a back room. Cole thought it more private than the boarding houses, and quieter than the hotels. He walked his gelding over to the livery on the way and had him put up. He saw Ira Priest examining the blaze-faced roan that Frank Straw had stolen from him—the one on which Cole had brought Frank back from Julesburg. Ira was a barrel-chested man with a thick head of carrot-red hair and freckled hands.

"Thanks for returning my horse," Ira said. "I'm glad you killed that son-of-a-bitch. He deserved shooting for stealing my horse." Then he added: "I heard he was wearing a dress?"

Cole didn't bother explaining that he hadn't killed Frank, or the reason for the dress. He was too weary and his bones felt like they still had rain water in them. The barn had the sweet smell of hay and horse and held a warmth that made his weariness even deeper.

Sun Lee was eating watery soup with a spoon when Cole came in. His dark, beaded eyes glistened within the folds of his narrow lids. His long, sallow fingers held the spoon in the way a child would. He was wearing a red silk jacket and cotton pants. He was a man of indeterminate age. The only clue to him was the iron strands that streaked their way through his hair and wispy chin whiskers. Cole calculated him to be several years older than Ike Kelly. That would have put him somewhere in his sixties, but he might as easily have been a hundred.

"Ah, Mistah John Henly . . . you back, eh? You catchee your man?"

"Yeah," Cole answered, not wanting to go into it. To explain how it was that Frank Straw was wearing a dress to a man with Sun Lee's orderly mind was more than Cole had in him at the moment.

"Your loom leady, like alays," he said, a smile like that of an emaciated jack-o'-lantern creasing his face. "You wanne some lice soup?"

"No thanks, Sun. I had something more substantial in mind . . . something that started out with horns and hoofs."

Sun Lee's laughter was a series of short, hard cackles like the laughter of a man who didn't understand something but was happy to laugh anyway. "Ah, Mistah John Henly, you a funny fellow!" The soup sputtered from his lips. It would be hard not to like a man like Sun. He was kind, decent, and hard-working—and he laughed at just about anything Cole said. Cole counted him among his friends.

Leaving Sun to his soup, he went to his room at the back of the laundry. It was small, but clean and well maintained by the old Chinese, and it had a window that looked out on the back alley—not much of a view, but a window nonetheless. He heard the tinkle bell ring out front over the door, heard Sun talking to someone about their laundry, heard the bell ring again, and the door close, then he heard Sun sit back down, heard the rattle of his spoon against the bowl.

He propped his Winchester rifle in the corner, dropped his saddlebags on a chair, and made sure not to lay his hat on the bed. A woman in Ardmore had once told him it brought bad luck, laying a hat on the bed, although he didn't think himself superstitious. Then he removed his Remington self-cocking revolver that he wore in a cross-over holster and the Colt Thunderer he used as a backup, feeling ten pounds lighter. It was a lot of hardware to carry, the Winchester and the two pistols, but not when you needed them. The next order of business was a hot bath and dry clothes.

The barbershop and bathhouse were just two doors down. He took a set of dry clothes along with him and asked Sun if he'd dry out his boots by the stove.

"Oh, yes, Mistah John Henly . . . certainly. Ha, ha, ha."

Ed Harris was a man who could talk milk out of a bull, but he knew how to cut hair and his baths were hot, and, if you got there early enough, the water was still fairly clean. A dollar would get you both a bath and a haircut. Cole preferred to do his own shaving. Ed plied his trade while his man, an old curved-back fellow known as Wayback Cotton—who claimed (every time he was sober or drunk enough to tell it) that he had fought the Blackfeet up in the great Stony Mountains and trapped enough beaver to make all the hats east of the Mississippi River—rasped in a breath that would cause a mule to faint: "I'm fond of fruit wine, you know."

Ed warned him not to disturb the clientele. Cole gave Wayback four bits and thanked him for hauling the water.

"You ought not pay that old man a tip," Ed warned. "It's like feeding a stray cat . . . he'll keep coming back for more."

"Maybe he really did fight the Blackfeet," Cole said.

"The only Indians Wayback ever fought were wearing doe-skin dresses . . . speaking of which, I seen you brought Frank Straw in. What was he doing in a dress and dead as last week's fish?"

"It's a long story. Remind me to tell it to you sometime. Right now, I'd just like a little privacy and to soak the ache out."

Ed was still fighting the temptation to persist when a gambler came in seeking a haircut and shave. It was someone Cole hadn't seen before, but then, that wasn't unusual with the way Cheyenne was filling up with new faces. It was on the road to the gold fields up in the Black Hills and about everything with two legs, a deck of cards, a gold pan, and dreams of growing rich was pouring through.

Cole sank into the water to his chin, then closed his eyes against the steam and let it drag all the weariness out through his pores. It felt like a thousand tiny pinpricks against his skin, but for him it was one of the best feelings in the world. He tried not to think about the long ride to Deadwood. He tried not to think about someone who would kill young women, no matter what the reason, and wondered if maybe the killings had something to do with their profession. Though Liddy Winslow hadn't said exactly what her business was in the letter, Cole had a good idea what it was judging from what Ike had said of her past. He thought of all the names working girls were called by the men who used them: brides of the multitudes, soiled doves, Cyprians, and whores. He thought of another name he'd heard them called, too—fallen angels. Nobody should have to fall that far, he thought, not even angels.

Maybe it was the hot bath water soaking into his tired muscles, but memory took him back to the day he'd received Ike's letter asking him to come to Cheyenne and work for the agency. He had been in Del Río at the time, wearing a badge for the past nine months for a man named Jess Benson, who headed up Del Río's Peace Commission, such as it was. Actually, the Del Río Peace Commission was just Jess and another man named Junebug Brown. The town was scarce on politicians. A week after they hired Cole as city marshal, Junebug Brown got drunk and fell from a wagon and died of a broken neck, leaving the commission a little smaller.

Cole had drifted to Del Río to escape the winters farther north; December and January in the Texas Panhandle can ruin a man on winters. For a time, being the law in Del Río was a nice change of pace from what'd he'd been doing—drifting. The weather was warm, the tequila good, and the *señoritas* plentiful.

One in particular held his attention. She was a working girl, tall and beautiful, with long black hair and deep brown eyes. Her name was Juanita Delgado, and she was all a man could imagine himself wanting or needing. As it turned out, he wasn't the only man who wanted or needed her, nor had he been the only man she had eyes for. That was when the beginning of the end came, the day she introduced him to Francisco Guzman, a border bandit who plied his trade up and down both sides of the Río Grande, but never in Cole's town. Either he had been too blind, or too trusting of Juanita when she said Francisco was a cousin she hadn't seen in a long time. They had spent lots of nights, the three of them, laughing and drinking and going to the local dances.

Cole remembered asking Francisco one night why he'd never pulled a crime in Del Río. He had said the reason was because of the old man, Jess Benson—the one that had hired Cole. Francisco had said he respected Jess and he would never do anything to dishonor him, such as committing a crime while the old man was head of the town's peace commission. He had said Jess used to come to the village when he was a boy and give him and the other children candy, and that Jess and Francisco's mother had once spoken of marriage after Francisco's father had been murdered by the *rurales* in a gunfight.

"Well, that's good to hear," he remembered having told Francisco. "I thought at first it was because you might be afraid of me." It had been a joke between them at the time, but Cole remembered the slightest twisting of his lips as Francisco had replied: "No, my frien', I am not afraid of you." The exchange had been lost in a blare of music, as Francisco had swept Juanita to her feet and onto the cobblestones of the square where the *bailes*, the local dances, were held.

"He ees oonly my cousin, Juan Enrique," he remembered her saying. "We've not seen each odder in a verry long time." He had lifted his glass and saluted them as they had spun to the music.

He had been in love with her. What did it matter if she had missed her cousin? But a week later, Francisco would lie dead on the cobblestones of that same square, and Cole would be nursing a bullet wound to his right leg from Francisco's gun. It was one of those things that happened when you were least expecting it, the sudden violence.

Francisco and Juanita were already dancing when he had arrived late from making his rounds. They had been drinking mescal, laughing, lost in each other's gaze. Cole guessed that's when he had realized that Juanita and Francisco were more than just cousins. How exactly it had flared up between them was still hazy. First there had been a little joking about this closeness of cousins, then a few more words that weren't jokes. Then Francisco had done something he shouldn't have done—he had spoken the truth about him and Juanita. Cole had had just enough tequila in him so that it had hurt, Francisco's truth. Francisco had pushed him. He had called Francisco a name. Francisco had reached for his *pistola*. Cole had reached for his. It had been over in an instant. Juanita had cursed Cole, had cried as she knelt over Francisco, her tears falling onto his face. Some of Francisco's relatives had come across the Río and had taken charge of his body and carried him home to his village in the back of a wagon. It was then that Cole began to hear the rumor that some of Francisco's people were vowing to avenge his death. That was the same week he had received Ike's letter asking him to come to Cheyenne and work as a detective for him. The timing had seemed right. He couldn't find any reason to stay in Del Río.

He remembered limping down to Jess Benson's saddle shop the same morning he'd gotten the letter and read it several times. He wanted to inform Jess personally that he was going to resign his position. Jess hadn't acted surprised. "It's just as well," he had said. "Trouble finds you like thirsty men find liquor."

Cole had thanked him anyway for having hired him and for his kindness.

"Where will you go, *senor?*" he had asked.

"Cheyenne," Cole had told him.

"How is the weather up that way?"

"I hear the winters are cold," Cole had said.

Jess had nodded his head as if that were all he needed to know about Cheyenne. A part of Cole had hoped he would try and talk him out of leaving, that he would make a promise that he and the others who lived in the dusty little town would stand behind him if Francisco's relatives did come and try to avenge his death. Something like: No, *Señor* Cole, you don't have to leave because of those grieving people of Francisco's. We will protect you. We will fight for you." But the only thing Jess had said when Cole had handed him his badge had been: "I have a brother-in-law who needs a job. I guess now I can give him yours."

So Cole had packed everything he owned into his saddlebags, threw his $40 saddle on his $20 horse, and said *adiós* to Del Río. But before he had cleared the town's limits, he had stopped by to see Juanita one last time. She was back working at The Conquistador Club when Cole had ridden up. It must have been a slow day because she wasn't with a customer at the time.

"I'm leaving Del Río," Cole had said.

"Do you expect me to cry, beeg me to stay?" she had asked sullenly.

"Why didn't you tell me the truth about you and Francisco to begin with?" Cole had asked. "It might've saved us all some grief."

"Because a woman has her beauty onnly soo long," she had said.

"What the hell does that have to do with anything?" he had asked.

"I wanted you both, because you both found me desirable, and I know someday I won't bee beautiful any loonger and no man weell want me when that day coomes. Ees there soometing wrrong in wanting what you want?"

Cole had thought that a good question. Three weeks later he had arrived in Cheyenne.

Now, he was sitting in a tub with the water growing cold and the whiskey bottle he had showing empty. It was time to go nab a few hours' rest before heading to Deadwood. He figured Deadwood couldn't be any worse than a lot of other places he'd been.

Chapter Four

Morning came with the shuddering force of someone opening a trap door and dropping Cole through it. He had
slept the sleep of the dead, and, when Sun Lee shook him awake,
he had fully forgotten where he was. His hands instinctively
searched for something with which to defend himself. The war
had done that to him. The war had done a lot of things to a man.

The war could make a man so tired he would gladly fall
asleep in a trench of rain water, caring not whether he drowned,
for sleep became everything. It wasn't just the exhaustion of the
limbs that made a man so tired; it was the exhaustion of the mind
as well. And when a man did fall asleep, it wasn't really like sleep
at all as much as it was a great falling into hell. That kind of sleep,
that temporary death, carried with it the shock of reawakening,
of being jolted back into the temporal world. And often, such an
awakening was to the thunder of cannon and a thousand butternuts coming out of fog-enshrouded woods, their voices raised
in a single yell that crawled down your spine and clawed at your
groin. And you knew they were coming to kill everything in their
way, including young Union boys in blue tunics who had taken
to sleeping in rain-water graves.

"Mistah John Henly, you gotte get up now. You telley me to
wake you up. It is Sun."

His hands stopped searching and he swallowed against the
thumping of his heart. The old Chinese grinned hugely at him,
then left and returned with a tin cup of coffee that was hot
enough to boil shirts in. He smelled like incense and his silk

jacket whispered against itself when he handed him the coffee. "You leave this morning, Mistah John Henly?"

"Deadwood," he said.

"Why so?" Sun was curious as a two-headed cat.

"Business," he said.

"Ah," Sun said, as though that explained everything. Then he grinned again and said: "You don't look so good, Mistah John Henly."

He got dressed, walked down to the livery, and got his saddle, and then walked over to the stage office. The air was fresh and clean, the sky crisp and blue. Far to the east he could see the fringe of the cloud blanket that had passed over the day before. He could smell autumn coming down from the aspens high up in the Medicine Bow Mountains.

A round-trip ticket was waiting for him, just as Ike Kelly had promised. The office contained two benches, a regulator clock with a brass pendulum, a calendar with a rendering of a young woman holding a can of Arbuckle's coffee, and a single spittoon that needed emptying. A small cast-iron stove with nickel plating and some of the isinglass busted out heated the room against the morning chill. The place was so dry you could smell the dust.

Cole looked over his fellow passengers. A gambler stood by the window. He was wearing a claw-hammer coat and carried a leather kit under his arm that probably contained the tools of his trade. The weight of a small pistol bulked the inside breast pocket of his coat. Sitting on a bench was a frail young man in buckskins whose fine-boned features were drawn tightly as though he carried with him troubles or was expecting some. He wore a tan Boss-of-The-Plains Stetson that looked too much hat for him. Across from him, sitting on the other bench, was a woman and what was obviously her daughter, judging by the way they each had the same corn-silk hair and china blue eyes. He guessed the woman to be in her late twenties, the girl six or seven. The woman wore a small black velvet bonnet trimmed in scarlet, and so did the little girl. They both wore cloaks over their tie-back dresses. It was hard to imagine why a woman and her daughter would be going to the Black Hills, unless she had a husband there—or was in search of one. A dark-skinned man of solid, square build squatted on his heels in the corner. He looked to be part Mexican, with some other blood thrown into the mix. He carried a blanket roll and wore a wide-brimmed sombrero of dirty gray that shaded a good part of his features. He watched Cole from under that hat and Cole had the feeling that he was having some hard thoughts about his presence. He wore a corduroy jacket over a threadbare cotton shirt and faded Levi's. His boots were scuffed and run-down at the corners of the heels. He seemed not to breathe.

Cole walked back outside, set down his Dunn Brothers saddle, and rested the Winchester rifle in the crook of his arm while waiting for the stage to come. He had taken the liberty to wear a linen duster as protection against the boil of dust the Concord would raise if the weather stayed dry. He was traveling light out of necessity. He carried only one extra shirt in his saddlebags along with spare ammunition, a Barlow knife, and clean socks. The duster would cut down on his need to change and still allow him a presentable appearance. He checked the time on his Ingersol: it was 6:50. He saw the driver, a man named Jake Goodlove, and his guard, a fellow named Gyp Taslow, leave the diner where they no doubt had eaten their breakfast. He watched as they shuffled across the street and down to the livery. Gyp Taslow carried a twin-barrel shotgun—the tool of his trade.

In twenty minutes, they brought the Concord up pulled by a four-horse team, all bay horses except the right lead, a thick-chested dun. In a half hour more, they were rolling out of Cheyenne on their way to the Black Hills and already were being bounced senseless. The road was a line of ruts and rocks. Cole had picked a seat next to the door. The woman with the blue-eyed child sat next to him, her daughter alongside her. Directly across from him sat the gambler, his eyes full of disinterest. Next to him sat the slender young man wearing buckskins. To his right sat the Mexican. Cole had gotten a closer look when he'd climbed aboard the stage. He had light gray eyes but the cheek bones of an Apache. He had been right about his mixed blood.

The sun chased them that day, and three times they stopped to change horses and twice to eat—except for the Mexican, who stayed to himself, whether too poor to afford the price of a meal or too disinclined, Cole couldn't be certain. He did notice that he wore a thin silver bracelet around his wrist and always kept his blanket roll close by. Cole figured the blanket held a short-barreled gun, maybe a carbine. Something small bulged in one pocket of his jacket—most likely a pistol nearly the same size as the one the gambler carried. Cole opined he was trouble waiting to happen.

At the last stop of the day, the stationmaster, a big German named Gauss, came out to greet them. A large-boned, apple-cheeked woman accompanied him. Cole took her to be his wife. She said her name was Helga, and then she showed them where to place their things inside the log hut that doubled as a hotel. Afterward, she showed them where they'd take their supper—at a long table outside fashioned out of lodgepole pine. There were the benches on either side of it. The shadows from the trees crossed the yard. Cole noticed while they ate that the German kept staring over at the kid in buckskins while the wife talked nonstop about the privations of living so far away from civilization.

"Der savages are on da loose, ya know," she said. "Dey could come any time and kill us all in our beds!"

Cole saw the way that took effect on the woman with the little girl, saw the way the little girl's eyes filled with firelight and fear.

"Helga! Shut yer damn' talk vid tellin' of der Indians, eh!" Gauss ordered, his mouth full of half-chewed food that flew from his lips when he spoke.

Then, as though unaffected by her husband's angry chastisement, Helga fell to talking about the dresses the woman and girl were wearing and about how she only had but a few flour dresses to wear herself, being so far out on the frontier and away from any of the towns. The whole while the German kept his stare on the kid.

The rain came hard that night again, a storm out of nowhere. The white flashes of lightning danced through the sleeping quarters, a long room divided by blankets strung over rope to provide the women with a modicum of privacy. The crash of thunder exploded overhead like cannon shot. Cole could hear the little girl crying because of the storm and knew her fear from a long time ago—the same fear he had heard when the thunder of real cannon and the rain of shrapnel had torn through the trees at Cold Harbor and other killing places. Fear comes to each in different ways. Cole wanted to draw back the blanket and tell the little girl that it was all right, that the storm wasn't going to harm her. Then he heard her mother say: "It's OK, Tessie, it's just rain. It won't hurt nothing. I won't let it." The little girl stopped sobbing and Cole wondered what fate awaited her in life, what other fearful things she might come to know.

Cole stepped outside and stood under the only overhang of the log structure and watched the silver wire of lightning dance through the sky. Like a photographer's flash against the landscape, the brilliance of the storm caused the rain to look like falling dimes. He made himself a shuck and smoked it, felt the dampness crawl against his skin, and remembered a surgeon's tent where he had lain face down on a table while pieces of Confederate lead were dug out of his back. A rain like the one that was falling now had snapped against the tent's canvas and spilled under the edges, turning the ground into a soup of mud and blood that slathered the surgeon's boots. He remembered thinking that it was his baptism into this world, or maybe the next.

He finished the shuck and ground it out under his heel. That was when he saw the stationmaster climb out of the stage, buckling his belt. His features were frozen under a sudden flash of lightning, making his big frame ghostly. Cole watched him head back toward the front of the hotel as he leaned into the shadows. Then the kid climbed out of the stage. He looked frail and thin, and he walked as if he was somehow wounded—his movements jerky, erratic in the popping light of the storm. Then the long darkness swallowed him, and, when the lightning flashed again, he was gone. It was something Cole wished he had not seen. He waited for a time until he thought everyone was settled back inside again, then returned to his bunk and grabbed what sleep was left to him. He tried hard not to think about the kid and the stationmaster.

The next morning, he saw the Mexican squatting by the water tank when he came out. The sky had cleared to a flawless blue and the hint of a warm wind blew out of the south, taking with it the heavy, sweet smell of the corrals. The Mexican looked at him without moving his head, his eyes shifting with Cole's movements. Cole washed his hands and face at a pump, ran fingers through his hair, and replaced his hat.

He saw the gambler stepping out of the privy; the woman and little girl went in next. The kid stood by the corrals, one foot hitched on the lower rail, watching the horses as though he did not want to show his face to the rest of the travelers. The smell of fried bacon came from the main room of the station; its scent crawled down into Cole's belly. He went to the kitchen and took a plate and filled it, then went back out and sat down at the long table. The kid stayed at the corral while the rest ate breakfast. Cole saw the German looking in the direction of the corrals several times. The German had close-cropped thick hair and a large forehead that rested atop a nose that was thick and flattened against his ruddy features. He had the sort of face you didn't enjoy looking at. His heavily muscled forearms rested atop the table as he ate. Cole saw fresh scratches on them. He thought of what he'd seen the night before. Then he looked at the German's wife. *The secrets we keep*, he thought.

In forty minutes, they were back to getting their bones rattled within the confinement of the Concord. The little girl whined, then slept with her head in her mother's lap. The gambler looked annoyed. Dust climbed through the open windows and the canvas shades were unrolled to keep it to a minimum. They went along another half hour like that, then it happened.

Cole heard the driver say—"Whoa!"—to the team, and the stage lurched suddenly, then slammed to a stop so hard it threw the gambler and the kid halfway out of their seats. The Mexican had somehow braced himself. The little girl instinctively started to cry. Cole's attention stayed on the Mexican. His face seemed to grow darker under that big hat and his eyes caught pinpoints of light enough to let Cole know he was watching Cole as well. Cole saw then that he had dropped the blanket off the carbine; he had it aimed at the center of Cole's belt buckle.

The woman coughed against the dust and the gambler's gaze was full of anticipation as he and the kid struggled to regain their seats. The kid kept his eyes lowered. The little girl said— "Mama?"—and she hushed the child with a finger to her lips. Someone outside the stage said—"Get the hell out here!"—then a face appeared just below the window where Cole was sitting. The face had a red kerchief wrapped over it, and, when he jerked open the door, the Mexican shot him through the kerchief. Cole had no time to figure it out as he pushed the woman to the floor. She pulled the child down with her. The Mexican dived out one side of the coach; Cole dived out the other.

There were three men still sitting their horses as Cole tumbled out of the coach behind the bandit the Mexican had shot through the face. Confusion helps the disadvantaged in such instances and Cole came up, firing the Remington. He saw two of his shots kick up dust from the coat of a man sitting a paint horse. He threw up his hands and fell backward over his mount's rump, and landed in a heap. The explosion of the guard's shotgun roared overhead, and Cole saw the effects of his Greener as it snatched one of the riders out of his saddle and flung him to the dust. He rolled over and tried to sit up. The front of his shirt was ripped by a dozen blood spots the size of nickels. He said nothing; he just simply fell back and died.

The remaining bandit fired off several wild shots at the only thing he was sure to hit—the Concord. He was still firing wildly as he wheeled his horse around and raked its flanks with his heels. He was maybe fifty yards away when the Mexican stepped into the middle of the road, and, as calmly as if he were aiming at a prairie chicken, fired his carbine. The rider slumped forward, nearly lost his seat, but somehow managed to hold on. Before the Mexican could reload another shell into the breech of the carbine, the wounded rider was too far out of range. Then the woman inside the coach screamed.

The kid sat slumped on the floor of the coach. A ribbon of blood trailed down from under his hat and over his smooth face, staining the front of his shirt. One of the bandit's shots had pierced the coach, and struck the kid somewhere in the head just above the hairline. The gambler, who had not left his seat, said: "I think that boy is as dead as a rose in winter."

The Mexican came around and with Cole they carried the kid out of the coach and laid him upon the ground. Cole had taken hold of the upper half of the kid, and, when he did, he felt something that surprised him—the kid had small but very firm breasts. The scene of the previous night between the stationmaster and the kid coming out of the coach flashed through Cole's mind. The bullet had plowed a deep crease across her scalp but left the kid's brain's intact—bloody but not fatal. Cole wiped her face with a linen hanky provided by the woman and wrapped the kid's head in a piece of the extra shirt he'd carried in his saddlebags.

"He'll live," Cole said, figuring it wasn't up to him to give away her secret. She obviously had her reasons for posing as a man. They put her back in the coach, and then took tally of the work upon the bandits. Two were dead. The one Cole had shot would be joining them soon, judging by the way the blood was frothing from his lips. Cole had seen enough men shot through the lungs to know he wasn't going to make it.

The Mexican knelt by the dying man and said in good English: "What is your name and who are these others?"

The man looked into his face and uttered: "Why the hell should I tell a damn' greaser anything?"

The Mexican reached over and took a Colt Army Model revolver from the man's outstretched hand and stuck it in inside his waistband. Cole guessed he figured the dying man wasn't going to need it any more.

"Well, you are dying, *señor*. And two of your friends are already dead, and the other one is carrying one of my bullets. It seems you have had an off day. Do you believe in God and Jesus Christ?"

The man's eyes filled with a mixture of contempt and confusion.

"Do you?" the Mexican repeated.

"Hell, no!"

"Then I feel sorry for you, *amigo*, for in a short time you will have to answer to Him. Maybe He will forgive you. I won't." Then the Mexican stood and walked back to the coach.

The woman asked if we would bury the dead men. The driver said he'd send someone back at the next stop.

She asked about the one who wasn't dead yet.

"We'll leave him a canteen of water," Cole said. "That is about all we can do for him. He won't live long enough to drink it all." He saw the way her eyes glistened with the tears forming in them. The terror had left her little girl mute and clinging to her skirts. Sudden violence has a way of blowing out the flames of innocence and leaving the soul a darker place. Yet such violence on the frontier was a common event, like a wildfire or a killing snowstorm or a cyclone. There wasn't much you could do about it when it happened. The mother would have to try somehow to explain it to the little girl once she understood it herself.

They lifted the kid back inside the coach, still unconscious. She didn't weigh more than a hundred pounds. With her hair cut short and her slender frame hidden under the buckskins, it was easy to see how she could pass for a boy. Cole wondered, if when she awoke, she would regret her decision.

The gambler volunteered to ride on top of the coach so that the kid had more room to stretch out. The Mexican started to climb in.

"Tell me something," Cole said.

He turned, looked at Cole with those dark expressionless eyes.

"Deputy United States Marshal Miguel Torres," he said. "I'm on my way to Deadwood on private business." When he saw the next question form itself in Cole's gaze, he said: "I thought maybe you were trouble from the way you were armed. This country's full of blood-letters. I thought maybe you could have been one of them. I'm a cautious man." Then he stepped into the coach.

The ride to Deadwood was proving to be full of surprises. Cole had started out thinking he was only going to be shaken to death over the next couple of hundred miles. Instinct and experience should have warned him that nothing is ever as simple as it first seems. Going to find a killer would be no exception.

Chapter Five

For the next three days, the routine changed little, except the dust and the heat seemed to chase them all day and everyone in the coach was smelling gamy because of the lack of facilities. The jolts and jars of the trip were enough to fray the nerves of a *padre*. The kid had regained her senses by late the same evening that she'd been wounded, but she said her head felt like it had been split open by a maul.

"You're lucky," the gambler had told her. "An inch lower and you'd have had a third eye to see out of." He wasn't much on sympathy or kindness, qualities unknown to his profession.

Deputy U.S. Marshal Torres continued to keep to himself, forgoing conversation or the company of the others. The woman, who had said her name was Suzanne Smith and that her child's name was Tess, made several attempts to engage Marshal Torres in conversation. He expressed little interest in her efforts. She was more than a little grateful to him for helping to save her and the child from, as she had stated in a whisper, "abuse of an unspeakable nature" at the hands of the men who'd held up the stage.

"What is your name, sir?" she asked Cole, after several failed attempts with the deputy as the coach rocked along a smooth stretch of the Belle Fourche—the first decent piece of road they'd encountered since leaving Cheyenne.

"John Henry Cole."

She seemed to roll the name over in her mind, as though testing the sound of it. Her dress showed white salt stains of sweat, and strands of her dark hair had come loose from under the feathered hat she wore. Dust smudged her cheeks. Cole had to feel for her; she looked like a woman that was accustomed to regular bathing and toiletry—uncommon luxuries on the frontier. The trip must have been harder on her than on anyone except for the child, who seemed each day to lose a little more of her energy and tolerance for the rough, hot ride. Finally she said: "Cole. That is a good strong name. Is it Irish?"

"No, ma'am. Mostly English . . . at least my elders were."

She smiled softly.

"I apologize for the error."

"No need," he assured her. "If the truth were told, there's probably some Irish mixed in as well."

"Well, anyway, Mister Cole, I want you to know how terribly grateful I am that you and Mister Torres fought off those men. There is no telling what might have occurred had they been successful in their attempt to rob us." Her eyes lowered, diverting away from the obvious thoughts she was tendering about the bandits. Cole wanted to say that there was little chance that the hold-up men would have taken advantage of her. He wanted to say that those poor bastards were just after the money, but he couldn't be sure that was all they were after. The little girl, Tess, rested her head on her mother's lap, her eyes half closed in that dreamy state of exhaustion and boredom that comes from a whole lot of doing nothing. "It's none of my business," Cole said, "but Deadwood seems like a hard place to take a child."

Her hand stroked the little girl's head, her long fingers pale against the child's raven hair. "My man is there."

She didn't say husband. She said *man*. Cole wasn't sure if the way she said it was intentional. He saw no wedding band on her finger. She seemed too fragile, like an expensive vase, to be going to a place like Deadwood, even if it was to meet a man. But he'd known women to be fools when it came to love. Then again, love often made fools of everyone. He thought briefly of Del Río and

Juanita Delgado. He smiled at her and said: "Well, I'm sure he is anxious to see you both again."

She didn't return the smile. He let the topic die in the air between them.

The last night on the road, they stayed at a way station twenty miles outside Deadwood. The Black Hills surrounded them, their slopes dark with the ponderosa pine that grew forty and fifty feet high; the sun cast their long shadows over the road. And when the sun set, the hills claimed their name, their blackness growing deep and complete.

Cole took his usual leave from the confinement of the station house and stepped out into a black night that was whitewashed end to end with stars. A cock-eyed quarter moon rested just above the spiny tops of the trees. The air was cold enough for him to see his breath and it made his heart beat just a stroke faster. He saw the Mexican lawman squatted at one corner of the log house, his blanket draped across his shoulders, the carbine resting across his knees. He walked over, knowing he was uninvited and held out his tobacco and cigarettes.

"Smoke?"

He took a short, sharp breath inward and let it out through his nose. "You don't look to me like a gambler," he said. "And you're sure not a miner." It was then that Cole could smell the whiskey coming off him. "I figure you for a *pistolero* . . . a hired hand of someone."

"I'm just offering you a smoke, Deputy," Cole said, wondering why he had bothered making the effort.

"You were cool under fire when those men tried to take the stage. You hit your man with both shots. I couldn't place more than two fingers between the marks. What's your game?"

"Nothing," Cole said. "Forgive me for disturbing your rest." He started to turn to find a quiet spot to smoke his shuck.

"Sure, I'll share your makings," Torres said. "I've tried to give up the habit, but I can't seem to find a good enough reason."

Cole extended the tobacco pouch and papers again and this time he took them, rolled himself a cigarette in neat fashion, and handed back the makings. He pulled a match out of his jacket pocket and struck it against the buckle of his belt. The flame danced white, then blue, in a flash of light, and, when he snapped it out, Cole eyes had to readjust.

"I'm a cautious man, Cole. I have to be in my business. It's caution or the boneyard for men like me. Don't take it personal that I'm trying to get a tag on you. I just need to know who I'm keeping company with."

He had a drawl to his voice that Cole had often heard down along the border and wondered what he was doing this far north. The tip of the cigarette glowed red against his dark features. He had a thin silky mustache, black, untrimmed. The mustache, along with those Apache cheek bones, added menace to his countenance. The smell of liquor on him just made him seem a bit more dangerous. "I'm not any of those things you mentioned," Cole told him. "I'm just a fellow doing a favor for an old friend." Lawman or not, Cole felt it necessary to keep his business private.

The lawman pulled something out from beneath the blanket, held it forth. Cole saw then it was a bottle. "Drink?" he said.

"What is it?"

He snorted. "It's commonly referred to as Mexican Mustang Liniment. It's better than most doctors you could get in this country. They claim it cures everything, including nightmares and carbuncles. It steadies the hand and steels the nerve, or so it is widely advertised."

It was cheap alcohol that burned the tongue and throat and sent a fire down into the belly, but it warded off the chill air. After taking a swig, Cole handed it back to him.

He tipped the bottle to his mouth and took a long, hard swallow, then wiped his lips with the back of his hand. "Night is a fascinating time," he said.

"It can be."

"Night is when the thief comes. The Bible says that death will come to us like a thief in the night. There is more to night than just the darkness. There is the darkness of men's souls." As he spoke, his voice was sinking in tone. "The darkness of the night attracts the darkness in a man's soul. Like attracts like. Night is the time of evil, is the time when the innocent sleep and the guilty do their dirty business. Predator and prey."

"You don't talk like a border marshal," Cole said.

Again he snorted, drew on the cigarette, blew it out through his nose. "I was educated back East at a school for Apache kids. I had four years of college and wearing shoes and neckties and white shirts and acting like a white man to prepare me for this," he said, waving the bottle in one hand, the moon's light reflecting off the brown glass. "Only thing was, I wasn't a white man and I wasn't an Apache, either, although I had a little of both running through my veins. Even got some German blood. Don't ask me how or when all those folks got together with my Mexican side, but they did. I learned to speak Latin in that school and can still speak it some, although I find little need for it in my line of work." He paused, drew in a breath of the smoke, put the bottle to his mouth, and took another swallow. "I also have the failing of talking too much when I have been drinking." If he was drunk, he held his liquor well. "I am the first Mexican Indian white man hired as a United States Deputy Marshal as far as I know. I guess they don't get many of my type applying for the job."

"I didn't mean to pry," Cole said.

He waved the hand holding the bottle, then offered it to again to Cole. When Cole declined a second drink, he had at it some more, his teeth flashing white in the dim light. He finished its contents in one long swallow, then dropped it to the ground where it clinked off a rock. "I like what I do, Cole. I'm good at it. I've got more education than most white men I know, but it doesn't mean spit. As far as most are concerned, I'm just a damn' *mestizo* . . . a man of color, less valuable than a mule. But wearing this badge changes some of that." He pulled back the lapel of his corduroy coat and touched a small nickel badge pinned to his shirt. "This," he said, "helps keep things even."

He stubbed out his cigarette, and Cole finished his. The blackness closed in on them again. The door of the hotel opened and closed again on a pair of dry hinges. Cole turned his attention to the sound. It was the girl in buckskins. She walked to the corrals where the horses stood, sleeping head to rump, and rested her forearms on the top rail. She looked small and shadowy in the night light. Miguel Torres had fallen silent, his breathing deep. The Mexican Mustang Liniment had done its work.

Cole walked over to where the girl was. She heard his approach and turned, startled.

"You don't have to be afraid," Cole said. "I was just having myself a smoke. How's the head feeling?"

She seemed to shrink in his presence and he wondered if it was a mistake to have approached her in such a manner. "You ain't going to hurt me, are you?" she asked.

"No. I just came out to have a smoke, like I said."

She touched the side of her face with her right hand as though it were hurting. Cole wasn't quite sure what to say to her. "It's none of my business," he said, "but this country is a hard place at best. I can help you get back to Cheyenne or Denver or wherever it is you are from, if it's a matter of money."

She looked at him, the moon's light touching her face, her head slightly tilted, the dry stain of blood dark against her buckskin shirt. "I need to get to Deadwood," she said.

"I can't imagine why."

She had the nervousness of a deer about to run off. "It's a personal matter," she said.

"It's not worth having to do what you've had to do to make it this far," he said. Her features grew stiff; he saw her swallow hard.

"What would you know about anything?" she asked.

"I know you are not a boy," he said. "And I saw you and the stationmaster the other night. I didn't want to see it, but I did. You're too young to have to prostitute yourself. Let me buy you passage back to your home."

Her shoulders slumped noticeably. Cole thought she might fall down. He took a step toward her, and she took a step backward. "Don't touch me!"

"I wasn't going to."

"I didn't prostitute myself," she said, her words fluttering out like wounded birds struggling for flight.

"It's none of my business," Cole said. "Life is hard enough for most of us as it is. I wasn't trying to judge you. I just wanted to help."

"I was out looking at the horses," she said. "He came out, took hold of me, told me not to fight him. I begged him . . ." The words caught in her throat, and she turned her face away from him.

"You don't have to explain," he said.

"No! I do. I have to explain to someone!"

"OK."

"He forced me into the coach. He knew. Somehow, he knew that I was a female."

"Maybe. Maybe not. Men like that . . ."

"No. He said he knew I was pretending to be a boy, but that he could see right off that I wasn't. He said that his old woman couldn't pleasure him any more, but that I could. He was too strong. He hurt me. He hurt me in ways I can't tell you . . ."

Cole reached out and put his arms around her. She trembled like the frightened child she was. "You don't have to explain any more," he said. Her crying was something soft, muted, like the wind stirring in the tops of trees. Only the sound came from a deep and broken place, a place that might never be mended again.

"I can't go back," she said. "Not yet, anyway."

"Then you'll need to protect yourself," he said.

"I don't know how."

"I'll show you."

"You won't tell anyone about me?"

"No. It's your secret. But remember, if Gauss could see through your disguise, so will other men like him. Keep a caution, always. Don't trust anyone."

She stepped away from Cole, looked at him with those innocent, hurting eyes, and said: "Not even you?"

"I think you already know the answer to that. I don't think you'll have to worry about Deputy Torres, either."

She reached out and touched the wrist of his left hand. The hoot of an owl drifted out of a tree; its sound was primitive and lonely and crawled under the skin.

"My name is Rose," she said.

Chapter Six

Before they parted, Cole took the Colt Thunderer backup with the two-and-a-half-inch barrel from his shoulder holster and gave it to Rose. "It's got small grips," he said. "But it's enough power to stop a man, even one the size of Gauss, should you need to use it."

She seemed reluctant to take it, her hands lying at her sides, not reaching for the nickel-plated pistol that looked like silver in the moonlight.

"You don't have to wear it openly," he said. "Wear it in the pocket of a jacket."

He opened the cylinder, showed her the empty chamber that he kept the hammer on and the five remaining shells. "It's a single-action. You need to thumb back the hammer before you can fire it." He ejected the cartridges and showed her how. "Just aim it like you would your finger, hold it steady while you squeeze the trigger." The hammer snapped down with a hard click. He took hold of one of her hands and placed the pistol in it. "It's up to you, Rose."

She tried it, her thin frame silhouetted like a black paper cutout, her arm extended, pointing the pistol toward nothing more than darkness.

"Just squeeze it slowly, don't pull," he said. The hammer fell on the empty chamber. She didn't flinch, but the barrel of the pistol dropped noticeably. "Try it again," he said. The second time was better; the third was better still. "How does it feel?" he asked.

"It's heavy for such a small gun," she said, lowering the revolver to her side.

"You'll get used to it."

"I don't know if I will," she said, looking at the pistol in her hand as though she couldn't comprehend its meaning.

"Remember what Gauss did to you," he said. "There are other men who would do the same if given the chance. It's your decision. I won't force you to take it."

Cole saw her close her eyes against the memory, the pain that came with the memory. He waited for her to decide.

She held out her hand for the cartridges. He placed them in her palm and watched her slip them, one by one, into the chambers, snap shut the cylinder. It looked larger than it was in the smallness of her hand.

"Remember, keep the hammer on an empty chamber," Cole said. "And practice shooting it so that you get used to the feel of its kick . . . and so you can hit what you are aiming at."

She looked doubtful.

"It's not that difficult," he said. "The trick is not to be afraid. A pistol is a close-range weapon. Aim at the largest part of your target . . . the chest. Not many shootists can hit anything with a pistol at more than forty feet. Not under fire they can't."

She let out her breath all at once.

"The thing is, you may not have to use it at all. But if you do, at least you'll have it, and, with some practice, you'll be able to hit what you're aiming at. Real important in a gunfight." He tried to put a touch of humor on it, but wasn't sure he'd succeeded.

She looked at Cole then, the faintness of her eyes seeking his own. Her breathing was soft, like the muted purr of a cat. "Why is it," she said, "that some men can be like Gauss and others like you?"

"The world is made up of all sorts of men, Rose. Why we are who we are is just a matter of luck of the draw, I suspect. I don't know the true answer."

"You are very kind," she said.

"I'm not a saint, Rose. I just don't like to see people get hurt. It's real important you learn how to shoot that piece and protect yourself, especially in a place like Deadwood. Don't count on the kindness of others to protect you. It's a hard fact, but one you need to be aware of." He saw the softness go out of her eyes.

"I suppose you are right, Mister Cole."

"You can call me John Henry, I prefer it. Mister Cole makes me sound old, even if I seem that way to you."

Again she touched the back of his wrist. The bones in her hand and fingers were as small and delicate as a bird's.

"I reckon we had better get some sleep," he said. "We still have twenty miles tomorrow in that Concord."

She hesitated before removing her hand. "I will pay you for the pistol once I get to Deadwood and get settled."

"No need. It was a gift to me in the first place." He didn't tell her that it had once belonged to a Creek policeman over in the Nations whose wife had used it to murder him in a quarrel over an octoroon woman. The wife had sold it in order to pay for her husband's funeral. It had cost Cole $25. He had liked the way it balanced in his hand and didn't mind paying the extra for it. He had owned it for several years as a backup.

"It's generous of you," she said. "I don't know how to thank you."

"Just stay alive, Rose. Don't let anyone harm you. And when your business in Deadwood is finished, go back home. Go back to people who love you and will care for you. This country is no place for someone like you."

Cole stood there in the cold night air for a while after she had left and thought about another young woman he had once known who was in some ways much like Rose in her delicacy and her pain, and in his wanting to protect her. Only he hadn't been able to. It was a memory he had tried hard to keep tucked away, like a tintype kept in a drawer under some shirts. But Rose's vulnerability had dredged up the memory of Zee Cole and he saw his late wife's face behind the lids of his eyes as he closed them. And the softness of her voice whispered to him like the wind easing through the trees.

John Henry, I don't want to leave you. I don't want to leave little Tad. Please, make it so I don't have to leave you both. John Henry . . . promise me that you will take care of our son and that you will never forget me and that you will tell him about me. Will you tell him about me? Will you remember me always as I was? Please, please, please.

They were her last words to him, and now they tumbled through his head like loose rock breaking down a mountainside, each word bruising his soul. She had died that night and took some of him with her. Their infant son died two days later, taking most of the rest of what was left of him. They called it the milk sickness. He had never understood it or tried to beyond what it had cost him. Someone once said: "That which does not kill you, makes you stronger." He was not so sure.

Cole could hear Torres's breathing from across the way. It was deep and sonorous now, the rhythmic sound of the exhausted or the drunken. But he had the feeling that he was a man who would awaken instantly if approached. Men like Torres never slept the sleep of the dead. Instead, they rested somewhere just below the surface of consciousness, their framework tuned to the slightest noises, their nerves frayed as the cuffs of their shirts. Men who could kill you while you were still sleeping.

The night was blue-black and empty, the stars pinpoints of light, and the chill air held in it a warning of an early winter. Cole smoked another shuck and let all that day's weariness creep in, not wanting to go to bed, not wanting to think about girls like Rose or those who were being murdered in Deadwood or men like Gauss and Torres. He didn't want to think about Zee, either, or a son he'd never get to see grow up. Maybe the dead were the lucky ones. That night he dreamt about Rose.

She was pointing the silver pistol at him, thumbing back the hammer. He could see the slow turning of the cylinder, see the blunted dull gray heads of the bullets, hear the clicking of the mechanism, her hand steady, her face a mask of deliberate calm, and he knew within that moment that she would kill him and there was nothing he could do to stop her—and he wondered why.

The following morning produced a sky that was swollen with the gray bellies of clouds the size of Conestogas, bunching together, crowding the cañon walls, obscuring the tops of trees that stood blue-green in the cold dawn light. They had breakfast outside at a long table and the child, Tess, told her mother she was cold and everyone else ate their meal in the silence of people who are uncomfortable and not much given to conversation at that hour of the morning. The driver and the guard went about their work of harnessing the team of horses without the benefit of exchanging words. Wood smoke rose from the stone chimney inside the log dugout where the cook stove was. Everywhere there was the smell of burning pine, thick and tangy in the chill air.

Rose sat directly across from Cole and several times he looked up to see the gratitude in her eyes and thought it was a good thing that other people can't know our fears.

The gambler ate with rapid deliberation. He wore a pinky ring that had a small diamond set in it and his hair was greasy from not having been washed. The pores of his skin were black from the road dust, and his growth of unshaven beard was a light rust that rolled with the movement of his jaw as he ate. Cole saw Torres, hunkered by the corrals, watching the driver and guard hitch the team. He looked no differently than he ever did, the sweep of his sombrero's brim low over his dark eyes, his heels lifted off the ground so that they could support his haunches, his back bent to the wind that blew down from the northwest. He seemed not in the least disturbed by the cold weather or the effects of the Mexican Mustang Liniment from last night. Cole saw then that he was chewing what looked like a strip of jerky. He was still curious about his business in Deadwood.

Soon they were once again inside the stage, including the gambler, now that Rose had recovered sufficiently to sit up. The road climbed farther into the Black Hills, the sides of the cañon walls closing in so that no two wagons could pass one other at various places. One time the stage had to be stopped so that the driver and guard could climb down and remove a lodgepole pine that had fallen across the road.

By noon they arrived in Deadwood. The last twenty miles of the journey had seemed the longest. Cole had done some prize fighting at one time in his younger days, and, after long bouts, his ribs and arms and chest would be sore for days from the blows of other men's fists. It was nothing compared to the pounding the stage trip had given him, only the pain was in different places.

He climbed down and waited for his saddle and Winchester to be handed down from the boot of the stage. The woman, Suzanne Smith, approached him, her daughter clinging to her hand. He saw the listlessness in the child's eyes—small vacant pools of blue that were absent of light.

"I want to thank you again for what you and Marshal Torres did to protect us," she said. "Perhaps later, after we've gotten settled, you will allow me the opportunity to show you my appreciation in a more tangible way . . . dinner, perhaps."

"Perhaps," Cole said. Her little girl looked up at him, the dark ringlets of her hair damp against her head, damp and uncombed and unclean, as was her dress and her shoes, which were spotted with dust. Then her gaze shifted impatiently to her mother.

"Have the driver tell you of a good hotel or boarding house," Cole said to the woman. "Your child looks as though she could use some rest and decent food and a bath."

"Yes," she said, "I will." She looked into his eyes a moment longer as though searching for an answer to an unspoken question, then turned and went over to where the driver was standing at the rear of the coach, talking to a man whose belly hung over his belt buckle.

Cole watched the gambler pick up his valise, saw the glint of his pinky ring, then watched as he marched off down the walk and become quickly lost in the flowing mass of humanity that crowded the streets of the ramshackle town of Deadwood.

"It looks like hell on wheels," Miguel Torres said as he stepped past Cole, his carbine in one hand, his blanket tied over his shoulders. Then he paused, leveled his gaze at him, and said: "Last night . . . I talk too damn' much when I drink. And I sometimes drink too damn' much. Don't get the idea we're friends. I don't make friends. To me, you are just like everybody else . . . potential trouble." Then he turned and walked away.

Somehow, Cole understood what he meant about friendship and not trusting and knowing what you were about in this life. It was a good way for him to be if Torres wanted to stay alive very long in his business. It was the same for Cole who hefted the Dunn Brothers saddle in one hand, the Winchester in the other, and asked the driver where he might find a livery. Before he could answer, Rose touched Cole on the shoulder.

"I'll keep your advice," she said. "I'll practice till I get it down. I just hope I don't ever have to use it." He started to say something, but she cut him off. "If I do, I do," she said. "I ain't afraid." When he shook her hand, he felt its smallness in his own, and said: "Good luck to you, kid." She smiled, the driver and the man with the big belly looking on. "Thanks Mister Cole. Thanks for everything."

The driver told Cole where he could find a livery and he walked in that direction.

Deadwood was laid out on a long narrow street that was without a straight line to it. Trailing off at angles were one or two other streets. Every building in the town looked like it had been put up in a hurry. Everywhere stood the enterprise of a boom town: saloons, honky-tonks, gambling dens, whiskey tents, crib houses, a couple of hotels, hardware stores, jewelers, restaurants, opium dens, gunsmiths, butcher shops, and a shoe repair—all jammed cheek by jowl in raw-lumber, false-fronted buildings, canvas tents, and hodge-podge structures of lesser quality. The street itself was clogged with teamsters, mules, horses, and oxen teams hauling more lumber and more mining equipment, all trying to pass and get around one another. The result was a lot of men cursing the air. The sharp report of hammers could be heard farther down the street. Still more permanent buildings going up. Men lounged about in bowler hats and claw-hammer coats—attorneys-at-law and real-estate agents. Only they had another name for them in the South; they called them carpetbaggers.

Miners in their stiff dirty clothing, their eyes hollow and streaked like raccoons, leaned against the support poles of overhangs and squatted on the steps of several establishments, watching the goings-on and each other. Other men stood around in doorways: pimps, gun punks, pickpockets, judging by their eager, expectant eyes and their slouching postures. Frontier flotsam—every town had them, just like every town had mongrel dogs and tame Indians. The foot traffic up and down the street was heavy with gamblers, faro dealers, vagrants, sloe-eyed women in colorful dresses cut high on the bottom and low on top. If there was a profession to be named, there was a face to match it somewhere in that crowd. Everyone wanted to strike it rich and take their share of the gold. Some took the yellow metal from the earth, others took it straight from the miners' pockets. That was life in the mining camps.

Cole found what he was seeking at the far end of town— Black Hills Livery & Rental. An old gent whose features looked as though they'd been cut out of the very rock itself sat a three-legged stool, his grizzled, craggy face tilted toward the sun that now appeared between a split in the clouds.

"I might need to rent a horse while I'm here," Cole said.

The livery man's eyes opened with the slowness of a yawn. Tiny lines of dirt were creased in the folds of his skin. He was bundled up in a heavy buffalo-hide coat that looked several sizes too large for him. His unshaven face was a patch of gray briar. His mouth twisted downward at the corners, the right side stained brown from a lifetime of chewing and spitting tobacco from that side. "A horse?" he said, as though he had not heard that word before.

"That's what you do here," Cole said, glancing up at the sign painted over the double doors of his barn, "rent horses?"

"'Course I do, when I got 'em to rent. Trouble is, I ain't got one to rent right at the present." He looked irritated that Cole had disturbed his rest. His eyes trailed over Cole and he held up the palm of one hand to shade the sun's glare so that he could better see who it was that had come to trouble him. "You're a long drink of water," he said, then spat off to the side from a cud he had stored in one cheek. "Ain't seen you before, have I? Folks coming in here a hundred a day to pan the gold. Cutters and shooters, there's a killing a night right out there on them streets. Had to carry two off just this mornin'. Somebody laid 'em out last night. Ain't nobody knows who done them boys. Ain't nobody even cares. Welcome to perdition, mister." Then he spat another watery brown stream and wiped his mouth with the back of his hand.

"When do you reckon you will have a horse for rent?"

He looked at Cole's saddle. "That's a double rig," he said. "We called them rimfires, down on the Brazos. A Dunn Brothers, ain't it?"

"That's right."

He smiled his approval. "I should have a horse or two due in later on today, or tomorrow. Cost you four dollars a day. And before you tell me how pricey that sounds, remember . . . I'm the only livery in Deadwood. You could always walk to wherever it is you need to go. You from down on the Brazos?"

"I've been in the neighborhood a time or two. Can I leave my saddle stored here?"

"You can. Set her down and I'll take her in soon's my *siesta* is up."

Cole looked at his hands. They were rough, the fingers twisted and knotted at the joints. "You cowboy for a time?"

Light came into his face, along with the first show of friendliness. "Man. I must've drove ten thousand of them god-damn' creatures. Five long, hard seasons. Drove them from the Río to Kansas and Nebraska and later on up into Montana. Now there is some damn' righteous country . . . Montana. Purtiest place I ever seen. Would've stayed, but I didn't." He spat again. "Come here instead. Tried mining gold and my hands froze up in the creeks. The arthritis crippled up my fingers, bummed my knees, crawled into my back. Then I took to this. Horses is all that I know any more, all that I care to know. It ain't a bad business." He spat out the blanched cud into his hand this time, looked at it, and threw it aside. "All gone," he said. "Dead as Yankee soldiers on Pea Ridge. Har! Har! Har!" He had a laugh like the bray of a mule.

"I'm looking for someone," Cole said. "A woman."

The angling light of sun caught in his gray-as-crawfish eyes as he squinted up toward Cole, his hands jerked up from his knees, and his throat seemed to slide down inside the loose skin of his grizzled neck. "Hell, mister, I hope you ain't set yer sights too high because there is only two kinds of women in Deadwood . . . fat whores and skinny ones. Take yer pick! Har! Har! Har!"

"Her name is Lydia Winslow." A wagon filled with freshly sawed boards of lumber rumbled past. The boards slapped hard against one another as one of the wheels hit a rock in the road. It sounded like pistol shots.

"To hell and Jesus!" shouted the driver, and he cracked a bullwhip over the head of a team of mules whose velvety ears shone golden in the sunlight.

Some of the joy went out of the old-timer's face at the mention of Lydia Winslow's name, his mouth stopped moving, the soft, pliable skin under the rasp of dirty whiskers lay still. "You talkin' of Liddy Winslow?" He brought a rough hand to his mouth, drew it down across his stained lips, and shook his head in a slightly agitated way. "God damn, mister, I was you, I'd steer clear of Liddy's fer a while. She's had some trouble lately. Fact, she's sorta suspended operations."

"How so?" Cole asked, watching the movement of the old man's eyes. The eyes of a man can tell a different story than his mouth. The eyes shifted past Cole. He could see black flecks floating in gray centers, jagged lines of bloody veins running through the white.

"They say some of her gals have been murdered," he said. The knot of his throat percolated, then settled back again just above the top button of his soiled shirt. "Last one they found had a butcher knife stuck in her." He shuddered his shoulders. His lids closed against the light, pulling his bushy brows downward. Then he shook his head once more, and opened his eyes again and looked at Cole. "There's plenty of other places a man could take his pleasure. I'd avoid Liddy's I was you."

"Why is that?"

"They say she's put out a reward for whoever it is killed them gals. Word has it King Fisher and some others like him has already hit town. You ever heard of King Fisher, mister?"

"Yeah, I have."

The old man spat again, even though he had no tobacco in his mouth, and rubbed the palms of his hands against the sides of his legs. "King Fisher is a killing son-of-a-bitch," he said, some of the words catching in the phlegm of his throat. "If Fisher has come after that reward money, he's liable to shoot somebody just to say they was the one who killed them gals. Anyone doing their business down to Libby's is liable to wind up on King's gun list. You wanna get your ashes hauled, I'd do it at Becky Cash's, or Big

Nose Nel's Queen of Clubs. Hell, I'd even take up with Calamity Jane first." He struggled with a chuckle. "She's less attractive than a chamber pot, even to an old coot like me." His eyes glittered. He was obviously enjoying whatever it was traipsing through his mind. "But at least with ol' Janey, you wouldn't run the risk of dying because of it, less it were from the clap, maybe." Then his laugh became lost in a wheeze. The old man reached in his pocket and took out a fresh plug of tobacco and set about filling his cud with it.

Cole was still considering the presence of King Fisher in town. He had the instincts of a bird of prey when it came to knowing where the reward money was being offered. If Fisher had come, it must be in answer to Lydia Winslow's newspaper advertisements.

The sun went back behind the clouds and, just that quick, drops of rain the size of half dollars clanged off the tin roof of the livery.

"Well, so much fer a pleasant day," said the old man, then grabbed up Cole's Dunn Brothers saddle and took it inside. He had the limp of a man who knew what it was to have horses fall on him.

Cole was left to his own fate, standing there in the sudden downpour. *Welcome to Deadwood*, he thought.

Chapter Seven

The rain lasted less than five minutes, then the clouds parted once more and the sun broke through beautifully against a sky as clear as blue glass and a rainbow formed itself at the far end of the cañon. It was a touch of rare beauty set against a backdrop of such a scarred place. Several patrons of the Jersey Lil Saloon had stepped outside to observe the rainbow. The air smelled clean and new, and the sun mirrored itself in the puddles of rain lying in the rutted street.

Among the curious clientele of the Jersey Lil that had been drawn by the spectacle of the rainbow was a slightly built man who wore blue-tinted spectacles. Cole gauged him to be about five-foot-six. He was well dressed in a frock coat, fresh white shirt, creased trousers, and polished boots. His features were sharp, bony, but the skin was sallow. He had a straight thin nose and heavy sandy mustaches. There were other things about him, too. Cole noticed that his hands were well attended, as was the rest of his appearance. He had clean fingernails, an unusual affectation on the frontier. But it was the blue-tinted spectacles that first drew attention. Not only did they hide the man's eyes, but also gave him an air of mystery. And though he posed no outward sign of threat, Cole got the feeling he was dangerous. Standing next to him was a woman of robust build; her left hand was hooked through the crook of his arm. The woman was paying more attention to the man in the blue spectacles than she was to the rainbow.

They seemed an odd couple, the two of them. He stood at least a head shorter than she and hardly matched her in size and bulk. She had thick, short-cut hair tinted a deep reddish color. She wore a black velvet dress that fitted tightly against her figure. The swell of her breasts was exposed by the low cut front of the dress. Her skin was slightly ruddy and healthy in appearance, unlike that of the man's. She had a plain but not altogether unattractive face, a prominent nose, and red full lips. She held a little yellow parasol in her right hand. Even though his eyes were hidden behind the blue-tint glasses, Cole knew the man had taken notice of him as he passed by. He heard the woman say: "Come'n, Doc, let's go back inside."

And then in a voice that was soft, almost feminine, he replied: "In a moment, Kate. I haven't seen a rainbow in years."

Cole knew then who the man and the woman were. He saw a sign across the street that advertised the Deadwood Hotel & Billiard Parlor. He needed a room and a change of clothes, although he'd have to buy another shirt after having used his spare as bandages for Rose. He needed a decent meal and bed that didn't hold the company of graybacks. These were just a few of the things he needed before introducing himself and his reason for being in Deadwood to Lydia Winslow. But the thing he most needed was a bath with enough hot water to burn through the soreness the Black Hills Stage Company had pounded into his carcass for the last two hundred and forty-six miles.

The man at the hotel counter looked him over when he asked about renting a room. "You're lucky," he said. "We got one vacancy on account of Juno Smoke being killed last night in the Variety Club."

"Unlucky for him," Cole said, "but lucky for me."

The clerk grinned. "Miner stuck him with a stiletto over a card game. They say Juno's blood squirted high as the ceiling. Juno fancied himself a prize fighter, but I guess he didn't count on fighting no knife."

"I'll take the room," Cole said.

"Don't mind his stuff. I'll come and pick it up later." The clerk handed him the pen to sign the register.

"How much for the room?"

"Dollar fifty a day, clean sheets included. We got the best rooms in town. Ask anybody."

Cole laid $5 on the desk. "I'll take the room for five days, and, if it's as advertised, I might stay longer."

The clerk stared at the money, knowing it was short of the asking price, then handed him a key.

"And if I fall to the same fate as Mister Smoke, you can keep the change and rent the room to someone else. How'll that be?"

That seemed to satisfy him. "Top of the stairs, down the hallway to your left. Last room on the end. There's a stairway just across the hall from you that leads down the back and out to the privy in the alleyway."

It was a skeleton key that would have fit any one of the doors. Cole took it and slipped it into his pocket.

"Anything else you'll be needing, Mister . . . ?" He glanced down at the signature on the register. "Mister Cole." Then he peered at Cole through the dark circles that formed his eyes. "A woman, maybe?"

"No, thanks," Cole said, and climbed the stairs.

It was a common room, bare of all but the essentials: a cotton tick mattress upon a bed of iron springs, a single plain chair, a tin wash basin, and a china pitcher of fetid water resting on a roughly hewn commode. Lying next to the pitcher were a towel and a yellow bar of soap. A small framed mirror hung from a nail above the commode where a man could shave if he wanted and had his own razor. And, of course, Mr. Juno Smoke's belongings, which Cole collected and piled in the hallway.

He laid his saddlebags on the bed, propped the Winchester in a corner, and hung his hat on the chair before pouring water into the basin and washing his face and hands, then strung wet fingers through his hair before drying with the towel. When he looked up, he saw his image in the mirror: the clear, almost colorless eyes of his father and his father before him, a square of face that needed the burned red stubble scraped clean, the sweep of mustaches of the same deep rust color that draped along the sides of his mouth. He saw weariness and a man who needed a shave and a bath and his mustaches trimmed—the face of the Cole clan. He saw what Zee Cole had seen the night she died, the same face that the man he had killed out on the trail to Deadwood had seen just before he died. It was the same face that some Confederate boys coming out of a stand of hardwood trees had seen as they swept down on the Union position at The Wilderness and a lot of other places where they had set about killing one another. It was a face less inclined to either sorrow or joy than it once was. *What had happened to all the years?* Cole wondered. How had it come to be that he was in this place at this time?

As he stood there, staring at the image that seemed both his and not his, he remembered one young boy in particular in that bloody campaign. He could not have been more than thirteen or fourteen and carried the Rebel flag on a tree branch. He was leading a small company of Rebs up the Union's right flank at Pickles Gap. He had lost his cap as he charged out of the trees, holding his flag, the wind tearing through his long wheat hair as he ran. His screams rippled through the meager gray ranks, and they, in turn, set their voices to the yell. It was not so much a yell as it was a howling curse. And in that small, spare, frozen moment, Cole could not bring himself to pull the trigger on him. He had seemed only a boy playing a boy's foolish game, and he could not kill him. All around him the crack and pop of rifle fire had pierced the air and the smoke from Union guns and Rebel guns had lifted over the Union line in a thick blue cloud that obscured vision and scorched throats. The whine of Minié balls had split the air, kicking up dirt and snapping leaves off the trees. It was a horizontal rain of lead, killing and maiming everyone in its path, cutting men down like marionettes whose strings were suddenly broken.

Somehow, miraculously, through a break in the choking smoke, the young flag bearer had emerged, the ragged bunch of butternuts behind him, and on they had come directly into the Union guns. And still Cole couldn't pull the trigger on him. He was just a boy. But someone did shoot him, for his head had suddenly jerked backward just as he was leaping over the dead body of a fallen Union man. A bloody spray of red had flown from his golden head. The flag he had carried fluttered to the ground like some great wounded bird. Dead or dying, his legs had continued to carry him several more paces. Then he had become entangled in his cherished flag, fell, and had come to rest just inches from where Cole had been kneeling. And for a long, full moment, the war had stopped. The flat pop of rifle shots had faded, and a calmness had descended upon that small square of ground there in front of Cole as he had looked down into the open eyes of the dead Rebel flag bearer. A halo of bright red blood had soaked the ground. His right hand was stretched out before him, nearly touching the toe of Cole's boot as if he were reaching for Cole, reaching for someone to take his hand and hold it in those final fateful seconds. Only death had come too quickly for such sentiments, and he, like a lot of other boys, had died alone.

As he stared into his own eyes in the mirror, Cole remembered something that he had long tried to forget. Just before the boy was shot, their eyes had met for the briefest moment and he had stopped yelling as though in that moment he'd forgotten that they were at war and that their only reason for being in that place was to kill one another because of the color of their uniforms. And for a long, fateful second, he was just a boy in the wrong place at the wrong time; they both had been. The memory touched a spot in Cole that caused him to take in a deep breath and let it out slowly. It was a spot next to the one he kept for Zee and his son Tad.

He was drawn up out of the well of remembering by a knock at the door. He slid the Remington out of its holster and held it behind his back before opening the door.

The man was tall, slump-shouldered, wearing a coat made out of dyed black sheepskin. He wore a pinch-brimmed fedora pulled down tightly to his ears. He had brown eyes that were flecked with green and pocked skin around his jaw and neck. His ears were prominent and he had the flat nose of a boxer. His thick, meaty hands rested at his sides. Before Cole could ask, he pulled back the lapel of his coat and showed a small badge cut from a silver dollar.

"I'm Constable Johnny Logan," he said. His long dark mustaches lifted, then fell back into place when he spoke. "I saw you get off the stage today." When Cole did not reply, he continued: "I watch and see who gets off the stage. It's part of my job . . . to see who's coming into town."

He fell silent, his eyes searching Cole, waiting for Cole to tell him who he was and why he was there. When he didn't, Logan said: "Ever since she put it in the papers about the reward she was offering, they've been riding into my town. I figure you're one of them. Tell me if I'm wrong."

He didn't say who *she* was, but they both knew.

"You're wrong," Cole said.

"No. I don't believe I am."

"Believe what you want."

His gaze slid to the hand Cole was holding behind his back with the self-cocker in it. "If you was just another gambler or a gold panner," he said, "you wouldn't be coming to the door, holding a pistol behind your back. I could arrest you, run you out of town."

"No. I don't believe you will do that."

"Why wouldn't I?"

"Because if you were going to, you'd have already done it."

Something determined left Logan's gaze, and the left side of his face twitched, stretching the muscles in his neck. "I've got my hands full here," he said. "I don't need men like you to make my job harder than it is."

Cole took the opportunity to ask him the obvious question: "Seems you could have saved yourself all this trouble of worrying about the gun artists showing up in town if you had found whoever it was that killed Miss Winslow's girls in the first place."

Cole saw the knot form along his jaw line, saw the color of anger rise in his face. "If you know that much," he said, "then I'm right about your reasons for being here. Your type always comes to gather over the carcass. And as far as those gals of Liddy Winslow's, they're just fancy whores whose living or dying don't mean a whit in the long scheme of things. People get killed here all the time and for a variety of reasons. I don't have the time or inclination to spend all my energies looking for someone who has a bent against sporting gals."

"It would seem to me the reward alone would make you interested."

He took a deep breath, then let it out, his irritation with Cole growing. "I get paid regular, mister, every week, for pinning on this badge, and I get to run a faro game over at the Jersey Saloon, and I get to go home and sleep at nights when I'm done working. It's honest, steady work. I don't need no more than that."

His answer didn't make sense to Cole, but he said nothing.

"I'll tell you this," Logan said. "I figure you for trouble. You and the others that already arrived and are bound to come. The way I see it, comes to trouble out there on those streets, I'll shoot you without warning, you give me reason."

Cole knew the type. Men who were brave enough to wear a badge and back up their authority with a gun, but not so brave they'd give an opponent an even chance. They were the kind of men who would walk up behind you and shoot you in the back of the head, then arrest you for whatever law it was they thought you had broken. He harbored no doubts that Constable Logan was probably very dangerous.

"I'll keep your warning in mind," Cole said. "Now, if you will excuse me, I'd like to see about the chances of a hot bath and a meal."

Logan looked at Cole with the dull, vacant look of a man who had already written him off as someone to share a drink with and a cigar. Then he touched the brim of his hat and turned and walked away. Cole could hear his heavy steps on the stairs as he descended them. Then he heard him say something to the desk clerk in a muted voice.

He closed the door and stretched out across the bed, suddenly weary from the stage ride, the sleepless nights, old memories, and thoughts of men like Constable Logan and Miguel Torres and King Fisher—any one of whom might kill him if given half the chance.

Chapter Eight

Sometimes a man sleeps the sleep of the dead, and other times he visits with the ghosts. It's those other times when he forces himself to come awake and sit on the side of the bed and smoke a cigarette. The times when he can't seem to escape the gloaming images, all the dead faces, and whiskey rivers. And in that hour of deep lonely, he also remembers the women, too. Women who've held him and loved him for a night at a time. Maybe he forgets most of their names, but he never forgets them completely. And remembering that much at least helps him get through the worst of it, the long nights.

In the nightmare Cole had just awakened from, the fuzzy-faced boys of the 32nd Michigan Volunteers had been crossing a low, swampy area, the fetid water up to their waists, the muck sucking at their boots, making every step an effort. Some of the boys were afraid cottonmouth snakes would slide through the coffee-stained water and bite their legs. They could hear the bull-frogs croak, then stop, then croak again. The mosquitoes rose like clouds off the water, taking their toll on their arms and faces and working their misery into their eyes and noses. Their clothes were damp and rotting away, their flesh sloughing off their bones. It was in the false dawn of morning, when the light tricks you into believing that you are safe from the night and a warm breeze plays among the Spanish moss that hangs from the cypress trees like the molted hair of dead Southern belles. Cole wasn't sure why they were crossing that swamp or how they had gotten there or what their purpose was for being there. But he knew that they were surrounded by the floating shadows of Confederates dressed in tattered uniforms as gray as the very dawn itself. And through the swirling mist he could see a gallery of faces, faces that were drawn with hunger and hatred, their yellow eyes burning brightly, their mouths set in ghostly grins of broken and missing teeth.

It seemed like they had been in the water a long time. No one talked. A great silence impaled them with fear, a fear so heavy it lay against the chest and pinched the heart. The water and the muck pulled at them, wearing them down so that once they made the other side, they'd be easy prey for the waiting Rebels. And then, suddenly, a large man in a slouch hat and a butternut jacket torn at the shoulder had hovered above Cole. And he saw what he was holding: a Springfield musket with a long, rusty bayonet attached to the muzzle. Before he could move, he plunged the steel into Cole's guts, pinning him to the ground, his weight behind it. Cole thought that it would hurt. Only he didn't feel any pain. He knew somehow that he was going to die. And in knowing that, he knew something beyond pain, something indescribable. He had looked up into his face and saw there was no hint of compassion, no expression of forgiveness in the glazed eyes of the man forking him to the ground, for the war had cost him what it had cost everyone. They were not brothers or men of the same color or even men of the same country. They were simply men who had lost themselves, who had come to understand only one thing: survival. And that need had brought them to this moment: one man killing the other so that one could live, for another day, another hour, another minute. Cole had closed his eyes and waited for the end.

He awoke against the pull of the dream, his mouth dry, the rest of him soaked in sweat. He sat up on the side of the bed, the room deep in darkness. He struck a match to the lamp on the little stand next to the bed. The flame guttered low, flared, and filled a corner of the room with dull buttery light. He adjusted the wick and closed the glass chimney down around it, his hands unsteady, his breath short, labored. Reaching into his pocket, he took out the Ingersol, checked the time. It was nearly 9:00 p.m. Then he rolled himself a shuck and used the lamp to fire it. The smoke felt good and powerful against his lungs and he realized that he was grateful to be alive—grateful and ashamed at the same time. He thought of those who were still lost and wandering aimlessly in the dreams of the living, those still seeking release from the world of his mind: Zee, Tad, the Rebel boy who had carried his flag, the men who'd died by his hand, faces and memories, hard to forget, hard to remember. *From the earth we are born, and to the earth we return*, he thought, *but what of our souls?*

He dressed, took his hat from the back of the chair, and left down the rear stairway. The night air was cold and black, the sky filled with stars. He walked out to the street, where a few heelers and loafers were hanging about. Almost everyone else was staying inside the dens of iniquity where they could indulge their desires and conduct their business, one seeking the other, desirous men and wanton women, Johnny-Behind-The-Deuce and bottom dealers, billiard boys and raccoon-eyed miners. Pieces of the dream were still with him like broken bits of glass shattered inside his skull, wounds that would never heal completely.

He stepped inside one of the saloons. Whiskey sounded good to him just then. The room was long and narrow, a fancy oak bar running down one side with a backbar, a mirror reflecting the bottles and the faces of the men staring at themselves as they stood, drinking their whiskeys, one foot resting on the brass rail. Suspended from the ceiling were old wagon wheels that supported oil lamps and could be lowered or raised by ropes. Opposite the bar were the poker tables. Farther down, a faro rig was set up and men were bucking the tiger. And in the back, a keno game was going on.

Cole noticed a chair hanging high up on the wall, suspended from a peg. On either side of the chair were the stuffed heads of a bison and a black bear. The black bear's yellowed ivory teeth were exposed in a frozen snarl, the glass eyes staring impassively.

One of three bartenders lifted his chin and said: "Name's Irish Murphy, what'll it be?"

"Whiskey," Cole said. "Mash whiskey, if you have it."

The bartender's eyes were blue, creased in a broad face, and he was wearing a white apron. "Sartainly," he said, and took a bottle from the bar behind him, poured a glass full of it, and shoved it across to Cole. "Will Jack Daniels do you, sar?"

"Tennessee whiskey, but it'll do me just fine."

He drank the first glass and had Murphy pour a second.

"Come for the gold, did ya?" Murphy asked, his face was as expectant as a child's, his accent cheerful, and full of Irish charm.

"No. I came for the whiskey."

Murphy's grin was huge, his cheeks florid. He had large arms and a thick chest beneath an apron that was tied around his neck and again around his waist. "Yer smarter than most, then," he said, tippling the bottle for a third time when Cole failed to protest. "Oh, some will get lucky, strike it rich. But most will end up with whatever gold they do manage to muck out of them blackened hills being taken by the professionals, the gamblers, and the sporting girls. Them's the real miners."

"Tell me," Cole said, "why do you have that chair hanging up there on the wall?"

Murphy's gaze traveled upward to the chair, and a pleasant expression settled into his face. "Oh, that's ol' Bill Hickok's chair. The one he was sitting in when Jack McCall came up from behind him and relieved him of his salad days." His right hand contained a damp rag and he ran it in circles over the polished bar. "He was quite a talent, you know," Murphy went on. "The boss says he's honoring Bill by keeping his chair up where nobody can ever sit in it again. Personally I think he keeps it there for show, to draw a crowd, don't you know? A fellow from Denver came in last month and offered to buy it for a hundred dollars, but the boss said he wouldn't sell it for a thousand. Although I think he would, if someone was to offer him that much for it. The man would be a fool not to . . . it's nothing more than an old chair."

"I heard they let McCall off on a verdict of self-defense," Cole said.

Irish Murphy nodded, his blue eyes crisp in the smudgy light. "That they did, and it's a crying shame, for the man was as guilty as Judas. It wasn't no legal jury, of course, just some drunks and miners who thought Bill was too much a dandy to begin with." Murphy was now looking up at the chair. "Jack left town right after. There was talk that some of Bill's friends would carry out their own justice. Personally I never believed it. There are very few tried and true men that come to Deadwood, Bill included, I'm sorry to say. God rest his soul." He snapped out the rag and flipped it over his left shoulder. "I'll tell you this," he said confidentially, leaning over the bar in order to speak low. "Talk has it that McCall was a hired man, an assassin for some of the hard element here in town that didn't want to see Bill become the law and take things over."

Just then, a commotion started up by the front door. Several miners led by a rowdy teamster swept into the place. The teamster was short, wiry, dressed in a butter-soft fringed jacket and canvas trousers stuffed into the tops of long boots. He wore a billed cap and the butt of a pistol was exposed from his waistband.

"Oh, piss and feathers," said Murphy at their appearance. "It's that damn' Calamity Jane and her friends!"

Cole looked but still couldn't make the determination that the teamster was, in fact, a woman. She had a narrow, homely face that was bereft of any femininity. The hair was short and dark and chopped and sticking out from beneath her cap. There was nothing in her gait or manner to suggest womanly qualities. Unlike Rose, this woman appeared to him to be a mistake of Nature.

"She'll cuss the air blue and try to pick a fight with any man that looks at her wrong," Murphy said. "And it don't take much for a man to look wrong at Calamity Jane."

"I've heard it said she and Bill were an item," Cole stated, turning his attention away from the arrivals that had taken up chairs in the back of the room.

"According to her version," Murphy said with a wink, "she and Bill were husband and wife. Longtime lovers. She saved his life, he saved hers." He hunched his large shoulders. "Depends on which night she's telling it, and to whom. Depends on how drunk she is or ain't and who she's trying to get to buy her drinks that night or bed down with. Me personally, I never seen the two of them together . . . would've been surprised if I had. Bill Hickok was sartainly no saint, but he wasn't no blind man, neither."

Cole's interest was more in the hard element that Irish Murphy had mentioned as possibly having a hand in killing Hickok. If there was a certain element trying to control the illicit trade in Deadwood, then maybe there was some connection to the killings of the women who had worked for Lydia Winslow. How, or who this element was, and what role they might have played in the killings, would only be an unfounded guess, but still the mention of such an element intrigued him. When he met Miss Winslow, he could ask her what she knew of such men.

"Tell me something, Irish," he said. Murphy's features were like tight muscles as he continued to stare toward the back of the room, where Jane and her crew were in the process of raising general hell.

"What's that, sar?" he said, twisting his head back around in Cole's direction.

"This hard element you spoke of, concerning Wild Bill's killing . . . do you know any of the parties that might be a part of this group?"

Cole saw the last traces of humor fade from Murphy's eyes as he blinked twice. "No, sar, I would not. Nor would I care to find out. Men that would lay Bill Hickok low are not men I'd want to make the acquaintance of. Bill may have had his faults, but he wasn't afraid of anyone. It would take some real nerve on the party that'd want to assassinate him." Then he leaned forward again and said: "If I were you, sar, I'd be watchful of who I asked about sartin matters, if you want to keep on breathing the air of our lovely little burg."

"To tell the truth, Irish," Cole said, "it seems strange to me that you'd have heard such a rumor and not have heard any names to go with it."

Murphy's gaze danced over the rest of the room beyond Cole's shoulder and down along the bar before leaning toward him again. "I only just arrived myself, a week or two before it happened. No one seemed to be all that stirred up over it. Except there was this one odd little fellow who claimed he was Bill's best friend, a man named Charley Utter. Colorado Charley, they called him. He told me soon after it happened that he thought Cross-Eyed Jack was put up to the whole thing by some of the local bosses, men who control most of the gambling and confidence games. Charley claimed they didn't want Bill to get elected as the law because of his reputation, and so they paid McCall to put a bullet through his brain, which he did right smartly. Anyway, Charley didn't say any names. He was commonly drunk the day he told me and it was not even yet ten in the morning."

"Why'd he tell you, if you were just new in town? Why not someone he knew and trusted?"

"Drunks talk to the men who pour them their whiskey," Murphy said. "It ain't unusual. I've had men tell me things I would be reluctant to tell a priest . . . things about their wives, for instance. Who can say what it is about liquor and loneliness that makes a man want to speak so freely?"

"Where could I find this Charley Utter?"

A slight bit of relief returned to Murphy's eyes. "Oh, that I couldn't tell you, sar, other'n to say he left town shortly after paying for Bill's funeral and seeing that he was properly buried up on Mount Moriah. Some say he left and went back to Colorado. Others have said he went back East, to Boston or New York, where he had come from originally. I haven't seen him around since that morning."

Just then, Jane was heard to yell an insult to someone in the back of the room and a voice yelled back for her to shut the hell up, followed by a lot of laughter and more swearing and more laughter. The mash whiskey had worked its wonder and Cole thanked Irish Murphy for his time and laid a pair of silver dollars down on the bar that Murphy picked up with fingers thick and reddened as sausages.

"Come back again anytime," he said, the Irish lilt of his voice ringing above the noise of the crowd.

Cole stepped back out into the night and felt the chill air through the linen duster, felt it crawl along the back of his neck. The whiskey helped warm him. Yellow light spilled from the windows of the hurdy-gurdies and saloons all up and down both sides of the street. The town was cranking up for another night of revelry and hell raising. Cole could hear the drunken, boisterous chorus of the miners singing their sentimental songs of home and sweethearts left behind. The lovesick and homesick men were joined in song by their chippies—the closest those men were ever going to get to a sweetheart in such a far-flung camp as Deadwood. But Cole knew the loneliness of such men, and he didn't blame them for wanting to raise a little hell and have the company of a woman, any woman, to share the long, cold nights with them. He wanted to go and join them and forget about the reason he had come to the gulch. Ever since he'd arrived in town, he'd been getting a bad feeling about the place. He didn't reckon it would get any better the longer he stayed. But the conversation with Irish Murphy had given him a hook at least to hang his hat on as far as the killings went, and he knew he needed to forget all about joining the rowdy miners and their painted ladies for at least this night. It was time to pay a visit to Lydia Winslow.

Chapter Nine

John Henry Cole found the address Lydia Winslow had given in the letter—24 Front Street. It was a small white clapboard house at the north end of the gulch, sitting by itself next to an empty lot. It was freshly painted, and its small square windows revealed light seeping through the parts of maroon drapes. There was a white picket fence guarding the structure. It might have been the house of a parson or a bank president.

He opened the gate and went in. There was a set of three wooden steps leading up to the door. Just as he reached the first one, the door suddenly opened to a quadrant of saffron light. A man, one hand still holding the doorknob, stood there, silhouetted against the light. For a brief moment he did not move. Then he descended the steps and walked past Cole without greeting. He wore a greatcoat, but Cole recognized him as he brushed past. He wasn't wearing his blue glasses now, but it was the same man who earlier in the day had been standing in front of the Jersey Saloon watching the rainbow—Doc Holliday. Although Cole had never personally met Holliday, his reputation as gambler and gun artist was known to him. He also knew that he supposedly was a consumptive and a drunk who had a penchant for meanness. He had never heard or read anywhere that Holliday had actually killed anyone in a gunfight, although he had read of a shooting scrape for which he had been run out of Dallas. The territory was full to overflowing with men like Doc Holliday, men of little known fact and a whole lot of rumor who did little to dissuade the public of their dangerousness.

A mulatto girl answered Cole's knock. She was tall but finely put together with a cinnamon skin and dark freckles dotting the bridge of her nose, her eyes a soft gray. She wore a dark blue blouse and a long black skirt, and several silver bracelets encircled her forearms. Large gold loops dangled from her earlobes.

"Yas, suh?" she said, her eyes fixed upon Cole.

"I've come to see Miss Winslow."

"Miss Liddy not be seein' any gentlemen callers tonight, suh." She had a voice that reminded Cole of bayous and tall cotton under a hot dry wind. It was a soft Southern drawl he'd not heard since the war.

He glanced down the street, and saw Holliday pause in the light of a saloon window to tip a small silver flask to his mouth as he leaned against the wall of the building. His cough erupted in the air, then he wiped his lips, and moved on into the waiting shadows. "That man," Cole said, "the one that just left here. He was a gentleman caller?"

Her eyes shifted downward. "No, suh, he a friend of Miss Liddy's."

"Well, you might go and tell her another friend is here to see her."

"Who should I say be calling?" she asked, her gaze once more lifting to meet Cole's eyes. Her lips were slightly separated and he could see the porcelain of her teeth, even and white against the dark ruby mouth.

"Tell her Ike Kelly."

"Yas, suh," she said. "You wait here." Then she closed the door gently, but all the way.

Cole glanced back down the street in the direction he had last seen Holliday. He was gone. The door suddenly flew open. The interior light shone brightly.

"Ike!"

Cole saw then why Ike Kelly had said the first time he met her, he knew he was going to fall in love. She was uncommonly beautiful. Her russet hair was combed straight back from her oval face, pinned by a pair of silver and abalone shell combs. Her eyes were the green of emeralds, her skin smooth and white and flawless.

When she saw that Cole was not Ike, she looked sharply at the mulatto girl. "Jazzy Sue, I thought you said . . ."

Cole stopped her. "My name's John Henry Cole, Miss Winslow. Ike Kelly received your letter and asked me to come in his place, at least until he could come himself."

She took her gaze off the girl and placed it back on the stranger. Her eyes were the sort of eyes a man could easily fall into and drown. "Ike never replied, saying he was sending someone in his place."

"He figured it was best to keep whatever business we might have as private as possible."

"Why didn't he come himself?"

"He was unable to just at the time."

There was an instant of doubt, but then the eyes relented. And this time, as she looked at the stranger, she really looked at him. "Ike must trust you a great deal."

"We go back some."

She took a breath and let it out again. "Come in, Mister Cole." She stepped back away from the door while the mulatto girl held it open for Cole. He followed her into a small, well-appointed parlor. A matching pair of green upholstered chairs sat facing each other. Across from them was a serpentine-back sofa with half-lyre-shaped armrests. A light brown Brussels covered the floor. The walls were done in flocked wallpaper; a pair of Currier and Ives prints hung on the east wall. A small tea table stood in the center of the room. Cole had seen one similar to it in a cathouse in Denver.

"Have a seat, Mister Cole." She was wearing a dark blue sateen dress that caused her skin to seem even more white and unflawed. The dress was clasped at the throat by a cameo brooch and the sleeves were decorated in an arabesque of black beads from wrists to elbows. The light in the room shimmered against the material, seemed almost to swim in it. "Jazzy Sue, bring us some cognac," she said to the mulatto girl, who turned quickly and wisped away.

The room was warm and comfortable and intimate and held the scent of crushed flowers. She sat across from Cole, her gaze never leaving his face.

"Tell me," she said, "how is dear Ike?"

"He's fine."

"And married?"

"No."

She smiled, her teeth even and white, her lips curved in a perfect bow around them. "I thought by now . . ." she began. Her voice still held traces of an Eastern accent running through its smokiness. Her hands rested in her lap, the long fingers bone-white against the blue dress.

"I think maybe he's waiting for the right woman to come along again."

She tilted her head just very slightly and everything softened in her face. "He's a fine man," she said. "I would wish him the best of everything." There was a tenderness to her words, and Cole felt she meant it.

"I read the letter," Cole said. "Do you care to tell me about what's going on?"

He saw the light fade from her eyes, the slight smile disappear. She swallowed, but before she could say anything, the mulatto girl brought in a cut-crystal decanter and glasses on a small silver tray, and set the tray down on the table.

"That'll be all, Jazzy. You can go on to bed."

Jazzy Sue said—"Thank you, ma'am."—twisted her eyes in Cole's direction, then slipped out of the room again as quietly as a whisper.

Cole waited while Miss Winslow poured them each a glass of the cognac; the amber liquid seemed alive in the soft light of the room. It had a smooth, unfamiliar taste to him, but he liked it. He watched her sip it as though it were something precious, something not to be disturbed in the drinking of it.

Without setting the glass back down on the table, choosing instead to hold it within both her hands, she said: "Someone is killing my girls."

"Yes, you stated that in your letter."

"Three so far, Mister Cole, since my arrival here this summer. At first, with Dotty, I thought it was a suicide. A bottle of poison was found by her bedside. Then, a couple of months later, Eva was found with her neck broken. . . ." Something caught in her throat, her gaze shifted to the right, a luster of wetness filled her deep green eyes. "Still, I did not think of a connection between the two," she continued, touching the tip of a finger to the corner of one eye. She didn't seem to Cole a woman who would cry easily. "But then about a month ago, another of my girls, Flora, was found stabbed to death. A butcher knife was . . ." She brought the glass up to her mouth again and drank from it, only this time she drank without the same restraint she had earlier. This time she drank like someone who meant to have the liquor take hold of her and tear her loose from soberness.

Cole watched as she refilled her glass and his. "I think it's a warning to me."

"What sort of warning?"

"I think someone wants me to leave Deadwood, to close my business."

"Why would someone want you to do that, Miss Winslow?" Cole asked, feeling the warmth of the cognac course through his blood. "I'd think a town like this would welcome your services."

Her eyes came to focus on his. He shifted slightly under her gaze. He knew it would be easy to cross over the line, to let the matters at hand become secondary in his thinking. There was something about her beauty, something vulnerable and insurmountable all at the same time, and everything about her seemed to lie just beneath the surface of those alluring eyes that made him want to go over and put his arms around her and kiss the smoothness of her jaw. "Let me make something clear to you, Mister Cole." The eyes that were drawing his down into them did not waver or blink as they stared into him. "I know what it's like to be a working girl. I've been one. But I was luckier than most . . . luckier or smarter, however you want to look at it. I saved my money and I didn't marry the first cowboy who came down the pike and asked me, and I raised myself up out of the life. But there aren't many ways for a woman to be independent on the frontier. And the life never lets you go, not completely it doesn't. I've seen first-hand what happens to most working girls." She paused, took another drink from the cognac.

She rested her dark fluid eyes on Cole again. "Have you ever been to the bottom of the barrel, Mister Cole? Can you possibly know what it is like to be twenty years old and have to sell your body to a dirty miner for fifty cents, or hope that a pimp likes you well enough not to beat you, or worse, scar your face?" Her eyes smoldered with old angers and hurts. Then she added: "No, how could you possibly know such things?"

"I know where the bottom of the barrel is, Miss Winslow. I've been there. Maybe not in the same way as you've described, but I've been there."

"I haven't," she said, her jaw jutting outward, her look one of self-possessed dignity. "I was lucky, and I was smart, and I was determined. And I never fell to the mercy of but one man, and just one time. But I've known lots of girls who weren't so lucky. By the time I left Dodge, I knew that I'd never again let a man control my life or my future. I came here to Deadwood with the express purpose of running an escort service. I brought with me five young women who wanted the same thing I wanted. I made them a promise that I would take care of them. I do not run crib girls or streetwalkers or women who will drug you and steal your money or have their pimps knock you over the head with a lead sap. A man knows that, if he is with one of my girls, he doesn't have to worry about such things. And my young women know it as well. That way, everyone is happy."

"In the end, though, it still boils down to the same thing, doesn't it?" Cole said. "The ladies still have to sell themselves to the miners, or anybody else who wants them."

"No, Mister Cole, it is not the same thing. The ladies who work for me have a choice in the matter, and *that* is the difference. The men who use my service know that they are to treat my girls with respect and charity, that they are not to abuse them. When it comes down to the more intimate details, it is by mutual agreement between the customer and the young woman. In return, the men pay handsomely for the privilege of a first-class escort for the evening."

"But it doesn't always work out that way, does it?"

"It had, until the killings began. Now the other girls are afraid. They want to leave Deadwood. But I have convinced them to stay, even though I've temporarily suspended operations."

"Maybe it's better they leave than be murdered."

"You don't seem very sympathetic to the situation, Mister Cole. Perhaps it is a mistake, your coming here instead of Ike."

"Don't misread me, Miss Winslow. I don't like to see people hurt. If three of your girls have been murdered, I don't blame the others for wanting to clear out. Whatever life they may return to has to be better than being murdered. Leaving might be something for you to consider as well."

"I won't run or be driven out of town," she said. "Whoever did this needs to be caught!"

"I agree, that's why I'm here. Tell me of your suspicions."

She sighed, sipped the cognac, fixed her gaze on him. "As I said, I think someone wants me out of business. I've thought about why. The reasons are few, if any. But there may be one or two."

"Tell me."

"Well, first, the best girls in Deadwood come to me because they know my policy. The second thing is, once men have been escorted by one of my ladies, they are rarely willing to settle for less the next time out. My girls remind them of the sweethearts and wives they left back home. Money to a miner doesn't mean a thing if he can't spend it on his own pleasure. I think whoever is responsible doesn't like the fact that the miners are spending most of their money on my girls. Maybe it's a pimp, or a joy house owner . . . I don't really know."

"And maybe it's someone who is killing them for his own strange reasons," Cole suggested.

She bit her lower lip, her eyes tearing over again. "Maybe it is," she said, her smoky voice barely audible.

"There is something I am curious about," Cole said.

Again she swallowed. "What would that be, Mister Cole?"

"How were you able to ensure that your girls were unmolested while escorting their customers?"

She drank the last of the cognac left in her glass and brushed at the corners of her eyes with her fingertips. "I pay a man to watch out for the welfare of my ladies. He is quite notorious. Very much feared."

"Doc Holliday?"

She looked surprised. "How did you know?"

"I saw him leave just as I came up."

"I needed someone of well-known reputation. He was in town. I offered him the job. It pays well."

"Which leads me to another question, then."

"Which is?"

"Why didn't you simply have Doc find the man who is killing your ladies, since he's already on the tab?"

"Obviously you don't understand," she said. "I pay Doc for his deadly reputation. He is not a well man. His vice is liquor, his energies limited."

"There sounds like more to it than that."

Her green eyes shifted away. "Perhaps there is, Mister Cole."

"What might that be?"

"I suspect Doc has a personal interest in me . . . one I'd just as soon not encourage." Her voice trailed off, but Cole knew there was more.

"That sounds like only half the reason. What's the rest of it?"

She seemed reluctant to speak about it further. But when she saw he wasn't leaving, she said: "I am not entirely sure that Doc isn't somehow involved with the killings. After all, his job was to protect the girls and that he failed to do, or so it seems. To be honest with you, I don't know of anyone here in Deadwood I can trust. It is why I have sought help from the outside."

"But you did more than that, Miss Winslow." Cole saw the uncertainty in her velvet eyes. "You advertised in the territorial papers. And now, men like King Fisher and Kip Caine will be coming and you'll have to deal with them."

The eyes snapped. "You seem to know a lot about my business."

"Have you ever dealt with a man like King Fisher?" he asked, and, before she could answer, added: "Do you know what sort of man King Fisher is? Do you know what the others who'll come for the reward are like?"

She looked at him as though he had thrown her an insult. But Cole felt she needed to know she was playing a dangerous game, if she was playing it with manhunters like King Fisher and the others that would swoop down on Deadwood like turkey buzzards on a dead opossum once they read her advertisement.

She quickly regained her composure. "I won't stand by and do nothing," she said. "I'll do whatever it takes to find the killer."

"Sometimes the cure is worse than the ailment."

"Maybe it is. But what choice have I?"

"None now."

"Are you certain you want to involve yourself in this, Mister Cole?"

"I guess I'm like you, Miss Winslow, I don't see any choice. I gave Ike my word." He couldn't tell if her eyes were grateful or unhappy. "I have one last question for you."

"What is it?"

"Why, if someone wanted you out of business, wouldn't they just come after you? Why kill three of your ladies instead?"

She shrugged her shoulders, her lips pursed into a momentary thought, and said: "I honestly don't know, Mister Cole. Maybe the angels are watching over me, the fallen angels of my girls."

"Yeah, maybe so."

"What will you do now?" she asked, as he stood and placed his Stetson back on his head.

"First thing," he said, "I'll go and find me a hot bath. I haven't had one in four days. Then, come tomorrow, I'll do what I get paid to do . . . I'll start investigating."

She stood and extended her hand. Cole took it in his and shook it lightly. Her fingers felt warm and graceful as they closed on his. He could smell the scent of her perfume and it did something to him, something that made him shift his weight and wish that he had found that hot bath earlier and scraped off the stubble from his chin.

"Then you'll remain in touch, Mister Cole?"

"You can count on it," he said. *Keep it business*, he told himself as he released her hand.

She saw him to the door, held it while he stepped out into the night. Cole turned then, looked at her standing there in the lighted doorway, and said: "Do you keep a pistol?"

She smiled and said: "Yes, as a matter of fact, I do. And I know how to use it."

"Somehow, I'm not surprised," he said, then bid her good evening.

"Good night, Mister Cole."

Her words trailed him down the steps. A raw wind had picked its way down through the cañon and blew trash along the street ahead of it. As he neared his hotel, a shot rang out of the darkness and clipped a chunk of wood from a post inches in front of his face. He was thinking about Lydia Winslow, about the way her perfume smelled and the way her hand felt in his, when the bullet whistled through the air and slammed into the post. Instinct put him on the sidewalk, the self-cocker already in his hand.

He had not seen the flash but knew by the sound that it was a pistol shot and not a rifle. The abrupt bang was lost within the din of the night's revelry. No one bothered to come rushing out into the street to investigate. In towns like Deadwood, pistol shots were as common as hogs at a trough. And by the time he was cocked and ready to defend himself, whoever had taken the shot had disappeared into the cover of night.

He felt the pulse thicken in his wrists and throb against his temples as he slipped the Remington back into the cross-draw holster. A few inches closer and he would have been tomorrow's gossip, displayed out in front of the local funeral parlor. He remembered on his way to catch the stage in Cheyenne how the undertaker had trussed up Frank Straw with baling wire and propped an empty Winchester through the crooks of his arms so that folks could have their photographs taken with the body for a dime. Death always seemed to magnify a man's celebrity. It wasn't the sort of attention Cole wanted.

Chapter Ten

Instead of going to directly back to the hotel room, Cole bought a bath and sank down into the tub of hot steamy water and paid the kid working the bathhouse $2 to bring him a meal. He wanted something that had beef on the plate and something to wash it down. He gave him two bits more to take his clothes down to a laundry and get them cleaned and wait for them. The steak was two inches thick and covered the entire plate and he ate it down to the bone, then washed it down with beer, and waited for the water to do its magic and the kid to return with his clothes. He thought of Billy Cook, reposing in the crimson water of his bloody bath, his expensive cigar floating on top. *One minute you're alive and the next you're dead.* He thought he could still hear the gunshot ringing in his ears.

He turned his thoughts elsewhere, to something more pleasant. Liddy Winslow's image filled his brain. He could still smell her perfume. She had stirred something in him that had long lay cold and untouched, something that went beyond the usual desire a man can get for a woman. And yet there had been that air about her that suggested she was a closed door, a door behind which no man was allowed. What really troubled him was that he wanted to be the one to go through that door. He thought of the women who had come along in his life after Zee died: the widows and the whores and the ones in between. It seemed he'd drifted between one and the other, not knowing which he preferred. Part of him wanted what he once had had—a good stable woman and a home where he could hang his hat after a long day—while the other part wanted just the opposite: a woman as wild as the West Texas wind and just as hard to hold, warm nights and tempting smiles and plenty of mescal. He wondered if Juanita Delgado had found herself a new man yet.

Lydia Winslow was another matter altogether. She was neither saint nor sinner, as far as he could judge. She wasn't needing or wanting. And now she was floating around in his mind in a way that good whiskey will, making him feel slightly off kilter and more pleasant than he had a right to feel.

The door opened with a slight click of the latch. He brought the Remington around from where it had been resting on a chair next to the tub; its action was smoothly mechanical, all its vital functions ready and set as he thumbed back the hammer. The man stood there, staring at him, the light soft in those nearly colorless eyes, eyes that were stern and without humor, the hollow cheeks puffing in and out below the prominent bones of his face. His mouth, partway open under the heavy sand-colored mustaches, showed a set of good teeth. His breathing was raspy and faint. The eyes shifted enough to see the self-cocker in Cole's hand, then drifted back.

"What'll it be, Doc?" Cole asked him. The front sight of the pistol was aimed at a spot just above his breastbone.

"It's not what you think," he said. "I didn't come to shoot it out with you."

"That's good. Because, if you had, I'd have to pull the trigger and I don't think you could stand the grief."

He coughed into a crimson-stained handkerchief, wiped it back and forth across his lips twice, and then balled it in his fist. "What's your business with Liddy Winslow?" he asked.

"That's just it, Doc . . . my business."

"That's not good enough."

"It has to be."

"You know of me? You know the type of man I am?"

"Yeah, I've heard the talk."

"Dying doesn't mean a damn' thing to me. Does it to you?"

"Did you come to discuss philosophy, Doc, or was there another reason for this unexpected visit?"

His gaze grew to fixed points within his skull, his hands flexed and unflexed by his sides. His cheeks worked hard, like a bellows against a fire, trying to work the air in and out of his weakened lungs. "I will ask you again," he said. His voice was raspy, full of phlegm, rough, the way a hard drinker's will get after a time. Still, it was a voice stubborn with a Southern accent—the voice of a Confederate gentleman who had maybe lost some of his gentility. "What is your business with Miss Winslow?" he asked again.

"Like I said, it's personal."

"Then you and I, sir, have a problem."

"Only if you believe so."

He stood there, unmoving except for the labored breathing. He didn't look like a killer; he looked like a man who had lost hope that he was going to live a long time.

"Someone took a shot at me tonight," Cole said. "Maybe it was you."

Something moved just under his left eye, a small twitch like a tiny worm working just below the skin. "Had I been the one," he said, "you would have now been wrapped in the arms of death."

Coming from him, the expression did not seem florid. "Well, Doc, I guess I was lucky, then, that it wasn't you."

"Miss Winslow is a special friend of mine. We enjoy a business relationship as well. It is incumbent upon me to see that she and her employees are not to be troubled. Do you understand my position, sir?"

"I know, she told me."

The spot below his eye twitched again. He swallowed, the paper collar around his neck moved, the string tie moved with it. His shadow hovered against one wall. Cole was fully prepared for him to produce a pistol. He was half expecting it.

"She told you," he said. It was not quite a question, not quite an assertion. Then, impossibly, the eyes became colder, more void of any emotion, and he said: "Then you understand?"

"I understand that your business with Miss Winslow is your own, Doc. I expect the same consideration."

"Then you understand?" he repeated.

"Let me ask you something, Doc."

He did nothing to invite the question, but Cole asked it anyway. "If your job was to protect the girls working for Liddy, then why didn't you?"

The slightest blush of color rose in his neck; the side of his jaw moved almost imperceptibly. These were the little things a man needed to be aware of when challenging a man of Doc's reputation. The hands will kill, but the look in a man's eye will tell you whether or not he's thinking about it. On the frontier, there were two types of men who would kill you: there were those like Doc, who might just pull their piece and have at it, and there was the other type, the ones that would lay for you in an alley, or shoot you in your sleep—fill your brains full of lead or shoot you in the kidneys and walk away. With Doc, Cole sort of got the sense he could do it either way. "You are intruding where you are not welcome," he said.

"You know about the reward she's put out for those responsible for killing the girls?" Cole said.

"You are here for that?"

"It's what I do, Doc."

Then the hard stare eased a bit and one corner of his mouth lifted into what could only be described as mild amusement. "I hope that your journey to this place was not a long one," he said. "For you have come here for nothing."

"I'm not the only who has come, or will be coming," Cole said. "One of them might already be in town. King Fisher. You ever heard of King Fisher, Doc?"

The small amusement fell from his mouth. "He is a low-heeled assassin," Doc said. He said it like a Southern senator denouncing an opponent. A cough rattled high up in his chest and bent him forward at the waist. The hand with the balled-up hankie jerked upward to his mouth and the veins of his neck distended into small purple ropes as the paroxysms rattled through him. He gripped the jamb of the door with his free hand in order to steady himself. Finally, after several seconds, the cough abated and he wiped his mouth and swallowed several times. He looked weak and frail, a man ready to step through death's door. "Do you mind not dropping the hammer on that piece?" he asked, his gaze falling to the revolver in Cole's hand. "I need a drink of my whiskey. I have it here, inside my coat."

Cole motioned for him to do so. His hand, a tremble of bones, reached inside the greatcoat and brought out a small silver flask that he held aloft and said: "I would offer to share it with you, but not many men will drink from the same container as a lunger, so I won't bother to extend the invitation." Then he tipped it to his mouth and Cole watched the sharp edge of his Adam's apple jerk in his throat as he swallowed. His breathing was labored, but he replaced the flask inside his coat, then swiped a finger across his mustaches, sweeping away the dew clinging to them.

"Your involvement with Lydia," he said, his voice a tinge weaker now, "will come to nothing. There are things that you do not understand."

"My water's getting cold, Doc." Cole felt there was nothing he was going to learn from him that he did not already know, except that Doc saw him as a rival, a threat to whatever it was he thought he had going with Liddy Winslow.

Doc blinked. Just once. He drew in a deep breath through his nostrils and let it out again. "Perhaps the next time we meet, sir, the odds will be more even between us," he said, again his gaze falling to the self-cocker in Cole's hand.

"Maybe so, Doc. You just never know."

He adjusted the greatcoat over his shoulders, pulling it tighter about him, then he turned and closed the door behind him, the scent of his bay rum still lingering in the air. Doc Holliday, King Fisher, Johnny Logan. The number of gun shooters Cole had to keep an eye out for was beginning to add up.

Chapter Eleven

The next morning Cole walked down to Johnny Logan's office. The sky was leaden, lying low over the cañon, and the streets were muddy from a late night rain. An icy wind blew down through the cañon and the pedestrians, what few there were that time of morning, were huddled against the cold, their hands bunched inside their pockets, their collars turned up. One man's hat was racing down the muddy street, its owner running behind it.

Constable Logan looked up when Cole entered. He had been drinking coffee from a tin cup, an unlighted cigar clamped between his teeth. The wind blew in behind Cole and stirred some papers on his desk.

"You mind?" he asked.

Cole closed the door as he straightened everything. Logan's coat was off, and through the tight fit of his shirt Cole could see the bulk of his shoulders and chest and arms. He was a man who could do a lot of damage with just his fists. Cole had been in the ring with men like him back when he did some prize fighting. He knew what it was like to hit a man like him and what it was like to be hit.

"I see you ain't left town yet," Logan said, blowing steam off the coffee as he brought it to his mouth.

"I came to get some information from you."

Logan didn't bother to invite Cole to sit down or have some of his coffee. Instead he said: "You've wasted a trip down here, then. I ain't in the information business."

"What do you know about a ring here in Deadwood?"

Cole waited for a sign of recognition: a muscle twitch along the jaw, a shifting of the eyes, the unsteadiness of the hand holding the cup of coffee. Either he was a good poker player or he didn't know what Cole was talking about, because he couldn't see anything in him that gave away whatever secrets he might be carrying.

"Cole, right?" he said. "If I read your name right, the one you signed on the hotel register, it's John Henry Cole?"

Cole waited for him to say what was on his mind.

"I got no time for gun artists and bounty hunters, just like I got no time for drunks and troublemakers."

"Does that include murdered prostitutes?" Cole asked.

Logan set the cup down. Some of the coffee spilled onto his desk, staining the edges of some Wanted posters. His lips compressed and his jawbone worked into a small knot under his left ear. "You've been warned," he said. "You go on back to the hotel and get your things and climb on the next stage out."

"I'm afraid not. My business isn't finished here yet."

He moved well for a big man, but Cole was ready for him. He ducked the first blow from Logan's huge right fist. The left one followed, angled downward, and grazed the side of Cole's face. Cole drove a right to a spot just below his ribs, the only place to hurt a man his size with a body blow. Cole heard him grunt, but at the same time he swung a looping left hand that missed but caught Cole with the elbow to the side of his head as it came around. It was like being struck with an anvil. As Cole stumbled sideways, stunned, the inside of his head ringing like mission bells, his old prize fighter's instincts took over. He lashed a left to Logan's cheek, felt it drive hard against the leathery skin, strike bone. He followed with a right and another left, then two more rights in rapid succession—each blow driving Logan backward. His face was cut high on the cheek from where Cole had hit him with the last right and a knot bulged over his left eye and blood leaked from his nostrils. But he was big and he was a gamer, and he hit Cole with a series of pounding blows that drove him back and into the chair of Logan's desk, Cole's feet tangling in the rungs. Cole slammed hard against the floor, the palms of his hands stinging from trying to break the fall. Then Logan hit him with something that shattered his senses and dropped him into a long dark well of nothingness.

* * * * *

Cole awoke to a drunken chorus of "I'll Take You Home Again, Kathleen". The voice was scratchy, raking like cat claws against his skin. He tried moving, tried sitting up, and, when he tried, his head felt like shattered glass. He reached up, probed for the sources of the pain. There were many. The worst, however, was at the back of his skull, where the constable had hit him with something he hadn't seen. His hair was sticky from where his scalp had been split, and, when he touched that place, it took his breath away.

The voice stopped singing long enough to say: "Looks like ol' Johnny Logan gave you the bum's rush and a whole lot more, mister." Then, without further pause, it broke back into song.

Cole adjusted his vision enough to see he had been locked up in a small cell with none other than Calamity Jane Canary. She was horribly drunk and reeked of anquitum, a common concoction used by miners to keep down the body lice population. She squatted in her bunk, howling the same chorus of the song over and over again. The room was small, maybe six feet by eight feet, with one window that had a set of bars that let in a small amount of light. Through the gloom Cole could see a heavy iron door that he didn't have to try to know was locked. Against his own better judgment, he managed to sit upright.

When Calamity Jane saw him do this, she stopped singing again. "Wah there, yer a damn' sight more alive than I would've guessed! You don't have no whiskey hidden on ya, do ya?"

Carrying on a conversation with her was not something Cole had in him just at the moment. And when she saw that he wasn't a talker, she took over.

"I'd 'a' nursed ya, if I had some bandages and bear grease. Hell, I've nursed a lot worse than ya. I've even nursed folks through the pox and measles. God damn if I couldn't stand a drink . . . 'scuse my French, in case yer a Christian . . . which I am most of the time myself, except when I'm drunk and feelin' blue. Which I am at the present."

Cole felt his only hope was that she would pass out, but she didn't.

"Hell, ya like singin', mister? I should've been a singer like one of them opry gals, travel the world over, see everything, do everything." Then her face shrank into a frown as she examined something on the front of her shirt. "Trouble is, my bosoms ain't big enough to be one of them opry gal singers. Ya ever notice how big a bosoms them gals have?" She tittered. "But I ain't missed much in life besides having big bosoms. I've seen and done things most folks couldn't even dream about." She laughed and slapped the top of her leg. "Whoo, boy! I mean I have *done* some things, believe you me." Her fringed jacket was stained dark in places and her canvas pants were muddy at the knees. "Ya ever hear of Wild Bill?" she asked. "Hell, of course ya have. Everybody's heard of Wild Bill." She had small, blunted teeth, evenly set but yellowed. Her eyes shone fiercely, alive with a restless energy. "Me and Bill was married," she said. "Oh, Gawd!" Her face twisted suddenly and she began to bawl aloud and flung herself across her cot in a highly dramatic way. Cole had seen worse performances. "Me and Bill have us a child, a baby girl, back East. And now Billy's dead and will never get to see her, and she won't get to see him, either! Oh, Gawd!"

Her grief was exaggerated, just as her singing had been. She may not have made an opera singer, but she might have made a pretty fair actress. Her loud sobbing went on for several more minutes as Cole sat there, trying to overcome his own grief—the grief of his injuries.

"Ya sure ya don't have a drink on ya, mister?" she said, suddenly changing moods again, wiping at eyes that were absent of tears.

When Cole nodded his head, she took on a forlorn look.

"If I was wearing some bloomers, I'd 'a' taken them off and made ya a bandage and wrapped that poor head a yars. Did I tell ya I used to nurse folks?"

"Look, I appreciate the offer, Miss Canary," Cole said. "But the truth is, I'm not up to conversation just now."

"Ya know my name!" she shouted. "Hell's bells! Then I guess ya have heard of me?" She seemed as delighted as a child that Cole knew who she was. "What's yar name, mister?" she asked, completely ignoring his request for some peace and quiet.

Cole gave up on the hope that she would settle down, at least for the present. "Cole," he said. "John Henry Cole."

Her gaze studied him for several seconds. "Nope! Ain't never heard of ya," she announced. "I thought fer a minute I might've known ya. I've known plenty a good-lookers in my time, shame to admit. Har, har, har." Her laughter was dry, shrill, something that seemed to crack against Cole's skull. "Ya ever consort with Texas Jack or White-Eye Johnson?" she asked. "Maybe that's where I might've known ya."

"Don't know either," he said.

She twisted the ends of her short, choppy hair; it was greasy and lank, what there was of it. "Whiskey gives me the blues," she said. "Having too much of it, or not having enough." She waited to see his reaction to her self-made joke, and, when he offered none, she slapped her knee and laughed. "Har, har, har. Johnny busted ya good, didn't he? Drug ya in here and tossed ya on the floor. I said to him . . . 'Johnny, what'd ya hit this feller with?' And he said . . . 'I busted him with the butt of my double-barrel whanger, and I'll do the same to you, you don't shut yer yap!'

Then I looked him in the eye and said . . . 'There ain't a day in heaven or hell that'll ever pass by when ya'd ever bust me like that, Johnny Logan.' Then he slammed the door and skulked off!"

For a long moment she stared at Cole as though seeing him for the first time. "It's a wonder he didn't bash out all yar brains!"

"Yeah, a wonder."

"It was me that lifted ya up on yar cot and put that blanket over ya so's ya wouldn't catch yar death."

"Thanks," Cole said, and meant it.

"Pshaw! Don't need to thank me. I nursed plenty like ya . . . or have I told ya that already? Anyway, ya wasn't the only one that paid the devil's price. Johnny wasn't lookin' so tip-top hisself. I seen how his face was all cut and his eyes all big and swellin' up. I'd 'a' paid to see that go 'round."

She fell silent for a minute, and the break from hearing her talk was a welcome gift for Cole, but it only lasted for a minute before she was back at it.

"They killed my Bill, ya know?"

"Who did?" Cole asked, slightly more interested now in what she had to say.

"Some right here in town. They paid that old ugly skunk McCall to kill him. Paid him fifty dollars and gave him a stolen pistol and sent him off to do it and he did, by Gawd!"

"Who paid him, Jane?"

But Cole could tell, looking into her startled eyes, that she was lost somewhere in her own fogged thinking, unaware of half of what she was saying.

"He wan't cross-eyed, neither, like they said he was. He could see good as you and me. He was just a plain damn' ugly sum-a-bitch, excuse my French."

"Jane, who was it that paid McCall to kill Bill?"

"Poor Billy, laid low like that! We was goin' to make a big score and go get little Janey and start a home, maybe in Nebraska along the Platte. Bill said how he always liked the Platte. Me, I never could see it, livin' up in that lonesome Nebraska. But I'd 'a' gone anywhere with ol' Bill." Her features grew genuinely sorrowful. "But that's all dried up dreams now, thanks to *Mister* Jack McCall . . ."

She wound down at last, sat silently, her head tilted over to one side, her mouth open, the blunted teeth showing behind her pale, thin lips. A string of drool leaked from one corner of her mouth, and then she slumped over, her eyes closing as she did so. In a few seconds she was snoring.

She may have been drunk and she may have been half crazy, but she was the second person to tell Cole that someone had paid McCall to assassinate Hickok. And if that were true, then maybe the same party had a hand in the killings of Liddy's girls. It was a stretch, but it was all he had to go on so far.

The heavy door rattled open. Two people stood in the frame of light. One was Johnny Logan, the other was Lydia Winslow. She waited for Cole to stand. The pain raced through him like a wildfire through dry grass.

"I've paid your fine," she said.

Cole looked at Logan. The damage he'd done to his face couldn't have hurt half as much as Cole's head did.

"Are you able to walk?" she asked.

"Enough to get to my room."

"Come, let's go."

Cole thought it strange that Johnny Logan would accept a fine and let him go, considering the circumstances, but he said nothing.

As they stepped outside, Cole could see that the jail was little more than a log structure set in an alleyway in back of Johnny Logan's office. Cole wasn't sure of the time, but the sun was already setting beyond the surrounding hills and the sky had begun to turn brassy.

"How'd you know where to find me?" he asked.

"Word spreads fast," she said.

Cole looked at her.

"Johnny's face," she said. "He couldn't hide it. The woman he sees when he's not seeing his wife told me about it. I guess after the fight, he needed some special comfort."

"Tell me," Cole said, "how was it you got him to let me go without a fuss?"

"It's a simple matter of economics," she answered. "Johnny has a wife and a mistress to support. He needs money more than he needs his pride. Besides, he knows that I know all about him and Lulu Divan, the other woman. He wouldn't want to risk my having a chat with his wife about the matter. I simply suggested that the whole affair of the fight between you two could be resolved in a peaceful manner and allowed him to suggest an appropriate fine for your indiscretion."

"Yeah. Well, thanks."

"Come back to my place. I'll have Jazzy Sue stitch your scalp and we'll get you cleaned up and feeling better."

The thought of turning down her offer never even crossed Cole's mind.

Jazzy Sue washed the blood out of his hair and with a needle and some black silk thread sewed the gash on the back of his scalp together while he nursed the pain with plenty of Liddy's imported cognac.

"What dat fool hit you wid?" Jazzy Sue asked as she stitched the wound.

"I was told the butt of a shotgun," Cole said. "It feels more like it might have been the roof."

"Lawdy, you lucky he didn't knock you silly."

"I'll let you know if he did in the morning."

She giggled.

Afterward, he sat and let the cognac work its magic. Liddy sat across from him. She had changed from the gray jacket and overskirt she'd worn to the jail into a soft long-sleeved white blouse that had a V down the front and was tied loosely with a loop of string. Her skirt was long and flowing and of a soft black material.

She held a glass of cognac, her long, slender fingers encircling it, the glass and the fingers equally delicate. "Feel better?" she asked him.

His head was filling with a light blue smoke that was both warm and gentle. The sharp edges of pain were slowly receding to another place.

"Yes," he said. "This cognac does wonders."

"I'm having Jazzy Sue fix us some dinner. I hope you like roast duck."

Cole sipped more of the cognac, and lost any thought about his fight with Johnny Logan as he looked into her green eyes that, under the low light, seemed more jade than emerald. He told himself through the warm fuzziness of the liquor that he was making a mistake. He told himself that a smart man wouldn't allow himself to mix his business with his pleasure. Then he thought of Billy Cook, sitting in that tub of bloody water. Lots of men had made that mistake. He told himself another thing. She had once been the woman Ike Kelly was in love with, and maybe still was. He had no right to violate their friendship. But right at that very moment, he wasn't able to take his eyes from her.

They ate, the two of them, sitting directly across from each other, Jazzy Sue serving them the meal at a modest table that was lighted by candles. Cole thought he'd seen Liddy's beauty already, but there, in the light of candles, in that very instant, she looked glowing. He ate the meal without tasting it. The conversation was kept to a minimum.

Then they adjourned to the parlor where they had first talked. "More cognac, or would you prefer something stronger . . . whiskey, maybe?" she asked him.

"My preference would be for something else altogether," he said. He felt like he was standing on the edge of a cliff and had decided to jump off just to see what it would feel like to fall a long way.

"I think the cognac has affected you," she said. Her presence seemed to fill the entire room. He could smell the perfume in her hair. He could feel its silkiness touch the side of his face. He could taste her mouth on his. Even though she sat there across from him and offered no indication that she was being anything more than polite and compassionate toward him.

"I think you're right," he said. "I had better go before I say or try something really stupid."

She sipped from her glass, her gaze fixed on his. "I'm aware of what is going on here between us, Mister Cole. But that doesn't mean I want it to happen."

"You're right," he said. "It shouldn't happen."

"You need to understand . . ." she began.

The cognac was really beginning to bury him beneath a warm, heavy blanket of sweet comfort. "No," he interrupted. "The reasons don't matter. I came here as a favor to an old friend, I can't betray his trust."

Her face seemed to soften under the shadows and light of the candles. "What was between Ike and me is in the past," she said. "It's not Ike standing in your way, is it?" Her voice was smoky and he couldn't think clearly and the room seemed to shift.

"Let's just leave it at that," Cole said. "There's no point in discussing what I want to happen and what you don't want to happen."

"I confess that I find you an attractive man," she said, lowering her glass of cognac. "But there are two reasons why I can't allow myself to become involved with you. I want you to know what they are."

Either he'd had drunk too much, or he hadn't drunk enough. John Henry Cole waited for Liddy Winslow to explain without wanting to hear what she had to tell him.

"The first thing you need to understand," she said, "is that I vowed a long time ago not to let myself get emotionally involved with anyone. Ike was the exception. I was young. He was tender with me. He needed me in a way no man had before. It was love and it was something more than that, but I wouldn't marry him because I wanted more from life than being somebody's wife. I wanted independence. Most men wouldn't understand that. And if they did, they wouldn't appreciate it." She paused, turned the glass of amber liquid between her fingers, and never once stopped looking into Cole's eyes. "The other reason I have for not wanting anything to happen between us is that I already have a male friend. A man who I see. It would not be fair to him."

"I thought you just said . . ."

"I didn't say I was in love with this man. He is a companion. Someone who doesn't question me or force his life on me. We share certain things. It's convenient and without too much demand. I like it that way."

"I see," Cole said. He must have showed his disappointment.

"Do you really?" she asked.

"Yeah. I really do." It was a lie, but he didn't have it in him to argue the point. "I better get going," he said, and stood, nearly forgetting that he had a head full of misery.

She rose from her side of the table, came around, and touched her hand to his wrist. "No, I don't think you fully understand what I've just told you," she said. Her face was inches from his, her eyes searching, and, when he breathed, her scent flowed into his senses and mixed with the cognac and left him unsteady.

"You're right," he said. "I don't understand."

"Maybe in time you will," she said, and released her fingers from the back of his wrist. "Good night, Mister Cole."

Then she was gone. He was still standing there, holding onto the back of the chair when Jazzy Sue brought him his curled Stetson.

"You goin' to be able to put that thang on your head?"

"I wouldn't go out without it," he said. She looked at him with the sweet curiosity of a child. "The trick is going to be taking it off later."

She giggled.

"Thanks, Jazzy Sue. Thanks for the supper and sewing my head back together."

She smiled a smile of bright teeth and her beauty was a comfort against his pain and weariness.

He was halfway to his hotel room when he ran into Miguel Torres.

"Cole," he said, his gaze assessing the damage Johnny Logan had done.

"Marshal," Cole said.

He shifted his gaze. "I'd just as soon you kept my position to yourself."

"Yeah, I forgot. You said you were on personal business."

"I'm looking for someone," he said. "I'd just as soon they not know that."

"You don't have to worry about me, Torres. I've got enough problems of my own."

"I can see that." There was no sympathy or compassion in his manner. He was a man of unchanging characteristics. "There's some bad business going on in this place," he said without bothering to elaborate.

Cole started to ask him what he meant when someone shouted: "Hey, ya!"

Cole turned to see Calamity Jane weaving down the street. She was in the company of a miner. They were both drunk. It was a day that seemed to have no end to it.

She crossed the street, nearly got run over by a wagon carrying nail kegs. Ignoring the curses of the driver, she came to stand just inches from Cole, her breath sour. "Jack, ya ain't got a dollar for me and my pal, Ted, over there, do ya?" When Cole hesitated, she winked and said: "Maybe I could rid myself of

Theodore and me and ya could go up to yar crib and have us a sweet time, eh?"

He gave her the loose change in his pocket and would have given her more if she had persisted. She shook his hand like it was a pump handle and she was dying of thirst, then rejoined her friend on the far side of the street. He saw them kiss. When he turned back, Miguel Torres had vanished. Suddenly he was alone and glad of it.

Chapter Twelve

The dreams came hard that night. John Henry Cole tumbled down into them and everyone was waiting for him. Zee held the shattered head of the dead Confederate boy, his Rebel flag wrapped about him like a bloody shroud. She kissed him delicately on the cheek, just below where the Minié ball had entered. His eyes fluttered and his breath came in gasps. Nearby a cradle carved of cherry wood rocked in the wind. In it he saw his infant son Tad. He could hear gunfire in the forests that surrounded the glade where Zee knelt holding the dead boy. The woods were full of Confederate soldiers. He could hear the Rebels howling, their shrieks causing the tops of the trees to explode with blackbirds. Some strange, powerful jealousy rose in his chest at the sight of Zee holding the boy, at the way she kissed him as though she were his lover. The boy turned his head and looked at him, his gaze a mixture of sadness and pain.

Liddy Winslow was there, too—reclined on a quilt of soft yellow flowers. She called to him, held out her arms. Zee smiled, content to hold the broken child that changed from the dying boy to their son Tad. Without willing it, a force drew him toward Liddy and away from Zee and his son. He knew that he was betraying them, but he could not stop himself from going to Liddy. She was warm and sensuous and he lay down atop her, her arms reaching around, holding him tightly to her. She kissed his mouth over and over again and his passion was on fire for her. But then he turned just enough to see Zee. She was crying, the hurt pouring down her cheeks. She was asking him why he was doing this to her. Why was he being unfaithful to her? And shame overcame him, but he could not bring himself to leave Liddy.

Doc Holliday stepped from the trees dressed in Rebel gray, the sunlight shattering off the brass buttons of his tunic. His right hand was perched inside the gray coat. Cole could see the outline of a pistol against the fabric. His smile was craven as his hand slid from inside the jacket, bringing a pistol with it. Liddy, now naked in Cole's arms, whispered things to him he could not understand. She clawed at him and thrust her hips against his, oblivious to Doc and the pistol he had pointed at them. Cole could not move, could not escape her or him or the Rebels who suddenly came pouring out of the woods from every direction, their heads bandaged and bleeding, their faces contorted in hatred and pain.

Zee's long, slow wail of anguish rose from an open grave. He struggled to go to her, to set himself free from Liddy. As he struggled, Liddy became Rose, the girl on the stage, and she was frail against him and she was crying and asking him why he was doing this to her. Why was he hurting her in this way? Then Doc pulled the trigger and the sound shattered the dream.

Cole surfaced from the dream like a drowning man, struggling against the smothering grip of some dark, bottomless river. His lungs ached for wanting air and his heart pounded. He lay there for a long time, waiting for the effects of the dream to subside.

When the world righted itself in his mind again, he made it to the wash basin and pulled water over his face with both hands. His head ached from the wound. He was soaked in sweat; his skin felt hot, feverish. He wanted to crawl out of it. The room was dark, full of stillness, except for his breathing. He didn't know what time it was. It felt like he was in a tomb. Someone knocked at the door. He didn't move.

There was another knock.

He withdrew the self-cocker from the holster, then opened the door. He eased the hammer down on the pistol when he saw who it was.

"Miss Winslow." At least, he thought he said her name. She looked at him.

"Can I come in?" she asked.

He stepped back. She saw the Remington in his hand. He replaced it in the gun belt and lighted the lamp. She stood there, looking about the room.

"What time is it?" he asked.

"Well past midnight," she said.

"What's wrong?"

"I couldn't sleep," she said.

The flame guttered in the lamp, its yellow tongue of light dancing back and forth as if it were alive, trying to escape its glass cage. The lamp was nearly empty of oil. She was dressed in the same clothes she had been wearing earlier, the cotton blouse and black skirt, only she was wearing a dark blue velvet jacket that was stitched with black beads across the front. Her hair was loose, cascading past her shoulders. Just to look at her took his breath away.

"I don't have anything to offer you," he said, looking around the room. "I don't even have a bottle of whiskey or a glass to pour it in. You'll have to excuse my accommodations."

"I didn't come for a drink," she said, slipping into the room. She was close enough to him that he could smell her perfume. Then her hands were touching his bare forearms.

He hesitated, then kissed her. Her mouth was as warm and sweet as he had imagined it to be. His fingers weaved themselves into the smooth silkiness of her thick hair. His left arm encircled her waist and she slid her hands to his sides. Her kisses were passionate, full, and he felt his own passion rising out of places he had long forgotten existed.

It felt awkward, eager, but somehow they managed, without letting go of one another, to make it to the bed. His mind raced with questions as to what had changed her resolve from a few hours earlier until now. But they were questions he didn't want to take time to ask. They didn't seem important. He unbuttoned the jacket and removed it from her. Then he lifted the cotton blouse over her head and the warmth of her breasts pressed down against his chest. Her hair fell down into his face, a silken shroud, as she leaned over him.

"I don't know why I'm doing this," she said, her voice as thick as smoke.

"Let's not talk."

Her face closed on his again, her lips brushed the side of his cheek. She kissed the bruise there, and ran the tips of her fingers over his lips, then down across his chest, and down farther still. He shuddered from a deep, deep place. His hands caressed the smooth curve of her back, touched the swell of her hips. Then she stood, removed the skirt and the underskirt, and stood naked before him in the dying, dancing light. She seemed more than his eyes could take.

She knelt before him, took one of his hands into her own, brought it to the side of her face, held it there. Then she looked into his eyes and said: "Is this what you want?"

"Yes."

He pretended not to see the small flicker of pain behind her eyes when he said yes. She held his gaze for a moment longer, then rose to the bed alongside him and kissed him again, a long, slow kiss that seemed to last forever.

On the bed she moved over on top of him with animal grace and at the same time reached down for him, touching him in a way that caused him to swallow the rush of pleasure it gave him. His hands floated upward, encircling her breasts. The pain from his injuries was numbed by her presence, by the sweet anguish of his passion for her. Her sweetness flowed over him and through him and he finally knew what it was like to stand at the edge of a cliff and jump off and fall freely through the waiting space.

* * * * *

Later, she lay silently in his arms, her breathing even, warm against his chest. Somewhere in the time since she had arrived, the lamp had burned itself out. The only light came from ghostliness of a full moon that crept through the window.

"Tell me about your friend," Cole said.

She took a long time before she spoke. "Why does it matter to you?"

"I don't know why it matters. I'd just like to know what sort of man you find interesting enough to share your time with."

She looked at him, withdrew her face several inches, and stared.

"What sort of man are you?" she asked.

"I'm not sure I understand the question."

"You asked me what sort of man interests me. What sort of man are you?"

"I meant other than me."

"If it is a problem for you . . ." she began, but he stopped her by kissing her gently.

"It's not a problem for me," he said then. "I'm just curious."

She waited for a long moment. "His name?" she asked. "Is it his name you want to know, or do you just want to know what he is like?"

"Both."

She sighed, and her hand rested on his chest. "His name is Winston Stevens." She added: "He's English."

"And probably very handsome."

"Yes, I suppose you could say that."

"Rich, no doubt?"

"His family is well off, but if you think that is why . . ."

"No, I was thinking it is just my luck."

"What is?"

"That'd you be interested in a rich English gentleman."

"You're talking foolishness." She said it half seriously.

"Deadwood is a long way from England."

"Winston has come here to invest in mining. He seeks to be his own person."

"Easy enough to do when you have money behind you."

"You're being unfair to the man. You don't even know him."

Cole started to defend himself. He didn't think he was being unfair to Winston. He thought he was just calling a spade a spade. But she stopped him by placing her fingertips against his lips. "Do we really have to discuss this?" she asked.

"Of course not. But I wanted to."

She leaned her face closer to his. "Remember, you wanted to know," she said.

"Yeah. I had to ask, didn't I?"

"Yes, you did."

"He's probably gracious and has good manners, too."

Her lips brushed the side of his jaw. "All that, yes."

"Damn, last time it was a Mexican bandit, this time a charming Englishman."

Her fingers crept across his chest. "What are you talking about, John Henry?"

"Nothing."

Her body pressed against his, warm and soft, the way a woman's body ought to be, and the passion reawakened in him.

"Let's talk about something else," she suggested.

"No," he said. "I'm tired of talking." He pulled her closer.

She floated above him, her hair dangling against his face. He could smell the scent of her, the womanly scent that could drive a man to madness. Her lips brushed his cheek, floated to his chin, then sought his mouth. "Yes, no more talk," she said.

Chapter Thirteen

Somewhere beyond the passion, Cole sank into a deep, undisturbed sleep. There were no dreams this time, no ghosts, no pain. There was just the sweet nothingness.

When he opened his eyes again, Liddy was gone. The scent of her lingered there in the bed with him, lavender and female. When he tried sitting up, something sharp and painful pierced itself behind his eyes. Temporarily he had forgotten his encounter with Johnny Logan. He felt around on his scalp, touched the stitches. They were stiff. His head still ached, but the rest of him felt all right.

He gritted his teeth and sat up, then stood. He felt slightly off kilter, but the pain and dizziness passed in a few seconds and he made his way to the wash basin. He drew water over his face and examined his image in the mirror. He looked like a scruffy hound, but at least a contented one.

He collected his straight razor out of his saddlebags and shaved, then carefully drew a comb through his hair. He strapped on the self-cocker, pulled the duster over it, and settled the Stetson on his head as best he could. By all appearances, he looked almost normal.

He left the hotel. The weather over the gulch had cleared and the sky was a flawless blue. The sun sparkled in the puddles of rain, reflected against the windows. The labor in Deadwood had slowed. And for the first time since Cole's arrival, the boom town seemed to have taken on a casual air. To him at that moment Deadwood didn't seem like such a hell town. It was Sunday morning. He realized then that he was hungry—hungry in a way he hadn't been in a long time.

Cole entered the first restaurant he came to—a place called Lou's Café. Even at that hour, it was doing a good business. The all-night crowd of red-eyed gamblers, weary prostitutes, and men who'd had their pockets cleaned and their souls tarnished were steeling themselves for another twenty-four hours on earth, if they could just make it through this one more morning. They sat, leaning over plates of yolky eggs and greasy hash and crisp strips of bacon. The steam from their coffee cups rose in tiny clouds and broke against their fatigued faces. Cole took a table near the window—an old habit lawmen get. Outlaws, too.

A young Irish girl who was plump and apple-cheeked and wearing an apron came and asked him for his order. He took the special.

He formed a shuck and smoked it and watched the street outside, but his thoughts were on Liddy and last night. A part of him didn't want to believe what had happened; it didn't seem real. He wasn't sure it had been. He wanted to believe that whatever had taken place between Liddy and him was something special, that it wasn't just another case of two lonely people burning up the night. He tried to think through it over the plate of fried eggs and slab of ham the Irish girl brought him.

He was still thinking about Liddy when a voice he hadn't heard in a long time called him out of the pleasantness.

"John Henry Cole."

He looked up and saw a face that didn't offer him any comfort—King Fisher. He laid his fork down with his right hand, and at the same time slid the self-cocker out of its holster under the table with his left. The red-checked tablecloth hid the action. The only problem, he reflected, was that he had never been able to hit anything using his left hand.

The dark blunt features of King Fisher were peppered with a wiry beard. Black, pitiless eyes, half hidden by hooded lids, fixed themselves on him. King Fisher was a tall man for one thing, real tall. He wore a greatcoat, dusty and heavy and down past his knees, which made him appear even taller than he was. Cole could see the bulge of his pistols underneath the coat—how many was hard to tell. His gaze drifted over Cole, over his food, like Cole was something he'd never seen before. He drew air through his nose.

"Why ain't I surprised you're in Deadwood?" he said with a voice graveled by too many cigars and snake-head whiskey.

"You're standing in my light," Cole said.

King Fisher shifted his weight. Cole knew that it's the hands that'll kill you, not the eyes, so he made sure to watch King Fisher's hands.

"You come for the reward money?" he asked.

"I like to keep my business my own, King. You can understand that, can't you? A businessman, like yourself?"

"It's why *I'm* here," he said, "the money." Then added: "I don't much care if you know that."

"Well, thanks for sharing the information, King." *Fourth button from the top of his coat, that's where I'd shoot him if I had to,* Cole thought to himself, hoping it wouldn't go that far.

"Recall the time you screwed me out of that reward money on Shanghai Doolittle over in Ardmore," he said. "Twenty-two hundred dollars."

"You got a good memory. That was five years ago."

"Told myself then I'd never let you screw me outta no more reward money."

"I've got a sore skull," Cole told him. "It makes me edgy, the headache I've got from it. I came in here for some coffee, a little breakfast, a little something to take the edge off. Now you show up, stand in my light, talk about the past like I care to hear it. I'm in no mood. What do you want?"

"I ought to just go ahead and plug you here and now, John Henry. You know, pull my pistols and air you out like a bachelor's bed sheet."

"It'd be a mistake, King."

"Mistake?" He grinned the stupid grin of a bully suddenly unsure of himself.

"I've got my self-cocker under the table here, and it's pointed at your buttons. I couldn't miss if I tried. Hell, if I was just to fall off the chair by accident, I'd probably kill you. It wouldn't even be a contest. You wouldn't want that, would you?"

Some of his features sagged, the hoods lifted over the eyes like shades going up. His gaze fell to the table. "You do, huh?" He cocked his head just a little, as though trying to see under the table but afraid to move too much.

"Yeah. Primed and ready."

Was Cole lying or wasn't he? That was the question dancing behind King Fisher's eyes. All that hardware he was carrying under his coat wasn't worth a tinker's damn. Even a fast man isn't that fast. Cole saw the truth of it settle in his gaze, the hard reality that he was beaten this time around. He gritted his teeth, trying to see under the table but not able to, and not sure if or when Cole might pull the trigger on him. Finally he quit trying to see. "There'll be another time," he said.

"My eggs are getting cold," Cole said.

His nostrils flared, then he let go of it, the temptation to see if he could jerk the pistols before Cole killed him. Men like King Fisher didn't wish for death so much as they sometimes invited it. Cole knew one thing, sooner or later he'd have to kill him, or be killed by him. It was just a question of when. Slowly his hands relaxed at his sides. Cole still held the self-cocker aimed at his coat buttons. King Fisher's mouth twitched.

"Next time, no talk," he said, then turned and left.

Cole let out his breath as he saw him pass by the window and walk out of view. He didn't know if he could have hit anything or not, holding the pistol in his left hand, but he was glad he hadn't had to find out.

He slid the gun back into the holster, and resumed eating. The eggs had lost their taste and the slab of ham was cold—so was the coffee. It was a bad end to what had started out to be a good morning. He reached for the money to pay his bill when something suddenly blocked the sunlight coming through the window.

Without taking the time to look, Cole threw himself sideways just as King Fisher fired his pistols. The window exploded into a shower of glass. Falling, taking the table with him, Cole saw a gambler grab his neck and slump face down into his plate of food. A ribbon of blood spurted through his fingers. The table Cole threw up as a shield took two of King Fisher's bullets before Cole could clear his own gun. Over the clatter of plates and tableware and scrambling patrons, he could hear King Fisher say: "It's time to finish it, Cole. I've come back to kill you! Just like I said I would."

He said it as calmly as if he were announcing the playbill at the local opera house. A shard of glass had buried itself into Cole's left wrist; a single drop of blood, bright and red as a ruby, oozed from the wound. Time seemed to stop, and for a long, frozen moment, Cole could hear his own breathing.

A bullet shattered the air, slammed into the table, splintered past Cole's face, and bore a hole through the floor. Cole knew when he raised up from behind the table, he'd have one chance, and only one chance, to kill him. Once he raised up, all he had to do was hit the mark. It wasn't a thought he had much time to dwell on.

King Fisher fired twice more just as Cole came up over the table. How he missed both shots, Cole never knew. Cole's shot took him dead center. It was as if some invisible hand had snatched him off the sidewalk and flung him into the street. He landed on his back, flopped in the mud, dead.

Someone shouted to get a doctor, but it wasn't for King Fisher. It was for the gambler who'd taken one of King Fisher's stray bullets in the neck. Cole stepped outside onto the walk and stared down at the body, the boots pointing skyward, the lifeless eyes no longer menacing, the hands no longer quick. He didn't feel good about it. He didn't feel bad.

Johnny Logan came charging up the street, his gun drawn. Cole wondered if maybe it was going to be a day of killing. He turned on him, held the self-cocker straight out, the front sight in a direct line aimed at the center of Logan's body. "Hold it there," he ordered.

Logan stopped short.

"It was self-defense," Cole said. "You can ask these others."

Logan looked uncertain. Several confirmed Cole's side of it. Logan slipped his own gun into his pocket. Cole lowered his.

Logan leaned over, looked at the face, straightened, and said—"King Fisher."—like a curse that had slipped out of his mouth in church. It sent a buzz through the crowd. Lots of folks had heard of the gunfighter. "God damn it!" Logan swore. "I don't need this aggravation."

"Nor do I," Cole told him.

"He won't be the last to show up," Logan said, his face patchy with dark bruises. "I want you out of town."

"Then you better make it happen here and now."

It didn't occur very often, but when a man tried to kill him, like King Fisher had just tried to do, Cole's blood got hot in a way that burned up all his reason. He was at that point now, ready to fulfill the destiny of any man who was looking for it, including Johnny Logan.

"You threatening me?" he growled.

"Take it how you will."

Cole watched Logan's right hand, the one near the pocket he'd put his gun in.

"I didn't come here to raise hell, but I'll take all of it you want to hand out, Constable. You want to finish it, finish it."

They were both at that point, ready to die in order to stand their ground. Neither cared any longer. Then a voice spoke from the crowd of onlookers.

"You ought to let it go, Constable. I saw the whole thing. This man was just eating his breakfast, just having some runny yellow eggs, when that fellow tried to shoot him through the window. I don't think you want to die over some piece of dog shit like King Fisher. 'Course, maybe I'm wrong. Maybe you do."

Cole didn't have to look to recognize the voice. It was Miguel Torres's.

Logan turned his attention to the Mexican-Apache-Caucasian lawman, saw the simple way he was dressed, the cold stare, the carbine cradled in the crook of one arm. "Who the hell are you?"

"That doesn't matter, does it?" Torres said. "A fact is a fact, and the plain fact here is, Fisher brought on his own trouble."

Torres glanced in Cole's direction. Nothing in his look told Cole he was being anything other than a truthful witness. He was hard to figure out.

Johnny Logan let go of it reluctantly, like a dog giving up a bone already chewed clean of its meat. He asked some of the more able-bodied to help him carry the tall, lank corpse of King Fisher over to the undertaker's parlor.

"I ain't known you but less than a week," Torres said, stepping closer to Cole. "And already I've seen you kill two men cold as ice beer. I know why I'm here. You want to tell me why you're here?"

Chapter Fourteen

"Why the sudden interest?" Cole asked Torres as they walked down the street.

"I could stand a whiskey, how about you?"

"It's early for that," Cole said.

"This looks like a good place."

It was Nutall and Mann's Number Ten, the place that had Wild Bill's bloodstain on the floor and his chair hanging on the wall.

"Sure, why not?" Cole said.

Cole noticed Irish Murphy was not yet on duty. Instead, there was another man rubbing glasses behind the bar. He looked tired and miserable.

"A bottle," Torres said.

The man looked at him briefly, just long enough to see the hard, frank stare, just long enough to see this wasn't a man he should ask a lot of questions, questions like why a man would want to drink hard liquor at that time of the morning.

Torres took the bottle, dropped $1 on the counter without asking the price, and poked his fingers in two empty glasses that the barman had just rubbed and set on the bar.

"Let's sit over there," Torres said, pointing with his nose to a table in the far corner. A man with his trousers rolled up past his knees was sleeping on the pool table.

Cole waited while Torres filled each of the glasses with Red-Eyed Jim. Torres tossed his down, looked at Cole, then at his untouched glass.

"Like I said, it's a little early for me."

Torres refilled his own glass, turned it between dark, blunt fingers. "So what's the story on you, Cole? You sure in the hell didn't come up here to muck for gold."

"You answer my question first," Cole said. "Why the sudden interest in me?"

Cole thought he saw something that could've passed for a smile play at his lips, but it would be a stretch of the imagination.

"I'm looking for someone," he said. "It's what I'm good at, looking for people."

"What's that got to do with me?"

"Tell me first why you're here."

Cole took a breath, thought about the whiskey, about whether or not he needed a drink this early in the day, decided he didn't. "There's been some killings," he said. "Prostitutes. I came up here to check into it for a friend."

Torres didn't take his eyes off him.

"The dead girls worked for a woman named Lydia Winslow. She's the one who wrote my friend, asking for help. I came in his place. He's in the detective business."

Torres still had that look of something near to a smile and his fingers continued to twist the glass of whiskey around between them without spilling any of it.

"That must be good drinking liquor, the way you're fondling it," Cole said.

"Detective, huh? That what you are, too? A detective?"

"I guess you don't think much of the title or the profession."

"First god-damn' detective I ever met," he said. "Would you believe it? All these years, and you're the first one. Your friend, he's a Pinkerton man?"

"No. He's in business for himself. His operation is a lot smaller than Pinkerton's."

"Who's your friend? Maybe I've heard of him."

"Ike Kelly."

Torres shook his head. "No, ain't never heard of him."

"Kelly Detective Agency, out of Cheyenne," Cole tried again.

Torres half rolled his eyes, trying to remember if he'd ever heard of it. "No. I ain't never heard of it."

"It doesn't matter."

"Well, what the hell does a job like detective work pay, anyhow?"

"Depends on the assignment," Cole said.

"What, maybe a hundred a month, something like that?"

"It's not regular pay. It all depends on the job."

Torres lifted the glass of Red-Eyed Jim, sipped it, held it out, looked at it, sipped it some more.

"How's a man get in that line of work . . . detective?"

"It isn't hard to get into."

"No, I bet it isn't."

"Why the interest?" Cole asked again.

"Just curious . . . about the detective work."

"What about the other?"

"You mean, my reason for being here?"

Cole nodded.

"Yeah, like I said, I'm looking for somebody. You could be him."

"How so? I rode up here on the stage with you. You'd know if I was the man you're looking for."

"No, not necessarily. It could be anybody."

"Why're you looking for somebody in the first place?"

Torres set the empty glass down gently, like it was an egg he didn't want to break. "I had a brother come up here nine, ten months back. Come up here to muck gold. Him and another man, a man named Shag Hargrove. The way my brother described this Shag Hargrove, he was a gold panner. Robertito was a fool. I told him that first off when he talked about it. But you'd have to know Robertito to understand why he wouldn't listen to me.

Robertito's young, full of piss and vinegar. A dreamer, that's what Robertito Torres is."

Miguel Torres didn't seem to be talking to Cole as much as he was to himself. Cole listened closely to the rest of it.

"Robertito and this fellow Hargrove, they came here saying how rich they were going to get. I heard from Robertito once. Said they'd found something, but he wouldn't say what or how much exactly. Then, a month ago, someone sent home his things. They were wrapped in butcher paper and sent home to the old woman. His shirt and extra pants and a dollar watch he owned. No money, of course. I went to the house and the old woman showed me Robertito's things, wrapped up in that butcher paper. She said to me . . . 'Miguel, Robertito's been killed, I know it. Go see if you can find your brother and learn what happened to him.' She cried a little. It's mostly because of her that I came here. For me, too."

Cole watched him pour another inch of the whiskey in his glass and take his time drinking it.

"I ain't sentimental, like some," he went on. "But god damn it, Robertito was my brother, the old woman's youngest boy. You can see how a thing like that would affect her, can't you?"

"Yeah."

He blinked, dropped his chin a little. "See, Robertito was always chasing after something that wasn't there. He was an unsteady boy, but damn if you couldn't help but like him the first time you met him. He was that way. Everybody liked Robertito the minute they met him." Then Miguel Torres stiffened in his chair and his eyes grew fixed. "They shouldn't have sent his god-damn' clothes home in butcher paper," he muttered. "Not even a god-damn' note to say what happened to him."

"Somebody must have cared enough about him to do that much," Cole said. "A woman, maybe. Sounds like what a woman might do if she cared about him . . . send his things home."

"Butcher paper . . ." He said it like they were the only words he remembered from a forgotten prayer. Then he drank the whiskey, drank it like there was a fire in his gut he was trying to put out with it. And for a long time, there was nothing but the sound of flies droning the air. "The writing on the butcher paper," he said after a while. "It could've been a woman's. I didn't think of that till just now, you mentioning it." The thought stirred behind his eyes, bringing some new hope. "Robertito liked women, and they sure as hell liked him." He lifted his gaze toward Cole as he poured some more of the whiskey into his glass a little less carefully than before. Some of the liquor spilled over onto his blunt fingers. "But if it's like you say, Cole, how come she didn't take the time to write a note with it, to say what happened to Robertito? How come a woman would take the time to send his things and not bother to tell his own family what happened to him?"

"Maybe she thought she'd done her share," Cole said. "Or maybe she was afraid of getting more involved if it was something bad that happened to your brother."

"Maybe that was it, she was afraid."

"Maybe so."

This time he drank the whiskey like he was just plain thirsty for it. "It's a damn' weakness," he said.

"What is?"

"Drinking."

"To some, maybe it is."

"To me," he said. "It'll get me killed someday. I know that as sure as I know anything."

"Then why do you do it?"

This time his lips edged into a genuine smile. "Two reasons," he said.

Cole waited for him to tell him his reasons.

"I can't stop. And it don't matter."

"Dying ought to count for something," Cole said. "The same way living ought to count for something."

"Not to me, it don't."

"No sweetheart waiting back in Texas?"

He grunted. "Do I look the type?"

"It was just a question."

"Yeah, I guess it was."

He poured out another glass, only this time he filled it all the way to the top. "I guess we both came here because of the killing going on in this town," Miguel Torres said, just before draining his glass.

"Maybe you should begin asking about the women Robertito might have been friendly with," Cole suggested, but he wasn't sure Torres had heard him, for his head had dropped slightly, like a weary old bull's.

Cole stood, and the chair scraping over the floor brought Torres around.

"Detective . . ." he said, staring up at Cole.

"Good luck, Mister Torres. I hope you find your brother."

The muscle below Torres's left eye became pinched, maybe from disdain. "What's something like that pay? That detective work?"

Cole left him sitting there, his hand gripping the half empty bottle. The company of Miguel Torres had suddenly lost its appeal.

Cole walked up the street to the stable where the old man was sitting, his face tilted to the sun.

"You get a horse in yet I can rent?"

The old man opened his eyes. "You ain't dead yet," he said.

"Was I supposed to be?"

The old man coughed a laugh, then spat, then wiped his mouth and nose with the back of his hand. His eyes searched around in Cole's face like a prospector looking for quartz in a field of stone. "I heard the shots," he said.

"About that horse . . . ?"

"Saw them carry a man over to Principal's funeral parlor. I thought maybe it was you."

"Well, you can see it wasn't. Do you have a horse to rent, or not?"

He scratched the loose skin of his neck. "Got a buckskin. He ain't fer beginners, ya know what I mean?"

"Bring him out."

The old man stood like it was the greatest effort in the world to do so, wiped his hands along the legs of his trousers, and disappeared inside the stable. In a few minutes he led out the buckskin. He had put Cole's Dunn Brothers saddle on the gelding. Cole appreciated the fact that he had.

"Four dollars," the old man said, holding out his hand. "Up front, ya don't mind."

Cole paid him and climbed aboard. He had barely got both feet in the stirrups and the buckskin was off. He gave him his head; it was the best thing to do with a horse that wants to run. Just let him. Cole wanted to run, too.

The buckskin ran for a long time, then Cole was able to slow him down to a walk. He followed a trail off the main road that led back in among the tall dark pines. They climbed a ridge, worked their way along it, and kept going until they came to a blue mountain lake that lay glittering in the sun. The buckskin was balky about the descent, but this time Cole was in charge, and together they went down—all the way down to the edge of the lake, then in, up to the buckskin's belly.

Cole let him drink, then rode him out and back up on the shoreline. There he dropped his saddle and let the buckskin crop grass while he pulled off his boots and everything else he was wearing.

The water was cold, nearly as cold as a knife, but Cole went in anyway, and it sucked the breath out of him and tempered the pain shrinking his skull. After a while, everything quit hurting and feeling bad, and he could breathe again. He soaked in the icy lake until he couldn't feel his legs and arms, then worked his way out and lay in the grass, letting the sun warm him. He refused to listen to the voices of the ghosts. Instead, he listened to the gentle cropping of the horse and the way the wind floated over the meadow grass and the way the water kissed against the rocks there at the shoreline. It was enough, just enough, all he needed. He remembered an old Baptist preacher telling him once that it wasn't what a man wanted in life so much that counted, as it was what he needed. And if a man just got that much out of life, he was well blessed.

Lying there on the sweet grass with the sun warming his skin and Deadwood a long way off, he had just exactly what he needed. He closed his eyes and was nearly asleep when he heard the drumbeat of riders approaching.

Chapter Fifteen

Cole rose up in time to see four riders pressed against the horizon, their horses throwing up clods of dirt. He could feel the pounding hoofs, rumbling up through the ground like a thumping heart. He pulled on his trousers and shirt and shoved the Remington into his waistband.

Three of the riders were wearing red shirts and the brims of their hats were flattened back against the crowns. They all had the same squinting eyes and long, wild mustaches and Vandyke beards. Quirts swung from their gauntlets, and their chaps flared and flattened as they lifted and fell in rhythm with their lathered ponies. But it wasn't the red shirts Cole was watching as much as the man who rode out front. He was riding a large blooded stud with four white stockings. A horse like that would cost $300 or $400. Then he noticed the saddle. It sure wasn't anything that the Dunn Brothers would've made. It had iron stirrups and a small flap of leather for the seat. It was the kind of saddle a man would want if his horse gave out on him in the middle of the plains and he had to carry it a long distance. It didn't look like it weighed anything at all.

His attention went from the horse and saddle to the man. He was tall and well built, wearing a tailored gray suit and a tweed cap. He would be hard to mistake for a frontiersman, and the way he rode told Cole he wasn't a Westerner. The riders drew up ten feet away, sliding their horses to hard stops, except for the dude riding the thoroughbred. He circled around Cole, then came to a halt.

125

The other three fanned out in a semicircle behind him. The three red shirts could have been brothers, for all their similarities. They looked on with curiosity while the dandy riding the big stud tipped his cap before addressing Cole.

"I say, my dear man, is it your habit to take your leisure on private land?"

Cole didn't have to guess to know who it was just by the accent—Winston Stevens, Liddy's English gentleman, he thought, for lack of a better term. He had soft brown eyes and a nose that had never been broken and a narrow, square chin and overall soft features. He wore a cravat, a bright blue one, and tall, polished boots with small silver spurs. Cole noticed the checkered stock of a sporting gun protruding from a hand-tooled scabbard just behind his right leg.

The stud pawed the ground and snorted and tried tossing its head, but the Englishman held him in check with total command. He might not have been a typical buckaroo, but he knew how to handle a horse. He wore gloves—nice soft kid gloves, expensive, like the horse and the rest of his outfit. He was the kind of gent you might well see at some cattleman's club, sipping port from a crystal glass, or relaxing in a private rail car, smoking $1 cigars while out shooting up a herd of antelope on one of Pawnee Bill's hunting expeditions. Cole was trying hard not to make a judgment about him, but it was difficult not to, considering how it'd gone between Liddy and him the night before.

He waited for Cole to answer his question. The other three sort of sat there, resting their forearms on the horns of their saddles, curious, like monkeys.

"Didn't know you could own this land," Cole said.

The gent smiled at that. "What makes you think not, sir?"

"Well, the last I knew, the Sioux owned it. I believe that is why they killed that poor crazy bastard Custer . . . because they were under the impression that the Black Hills was still theirs."

"Ah, I see," he said, almost politely. "The Sioux, that would be the red men in this part of the territory, is that it?"

"Yeah, that'd be them."

Cole could see the red shirts were enjoying the conversation. "Full of it, ain't he?" one of them said to the other two. They all grinned like can-eating goats.

Winston Stevens looked at his hands as though he were admiring them, or the kid gloves he was wearing. He looked at them a moment, then back at Cole. "You see, my dear man, this *is* private land. I've purchased it."

"The hell you say." Cole spoke with mock surprise. "How'd you manage that?"

One of the red shirts edged his horse closer to get between Cole and the Englishman.

"Hold on now, Mister Coffey," Winston Stevens said.

The mention of the name rang a few old bells for Cole. He looked at the man and the man looked back. Charley Coffey had grown some since the last time Cole had seen him. He'd grown a mustache, for one thing. It made him look foolish. The last time he'd laid eyes on him was when he'd been locked up in a Kansas jail for stealing a man's union suit off a clothesline. Charley was just a kid then, fourteen, fifteen, maybe. No one thought he'd amount to much. But Charley'd proved them wrong. He had made himself into a gun artist of sorts. He had killed a few old outlaws on his path to glory—a petty thief in Fort Riley, two Army deserters in Hays City. Off and on over the years, Cole had heard rumors about Charley Coffey. Kid Charley, some called him. Then he'd heard, last winter, that he'd killed Jim Ketchum in Telluride. Some claimed it had been a fair fight. If it was, that would make Charley the genuine article. Jim Ketchum was no slouch with a gun.

"No sense in letting this man backtalk you, Mister Stevens," Charley said, feeling brave, with the others there to back him up.

"No, Charles, I don't think that is what the gentleman was doing. I simply think he is misinformed about matters. Wouldn't you say that was the case, sir?"

It hadn't taken Cole long to dislike him, the manner in which he spoke. "You're Winston Stevens," he said.

The Englishman offered Cole a look of mild surprise. "I am, sir, and might I ask who you are?"

"Name's Cole. John Henry Cole."

Charley Coffey lost that slouched, surly look he'd had when he heard Cole tell Winston Stevens who he was. "I know this sum-a-bitch!" Charley declared.

"Watch your mouth, boy," Cole warned. "Only my friends call me sum-a-bitch."

Coffey wasn't quite sure how to take that—as a joke or not. His holster was half turned around from the hard riding he'd just done; his pistol was resting just about the middle of his spine. Cole could see he was trying to figure out a way to reach it without being shot first, but there was no way. He knew it and Cole knew it.

"Hold up, Charles," Winston Stevens ordered.

"Take his advice," Cole told Coffey. "Even you're not that fast, and I'm not that slow."

The other two were waiting for the play to begin. Most men won't enter a fight that's not their own—not for $30 a month and board, they won't. One spat; the other scratched his jaw. Cole guessed both were a little more than disappointed that Coffey hadn't shot him or he hadn't shot Coffey, or somebody hadn't shot somebody. They'd probably been having a slow week until Cole had come along.

"Have we met, sir," Winston said, "you and I? Have we met somewhere along the way?"

"No, I don't believe we have. But I met a friend of yours and she mentioned your name."

A quizzical look troubled his brow.

"It's the accent. It stands out in this country."

He smiled, showed Cole his teeth. He had a lot of teeth, Cole thought. "Jolly well," he said.

"Well, now what?"

"Well, I hate to seem an old fussbudget about it all, Mister Cole, but, if I allow you to stray onto my property, then I invite everyone, don't I? And then you can see how that would become a problem, can't you?"

"Is it the grass?" Cole wondered.

"Pardon?"

"Are you worried that someone will steal your grass?"

Again that furrowing of the brows. He didn't quite get it.

"I mean, is that what you're worried about, a man comes and takes a swim in your little lake here, rests himself, then, when he's ready, he'll steal your grass? Because to tell you the truth, I don't see anything else a man would want with this country other than to look at it. So I guess I don't understand your concern about trespassing."

"Let me handle this, Mister Stevens," Charley Coffey said.

For a long moment, Winston Stevens didn't say whether or not he would let Coffey try and handle Cole. Then he laughed hard and loud. "Grass! Steal my grass, indeed!"

Cole saw the other two red shirts grinning. They weren't quite sure what the joke was, but, if Mr. Stevens found it funny, then they reckoned it had to be funny. Cole thought again that it must have been a slow week around Deadwood before he had come along to cheer everyone up.

"Can't you see, Charles, that Mister Cole is implying that the reason I don't want trespassers on my land is that I'm worried they might steal the grass?" This was followed by some more of the deep laughter.

Coffey said: "No I *can't* see, Mister Stevens. It don't sound like no god-damn' joke to me!"

"Oh, but it is, dear Charles," Stevens said. Then his laughter drifted away like a hot wind that dies out at sunset, and his gaze narrowed sharply. "You see, Charles, Mister Cole here obviously cannot see the point of why I don't allow trespassers and he has made some sort of a joke about it. A rather sly joke, I must admit. But a joke nonetheless." Then the nostrils of that unbroken nose of his flared and Cole knew Stevens no longer appreciated either his humor or his presence. "Tell Mister Cole what the usual penalty is for men who trespass on my property, Charles."

This time it was Charley Coffey's turn to look happy. "Well, Mister Stevens, usually you have me and Fork and Tolbert whup a man with our quirts. Whup him all the way back to the boundary line where your property begins."

"Indeed I do, Charles. Indeed I do. What do you think of that, Mister Cole? Charles . . . Charles and Mister Fork and Mister Tolbert punishing trespassers in the way just described to you?"

"I think a man who would allow himself to be whipped by these sisters of yours isn't much of a man."

Winston Stevens straightened slightly in his saddle. "I see. You're portending that you won't allow my men to mete out the usual punishment on you, is that it?"

"If you mean to order them to whip me, that's it exactly."

He swallowed. He was close to the edge. Cole could see that veiled anger just behind the glass of his eyes. Anger just waiting to be set loose from under all the breeding and fine rich upbringing he'd had. Cole figured a man like Stevens enjoyed it more than most, seeing a man whipped, broken down. All his refinement didn't stop him from liking the taste of a little blood now and then. He probably saw it as some form of high sport. "Well then," he said, adjusting his jaw. "It would appear we are faced with a dilemma."

"Call it what you will."

"What say you, gentlemen?" he called to the other two red shirts, Tolbert and Fork. They offered him looks of uncertainty.

Then Tolbert said: "Whatever you say, Mister Stevens. We work for you."

He looked pleased to hear the right answer. He was a man used to hearing the right answers to his questions. "There, you see?" he said, turning his attention back to Cole. "My men agree with me."

"Then let them begin," Cole said. "But first, I'll shoot Charley there, then you. Him first, because I figure he's the fastest. Then you. I'll take my chances those other two won't have the stomach for it. How'll that be, Stevens?"

Cole saw the effect of that, how it settled in those eyes that had been enjoying everything so much up till then.

"That sound all right with you boys?" Cole asked, without turning his attention completely to Tolbert and Fork. He could hear the way the leather of their saddles creaked when they shifted some of their weight. The sudden prospect of a gunfight was something they hadn't counted on. Charley was another matter, however. He wasn't a real smart boy, judging by the looks of him; most gun punks lacked good sense but made up for it with pure meanness. But the fact was, Charley was still sitting there with his Peacemaker halfway up his butt, so it wasn't doing him much good just at the moment. Still, the odds were long in their favor if they did decide to fight.

"Is it worth it?" Cole asked, pushing the point home, because a situation where men are being tested can turn south real quick.

"I seemed to have misjudged you, sir," Stevens said, after a long, unsteady moment. "I don't enjoy this business with trespassers, but, then, a man must protect what is his, wouldn't you agree?"

"Depends on the price he has to pay," Cole said.

"Quite true. And in this particular case, the price would most certainly be much too high. I will, however, insist that you vacate my property immediately."

"I've never been one to stay where I'm not welcome."

"You won't mind if I have Mister Fork and Mister Tolbert and Charles here escort you to the boundary line?"

"Not Charley," Cole said. "You want those other two to ride along, that's fine with me, but not Charley. I don't care for the man's company."

Cole could see Charley Coffey would have given up his mother's virtue just for the opportunity to reach that .45 slid around to his tailbone, but his mama could rest easy; she wasn't going to have her reputation stained this day.

Cole cleaned camp, mounted the rented horse, and turned back in the direction he'd come, with the two red shirts in tow. One was smoking a shuck and the other rode with his right leg wrapped around the horn of his saddle, bored men doing a boring job.

They reached the boundary of Stevens's property just above the tree line, high up the ridge Cole had descended earlier.

"This is it, Cole," the one smoking the shuck said. "Don't come back here, OK?"

"What's a job like this pay?" he asked.

The other one dropped his head and said: "Thirty-five a month, and board."

"Somehow, it don't seem worth it," he said, "you want my opinion."

The first one said: "It's steady work, though, working for the Englishman. There ain't many good jobs to be had. Not around here, there ain't."

"You mean as long as you don't mind whipping a fellow with quirts for stretching out on some grass, maybe watering his horse?"

Neither of them took any offense, but they were plainly uncomfortable with Cole's end of the conversation.

"We do what we're told," the one smoking the shuck said. "There's plenty of hands'd be willing to take our places, we don't take orders. You can understand that, can't you?"

"No, I can't."

They looked off, back toward the lake.

"Tell me something," Tolbert said. "Were you really going to shoot Stevens and Charley and me and Fork here? Were you going to go up against all four of us?"

Cole looked him in the eyes. "What do you think?"

They both looked sheepish.

"A man'd have to be crazy going against four," Tolbert said. "You don't act like somebody that's crazy."

"Well, that's the thing. You just don't know about a man, do you?"

Cole could tell by their stares they weren't certain.

"We better be heading back," the one called Fork said. "You ain't intending on coming back this way, are you?"

"If I do, I'll let you know."

"Most likely you do, Mister Stevens'll have us whip you. That's if Charley don't shoot you in the head first, or the spine."

"I'll take my chances with Charley Coffey," Cole said. "I knew him when he was stealing other men's underdrawers from a widow's clothesline."

That raised a couple of smiles.

"He'd be the type," Tolbert said.

The three shook hands.

"There's work down in Texas," Cole offered, as he turned his horse around in the direction of Deadwood. "A top hand might do well for himself a little farther south."

They didn't reply.

As Cole rode toward Deadwood, he knew that those two boys had one thing and only one thing on their minds—counting the number of days left till payday. That and maybe some plain-faced gal waiting for them down in the low country somewhere. He didn't hold anything against them. They were just a couple of good men doing a bad job.

Chapter Sixteen

By the time Cole rode back into Deadwood, the sky was bunched with heavy gray clouds and the wind drew, sharp and cold, down through the gulch. The old man was still sitting out front of his livery when Cole arrived. It was as if he hadn't moved since Cole had left that morning.

He eyed the horse. "You come back," he said, like it was a surprise to him.

Cole dismounted and handed him the reins. He ran his hands over the haunches.

"You looking for dents?" Cole asked.

He grinned, showing Cole his missing teeth. "Just an old habit I picked up in my droving days," he said, "running my hands over 'em, checking their legs and such." Then he jerked the saddle free, set it up on a barrel, and led the horse inside.

Cole was hungry, but he wanted to swing by and see Liddy first. He didn't have to give himself a reason. He already knew the reason.

Jazzy Sue opened the door a minute after he knocked. "Mistuh John Henry," she said. Her smile was pleasing. She was an attractive girl.

"Is Liddy home?" Cole asked.

"Miss Lydia be with somebody."

"Oh."

"Some young man," she said. "Wanted to talk to Miss Lydia."

Dust blew up from the street. The gusts of wind pinned some pages of yellow newspaper against the white picket fence.

"You want to come inside?" Jazzy Sue asked. "Look like a storm fixin' to come."

"I'd like that."

She stepped back, led Cole into the front parlor. "I can take your hat for you," she said.

"That's all right," he said. "I take it off, I'll just have to go through the grief of having to put it back on."

When she smiled, so did her eyes. "Would you like me to bring you something to drink, Mistuh John Henry?"

"A little of that cognac would do the trick."

When she returned, she was carrying the crystal decanter of cognac and two glasses on a silver serving tray. She set the tray down on a small black walnut table in front of him.

"There you go," she said.

"You want some of this?" he asked, pouring out a couple of inches of cognac.

Jazzy Sue's hand flew to her mouth and her eyes grew wide. "Oh, no, suh. Miss Lydia'd whup my bottom she was to catch me drinking that devil water."

This time it was his turn to grin.

"I could dust off your coat while you was waitin'," Jazzy Sue offered.

He was about to decline the offer when a door across the hall opened. He stood, thinking it was Liddy coming out of the room. But he was a little more than surprised to see the kid, Rose, coming out of the room. Liddy appeared just behind her, supporting her by the elbow. Cole stood and went to the hall to meet them.

Rose saw Cole, stopped, looked uncertain. "Mister Cole, what are you doing here?" she asked. Her cheeks were strained with tears, her eyes red and full of hurt.

"I was going to ask you the same thing," he said.

Rose looked like she was about to come apart. She looked at Liddy, then back at Cole. "Oh, Mister Cole!" she cried, then threw herself at him, and suddenly he was holding that frail body again, uncertain about the cause of her pain and grief.

His gaze lifted past Rose's shaking shoulders and was met by Liddy's questioning stare. "What is it, Rose? What's the matter?" he whispered to her.

"Maybe we should all go in there," Liddy said, pointing to the parlor.

Cole led Rose into the room, helped her to the settee. She didn't want to turn loose of him. He looked at Liddy again, looked for answers.

"Jazzy Sue, bring some water," Liddy ordered.

Jazzy Sue brought a glass of water, offered it to Rose. She wiped her eyes with the back of her wrist and sipped some of the water. She looked up at Cole, then at Liddy.

"It's my mama," she said.

"What is?" Cole asked.

"She's been killed . . . murdered," she sniffed.

Cole glanced across the room at Liddy. She nodded. "Do you remember the matter we discussed," Liddy said, "the reason you've come?"

"The killings?" he said.

"Yes. Rose's mother was one of them."

"Her name was Flora," Rose said. "Mama's name was Flora."

"She worked for you, Liddy?"

"Yes. She was the last one to . . ."

Cole remembered what Liddy had said, how they'd found the last woman murdered by a butcher knife. He knew Liddy wouldn't have gone into detail with Rose about it. At that moment, he felt as sorry for Rose as he had ever felt for anyone. She was frail in lots of ways.

Rose's hands trembled as they tried to cling to him. "That's why I came, Mister Cole. I came looking for Mama . . ."

"I'm sorry, Rose."

She had the look of the lost now, the look that comes when the hard cold reality of a loved one's death sets in.

"I didn't know Flora had a daughter," Liddy said hesitantly. "She never told me."

"Mama left me when I was little," Rose uttered. "But I was old enough to know she was my mama. She promised she'd come back. Left me and Daddy 'cause Daddy went a little crazy with drinking and quoting the Bible all the time and swinging his fists at her. I guess Mama couldn't take no more of Daddy hurting her. But I remember her saying she was coming back. I remember her saying that to me. . . ."

Liddy's hand closed over her mouth, the fingers pressing her lips.

"Maybe you ought to lay down for a little while, Rose?" Cole suggested. "Just rest a little. Liddy, how would it be if you poured a little glass of that cognac for Rose?"

Rose was still staring into that netherworld, talking the whole time about her mama leaving her and about her daddy and how he went crazy afterward. Cole put the glass to her mouth and encouraged her to drink it. She made a face, but drank it, anyway. Liddy asked Jazzy Sue to make up a bed for Rose.

"Don't leave me, Mister Cole," Rose pleaded. "Don't leave me here in this room alone."

Cole helped Rose to a nearby bedroom, Jazzy Sue's. Jazzy Sue partially undressed Rose and helped her into the bed.

The light outside had grown dark from the coming storm and the room had a gloomy cast because of it. Cole pulled up a chair next to the bed.

"Let yourself rest, Rose."

She looked up at him with those sad, bittersweet eyes of a woman who was not quite a woman yet and not quite a girl any longer. Cole didn't know the words to say to her, at least the ones that would make it better, make the ache go away. So, instead, he held onto her hand, and she to his. And they stayed like that until the bedroom grew dark and the silence and the cognac soothed her and her fingers grew limp in his. She fell asleep like that, with him holding her hand.

"How is she?" Liddy asked, when he rejoined her in the parlor.

"Resting."

"How do you know her?" Liddy asked.

"We rode here on the stage together."

"Just that?"

"There was a problem out on the road. I offered my help. That's all."

Liddy handed him a glass of cognac. He drank it down.

"She showed up at my door an hour ago," Liddy said. "She told me she was looking for her mama, Flora Pride. It was totally unexpected. At first I thought she was a boy, in those clothes she's wearing. But then I could see, when she took off that big hat, that it was Flora all over again, only younger. Only her name wasn't Flora Pride when I knew her, it was Flora Reed."

"How'd Rose learn of it?" Cole asked.

Liddy shrugged her shoulders. "She had a small tintype, showed it around to some of the locals. Flora was a pretty girl, the kind men wouldn't forget seeing."

"How much did you tell her?"

"The truth, but not all. She didn't need to know it all," Liddy said.

"I met your friend today," Cole said, pouring himself a second glass of the liquor, feeling a need to change the subject.

"Oh," she said, her eyes widening slightly.

"A real son-of-a-bitch," he said.

Cole saw how that took effect. Her face flushed red, those lovely green eyes turning more jade. "You don't have the right . . ." she started to say.

Cole cut her off: "Why'd you leave before I woke this morning?"

"I thought it was better I did."

"Better for you? For me? Better for who?"

"For everyone concerned."

"I don't understand you," he said, feeling an anger toward her that he didn't want to feel.

"Would you be happier if everyone knew that I'd spent the night with you? Is that what you want, for everyone to know?"

Cole wasn't good at this sort of business, of dealing with feelings he knew he shouldn't be having. He didn't want to get into a fight with her over something that wasn't her fault, or his. It'd been a bad day all around, and he was carrying a lot of anger from a lot of different sources, and the day didn't seem to be getting any better.

He drank half the cognac. He didn't know if he wanted to walk out the door or pull her to the floor. He wanted to do both, but found he couldn't bring himself to do either. "I've had a long day," he said.

"I heard about the shooting this morning," she said. "Why didn't you come to see me?"

"I needed time to think about things, to get away."

"Everything's becoming entangled, isn't it?" she asked. "Us, the killings, now Rose?"

"It's my fault," Cole told her. "I shouldn't have allowed things to get out of hand . . . I mean, between you and me."

"Could you have stopped it?"

He looked at her, looked into those ever-darkening green eyes that he'd never seen on any other woman, and knew the answer. "No, I couldn't have stopped it."

"No one could have."

He wanted to kiss her mouth, kiss it and never come up for air. "It's going to get me killed," he said, "the way I'm feeling about you."

"No, don't let it."

"I didn't tell you the other night, the first time I met you, that on my way home someone took a shot at me. I was thinking about you when it happened."

Her hand reached up and touched the side of his face, her fingers cool and graceful, lightly against his jaw. "Then you must leave Deadwood," she said. "I can't ask you to stay any longer. There will be others to help me, but not you."

"Others?"

She nodded. "A man named Kip Caine stopped by at noon. He said he was answering the ad I'd placed in the *Rocky Mountain News*."

"Jesus, Liddy, another gun hand."

"He said he was a detective, a Pinkerton man."

"Christ!"

"Just go, John Henry. Leave Deadwood. Tell Ike there was nothing you could do for me. Tell him I decided to leave and the matter resolved itself."

"Have you?"

"No. I won't be forced out. I won't start my life over again, go on to the next mining camp and the next, until I turn myself into a crib whore just to survive."

"Christ, Liddy, you're going to wind up dead if I can't find out who it is killed those women!"

"No, you don't owe me that. You've risked your life enough."

"That's it?"

"That's it. I want you to leave Deadwood as soon as possible."

"Makes no damned sense. I thought there was something more between us."

"Does it matter?" she asked.

"It matters to me."

"But if you or I die because of it, what have we gained?"

"How can I protect you, Liddy?"

She shrugged, studied him, shook her head. "I don't know," she said, her hands cradling his face, her eyes brimming with tears.

Cole thought about Winston Stevens and that tailored suit and $400 horse and all that grass he owned, and all the rest of it. He thought about the two of them together, riding, picnicking, in bed. It made him feel brutal and angry and helpless. He felt Liddy was right, everything had become entangled. He'd come here to help an old friend and instead had betrayed him with the woman he had once loved and maybe still did. And worst of all, he was still no closer to resolving the murders than the day he'd stepped off the stage. And his mind was full of this woman.

"Do me a favor, Liddy. Take care of that kid in there. See she gets a stage ticket back to Cheyenne."

She looked at Cole, and for a minute he thought she was going to kiss him, to tell him not to go. But she didn't.

He stepped out into the cold wind that was sweeping down through the gulch. One day rainbows, the next storms. That was the way life seemed there in Deadwood, no matter how he looked at it—rainbows and storms. He wasn't even sure where to begin. Then he saw what might be an answer, standing in the opening of an alley, cussing two cowboys a blue streak.

Chapter Seventeen

The cowboys were half drunk, and Calamity was completely so. They had pinioned her up against the wall of a harness shop just inside an alley. It was the supper hour and there was hardly anyone on the street except for Jane Canary and those two cowpokes.

"God damn ya to hell, mister!" Jane was saying as they held her there.

"Look here, gal," one of the cowboys said back, as he struggled to hold her wrist and keep from getting kicked in the groin.

"Look here yarself!" Calamity screeched.

"We paid you five damn' dollars for what you're wearing under them buckskins. Five dollars and a whole lot of good liquor, now it's time you paid up."

Jane was stomping at their feet with her heels and thrusting her legs out in kicks, and every time she cursed them spittle flew from her lips and sprayed their faces. John Henry Cole could tell they weren't enjoying it much.

"What kinda gal ya think I am?" Jane cried.

"Hell, darling, we already know what kinda gal you are," one of them said, trying to hold her and wipe some of Jane's spit from his eyes. "It's just a case of proving it, that's all."

"Let her go," Cole said.

Their heads jerked around like he'd roped them. "Who the hell . . . ?"

"A friend," he said. "I'm a friend of this woman's, and I hate to see her being abused."

Jane smiled hugely in that sloppy way a drunk will when she recognized him.

"Jack!" she shouted. "Get these apes off me, will ya?"

They were just boys, bare-cheeked, freshly shorn boys just off the range, with their new haircuts and big bandannas hanging from their necks. The haircuts made their ears stick out from under the brims of their Stetsons. Tricked by Jane, their big ears were red with anger. One was buck-toothed, and Cole would've been willing to bet, neither of them had ever had a woman before. Now they'd picked the wrong one to marry for an hour. "She's got five dollars of ours, mister," the buck-toothed one said. "Said she take us both on for five dollars cash."

"Yeah, and we bought her drinks all afternoon, too," the other one said.

"You gentlemen new in town?" Cole asked.

"Got here today," Buck-Tooth said.

"Kansas, somewhere like that?" Cole asked.

They traded glances.

"How'd you know we was from Kansas?" Buck-Tooth's friend said.

"Just a guess."

"Well, that don't change anything," Buck-Tooth said, "just 'cause we're from Kansas."

"Just that you've been bamboozled by the best," Cole said.

They blinked hard, like startled owls.

"You gents know who you're holding there?"

"Damn' flim-flam artist," Buck-Tooth said.

"That, gents, is Calamity Jane Canary. She can outdrink, outfight, outshoot, and probably outlove any man in the territory. You are both lucky you didn't get what you paid for. And equally lucky all she got from you was five dollars."

They seemed uncertain. Jane was grinning like a weasel.

"Jane, give these boys back their earnings," Cole said, "and maybe they'll turn you loose."

"Ain't got but three damn' dollars left, Jack!" she shrieked.

"I'll make up the difference, if that's all right with you gents."

"Well, what about all the whiskey we bought and poured in her?" Buck-Tooth's friend asked.

"What about it? You want her to puke it up?"

Still they seemed reluctant to let it go at something that simple.

"Take your money and go over to the Number Ten," Cole said. "Ask for Irish Murphy. Tell him to line you up with one of the regular girls, one that won't cheat you or have her pimp knock you over the head. Tell him John Henry Cole sent you. You'll both feel better for it come tomorrow morning."

"Wadda you say, Elbert?" Buck-Tooth asked his friend.

"Sounds good to me." Then, looking at Jane: "Probably beat this homely sot any day."

"Say! Watch yar god-damn' mouths!" Jane cursed.

"Go ahead, turn her loose," Cole said. "Jane, give them the money."

She looked at Cole like he'd just announced her sister had died, but dug down into her greasy buckskins and produced three silver dollars. Cole gave the cowboys two more and watched them head off for Nutall and Mann's.

"Well, hell, Jack," Jane blubbered. "I'd 'a' whipped them boys' butts, ya hadn't come along and stopped me."

"Yeah, I know, Jane. That's why I did it. I just couldn't stand by and watch those two youngsters take a whipping."

She laughed, slapped her leg with her miner's cap, and said: "Hot damn, let's go have ourselves a drink. Whadda ya say?"

"I need to ask you some questions."

"Honey Jack, ya can ask me any damn' thing ya wanner, just buy me a round first. Wrasslin' them boys has made me as dry as a dead man's pecker. They was damn' lucky ya showed when ya did, or I'd 'a' whupped 'em like puppies."

The Zenobia Saloon was just across the street.

"How about over there?" Cole suggested.

"Sure, sure," she said, "any ol' damn' place 'at's got a fresh bottle of ol' John Barleycorn will do." She tried hooking her arm in Cole's, but he side-stepped her effort. She didn't seem to notice.

It was a big open room, the Zenobia. Full of blue smoke and noise. The usual kind of noise heard in a saloon: glasses clinking, rough talk, laughter, the sound of a piano being played by a professor. Jane slapped a few of the gents standing along the bar as they made their way to an empty table toward the rear. Some of the ones she slapped on the back turned and greeted her and tried to grab her, others tossed her angry looks.

Cole ordered a bottle and one of the bartenders brought it over to their table along with two glasses that were still wet from the last washing. Cole didn't think she needed anything more to drink, but it was plain she talked best when her tongue was being oiled. She eyed the operation while Cole poured them each a jigger's worth of mash, then her hand snaked out, and snatched up one of the glasses. She downed it like she was desperate, then set the glass back down all in one swift, sure motion.

"'Nother," she said.

"I need to talk to you, Jane."

"Sure, Jack, like I said, 'nother if ya damn' please."

"Can't talk if you're passed out on me, Jane."

She licked her lips and spread her fingers atop the green felt of the table. The nails were dirty, the ends blunted. "Ya married, Jack?" Her voice went from high-pitched to nearly hoarse when she spoke slowly, which was seldom.

"Let's discuss other things," Cole said, taking a sip of his drink.

She took the bottle from his hand and poured a good portion of it into her glass. "Handsome racehorse like ya. I wouldn't be 'tall surprised ya was married to two er three women. Har! Har!" Her laughter was harsh, unpleasant to the ear.

"I'm not one of those fresh-faced cowboys," Cole said.

"Whadda ya mean, Jack?"

"I mean, I'm not going to sit here all night buying you drinks and not get anything for it."

She grinned lasciviously. "What is it ya want there, Jack?"

"You know what I'm referring to."

She offered him a sly, hesitant look. "Go ahead, ask me anything ya want, Jack."

Cole watched the knot of her throat slide up and down as she guzzled another glass of the liquor. It gave him time to take her in more carefully. She was larger than she first appeared. And when her hand reached out for the glass, he could see her forearm was knotted with muscle. But she was thin, too, sickly. "Back in the jail, when we were locked up, you mentioned something about how Jack McCall was put up to killing Wild Bill. . . ."

She looked at Cole over the rim of her glass without removing it from her mouth, her eyes wide, staring. "I said that?" She lowered the glass an inch or two.

"Yeah, that's what you said, Jane. You were hung-over at the time, a little drunk, maybe, but that's what you said."

"It's true, god damn it!" she blurted suddenly, then looked around, then jerked her eyes back in Cole's direction.

"Tell me," he said.

She looked around again, squinted as though trying to see through the haze of the miners' cigars. "Gotta be careful what ya say around this place," she said, lowering her voice.

"Why?"

She looked at him dumbly. "'Cause, ya get heard by the wrong people, ya wind up dead like my darlin' Billy." She leaned forward across the table, nearly spilling the bottle. "Oh, Judas," she said through a short, hard sob, "they killed him. And they'll kill me, too, I don't clear out soon."

"Who are *they*, Jane?"

She blinked several times. "See, that's the damn' worst of it, Jack, ain't nobody knows who *they* are."

"But somebody suspects something, don't they, Jane?"

She looked around again. "Names," she said. "Lots of names get said around."

"Like which ones?"

Her hands shook. She poured another glass, downed it, wiped some of the dribble from her chin with the heel of her hand. "All kinds of names."

"Come on, Jane."

"Why ya want to know for?" she said, suddenly sounding wary of him.

"Just interested, that's all."

She scoffed at that. "Not ya, Jack. Ya don't seem like no kinda man that'd ask questions just to be askin' 'em."

"I'm looking into it for a friend of mine," he said. "He's the one that's curious."

Cole could see he was losing her to the whiskey again. Her gaze had grown suddenly unsteady and her lids drooped and her jaw became slack.

"Jane!"

Her eyelids snapped open. She looked at Cole. "What?"

"Names. Tell me what names you've heard."

"God damn, Jack, I loved ol' Bill. I surely did. He had his ways, god damn if he di'nt. Fussy about his appearance, fussy about his hands being clean, fussy about his guns. Fussiest man I ever knew. But god damn if I di'nt love him much as I ever loved any man."

"Then why not help me out here and give me the names you've heard?"

"McCall," she said. "He was in on it."

"Not McCall. Everyone knows he shot Bill. Give me some other names."

Her eyelids were drooping again and her head lolled to the side. "Loop," she muttered.

"Loop? Who is Loop?" Cole asked, shaking her by the arm.

Her eyes came open part way, began to close. "I heard maybe Leo had some hand in it. . . ."

Her hands slid off the table, dangled by her sides. Cole wasn't going to get anything more from her.

"Come on, Jane," he said, lifting her under the arms. It didn't take much effort, as thin as she was.

He hustled her out the door and down the street to the Custer Hotel, a one-story flophouse catering mostly to miners. The desk clerk looked up when he saw them enter and laid his copy of *DeWitt's Ten Cent Romances* face up on the counter. The cover featured a story about Wild Bill: *Wild Bill, The Indian Slayer.* He looked at Cole and he looked at Jane.

"It's not what you think," Cole said.

He grinned sheepishly.

"She'll need a room for the night," Cole explained.

"Two dollars if you bunk up together," he said.

"It's just for her," Cole told him flatly.

"Dollar," he said.

Cole paid him, took the key, and dropped Jane on the bed in the room, then covered her with a blanket.

"See she gets some breakfast in the morning," he told the clerk on his way out.

"You ain't staying?"

"Does it look like I am?"

Maybe it was the long day or his own weariness, but when Cole stepped back outside again, the wind seemed cold and his duster too little protection against it. If he was going to stay in Deadwood, he'd need a better coat. He made a cigarette and smoked it on his way back to his own hotel room. The name Jane had given him rolled around in his mind. Leo Loop. Who the hell was Leo Loop?

Chapter Eighteen

A hard cold rain began to fall, the kind of rain that stings the flesh and seeps into the bone. Cole ducked in under a butcher shop overhang. Inside, a man was dressing out an antelope. He watched the loafers and the heelers duck doorways, trying to avoid the same cold rain. Then the rain changed to sleet and he could hear it pelting the windows up and down the walk. A man rode his horse at full gallop down the middle of the street, trying to get home.

Cole rolled myself another shuck, hoping the rain would let up before he started for Liddy's place. If anyone would know who Leo Loop was, he figured Liddy would. The smoke tasted good and the whiskey he'd had with Jane earlier had warmed his blood just enough against the chill dampness. Then something drew his attention to the front of the Number Ten. He saw two men standing there in the low light of the doorway, talking. Normally he wouldn't have paid them much attention. But then he saw who they were. Johnny Logan was one of them. He was wearing a yellow rubber slicker against the cold rain, saying something to the other man, his head tilting from side to side as he talked. Cole was too far away to catch any of their conversation, but Murphy was standing there, listening, his hands plunged into his pockets, no doubt because he was cold. He was standing there in just his shirt sleeves, and it made Cole wonder if Johnny had called him outside, out from behind the bar, for the express purpose of talking to him in private.

Murphy started gesturing with his hands, as though he was explaining something to the lawman difficult to grasp. Then, stepping from the shadows, a third man joined them—Doc Holliday. Rain spilled off Johnny's hat brim every time he tilted his head. He towered over Doc, but somehow Doc still seemed the more imposing. Johnny immediately turned his attention to Doc. Doc stood there listening, then said something to the lawman. Johnny cranked his head around, looked over his shoulder, turned back to Doc. And for a minute more, they stood there, Johnny still talking. Then all three went inside the Number Ten.

The rain slackened and Cole flipped the shuck into a puddle and headed for Liddy's. He got almost as far as the front gate, then stopped short. Tied up outside was Winston Stevens's blooded stud horse. The feeling Cole got left him colder than the rain had. He could see a light on in the front parlor, between the split of the drapes. He saw another light on toward the back, where Jazzy Sue's room was, the one where he'd taken Rose earlier. Liddy knew how Cole felt about the man. That she'd chosen to entertain him after what he'd told her left him angry. The truth was that he felt betrayed and was tempted to confront them.

He waited for a time, thinking Stevens would emerge, but when he didn't after several minutes, Cole gave it up and headed back to his hotel room. The rain started up again and he did his best to stick to the sidewalks and whatever cover he could find, ducking in a doorway here, another there. Between his anger and trying to stay dry, he failed to notice the shadows that moved on him.

There was the sound of shuffling boots on the boards, and, as Cole reached for the self-cocker, he was hit from behind and sent off balance. He was quickly shoved into an alleyway into the darkness of cover. He guessed there were at least three of them, maybe four. The blows were delivered with short, hard grunts, and each one seemed to find a new spot against Cole's ribs and kidneys. Two or three times a boot found its way into his shoulders and back as he rolled around in the mud, got to his hands and knees, and was knocked back down again. A kick to his chest knocked the wind out of him and he stopped trying to get up.

The rain boiled up in the mud, next to his face. He could feel the blood leaking from his nose and lips. It was hard to breathe, and he clawed at the mud, trying. Then he heard the double click of a revolver being cocked just above him and knew he was going to be shot in the head. He closed his eyes and waited for the journey to begin. He didn't know if he was ready to die, but a great peacefulness came over him, knowing that the time had finally come. Like a dream, only this time it wasn't a dream. This time, he pressed his palms into the mud trying to raise himself up, to see the man who would do it, but a foot pushed down hard in the middle of his back, pinning him. He waited for the explosion of the pistol, wondering if he'd even hear it. *Bang!*

It didn't hurt. Then something slammed to the muddy ground next to him. He opened his eyes and saw the shadowy details of a man's bloody face under the pallor of yellow light coming from a second-story window of one of the buildings lining the alley. The dead man's features were distorted, the eyes frozen in a surprised stare. Cole could hear the sound of boots splashing through the mud, followed by the distinct metal click of a shell being ejected and another being jacked into the breech.

He lay there, trying to breathe, staring into the face, what was left of it. Then he heard the unhurried approach of footsteps, the sucking sound of mud. He waited. Maybe it wasn't over. He saw the muzzle of a carbine dangle in front of his eyes for a brief moment, then watched it swing over and poke at the dead man.

"You still alive?" the voice of Miguel Torres asked.

"I think so," Cole managed to whisper through the shortness of breath that'd come with being kicked in the chest.

"I could only get the one," he said. "The others scrammed into the dark. I guess, if I'd been carrying a repeater, I might've got more. But this old single-shot . . ."

"That's OK," Cole said. "One seems enough."

"You know that man?" he asked, poking with the muzzle.

"No. But then, there's not a whole lot left to identify."

"Yeah," he said. "Those big grain bullets create a lot of damage. Can you get up?"

Cole nodded. He felt Torres lift him under his arms until he could sit up. Torres leaned him against the wall of a building, squatted down, took stock.

"I seen worse," he said. "You were lucky."

"How so?"

"That one there, the one I shot, he was about to cap you." He stood, went over to the dead man, bent down, and picked up the pistol still clutched in his hand. Miguel held it aloft where the light was better under the upper window. "Forty-Four-Forty. Merwin and Hulbert model. Don't see many around. Mean little bastard of a handgun." He shoved it into a pocket.

"You think you could help me up the rest of the way?" Cole asked.

Again he squatted in front of Cole, looked into his eyes. "Somebody wants you dead, why?"

"I don't know."

"Because you came here looking into the killings," he said. "That why they want you dead?"

"It would be my guess, if I had to make one." Cole looked back at the dead man briefly.

"Whip you, then kill you," he said. "They wanted to make you suffer a little before they capped you with that Forty-Four-Forty. I'd say you've made some real enemies."

In spite of the beating, Cole didn't feel there was anything broken—no ribs, no bones. "I think, if I can stand, I'll make it back to my hotel room all right."

"I'd think you'd want to wait right here until the next stage left tomorrow," Miguel said, "then crawl on it. You look like a man who's running out of chances. Maybe the next time I don't come along, then what?"

The rain splattered off the brim of Miguel's hat, danced in Cole's eyes, along his skin, feeling good and cool and welcome. Cole pushed against the wall, worked himself upward.

Miguel watched as he did. "It's a hard rain," he said, "cold."

"Yeah," Cole agreed.

Cole looked around for his self-cocker, saw it lying in the mud a few feet away. It took some doing, but he managed to bend and pick it up and straighten up again without falling down.

"You better clean the mud outta that before you try firing it," Miguel said. "Blow up in your hand."

It was hard for Cole to breathe through his nose. Maybe he had been wrong about nothing being broken. He pinched off the blood between his thumb and forefinger. "You just happened to come along?" he asked.

"I was over there," Miguel said, nodding toward a bagnio across the street. Cole could hear the laughter of women, the bark of eager men.

"Drinking?"

"Yeah . . . that, and keeping an eye on things," he said, looking across the street. "I heard there was a girl that maybe knew Robertito who works in there."

"The same girl who sent your brother's clothes?"

"Maybe."

"She admit to it?"

He hunched his shoulders. "I didn't ask her anything yet."

"Then you just happened to be over there, watching, and saw this?"

"Something like that."

"Lucky for me," Cole concluded.

"That's what I said."

"I owe you."

Miguel didn't say anything, whether or not he thought Cole owed him. He said: "Like flies and shit."

"What is?"

"Trouble and you."

"Maybe I'm just having a bad week."

"Man"—he shook his head—"nobody has that bad a week."

"Like you said, I'm lucky."

"Yeah, you are."

"What about him?" Cole asked.

Miguel looked at the dead man. "I guess it's too late for him. I guess he had a worse week than you."

"No, I mean, you just going to leave him there?"

"Well, I guess his friends will figure it out, come back for him soon as they think it's safe. I guess it'll be up to them to see he gets buried. I don't see where that concerns me."

"What about that girl?"

He looked over at the house across the street again, the laughter from the women louder, pitched, like someone was tickling them, the men barking like dogs. "I'll probably go back over, hang around a little, see what I can see."

"Remember, she probably had some feelings for your brother," Cole said. "Why else would she have done what she did? Go easy, if you find her."

Miguel cocked his head, the rain slanting off his hat brim to the side, sluicing down over the shoulder of his coat. "You think just because I was never married to one, I don't know how to handle a woman when I have to?"

"No, I just meant that you need to remember that whoever sent Robertito's clothes back to you probably didn't have anything to do with his disappearance."

"That's what being a detective teaches you? To think that way?"

"You're a smart man, Miguel. You want to find out about your brother, do it the right way."

He looked at Cole with those fearless dark eyes that were hidden in the shadows of his face. Cole could hear his breathing. He started to turn to the street, everything feeling loose, unattached. "Another thing," he said. "You need my help, let me know."

Miguel didn't say anything. Cole didn't expect he would.

Chapter Nineteen

John Henry Cole asked Graves, the hotel clerk, to have a boy get a bottle and bring it to his room.

"Looks like you fell down in the mud," he said.

"Make it mash whiskey."

He climbed the stairs; they might as well have been the Rockies. He fumbled with the key to his door, found it already unlocked. The lamp didn't need to be on for him to know there was someone in the room. He could smell her fragrance.

"What do you want?" he asked, without bothering to reach for the lamp. He struggled with his duster, wet and heavy with rain and mud, as were all his clothes.

"Mister Cole," she said. From the sound of her voice, she was sitting on the bed.

"Who are you?" he asked, pulling out the tails of his shirt, working the buttons with his muddy, cold fingers.

He heard the glass chimney being raised. Then a match flared and the flame touched the wick; the room slowly filled with soft, warm light. It illuminated her face. It was a face he hadn't expected to see again: Suzanne Smith's. She looked different than on the stage, less prim and proper, less plain. Her hair was loose and down around her shoulders. She wore a waistcoat over her blouse and a long heavy skirt.

"What're you doing here, Miz Smith?" Cole asked, still struggling to get out of the wet shirt. No matter how he moved, it hurt.

"I know this seems odd, my being here in your room like this, the light out," she said.

"No, the way things are going, there's not much I find odd. But it still doesn't answer the question of *why* you're here."

"I don't know . . . where else to be," she said.

Then he saw, on the bed beside her, bundled under the blankets, the small, still form of her daughter, the toss of dark ringlets upon the pillow.

Suzanne Smith saw Cole's gaze, and said: "She's exhausted. I'm sorry . . ."

"Don't be."

"I had no intention to impose myself on you. . . . I barely know you. But you see, Mister Cole, I have no one else to impose myself upon."

"If you don't mind, I need to get out of these wet clothes." He waited for her to avert her eyes, but she didn't. The room was small, not built for privacy.

Cole pulled off the shirt, then the boots, and then his pants. He was still in his underdrawers, but they'd need to come off as well. He reached for a towel, turned his back to her, and with as much dignity as he could manage traded the drawers for the towel. When he turned back, she was still staring at him.

He scrounged a shirt out of his saddlebags, the one purchased to replace the one he had torn into bandages for Rose. He put it on, keeping the towel tied around his waist.

"You mind if I smoke?" he asked.

She shook her head.

"Normally I wouldn't in the presence of a lady."

"No, go right ahead, Mister Cole. It is your room, after all."

Mud was clinging to his hair. He ran his fingers through it.

There was a knock at the door. She started, her right hand coming to her throat, just above a cameo brooch she'd pinned there.

"I think it's the bottle I ordered," Cole said. He reached into the pocket of his wet pants and pulled out the money.

The kid had corkscrew red hair and he tried hard to look past Cole into the room. Cole saw him grin when he spotted Suzanne Smith, the freckles spreading out across his nose. "Anything else you be needing, you just let me know, sir. Name's Deke. Just ask Mister Graves downstairs to have Deke get whatever it is you be wantin'. I'll do it."

Cole closed the door with him still trying to get a better look at Suzanne Smith. He pulled the cork on the bottle, found the water glass, wiped it out with his fingers, and poured enough of the mash to get his blood circulating again. Then he remembered what manners he still had. "You?" he said, holding the glass forth.

She nodded just a little. He handed her the glass, watched her sip the mash, saw the flinch in her eyes as she swallowed it. She steeled herself, drank the rest, and handed back the glass. He poured another one for himself.

"So what's this all about, Miz Smith?" he said, feeling the liquor rip through him.

She lowered her eyes at last. Her hands fidgeted, one against the other, the gray gloves she was wearing thin and tightly formed over her long, slender fingers. Cole imagined those gloves holding a parasol as she strolled along a tree-lined lane, a beau at her side, eager to please, a gentleman, and she as delicate in her manner as spring rain upon pretty flowers.

"You see . . ." she began, then drew a sharp breath. "I have no one to turn to, no place to go with my child, no one to take me in. And worst of all, Mister Cole, I have no money left."

Her voice stumbled and she gripped the bedpost with one hand, the knuckles showing through the cotton glove. Then she lifted her gaze with as much pride as she had left.

"It's not much of a reason," she said, "but you're the only one I could think of."

"You mind?" Cole said, indicating the foot of the bed.

"No, please, sit down." Then, as he moved closer, she said: "Your nose, it's bleeding."

He touched the back of his hand to it, pulled it away, saw a smear of blood. "I fell down. It was an accident."

She looked at him a minute longer, knew he was lying about falling down, then swallowed, willing to let go the rest of the questions she had about what had happened to him.

"I thought you said on the trip up you were coming to meet someone, a man," he said, sitting now on the bed. "What happened? Didn't you find him?"

"I found him," she said.

"And he disappointed you?"

She blinked several times, trying to hold back the tears that were building just behind her pale blue eyes. "You see," she said, her spine suddenly becoming a rod of stiffness, her chin jutting forward in an effort to compose her dignity. "John has already married someone else. He said he sent a letter, explaining it to me. But I never received it. At least, he claims to have sent a letter."

"The little girl?"

She turned her attention to the sleeping bundle of child beneath the blankets. "She's his daughter," she said. "John's and mine."

"That didn't seem to bother him? That you came all this way, brought her with you?"

"She was three when he left us to . . . as he put it . . . find a better life for us. That was nearly two years ago. I couldn't wait any longer in Denver. We were nearly out of money then."

"So you thought you'd just come and find him, and everything would be all right after two years?"

She turned her face away. "I thought that it would . . . yes."

"But you were mistaken about this John?"

She took a deep breath and let it out, her eyes wet, still wanting to be fiercely loyal, it seemed, to a man who'd abandoned her and their daughter. "He promised me . . ." It was like an unanswered prayer, the way she said it.

"Look, I'm sorry, Miz Smith. You and your daughter can stay here the night. In the morning, I'll see what I can do to get you tickets back to Denver. You have people back in Denver, folks that could help you and the little girl?"

She shook her head. "No one."

She was doing her best to maintain herself. He was doing his best to keep from closing his eyes and falling into the exhaustion that was pulling at him. "Well, try and get some sleep. We'll discuss it over breakfast in the morning, what you and the little girl are going to do."

"I'm a proud woman, Mister Cole. At least, I always was until now. If it weren't for Tessie . . ."

"Don't think about that right now, Miz Smith. I'll go out in the hallway and finish my smoke while you get yourself ready for bed."

Cole felt it was the worst kind of way to be, to be beholden to strangers, and he didn't want to make it any harder on her than it already was. Besides, he thought, he had the bottle of mash and his makings, and for him, right then, that was just about all he needed. He stepped out in the hallway and smoked the cigarette slowly, taking turns with the mash, trying not to think about anything beyond the moment, trying not to think about Liddy and her visitor and Rose, or the men who'd nearly killed him out in a dark alley, or even why they'd tried to kill him. His exhaustion was so deep that events seemed to be turning faster than he knew how to keep up with them.

He waited for what he thought was long enough for Suzanne Smith to get undressed and into bed. He knocked lightly before stepping back inside. The flame of the lamp guttered low and he could barely see her face. He unrolled his sougan, stretched out on the floor, propped his back against the wall, still holding onto the bottle. He closed his eyes, listened to the buzz inside his head, medicated himself with the liquor, shifted his weight now and again whenever one spot got to bothering him. He let the whiskey begin its journey through his flesh and soul, let it carry him on a long, slow ride down a peaceful river. He didn't mind resting that way. He'd done it a hundred times before in his life. Sleeping in places a man wasn't meant to sleep: the hard ground, trenches filled with rain water, and saddles. Sleeping on the floor was hardly an inconvenience. He heard the little girl cough in her sleep, and it pulled him up a little, then the whiskey river carried him back down again.

He was nearly asleep, not quite, but just at the edge when he heard Suzanne Smith say something.

". . . You want, it's OK."

He thought she was saying something to the girl. His mind was adrift, thick, heavy with exhaustion, the numbing effect of the whiskey. He thought maybe he'd been dreaming that she'd said something. Then she said it again.

"It's OK if you want to lie here in the bed next to me, Mister Cole. I don't mind. You don't need to sleep there on the floor."

It was soft, her voice, soft like a butterfly landing on the petal of a flower, soft and gentle and sweet. It drifted through his weariness. He thought about her in the bed. He thought about accepting the offer.

When he didn't move or say anything, he heard her say: "I wouldn't mind if you were to come and lay here next to me, Mister Cole. After all, it's your bed."

"Miz Smith . . . ?"

"You don't have to say anything," she whispered. "Words aren't necessary. Not tonight they're not."

He remembered how she looked with the shadows of the light from the lamp edging over her face. She'd proved to be an attractive woman with her hair loose and free like she'd had it. At first, he told himself it was the whiskey, or maybe the exhaustion, or even the whipping he'd taken in the alley. He was hurting and halfway to being drunk and maybe that was all part of it, thinking that perhaps she was offering more than she was, lying next to little Tess in the bed. "It's been a long day, Miz Smith. I need to sleep."

"I must sound needy to you, desperate."

"No, Miz Smith. You don't sound that way to me at all."

"I'm sorry," she whispered.

"Don't be."

For a long time more she didn't say anything. He could hear the soft breathing of the child next to her, sleeping the sleep of the innocent, and he thought that must be the way an angel sleeps, soft and still and undisturbed like that.

"Mister Cole . . . ?"

"Call me, John Henry, Miz Smith. I guess we've gotten to know enough of each other in this short time you can call me that."

"I just wanted you to know, I'm not needy. Not like that."

"I know, Suzanne."

He closed his eyes. Even though the flame had burned out and the room had become dark, he still closed his eyes. Something about her had touched him, her and the little girl. They were like angels that had fallen from the sky, their wings broken, unable to fly any farther, brought down by the false promises of a dishonest man and the unshakable weight of disappointment, their wings broken by hopelessness and despair.

"Suzanne?" he said. "What's your man's last name?"

"I thought I told you," she said.

"No, you just said . . . John."

"Oh," she whispered, "it's John . . . Johnny Logan."

Chapter Twenty

Cole left the room early, dawn just breaking over the Black Hills. The pine trees along the slopes stood shrouded in a languid mist. That hour of morning, the air was cold and sharp. Suzanne and her daughter had remained asleep as he'd gathered up his things and quietly dressed. Every piece of clothing but the clean shirt he'd put on the previous night was stiff with dried mud.

He saw a few miners heading off into the hills, their mules loaded down with gear, pickaxes, shovels, tin pans, their beans and bacon and dreams. But with the exception of those few eager men, the town itself was as quiet as the little cemetery up on Mount Moriah where Bill Hickok's bones were resting the eternal rest. He walked to Nutall and Mann's Number Ten.

The place was all but empty, the heelers and loafers having long since fled to their tents and shanties. The smell of stale smoke still clung to the air, stale smoke and stale beer—it was a smell he'd long been familiar with, and first thing in the morning not a smell he appreciated.

Irish Murphy was there, lying on the bar asleep, stretched out fully on his back, his arms folded across his chest, his shoes lined up neatly by his head, the laces left untied. Cole bounced a silver dollar off the oak.

Murphy opened one eye, screwed it around until he saw him standing there. "Mister Cole," he muttered, half sitting up, wiping drool from the corner of his mouth with his shirt cuff. "Are we open yet?" he asked with uncertainty.

"I'll have coffee."

He looked around the empty room. "I'd say either we ain't open yet, or we've lost all our business."

"No jokes this early, Irish. Make the coffee, if you don't mind."

He eased his bulk off the bar. "Damned poor bed, oak is," he grumbled.

Cole waited while Murphy got the Arbuckle's going, then watched as he combed fingers through his thick red hair, saw the muscled forearm as he did, the arm itself thick as a piano leg. He seemed less inclined toward chatter this time. He excused himself to go out back. When he returned, he poured Cole a cup of the pitch-black coffee. It looked and smelled like something other than coffee. "I never claimed to be any sorta cook," he said as he poured. He pushed the coffee and the silver dollar Cole's way. "On the house. How could I charge anyone for that poison?"

"Tell me something, Irish," Cole said, blowing off the steam. "You a friend of Doc Holliday's?"

That opened his eyes a little wider. "I know of the man, yes, sar."

"That's it, you just know *of* him?"

"I've seen him around, spoken to him once or twice, that'd be about it, sar."

"So you're not a friend of his, then?"

He shook his head. "No, I don't think anyone would classify me and Doc as chums." Then he seemed to think it was his turn to ask questions. "You look like you've had yarself a bit o' trouble, sar?"

He was staring at Cole's mud-stiff clothes, the nick above his eye, the nose that was maybe broken from the fight last night—if it could be called a fight—the bruises that were beginning to turn plum color just below his skin. Something told Cole he already knew about the trouble he'd had. "How about Johnny Logan?. You a friend of Johnny Logan's?"

Trouble filled his eyes. "Why you so interested in who my friends are, Mister Cole?"

"Just that I'm trying to get a handle on things around here, Irish, trying to figure out who's who, who it is I've got to watch out for, who I don't."

"Well, sar," he said, picking up a rag from under the counter and wiping the bar top with it, "I ain't but fairly new in town myself, like I told you already. I don't know very many folks I'd call friends of mine."

"So you're not a friend of Johnny Logan's, either?"

It wasn't setting well with Murphy, the questions Cole was asking. Cole could see that by the way he stiffened, the way he pushed the rag over the bar, the coldness that crept into his gaze, the way a man will look if you start to push him too far in a direction he doesn't want to go. "I know Constable Logan, if that's what you mean."

"Know him well enough to have private conversations with him? How about Doc? You know Doc that well, too?"

Murphy obviously thought the bar was clean enough, because he stopped wiping it with the rag. He placed both hands on the oak, his thick arms showing through his shirt. "Finish yar coffee, sar, and leave. We ain't opened yet."

It was what Cole had wanted, a place to start. "They in on it?" he said, setting the coffee cup back down along with the dollar.

"What would that be, sar?"

"The killings."

Murphy's head twitched, just a little. "You're trying my patience. I don't know nothing about the killings of those prostitutes. That's what yar talkin' about, ain't it? Those girls being murdered?"

"Yeah, Irish, that's what I'm talking about."

Cole figured he could do it one of two ways: he could just come over the top of the bar and brawl, or he could reach below the bar by his knee and snatch the hickory billy. Cole was prepared for him to do it either way. He was surprised when Murphy only spoke: "Looks like you've already had your share of misery and hard times, sar. I was the boxing champ of my county, Cork, back home. You wouldn't want to test me. Not in a fist fight you wouldn't."

Cole figured now he had three choices. He could shoot him, fight him, or leave. He decided he'd gotten enough of what he'd come for. An old Texas Ranger he had once known had cautioned him on the virtue of not becoming greedy by saying in a simple drawl: *Hogs get et.*

"Your coffee-making," Cole said, turning to leave, "it needs practice."

He stepped outside, rolled a shuck, and watched as the sun lifted over the Black Hills, its light shattering against the tops of the spiny pines and splaying out in long golden shafts. He thought to himself: *I've survived another night in Deadwood, thanks to Miguel Torres. The real question is, how many more nights will I be able to survive?* He wanted to go see Liddy, ask her about last evening, about the visit of Winston Stevens. But then he thought to hell with it. If she wanted, she could find him and tell him about Winston Stevens and his visit.

He started down the street, back toward the hotel. Maybe Suzanne and the little girl, Tess, would be up by now, maybe they'd have had enough time to get dressed.

Miguel Torres stepped out of the front door of the bagnio he'd been standing in front of last night when he saw whoever it was push Cole into the alley. This time, he was still putting on his coat.

"Torres," he greeted him.

Miguel seemed uneasy. He finished buttoning his coat, acting like it was a common occurrence, a man like him coming out of a cathouse. "What're you doing out this time of morning?" he asked. "You didn't manage to get yourself shanghaied or killed after I left you last night?"

170

"I didn't know you were given to humor, Deputy."

"I ain't."

"How'd you do last night, with the girl? You find her?"

He shifted his glance. "I might've found her."

"You're not sure?"

"I said maybe I did."

Miguel shifted his gaze to up the street, refusing to acknowledge much of whatever he'd discovered in the fleshpot, though it was obvious he'd spent the night inside.

"You find something in there besides information?" Cole asked.

"Hell, Cole, you're just full of damn' curiosity, ain't you?"

"There's nothing wrong with a man needing the company of a woman."

Torres looked hard at Cole then. "Jesus Christ, you must've gotten your brains scrambled in one of those fights you're always losing."

"Look, Miguel, it doesn't matter to me what you do . . . in there, or anywhere else. I was just asking if you'd found out any more about your brother, that's all. You want to take it a different way, go ahead. There's no shame in bedding a whore."

"Well, thank you very god damn much for the lecture," he said.

"You know, Miguel, you are about the touchiest man I ever met."

Torres shook his head, like a man in disbelief. "I'm starting to hear things about you, Cole," he said.

"What sort of things?"

"All sorts of things. Your name's become a cuss word in this town. There's talk you're dangerous, spoiling for any fight you can get into. Especially since you doused King Fisher's lights the other day. That lawman, Logan, he's been throwing your name around to his friends. You wouldn't exactly get elected mayor if you were to run."

"That means I'm stirring the pot."

"What pot?"

"The one where I find out who killed those women."

"Yeah, well, if you're not careful, you're going to wind up in that pot with them."

"Not as long as I've got you around watching after me, Miguel."

"I wouldn't count on it, Cole, about my being around next time."

"I'll see you later, Miguel. Good luck with finding Robertito, huh?"

Torres looked back at the bagnio, the one he'd just come out of, and tilted his head up toward a second-story window, one that had lace curtains hanging in it. Cole saw one of the curtains draw back just a little. A face appeared—young, pretty, dark.

* * * * *

Suzanne and Tess were up, sitting there dressed, waiting, by the time Cole reached his hotel room.

"How about some breakfast?" he offered.

Tess looked at Cole, looked at her mother. "Mama?"

"For her," Suzanne said. "Maybe a little something to eat for her."

"For both of you," Cole said.

"No, just for her," Suzanne insisted.

"Come on," Cole said, opening the door for them.

"What about our things?" she asked, pointing to the two small trunks in the corner of the room.

"Leave them. We'll pick them up later."

They found the café, the one Cole had been sitting in the day King Fisher had tried to kill him through the plate glass. There was a new window already installed, the putty still fresh along the casing. Tess ordered flapjacks and maple syrup and a glass of goat's milk. Suzanne ate little of her eggs, nibbled at her toast, sipped her coffee. She was prettier sitting there in the light of day. Cole remembered their conversation of the night before. He was struck by how much his opinion of her had changed since the stage ride up from Cheyenne. He enjoyed watching the child eat, hungry, full of energy, the way a person should eat a meal. He watched her pour too much syrup on her flapjacks. It ran off the sides before she cut into them with her fork. She grinned with each mouthful.

"I'll find a way to repay you," Suzanne said.

"No, you don't have to concern yourself with that."

"But . . ." she tried to persist.

"Look, Suzanne, it's really not a problem for me to help you and Tessie out. Why turn it into one?" He saw the way her soft blue eyes searched for an answer to his question. "I had a son once," he went on. Why he said it, he didn't know, but he said it as he watched Tess eat her flapjacks. Maybe that was it, watching a beautiful child enjoying herself, thinking how it would've been if he'd gotten a chance to watch his own son doing the same thing, pouring too much syrup over his flapjacks. "I'd like to think, if it were my wife and child needing it, someone would be willing to help out," he said.

"You said once," she said. "What do you mean . . . *once?*"

"He died of the milk sickness just after he was born. Him and my wife both died of the same thing."

She didn't say anything; she didn't say the usual about how sorry she was to hear of his loss. She didn't make words just to make them. She just sat there, looking at him with those soft sea-blue eyes that let him know she understood in ways that words could not.

"What I mean to say is, Suzanne, it is not a bother to me to help you and Tess. Don't let it be a bother to you, OK?"

She nodded. "I accept your kindness," she said.

"Good. Soon's we're done eating, we'll go over to the stage line and see about a pair of tickets to Denver."

Suzanne reached across the table and touched the knuckles of Cole's hand with her fingertips. "Mister Cole . . ."

He didn't move his hand away.

"About last night . . ."

"I know."

"I didn't mean it to sound . . . Her lower lip quivered slightly, the eyes misted over. "I just meant to say that I didn't want to sound needy to you. . . ."

"To tell the truth, it felt to me more like needing and not being needy. There's a difference."

"You're an unusual man, Mister Cole."

"No, not so different than anyone else."

Tessie asked if she could have a second glass of goat's milk. Cole ordered it for her.

"I can't go to Denver," Suzanne said.

"Why not?"

"What would I do once I got there? I've no money, no family, no one there waiting for us."

"I'll give you enough to rent a place, tide you along until you can find something."

"No. Why squander the money it would take to travel to Denver when I can stay right here, find work here."

"You've seen Deadwood, Suzanne. Is this a place you want to raise your daughter in?"

"It will have to do until I can get myself square again."

"Suzanne, I don't even think they have a school here for Tess."

"Then I'll tutor her myself."

"What sort of work do you think a town like this would have to offer a woman? He was blunt. "You've seen the female population here. What do you think those women do for a living?"

"There are other things a woman can do besides what you're referring to, John Henry."

"Glad to hear you call me by my first name." She gave him a weak smile. It felt awkward for him to be lecturing her on the vices of Deadwood. "Suzanne, if it hadn't been for Tess, I would have kept my opinions to myself. Besides the obvious, what sorts of other things would there be for a woman to do here?"

"I can take in laundry and sewing," she said. "I'm a very capable seamstress. With all these bachelors here, I would think there would be plenty need of my services."

"And Johnny Logan," he said. "What about him? He's still the law in Deadwood, in case he didn't tell you."

"What about him?" she said, stiffening her lower lip.

"You don't think that'd make him uncomfortable, to have you and Tessie living here in Deadwood, under his gaze?"

"I hope it *does* make him uncomfortable . . . John Henry. Besides, what's that to me? I have my daughter to look out for, that's my main concern."

"I don't think its a good idea, Suzanne. That's all."

Now her fingers did more than just glide over his knuckles; they encircled his wrist. "Your wife," she said. "Did you always give her your opinion on matters you felt strongly about? Did she ever disagree with you?"

"Yes. Matter of fact I did, and she did."

"And how did you take that, when she disagreed with you?"

"I respected her for having strong beliefs," he said, unashamed.

"You see, John Henry, that's the way good women are. They stick to their beliefs, no matter what anyone else tells them."

"You can have my room at the hotel," he said, not seeing any reason to continue trying to talk her out of leaving Deadwood. "I've already paid a week's rent. It'll give you time to get settled, maybe find something better, a small house, maybe."

"No, I won't see you out on the streets because of me," she stated firmly.

"Just till we find you something better," he said. "You and Tess."

Chapter Twenty-One

Cole told the clerk at the hotel the situation, and gave him another $5 to extend the room stay, in case Suzanne needed more time to find her own place.

"She your missus?" the clerk asked, looking at Suzanne and Tess waiting in the lobby. "That your little girl?"

"Mind your own business, friend," Cole warned.

The clerk shifted his gaze back to the money. "Sure, sure. It's your room. I reckon you can have who you want in it. You can keep an ape in it, you want. It wouldn't make no difference to me."

"See that she gets fresh towels, sheets," Cole said. "Soap for her and the little girl. Have your boy, Deke, take their clothes down and have them laundered. Have him bring some fresh fruit up to the room." He laid another $10 down. "Meals as well, in case Miz Smith chooses not to go out." The clerk looked at Cole who could see what was running through his mind, the name, the questions that came after it. "You make sure Deke takes care of it, OK?"

"Sure, Mister Cole, anything you want for Miz Smith, I'll see it gets done."

Cole told Suzanne he'd check on her later. Tess held her hand, looked up at him: "Thank you for the flapjacks, mister." She smiled, showing a missing front tooth.

Cole went outside, pulled his makings, rolled a shuck, and wondered what the hell he was getting into here. He decided it was time to wire Ike, asking him when he might be coming to Deadwood. There were some things Cole wanted to tell him about—the situation between him and Liddy, for one. He also could use the help, after what'd happened last night in the alley. He needed someone to watch his back. He'd been lucky so far, thanks to Miguel Torres, but how much longer he could stay lucky was another question.

He started to cross the street when he heard his name called. "Cole!"

He turned to see Johnny Logan coming down the street, a skinny deputy hurrying alongside him. By the way he was walking, in that stiff-legged manner of a man going somewhere, it was plain to see that Johnny wasn't just out for his morning rounds.

"I need to talk to you, Cole!"

Cole turned in his direction. His duster was unbuttoned. Johnny Logan could see the butt of the self cocker. Cole didn't mind that he could. "What is it?"

"In private." Johnny said. "I wanna talk to you in private."

Cole looked at the other man.

"Around here," Johnny Logan said, thumbing toward the alley.

"The alley? You've got to be kidding."

"What the hell's wrong with a little private conversation in an alley?" he asked. The blood had gathered just under his skin, along the jaw and cheeks and neck, the way a man's will when he's angry and heavily built like Johnny Logan was.

"You first," Cole said, and waited until he and the other man stepped into the ally. He followed but kept a distance between them. "OK, we're here, private, like you wanted, Logan," he said, after Johnny and the other man had gone in a short way and turned around.

"Tell him, Skinny!" Johnny said to the man.

"Saw you and that woman over to the café," the deputy constable said. "The little girl, too. Eating."

Cole looked at Logan. "Is there a crime in having breakfast in this town?" He now knew what it was that'd made the blood crawl up into Johnny's face and turn it plum-colored.

"You know what this is about!" Johnny said.

"Don't tell me," Cole said. "You're the jealous type."

"I don't need a reason to kill you, Cole."

"Get in line, Constable."

Watch the hands, that's what was going through Cole's mind. *His hand moves, shoot him! The other one, too.*

"Stay away from Suzanne!" Johnny said. "I won't tell you twice!"

"What is it with men like you, Logan? You won't keep to a woman, you won't let her go." Cole didn't mind airing Johnny's dirty laundry if he didn't.

"Get lost, Skinny," Johnny ordered the deputy.

"You sure, boss? You sure you ain't gonna need me in on this?"

"Get lost!"

Skinny retreated like a dog that had been kicked by its master, a little at a time.

"What do you want, Cole? You want to kill me, blow a hole through me with that big Remington? That what you come here for?"

"You know why I came."

"No. I know why you *said* you came. But ever since you've arrived, you've done everything you could to test me. Now it's Suzanne you're testing me with. I whipped you once. Maybe I should've killed you. But I didn't. I gave you a chance. And look what it's brought me. You see how that is, me giving you a break, not killing you when I could have? Now Suzanne shows up out of nowhere, and you and her are all of a sudden cozy, sitting down, having breakfast together. Skinny seen you coming out of the hotel with her. That's how you repay me for not killing you, squiring around my woman?"

"You left her in Denver. You forget that?"

"Stay out of it, Cole, that's between her and me."

"No, not any more it isn't."

"Since when?"

"Since she asked me."

Logan walked around in a tight little circle, hands on his hips, bent forward at the waist. Then he stopped walking in the tight little circle. "You don't know," he said. "You just don't know a damn' thing about anything! You leave Suzanne alone!"

Cole had grown tired of Johnny Logan's threats and his bullying. "It's too late for that."

Johnny cocked his head to one side, his face flushed with anger.

"You want to end it here and now?" Cole asked. "Go ahead, pull your piece. This conversation is getting old."

For a long, drawn-out moment, Cole thought Logan might just pull his pistol. He was breathing hard and the sweat was beading on his forehead. Then the air seemed to go out of him. "Why don't you just climb on the next stage and go back where you came from? Why do you have to try and bring more trouble to this place than what's already here?"

Cole felt something had changed in Johnny Logan, the voice, the stance, the eyes. Whatever it was, it had changed him from just two minutes before. He looked suddenly like an old bull all worn out, ready to lie down. "I lost track," he said. "I lost track of who I was. Lost track of Suzanne and Tess . . . everything. I came here, found it to my liking, married a woman. I figured Suzanne . . . a good-looking woman like her . . . wouldn't have trouble finding another man. Me, I didn't consider myself that much of a find. You can understand that, can't you, Cole? How a man can get like that, start thinking like that?" He looked at Cole, the eyes set close together in that brutal face. "I'd almost forgotten about her. Now she shows up outta the blue. Her and Tess. What'm I supposed to do? Leave the woman I married?

Leave Deadwood, my job? Give everything up for a woman I ain't seen in three years? Someone I'd written off?"

"Suzanne will take care of herself," Cole said, "as long as you let her alone."

"First you, then her . . ." he said. "Things was going good for me. Now all this has to happen."

"It could get worse."

"How?" he muttered. His brooding face was full of anguish.

"I could find out you were involved in the killings of those women."

"Liddy Winslow's girls? You accusing me of being part of that? Who're you to accuse *me* of being part of *that?*" The right hand shifted slightly.

"Don't!" Cole warned.

"You come into my god-damn' town and accuse me of murdering whores!"

"I'm not accusing anybody, Constable. Not yet I'm not. But it doesn't matter to me whether or not you wear that badge if I find out you were involved. I'll take you to the nearest court and see you hanged."

"You're not just some damn' bounty hunter, are you?"

"I didn't come for the reward, if that's what you're asking."

"You're a federal man?"

"No."

"Who sent you, then?"

"It doesn't matter."

"I didn't kill those damn' whores."

"If you didn't, I'm willing to bet you know who did."

A muscle in Johnny Logan's cheek twitched; his hand held steady. He was thinking, wondering if he could pull his piece and fire it into Cole before Cole could pull his and do the same to him. A man can only think about something like that for just so long. If he waits too long, more than a second or two, it's too late. Anybody that's ever been there knows that much. Cole could see it in Johnny Logan's eyes. He recognized that it was too late to threaten Cole any more.

"If I knew who killed them," he said, "I'd have arrested them."

"I'm not convinced," Cole said.

"What, that I didn't do it, or that I'd have arrested them?"

"Either one."

"Believe what you want," he said. "But proving it is another matter. You won't be able to prove anything in this gulch. Hell, there's not even any law here, other than me. Or did you forget that?"

"The law is whoever is willing to enforce it," Cole said. "I don't think that's you. You want to tell me anything, now's the time."

"You're 'way off, Cole. 'Way off."

"Jack! God-damn, honey, what're ya and Johnny doin' back here, the dosey-do?"

Calamity Jane came down the alley, swinging her arms in that exaggerated way she had, a half-used whiskey bottle in one hand.

"We finished here?" Logan asked.

Jane had been drinking. It was plain from the way she strutted, the way her face was flushed pink. She had a Navy revolver stuck inside her belt.

"'Mornin', Johnny," she hooted, and did a little dance around him.

"Go to hell, Jane!"

"Well, ain't ya just the most gracious thing?" She grinned as he stepped past her. "How's Lulu Divan? And how's the wife?"

Johnny threw her a hard look. Cole could guess what he might have done to her if Cole hadn't been there.

"That Johnny's lost his sense of humor," Jane said, twisting slowly around in a circle, her arms spread wide, like wings.

Seeing her again called up the name she'd given Cole the night before—Leo Loop.

"Good to see ya, Jack! Ya ready for a real woman yet?"

"Tell me about Leo," Cole said.

She didn't stop twirling, lost in her own revelry. "Leo? Where'd ya hear that name, Jack?"

"You. Leo Loop. You remember, Jane?"

She stopped twirling and pulled the cork out of the bottle she held in her hand. Fumbling, the bottle slipped from her hand and the contents leaked out. She fell to her knees, trying to save some of it, the whiskey dribbling through her fingers. "Jeezus, Jack!"

Cole pulled her to her feet, still clutching the bottle and what was left in it.

"Who's Leo Loop, Jane?"

She looked at Cole with eyes like those of a terrified bird. She felt puny, all bones, her body wasted away from the drink and the life. "I need a drink . . . Jack," she said, those wild-bird eyes peering down to the bottle in her hands.

"No, you don't need a drink, Jane. You've had a drink. You don't need another, not right now."

Her mouth drew down. She squeezed her eyes shut like she was about to be hit. Cole eased up on his grip. She shoved the bottle to her lips and drained what she'd saved from spilling into the dirt.

"Tell me about Leo Loop."

"Jeezus, Jack." Her mouth opened and closed like a fish out of water. "Leo's 'bout the majorest player in the whole damn' gulch, that's all."

"Go on."

She reeled away, now that Cole let her. "Billy knew Leo. Leo wanted Billy to front fer him. Wanted Billy in his vest pocket 'cause of who Billy was, 'cause of Billy's rep. But Billy told Leo to kiss his white shiny behind, that he wasn't no shill fer nobody. Leo told Billy, he di'nt go along with things, Billy wa'n't goin to be around long in Deadwood." She paused, put the bottle to her lips, but it was empty. She held it out in front of her, looked at it, then flung it aside. "Damn and hell!"

"You know for certain this conversation took place between Bill and Leo?" Cole asked.

She looked at him the same way she looked at the empty bottle, with a lot of disappointment, like both of them were something to be pitied. "Know? Di'nt I tell ya me and Bill was married? Di'nt I tell ya that? Don't married folks tell one another things at night when they're laying in bed together? Billy told me all about Leo Loop and his offers to have Bill shill fer him. Bill said it'd be a cold day in hell befer he'd shill fer a pimp like Leo."

How much was the truth? From what Cole knew, Jane and Bill were never married. And there was little evidence to prove that they were anything more than casual acquaintances. How much was the truth, and how much had Jane made up in her own besotted mind? "Where can I find this Leo Loop, Jane?"

She stumbled toward Cole and got close enough for him to have to turn his head to keep from breathing her breath. "Ya don't want to find him," she whispered in a voice that was near a growl.

"Why is that?"

"'Cause he'll kill ya, just like he killed my darlin' Bill." She let out a groan, caught the brim of her hat in both hands, and danced around in a circle. "'Cause he'll kill ya just like he did Bill . . . just like Bill." Her voice had turned sing-song.

"You've never met him, have you, Jane, Leo Loop?"

She stopped circling long enough to glare at him, squinting her eyes, unsquinting them. "Ya sayin' I'm a damn' liar, Jack?"

"Did you ever meet this man?"

"Ain't no one calls Jane Canary a damn' liar!" She tried jerking the Navy from her belt. Cole grabbed her hand, twisted the gun free, looked at it. It was rusty, pitted, the hammer missing. She couldn't have shot him with it if he had pulled the trigger for her.

"Jane, you're not only drunk, you're crazy, pulling a busted pistol on a man."

She sat right down on the ground and began to bawl. Whether the performance was real or not, Cole couldn't tell. Whether or not what she'd told him about Leo Loop and his threats toward Bill Hickok was something else he couldn't be sure of. He waited for a few minutes to see if Jane would come around again, talk a little sense, stop the play-acting, if that was what it was. But when she didn't, Cole offered her a hand up.

"Don't need no dang' help," she bawled.

She was wretched and sad, and who knew exactly what secrets she kept within that frail and fragile heart? Cole pulled her to her feet in spite of her protest.

"I'm sorry you spilled your bottle," he said, reaching into his pocket. "Here, buy one on me, for the one you dropped."

She blinked, and brushed back the tears that had been forced from her eyes. "I ain't no charity case, if that's what yar thinkin'."

"Did I say that?"

She narrowed her eyes. "I ain't no liar, neither."

"No one said you were, Jane."

She looked at the money he was holding out to her. "I di'nt mean to pull my Navy on ya, Jack. Ya know I'd never shoot a friend."

"I know."

"Ya believe me, don't ya?"

"I believe you wouldn't shoot me, Jane."

"No, I mean about that other, about what Billy told me about Leo."

"I'll follow it up."

A crooked smile eased itself across her mouth and suddenly she was child-like again. That was the best way to describe her at times, child-like. She scratched at her hip. "I could use a loan," she said. "But it'd be just a loan, ya unnerstand?"

"Sure. Pay me back when you get it."

"Yeah, Jack. Jane don't welsh on her loans, ya can ask anybody."

She took the money carefully from his hand, like it was a fresh bottle of whiskey and she didn't want to spill any of it. She patted Cole's hand. "Yar all right, Jack."

He watched her strut down the alley toward the street. "Jane?"

She half turned around, nearly fell.

"Maybe you could use some of that money to buy yourself a meal. It might not hurt you to eat a little something," he suggested.

She nodded her head. "Ah, Jack, I'll consider it. Ya know, I ain't ever had much of an appertite."

Cole made himself a cigarette and smoked it as he headed for the telegraph office. It was time to send that wire to Ike Kelly.

Chapter Twenty-Two

John Henry Cole sent the wire to Ike Kelly, told him what he'd learned so far, and urged his presence as soon as he could free himself of his obligations in Cheyenne. He needed to explain some things to him, the part about Liddy, only he didn't mention any of that in the telegram.

His next move was to try and locate Leo Loop. He began asking around. It didn't take him long to learn Leo owned a place called the Lucky Strike Saloon, up the street from Nutall and Mann's Number Ten. At least he'd learned that Leo Loop actually existed. He had to admit—entering the Lucky Strike—that it was a lot more elegant than anyone would expect in a town like Deadwood.

Shafts of light filtered in through the front windows and angled across the floorboards coated with sawdust, tobacco plugs, and brass spittoons. Hanging over the backbar was a large painting of reclining nudes, their eyes cast heavenward. The place was quiet at that time of day, except for a back table where four men wearing plug hats were conversing with one another. A swamper was going around, carrying out the spittoons. He limped—another busted-down cowboy doing the only work left to a man whose only education was horses and cows. Two burly bartenders were carrying in barrels from a beer wagon parked out front.

Cole waited until one of the bartenders took a break, wiped his brow with a kerchief, and said: "Wadda'll it be?"

"Coffee, if you've got any."

The bartender looked perturbed. "Nickel," he said. "That's how much a cup of coffee is." When Cole tossed a nickel on the bar, he said: "Refills are free." His shirt was soaked with sweat from carrying the barrels. "Anything else?" he asked as he took the nickel off the bar and looked at it like it wasn't worth his time.

"Leo Loop," Cole said. "You know of a man named Leo Loop?"

He cocked his head, looked at Cole with tired eyes. "You gotta be joking."

"Why's that?"

"Everyone in Deadwood knows Leo Loop."

"I'm new."

He grunted. "You and a hunnerd others that pour in every day. That's Leo in the corner . . . he owns the place."

"Which one?"

"This one," he said.

"No, I mean, which one is he?"

"Oh, the fat one with the fancy vest and the cookie duster."

"Thanks."

"Don't mind, I'll be gettin' back to work now. Red gets peeved if he thinks I'm slacking."

"A couple of more questions, if you don't mind?"

He showed a look of impatience. "Mister, Red won't like me standing around yakking. It's delivery day, or didn't you notice?"

Cole laid a pair of silver dollars on the bar. "That's for you if you'll answer a couple of my questions."

He picked them up and slipped them into his pocket, making sure the other guy hauling the beer barrels didn't see him do it.

"Say, Harve, what's up, ya helpin' out here or not?" the other barman asked.

"Can't you see I got a customer, Red?"

The guy grunted, settled the barrel behind the bar, and went back outside, muttering something to himself.

"Hurry up, ask your questions," Harve said.

"I hear Leo is the boss dog around Deadwood. If you want to do any business in this town, you need to get Leo's blessing first."

"Depends on what you mean," Harve said.

"Don't be coy," Cole warned. "That's good money in your pocket."

"Yeah, maybe you heard it right," Harve said, leaning over the bar and speaking softly. "Leo's sorta the man in town, you want to put it that way."

"He runs things?"

"You could say that."

"I'm asking."

"Yeah, I'd say he pretty much run things."

"Gambling, whores, things like that?"

Harve nodded.

"Somebody want to set up a game, maybe run a few of his own girls, they'd have to see Leo first? Suppose a man skipped seeing Leo and just set up his operation? What then?"

"Look," he said, keeping his voice low, "I could lose more than just my job here for being out of line about things . . . you understand?" He swallowed, looked over at Leo Loop and the other men with him. "Maybe you ought to go talk to him." Harve nodded in the direction of the fat man at the rear table.

Then Red, the other bartender, brought in another barrel of beer, set it down, and wiped his face with the sleeve of his shirt. "This going to take all day?" he asked Harve. "You serving this fellow a cup of coffee or planning an evening out at the opera?"

"I gotta get back to work here," Harve said.

Cole took his cup and walked over to the table of the men wearing the plug hats.

"Mister Loop," he said.

Four unhappy faces looked up at him, Leo's being one of them. They were all well dressed, clean white shirts, cravats, claw-hammer coats. Their hands were soft, the nails neatly trimmed, hands that didn't know work, other than the work it takes to count money or cut into an expensive steak. The fat man with the cookie-duster mustache said: "We're having a business meeting here, sir."

"Your bartender makes a good cup of coffee," Cole said.

Leo Loop didn't try to hide his displeasure with the interruption. His soft gray eyes shifted toward the two men carrying in the barrels. "Yes, well, I'll bring that to his attention the next opportunity I get," he said sarcastically.

"I'm new in town," Cole said, before he could turn his attention to the three others with him.

The soft gray eyes shifted, grew agitated. "That's all very interesting," he said. "I applaud your enterprise!" Then he returned his attention to the others, grinning like he'd made some sort of joke. They chuckled, two of them. The third man looked like he'd never know a moment's worth of pleasure in his whole life. He was a lean, cadaverous man with drooping bloodhound eyes and a sagging face, long and folded in lines. Probably on a full moon, he bayed.

"I'm thinking of going into business," Cole said.

That got Leo's interest just a little. "What sort of business would that be?" he asked, without bothering to look up.

"A gambling operation, maybe some joy girls. I heard I ought to see you first. So now I've seen you, now you know."

Leo Loop turned his head, the thick flesh under his chin bulging over his tight paper collar. His skin was an ash gray, smooth yet from a morning shave, no doubt from the local barber, not his own hand. He smelled of bay rum and sweat. "Who told you that you needed to see me?" he asked, his manner nonchalant, but still curious.

"Let's just say that's the word on the street, that if I want to do business in Deadwood, I should see you first."

"Gentlemen, if you'll excuse me," he said, scraping his chair back away from the table. "It seems this gentleman and I have a matter that needs discussing."

They all muttered their assent like the fine businessmen they were.

"My office is back there," Leo said as he stood up, his bulk pressing against the wool jacket he wore.

Cole followed him back to a small but well-appointed room. A large desk took up most of it. He took up residence in a brass-tack leather chair and indicated for Cole to sit in the one across from him. The chair was made of elk horns, the seat covered in hide.

"I didn't catch your name, sir," he said.

"John Henry Cole." There was no point in lying to him about it when he could find out if he wanted to.

He rubbed a place behind his left ear with his forefinger. "So you've come here to Deadwood to get rich, have you?"

"Something like that."

"And you aim to do it by setting up your own operation . . . gambling, prostitution, that it?"

He had a smooth voice, oiled, like a man that sells curatives off the back of a wagon, elixirs that he mixes up out of coal oil and alcohol and snake heads, promising the customer that it will cure lumbago, dropsy, and waning sexual desire. Cole thought a man like Leo Loop with that smooth voice could sell a lot of snake oil. "Something like that."

"And you were told you needed to check with me first?"

"That's why I'm here, to let you know."

"Because I sort of control things, is that what you heard?"

"Yeah, that's what I heard."

"Indeed." He smiled, the fatness of his face becoming a gray moon.

"So, if it's not true," Cole said, "then why the private meeting?"

Loop removed a cigar from a hand-carved box atop his desk. He bit off the end of the stogie and held a match an inch under the tip until it caught fire, then he drew in a long, deep lungful of smoke before slowly blowing it out in a blue stream. He held the cigar between his fingers and rolled it back and forth as he took stock of Cole. Finally he gave a smug smile. "I have to plead innocent," he said, his gray eyes expressive. "What can I tell you? The things you've heard about me are false. I have only this modest club, a small, simple operation out of which I do a meager business. I am, like everyone else who has come here to Deadwood, merely a man looking for the golden promise."

"So, then, I guess it doesn't matter to you that I start up my own operation, go into competition with you?"

His left hand slowly came up, the fingers touching the ends of the cookie duster as though testing to see if the barber had waxed them well enough that morning. "I have no concerns about your wanting to become a businessman in our booming little town, Mister Cole. What you do is strictly your business."

"Then I was misinformed," Cole said, not buying it for a minute. "Sorry to disturb your meeting." He stood, ready to leave.

"Ah, there is just one little matter, however," Loop said, clearing a throat that didn't need to be cleared.

"Go on," Cole said, waiting to hear the rest of it.

"You see, I am the head of the business council here in Deadwood, elected by the Deadwood Business Commission, some of whom you met out there at the table. And as such, I am responsible for making sure that any new business that goes up here in town has a proper business license. And of course there is the matter of monthly association fees that must be paid as a member of the council. It helps to regulate the town's growth, and also to police our own, you see."

"How much?"

He beamed. "A man who gets right down to it . . . I like that," he said, clearly pleased that Cole had not challenged the obvious shakedown.

"How much?" Cole repeated.

"The license will cost you a thousand dollars. The monthly fee will be twenty-five percent of your gross take, as audited by me personally. It's what I do best . . . count money."

"And if I fail to buy a license and pay the monthly dues?"

"Then, sir," he said with feigned disappointment, "you sha'n't be doing your business here in Deadwood, or anywhere else in the gulch, for that matter."

"How long do I have to think about it?"

"Take all the time you want, Mister Cole. Only don't attempt to open up your operation until you've paid your fees."

"I'll let you know."

"Yes, do that. And best of luck to you, sir."

Harve and Red were going at it outside near the beer wagon. A smashed barrel lay in a pool of foam near the back of the wagon. Both men had their fists raised like prize fighters, dancing around each other in a small circle, cussing each other, and making lots of hard threats. Cole side-stepped them and headed for Liddy's, now that he had something solid to go on. He needed to put the next piece of the puzzle into place. At least, that's the reason he gave himself for going to see her.

Chapter Twenty-Three

Jazzy Sue opened the door to Cole's knock.

"Mistah John Henry," she said, her smile telling him she was happy to see him.

"Miss Lydia home?"

"She's taking her bath."

"I can come back."

"Oh, no, suh. She say that, if you come, to send you to see her."

"You're sure?"

She grinned. "Yas, suh, I'm sure."

Jazzy Sue took his hat. Cole's head was nearly back to normal, so he didn't mind taking the hat off.

"My, your clothes sho could use a cleaning," Jazzy Sue said. "Looks like you been rolling around in the mud, or somethin'. An' look at that face! Mistah John Henry, you've been in trouble again, ain't ya?"

"Accident this time," he said, choosing not to go into it again. He took off the duster and handed it to her. She held it out away from her and wrinkled her nose.

"Well, at least you wearing a nice clean shirt," she said. "That's the gentleman in you. A gentleman always makes sure he's got on a clean shirt, if nothin' else."

"I'll have to take your word for it. I've never thought of myself in quite that way, as a gentleman."

She giggled. "Miss Lydia is back there. Just knock on the door."

"Maybe I should wait."

"No, suh, I don't think so. She say that, if you come, to send you back."

He knocked lightly.

"Come in."

Lydia Winslow was reclined in a tub of water and soap bubbles that reached the notch just below her throat and hid her beauty. A bare knee protruded from the water, wet and shiny. Her hair was pinned up, drawn away from her oval face, the milk-white skin. Her arms rested along the top of the tub, the hands dangling over the sides.

"I wondered when you'd be coming," she said.

"I don't like having to stand in line."

Those beautiful green eyes narrowed at the remark, darkened just a shade. "What's that supposed to mean?"

"Last evening. I came by last evening, but you already had company."

She didn't say anything. One of the hands reached over and took a glass of red wine that had been sitting on a small marble-top stand next to the tub. She brought the glass to her mouth, the wine deep red against the light in the room. She touched the glass to her mouth, to the curved lips that Cole remembered so well for their sweetness and delicacy.

She held the glass of wine to her lips, her eyes watching Cole. He waited for her to say whatever it was she wanted to say. But instead she just stared, the lips pursed to drink, the long, slender fingers wrapped around the glass's stem. "Winston came to visit."

"Yeah, I know."

Her gaze refused to look away, almost as if it were challenging him. "That bothers you, that Winston was here?"

"Hell, yes, it bothers me."

"It shouldn't, John Henry."

"I'm sorry I can't be as casual about it as you."

This time she flinched just a little. "You make it difficult between us," she said softly.

"What am I supposed to feel?"

"I don't know, Cole. I've never lied to you about who I am. You're free to believe whatever you choose. But I thought I made it clear the other night how I felt about you."

"I won't apologize for how I feel about you seeing him," Cole said.

"No, I didn't think you would. But you're making something of this that doesn't need to be."

Cole was tired of talking about Winston Stevens. "Tell me what you know about Leo Loop," he said.

She shrugged, her bare wet shoulders lifting slightly out of the bath water. "I don't know that much about him. Leo and I are somewhat in competition, I suppose you could say. But not really. As I explained in our first conversation, I'm not a madam and my girls aren't what Leo's girls are. There's a big difference between us."

"How come you didn't mention his name the first time we talked?"

One long fingertip trailed itself around the rim of the wineglass, a light, delicate movement. "There was no reason to mention his name. He does what he does, and I do what I do."

"He does more than just that. The way I hear it, he controls the pleasure trade in Deadwood."

"Yes, I've heard that, too. But it has nothing to do with me."

"It seems to me it has everything to do with you, Liddy. If it's true, then you would've had to pay him off in order to run *your* business. That seems to me like an important piece of information you left out of our conversation that first night."

Her gaze settled on the glass again, watching the tip of her finger rub the lip. Cole remembered just how delicate those fingers felt, the way they traveled over his bare skin, pressed into his back. He remembered at one point kissing her hands.

"Mister Loop paid me a visit when I first arrived in Deadwood," she said, the tip of her finger touching her upper lip to remove a bead of wine. "He stated that his position was as head of Deadwood's business commission, I believe he called it. He said that I would need to pay a licensing fee to him and his group. He also said that, in addition, I would be obligated to pay a percent of my gross income as a monthly fee. I told him I wouldn't be much of a businesswoman if I were to pay such exorbitant fees."

"And?"

"I declined his . . . offer."

"Just like that? He didn't do anything about it when you started your escort service?"

She set the empty wineglass down, the fingers reluctant to let go, always reluctant to let go of whatever they might be in contact with. Cole could feel his skin tingle.

"Oh, he came a time or two after that and restated his position on the matter. Each time, he was a little more insistent that I buy a license. But I simply refused."

"Wait a minute. You mean he let you operate your escorts without a problem?"

Her eyes widened just a bit. "I'm not as naïve as you may think, John Henry. I hired Doc to protect my interests and my business. I'm sure without someone like Doc to represent me, Leo Loop might have been less amicable about my doing business in his town."

"So he left you alone because Doc was working for you?"

"Yes."

"No, he didn't. Three of your young women have been murdered. Doc didn't stop that." He saw the wounded look invade her eyes.

"You think Leo killed them? Dottie and Eva and Flora . . . ?"

"You said it yourself the first time we talked, that it could've been a joy-house operator, someone warning you to take your business elsewhere. Leo seems the logical choice, don't you think?"

"But as you stated," she intoned, "why not just kill me if that was the purpose . . . to put me out of business, why the others? They were just working for me."

"I don't know. But I'd say Leo Loop is the man who's behind it. Now, it's just a matter of proving it. And in this town, that's going to be a little difficult. Everyone seems to be in everyone else's pocket, and there is no law here except for Johnny Logan. And unless I'm wrong about him, he's in Leo's pocket as well."

Suddenly she stood up, the soap and water sliding off her except for the dark triangular patch of her womanhood. She stood there unashamedly allowing him to look at her, wanting him to look at her, it seemed.

"Would you hand me the towel, John Henry?"

He handed it to her. She waited to see if he would do anything else as she hesitated in taking it. When he didn't do anything else, she took the towel and wrapped it around herself, strands of her russet hair clinging to her neck and in places around her face where it'd come loose from the combs. Still she stood there, looking at him, small puddles of water collecting around her feet.

"How *will* you prove that Leo Loop was responsible for the murders?" she asked.

Cole pulled his makings and started putting together a shuck, something to occupy his hands, his mind, his thoughts from what he really wanted to be doing. He put the smoke together, spilling just a little of the tobacco, and fired it with a match, snapping out the flame, then taking in a deep breath of the blue smoke before answering her question. "The way I see it," he told her, "Leo's not the type to do his own killing. He hires it done."

She moved the towel, using a loose end to touch the damp strands of hair along her neck. He wanted to take it from her and drop it to the floor.

"So, you'll find whoever it was that Leo hired and get him to tell you the truth," she said. The way she looked at him, Cole was willing to bet she knew exactly what he was thinking about the towel. "And then, when you do," she said, stepping closer to him, "you'll have enough evidence to see that he's arrested."

"I'd like to think that's how it will go."

"Yes," she murmured, "that is how it will go."

She dropped the towel. She was still wet in places, places that soaked through Cole's shirt when she kissed him.

"Is this a good idea?" he asked.

"Do you think it is?" she whispered.

"Probably not . . ." His face was buried in the softness of her hair as she reached up and unpinned the combs and let her hair fall free.

"We agreed, didn't we . . . ?" she said softly.

"Yeah."

Her mouth was wet, her skin dewy, soft, warm from the bath. He could taste the wine on her lips, her tongue as it searched his mouth. "I'm glad you're here," she whispered.

Those fingers, the ones that were holding the glass a minute ago, circling the rim so delicately, were tracing over his chest now, down along his ribs as she reached her hands inside his shirt, undoing the buttons. His skin prickled from her touch. "You like being here, don't you?" she said, the throaty whisper of her voice intoxicating him.

"Yes, I like it."

Her teeth bit into his lip, then she kissed him again, only this time the kiss was wetter, fuller, more wanting. And so was he.

The bath water was still warm when he slipped into it. Liddy insisted Cole enjoy the luxury while she had Jazzy Sue take his clothes and clean them.

Liddy sat by the tub and washed his hair, back, and chest. She paused several times, kissed his jaw, his chin, his mouth in little light ways, while her hands slipped below the water to tantalize him. It seemed he couldn't get enough of her.

"I wired Ike," he said, feeling the need to be completely honest with her, and maybe with himself.

The caressing paused for a brief moment, then continued.

"I asked him to finish up his business in Cheyenne and come here. That was before I found out more about Leo Loop."

"So now you won't need him to come," she said.

"Maybe not. If I can get this cleared up before he leaves Cheyenne."

"You will . . . I'm sure of it, John Henry."

"I need to be honest with Ike," he said. "If he comes to Deadwood, he might be expecting to renew old feelings with you, Liddy."

Again the hands stopped, but just briefly. "I doubt that he would still have an interest in me after all this time," she said.

"Either way, Liddy, I need to tell him."

"Do whatever you want, John Henry. Tell him whatever you must."

Her lips brushed his throat as he leaned his head back to look up at her. He reached up and brought her mouth around and kissed it.

She seemed perfect in every way. And that's why he couldn't understand that one little part of him that was holding back, a feeling he couldn't quite pin down. He wondered if maybe it was because he'd been too long without the right woman in his life, or spent too many nights with the wrong women. He even wondered if it had something to do with his late wife, his reason for not completely letting myself be swept up in Liddy. Whatever it was, it was something disturbing, subtle, like a knock at the door in the middle of the night. It was something he wished he hadn't felt.

They finished up the bath, and Jazzy Sue delivered Cole's clothes, fresh and clean, smelling like they were full of wind and sun.

They ate a nice lunch of oysters and cheese and drank glasses of red wine and spoke without speaking, talking with their eyes. The sun outside was giving way to more storm clouds. Jazzy Sue brought them coffee to go with a cobbler she'd baked.

"They say the snow comes early to the Black Hills," Liddy said as they watched the clouds gather over the gulch.

"I ever mention I don't care for winters?"

She smiled. It was small innocuous talk, the sort of talk lovers engage in after they've made love, but not the sort of talk that people who are *in love* have. Maybe it was just Cole, his jaded history since Zee had died. Lots of women, lots of failed attempts at happiness, had left Cole lacking in the conversation department. He wasn't sure that Liddy was any more comfortable than he was with the small talk.

They were sitting there like that, watching the storm, sipping their coffee, when Jazzy Sue knocked at the door, then opened it and said: "Look who's up and about."

Jazzy Sue had Rose with her. Rose looked wan but rested. Her eyes were still rimmed red, but she offered Cole a smile when she saw him.

"I guess I slept like crazy," she said.

"Won't you have some lunch?" Liddy offered.

Rose looked first at Cole, then at Liddy, then back at Cole. Unless Cole was wrong, he thought he could see the fleeting disappointment in her eyes as she sat down between them.

Chapter Twenty-Four

The skies over Deadwood had turned almost black, the clouds bunching up like they were trapped. Then it began to snow. Cole excused himself from the company of Liddy and Rose. Jazzy Sue brought him his duster, most of the mud brushed out, and he put it on before going outside. He thought again about needing a heavier coat, now that the weather had turned bad.

The wind kicked up and the snow swirled down in large flakes and some of the town's citizens came out on the street to watch. Kate Elder and Doc Holliday were among the spectators. Kate was dressed in a long ash-gray coat with a black fur collar and black fur trim around the cuffs. She wore a small gray matching hat. She had an arm through Doc's, looming over him. He seemed frail by comparison.

"Oh, look, Doc! It's snowing!" she said jubilantly as Cole came within earshot.

"I can see that, Kate," he said, his voice barely audible. He coughed and she supported him against the spasms.

The way she looked at him during that moment was with the same wistful look of love a woman has for a child. She looked at Doc like he was her man-child. Doc's face was ashen, with a bluish tinge to it, and his hands shook as he fought the coughing spell and Kate kept saying: "That's all right, Doc, that's all right, baby."

Cole didn't know if they had seen him or not, and he didn't much care. He felt sorry for Doc, but they weren't friends, and they were never going to be friends. As he started across the street, he saw another old face from the past. It was like someone had called a convention in Deadwood for every gun hand, pistoleer, and shootist in the territories. It was a credit to the damnable advertisements Liddy had put in the territorial newspapers.

Kip Caine rode a tall piebald mare. He drew back on the reins when he saw Cole.

"John Henry," he said, sitting there high up on that sixteen-hand horse.

"Kip."

"You come too, huh?"

"Not for the same reason."

"Not the money? Then why?"

"As a personal favor for a friend. You know him, Ike Kelly."

"Yeah, I know Ike. How's he play into this?"

"It's a long story, Kip, and it's snowing, and I'd just soon get down the street to the mercantile and see if I can find me a warmer coat."

"I talked to that lady yesterday," he said. "That Lydia Winslow. She's a looker, damned if she ain't."

"Yeah, well, Kip, like I said, I'd like to see about that coat, if you don't mind."

Caine walked the tall piebald alongside Cole as he continued down the street. It was already beginning to turn muddy, that's how heavy and fast the snow was falling.

"Heard you killed King Fisher," he said.

"News travels fast," Cole said, without any interest in discussing the matter with a man that was cut from the same cloth.

"Well, I don't suppose the world's going to mourn his loss," Caine said in a joking manner.

"I wouldn't know," Cole said, trying his best to keep the conversation between them at a minimum.

"I guess it couldn't be helped," Caine said.

"He brought it on himself."

"That's what I heard. Tried to shoot you through a winda glass." Kip's laugh broke through the crust of his beard. "Son-of-a-bitch never did have much sense. Shoot at you through a winda glass!"

Cole arrived at the mercantile only to find a sign hanging in the window: **Having a Tooth Pulled, Come Back Tomorrow**. *Just my luck*, Cole thought, *to run into Kip Caine the same day the only man I could buy a coat from was having his tooth pulled.*

"Looks like you're outta luck on that new coat," Kip offered. "Cold as a sucker, ain't it?"

"Let me ask you something."

"What's that?"

"What would it take to get you to leave town?"

Caine stood in his stirrups, stretching his legs, scratching at his backside. "Carbuncles," he said. "I get carbuncles rubbed on my ass from these long rides." Cole waited for him to answer the question. Finally, after he'd stretched his legs enough, he said: "It'd take me getting that reward money that woman's offerin'. I come all the way from Oglalla. You know how far a ride that is, Oglalla? Especially for a man that's got carbuncles?"

"How much would it take, Kip?"

"Two thousand, that's what she said."

"How about five hundred and you don't have to do a thing but leave town? How would that be?"

He sat down again in the saddle, the snow collecting on the shoulders of his capote, in his beard. "Well, now that's a tempting offer," he said. "But it still ain't no two thousand, is it? It's a dang' long ways from two thousand."

"So is a bullet in the back of your skull," Cole said.

His eyes grew larger under his heavy lids. "You ain't trying to scare me, are you?"

"You know this business. You're not the only gun in town wanting to collect that money."

Caine's mouth curled up through the hair of his face. "I'll take my chances, same as you,"

"I'm here for a different reason, Kip, like I told you. I'm not here for the reward money."

"Yeah, and I don't piss yellow, John Henry. Same as you."

"Suit yourself," Cole told him. "Five hundred for leaving Deadwood isn't the worst offer I ever heard of."

"See you around, John Henry," he said, and turned the piebald's head back toward the direction of the saloons and whorehouses.

Kip's presence in Deadwood was just one more complication, the way Cole saw it. But what else was new? He continued on to the livery. The old man was standing out front, staring at the storm. He had an old wood burner pulled out front, its door busted off, the flames cooking a pine log he'd been feeding it.

"Hey, sonny," he said. "Look at that damn' snow, would ya?"

"How much for that coat?"

He looked at Cole, the watery eyes pulled back within the bony brow of his skull. "How much fer the coat?"

"Yeah, the one you're wearing."

He looked at it, back at Cole. "Hell, I wouldn't take a hunner dollars fer it . . . can't you see it's snowing? It'll be colder than a well digger's nuts around here, now that the snow's come."

"Tell you what," Cole offered, "I'll give you twenty-five for the coat, and, when I leave here in a few days, I'll sell it back to you for five. How'll that be?"

The old man twisted his lips, thinking about it. "That for sure?" he said. "You leaving in a few days?"

"For sure," Cole said, and meant it.

"Done!" he said.

It was a lot of coat, heavy as hell, but it was warm. The main trouble for Cole was that it would take some doing to reach the self-cocker under all that curly hair. So, he took the pistol out and slipped it into the pocket of the coat.

He left the old man counting his new money. He didn't seem to mind that it was snowing and he was only in his shirt sleeves.

Cole decided to go pay Irish Murphy another visit. He needed to find out who was doing Leo Loop's killing for him.

"Irish ain't here," the man behind the bar said, when Cole asked for him.

"When will he be here?"

The man was of slight build, nervous with a bad tic just below his right eye. His hair was long and straight and plastered down with rosewater. Cole could smell the cheap scent of the rosewater.

"About never," the man said. "That's when Irish'll be back. He left town this morning on the stage for Cheyenne."

The bartender's manner was like that of a small, unpleasant dog.

"He say anything?" Cole made one final attempt. "Irish . . . why he was leaving?"

"Yeah, he said . . . 'See you around, sucker.' That's what he said."

"Just like that? Irish ups and leaves his job?"

"You think pouring drinks for miners and whores is some sort of a plum job?" he said, his arms crossed over his chest, "standing on your feet ten hours a day, cleaning up men's puke 'cause they don't know when to give it a rest? You think that's a job a man would hate to leave?"

Cole had grown a little tired of the man's attitude; he was a man easy to dislike the instant you met him.

The doors suddenly blew open to a gust of cold wind and swirling snow trailed by a lone figure who stood for a moment in the quadrant of pewter light. He paused long enough to let his eyes adjust; the carbine he carried rested in the crook of his arm.

Then, when he saw Cole standing there at the bar, he crossed the room. He ordered a whiskey and drank it, then ordered a second before turning his attention to Cole.

"That little gal on the stage, the one dressed in buckskins pretending to be a fellow," Miguel Torres said. "She just blew out Johnny Logan's lights. Thought you might want to know."

Chapter Twenty-Five

By the time they arrived on the scene, a sizable crowd had gathered around the stricken form of Johnny Logan. He was lying there in the mud, stretched out on his back, his arms flung wide, the snow gathering darkly on his mustaches, glazing his eyelashes. His mouth was partly open, his eyes wide and staring at a sky he could no longer see. A neat dark hole trickled a ribbon of blood across his brow. His head was slightly tilted to the side, like he'd tried to duck away from the bullet.

"How'd this happen?" Cole asked Torres, pulling him aside.

"I was over there," he said, indicating the front of the bagnio he'd been hanging around since the other night. "I was keeping an eye on things. I saw your man here coming down the street. I guess he was making his morning rounds. It was quiet, me and him were the only ones out here."

The part about Rose hadn't made any sense to Cole the instant Torres had said it was she that'd killed Logan. "Then what?" he asked.

"He got to this point here," Torres indicated with a thrust of his jaw. "She come around the side of that building, just there. She said something to him, he said something back. I didn't hear what they were saying, but Logan there seemed to get upset with her, raising his hands. That's when she shot him. Once, in the head, like you see."

"Anyone else see what happened?" Cole asked.

He shook his head. "Like I said, the streets were clean, except for the three of us."

"Then what," Cole said, "after she shot him?"

"She went that way." Torres indicated the direction with a nod. Cole knew where she'd gone. "I saw you talking to her alone that night out on the trail. I saw how she looked at you the rest of the trip. I figured maybe you'd want to know about this first."

"Look, Torres, I know you're a federal lawman, but I'm asking you to steer clear of this. At least give me a chance to talk with her, find out *her* side of the story."

He looked at Cole, those lawmen's eyes questioning what was legal, what was duty. "You want me to let it go, pretend like I didn't see anything, that it?"

"For her," Cole said. "Do it for her, not me."

He glanced at the crowed gathered around Logan's body. Some of them were talking about revenge, about hanging whoever had done it.

"I've got no interest in this damn' hell hole," Torres said without changing his expression. "Other than to find out what happened to Robertito, I don't give a 'coon's ass about what goes on here."

"Thanks," Cole said. He turned to go.

Torres said: "Here."

Cole looked.

He had the Colt pistol in his hand. "She dropped this afterward," he said.

Cole took the gun and slipped it inside the pocket of the curly coat. Torres turned his attention to the crowd, walking over and pushing them aside.

"Well, you men going to stand around gawking?" Cole could hear Torres chiding them as he headed toward Liddy's. "Or is someone going to carry this poor son-of-a-bitch over to the undertaker's?" He was a strange and unpredictable man, Deputy U.S. Marshal Miguel Torres. Cole could still hear him berating the gawkers as he made his way down the street: "He's not a god-damn' circus to be looked at! Pick up his arms and feet!"

The same question kept running through his mind every step of the way: *Why had Rose shot Johnny Logan?* As far as Cole was aware, she didn't even know the man. And even if she had, it made no sense, not Rose, not that shy, troubled creature.

He knocked on the door. This time it was Liddy who answered, instead of Jazzy Sue.

"Thank God it's you, John Henry. She's in Jazzy Sue's room."

He went in and instinctively took off his hat when he saw her sitting there on the side of the bed, her head down, her body shaking. Jazzy Sue was sitting next to her, trying hard to comfort her, her arm around Rose's shoulders, saying: "Now girl, now girl, just calm yourself down."

"Rose," Cole said.

She lifted her face to look at him. "Mister Cole . . ." Her lips trembled; her hands shook.

"What happened out there, Rose?"

Her eyes were full of fear, tearing as she looked at Cole. "He hurt . . . Mama," she stammered.

Cole looked at Liddy for an explanation.

"She found a diary Flora kept among her things. It was in a trunk of Flora's effects. I had it stored since her death. I gave it to Rose."

"Rose," Cole said, sitting next to her on the bed, "is that what the diary said, that Johnny hurt your mama?"

She nodded and bit her lower lip until it turned white.

"Where is it?" Cole asked Liddy.

She pointed to a pile of things exposed in a small open trunk sitting in the corner. A brown leather book lay atop the clothes; its pages were marked by a thin red ribbon. Cole took the book and opened it to the place where the ribbon lay between the pages. The handwriting was delicate, small, a little difficult to read. But there it was, the part about Johnny's abuse of Flora; how he'd beaten her on several occasions; how he'd always apologize for the beatings; how much she was in love with him; how he'd promised to leave his wife for her. It was a tale of a woman left longing, clinging to unkept promises, to unrequited love, to pain and shame.

I hate him and love him, the first line of the last paragraph began in that tender, unschooled hand. *I wisht he woodn't hurt me so bad. I wisht he'd love me more and marry me like he said. I don't know if I can stand much more of this life! Oh, Dere Johnny, please, please don't hurt me no more!*

Cole flipped a few pages more, to the last entry. It was dated July 4th, 1876.

I asked Johnny last night when he was going to leave! I told him if he didn't leave her, I wood make things hard on him (tho I didn't really mean any of it). Johnny knows I know all his dirty secrets. Secrets about this town, not just about him. He got real mad when I mentioned it, about his dirty secrets. We had quite a row because of it. He slapped me and threatened me, said he would kill me if I said anything! I was sorry to have upset him so. I cried, but it did no good. He called me a b—! & cussed me in terrible ways! I'm worried that now I've gone and done it. Johnny can be a terror. Still, I love him. . . .

Cole closed it and handed it to Liddy. "You didn't know?"

She shook her head. "It was among her things. I didn't bother to go through them, considering the circumstances. I'm not even sure why I saved them."

"I need a word with you," he said.

They stepped outside in the hall.

"I thought you told me you never allowed your girls to be abused."

"I didn't. This was something different, something I didn't know anything about. I knew Flora was seeing someone privately, but a girl's private life is her own. I never get involved with that. Johnny was not a customer as far as I knew. They could have met anywhere. Johnny liked women. Flora was the type to be taken in by a man like Johnny. She always had these romantic notions that someday the right man would come along and he would be the answer to all her problems."

Cole could see that Liddy was shaken by the sudden turn of events. He felt that no one, seeing the anguish of the young woman sitting on the side of the bed, could help but be drawn into her suffering.

"Where'd she get the gun, John Henry?"

"I gave it to her," he admitted.

"Why? Why would you do a thing like that?"

"I told you, there'd been some trouble on the trail. I wanted her to be able to protect herself."

"Well, she's done more than that now. She's killed a lawman. They'll probably want to hang her for it."

"That won't happen."

"What makes you think it won't?" she asked, her words sharp, angry. "Johnny has lots of friends in this town."

"I'll need your help on this, Liddy."

She cast a fretful glance toward Rose's room. "God, John Henry, this whole thing has become such a mess."

"I know, but we've got to finish it, not let it finish us."

"What is it you want me to do?"

"I want to keep her here, out of sight. Don't let her out of the house and don't let anyone in. I need time to tie Johnny to Flora's murder," he said.

Liddy looked confused. "I thought you said it was Leo you suspected."

"I think Leo was behind it, but he's not the sort that does his own dirty work. He hires it done. I think he had Johnny on the payroll. I think Flora was getting too much under Johnny's skin, and, when she threatened him with the secrets he'd told her, he went to Leo with it, and Leo ordered it done."

"Flora I can understand, maybe," she said. "But why would Leo and Johnny have the other girls killed? Why wouldn't they just kill me if all it came down to was wanting me out of business?"

"That's something I'll have to ask Leo. Johnny's in no shape to tell me."

There were other possibilities running through Cole's mind—Doc Holliday, for one. The other night he'd seen him and Irish Murphy and Johnny having a private conversation out front of the saloon. Now Irish had left town suddenly and Johnny was dead. But that still left Doc, the man Liddy had hired to protect her girls, but hadn't. Doc was still on Cole's list of suspects along with Leo. Somebody knew something.

Liddy's eyes were full of concern. "Maybe I . . . we . . . maybe we should just get out of here."

"You know you don't want to do that, Liddy."

She placed her hand on Cole's arm, stepped close. "I might. I've been thinking a lot about us."

"What about your friend, Winston?"

"John Henry . . ."

"Its gone too far, Liddy, we've gotten too close to them."

"I'm afraid. For the first time, I'm really afraid."

"Maybe it's not so bad a thing, being afraid. Maybe it will help keep us alive."

She pressed against him until his arms reached up and held her. He could feel her heartbeat, her warm breath against his neck. "I'm afraid for you," she whispered.

"Don't be. Just keep a watch on things here, Liddy. Buy me some more time."

She kissed his jaw.

The feeling came over him again: *What is it between us that won't allow me to be completely free with her?* It was a question he still didn't have an answer to, and just at the moment he knew he couldn't afford the time to figure it all out. There were other things to worry about, like keeping a vigilante mob of Johnny's friends from finding out it was Rose who'd killed Johnny. Then he needed to tie Johnny to Flora's murder, and maybe tie Johnny to Leo Loop. Doc Holliday was still a candidate to be a part of the killings. Plus, someone had been doing their best to kill Cole ever since his first night in Deadwood. And even with all that to think about, there was still the matter of Suzanne Smith. What would become of her and Tess?

As Cole headed to the Lucky Strike, he passed the place on the street where Johnny Logan had been shot and killed. There was a pink stain in the snow with new snow falling to cover up even that small trace of a man's death. It reminded Cole of just how quickly the land devours the evidence of our existence once we're gone.

When he arrived at the Lucky Strike, Leo wasn't there. The bartender, Harve, stood glumly at his post, a white apron tied around his bulging waist. His eyes were puffed, his lip cut, the dark bruises starting to form under his flesh from where Red had punched him a good number of times. Cole guessed it'd turned into a real fight after all, at least from looking at Harve.

"Where's Leo?"

Harve shook his head. "Don't know."

Cole placed some silver on the bar. "Would that help you to remember where Leo went?"

He touched fingers to his split lip. "That Red, he hits like a son-of-a-bitch."

"Leo. Where'd he go?"

Harve swept up the coins, held them in his hand; his knuckles were scraped. "Left about an hour ago," Harve said, checking the looseness of a tooth. "Climbed in his hack and took the north road. Ain't seen him since."

"Tell me something. You get in any punches?"

Harve winced. Cole headed for the stables.

The old man was perched outside on a three-legged stool, rubbing his hands over the stove to which he'd been feeding the pine log. He was wearing a blanket around his shoulders.

"Come to sell me back my coat?" he asked, his rheumy eyes expectant.

"Not yet. But I'll rent that buckskin off you again."

"Awful damn' weather to be going fer a ride, ain't it?"

"You want to rent him, or not?"

"Sure, sure. If I don't, he'll just stand around and eat hay and drop horse apples I'll have to clean up."

The old man went inside, saddled the buckskin with Cole's Dunn Brothers, and brought him out. "Four dollars," he said. "Or did you forget?"

Cole paid him.

"I'd be back before dark, I was you," he said. "Storm like this could get a hellava lot worse before it's done."

"What's up that north road?"

He looked at Cole, gave that toothless grin. "Hell, nothing but them hills. But if you foller it fer enough, you'll be crossing onto Mister Stevens's land. You know Mister Stevens?"

"Yeah, I know him."

"Private son-of-a-bitch!" the old man said. "English. Don't 'low nobody to trespass. Say he's had men whipped fer trespassin'. Got gold mine claims all over up there. I'd stay away, I was you."

Cole didn't wait around for more advice.

The snow continued to fall in large, swirling flakes, just like everyone had said it would. The snow was piling up fast, and by the time he'd gone as far as what he figured was Winston Stevens's property line, it was nearly a foot deep. The snow lay in white bundles on the boughs of the pines and was draped over the rock outcroppings. And where Cole crossed a stream, the water looked black against the whiteness of the banks.

It was deceptively beautiful, snow in the Black Hills. Cole could see why the Sioux were reluctant to give up this land. He could see why the white man wanted it. But the white man didn't want it for the same reasons the Sioux did. But any man with eyes could see how such beauty could seduce as well as any woman, any sin. All you had to do was take a deep breath and let your gaze travel over those black, black hills.

Cole didn't hear it, the bullet that struck him. It was a blow to his upper body, hard and sudden, and it carried him out of the saddle and flipped him over and over, tumbling him down the side of the ridge he'd just ascended and into a snowbank that swallowed him whole.

Cole lay stunned for a second, waiting to die, trying to suck air into his numbed lungs. It was a silent world, there under the snowbank, silent and peaceful, and for a few long moments he was willing to let it take him to that place where Zee and Tad and the Rebel flag bearer were waiting for him. It seemed he was at peace. He tried not fighting it, the dying. But then his lungs caught fire and instinctively he clawed through the smothering tomb of snow and gasped in a lungful of cold air.

He dug the snow out of his nostrils and rubbed it free of his eyes and sucked air until he didn't need to any longer. He could see farther up the hill that the buckskin had run a short distance, then stopped. The snow was too deep for him to want to run far. He stood there as though waiting for Cole to come get him.

He unbuttoned the woolly coat and looked for the bullet wound. He couldn't find one. He checked the coat and saw a small, flat matted spot where the bullet had struck but must have bounced off. Either the bullet had been of a low caliber, or it had been fired from too long a distance to go through the heavy coat. Either way, the buffalo coat had saved his life, and he was very glad it had. He was sorry now that he'd promised the old man he'd sell it back to him.

He scrambled to a nearby rock outcropping and crawled under it just as a second shot kicked up a spray of snow inches from his face. The sound of the shot echoed down the mountain and he saw a shower of snow break from a pine bough about two hundred yards from up above where he was. The buckskin was startled by the gunfire and crow-hopped through the deep snow a few paces before stopping again.

There was no point in returning fire with his self-cocker at that distance. In his haste to find Leo, he'd forgotten to bring the Winchester with him. He might as well have tried throwing rocks as to try and hit anything so far away with just a pistol.

He hunkered down and waited. If they wanted him badly enough, they'd have to come down the mountain and get him. That's the way he saw it. He waited a long time, listened, and kept an eye on the buckskin, which was eventually working his way back down the slope, pawing through the snow, looking for grass.

Cole figured it was Charley Coffey up top, maybe Fork and Tolbert, too, but at least Charley. It was Charley's way—shooting a man from cover. As for Fork and Tolbert, Cole could only guess. But if they worked for Stevens, and Charley was riding ramrod over them, maybe they weren't above bushwhacking, either. He checked the loads in his self-cocker, made sure they were dry by putting in fresh ones, checked the Colt Thunderer Torres had retrieved and given back to him. He kicked out the spent shell, the one Rose had popped Johnny Logan with, and put in a fresh one.

He waited some more, and finally they came, the sound of boots crunching in the snow. Little trailing balls of snow rolled down the slope ahead of whoever it was that was coming. Little by little they were coming. Cole got ready.

From where he was squatting under the rock outcrop, he saw Charley Coffey run out from the trees and snag the reins of the buckskin and lead him back toward the sheltering pines. Cole thought about swinging around and firing off a shot, but it was too far off, and he figured the others, Fork and Tolbert, were perched up above, waiting for him, just waiting for such a chance to put some of their own rounds into him. *Not today, boys.*

After several minutes more, they got close enough so that Cole could hear them whispering back and forth, asking one another had they seen anything yet, any blood, a body laid out stiff. They hadn't seen anything. He had to be down there some-where, they assured themselves. Cole was.

Tolbert stepped onto the rock outcropping Cole was under. He knew it was Tolbert when he raised up from below and shot him in the only place he could—through the groin. He didn't aim, didn't try to pick the right spot, just swung up and shot him. Tolbert toppled headlong out into space and landed with a thud ten feet away, clutching himself, squirming in the snow, his blood turning the snow crimson between his legs.

A shot rang off the rocks and Cole could feel the sting of shattered stone against his cheek. He ducked away again, heard Fork shout back up the ridge that Tolbert had just been killed. That wasn't quite true. Tolbert was dying, maybe, but Cole hadn't killed him yet. Then he heard Charley Coffey call back down for Fork to close in, finish him off, and Cole thought: *Yeah, Charley, why ain't you doing it?*

It was a little bit of a risk because Tolbert was lying ten feet away and exposed in the open, but his Winchester was lying there at his feet, and, if Cole could grab it, he increased his odds a good bit. He gave it a count of three, then went for it. Two, three shots cracked the air. One of the rounds slammed into Tolbert's back and he stiffened, sucked in a lungful of air, and died. *Nice going, Fork.* Cole grabbed the Winchester and missed getting killed by luck or poor marksmanship, maybe both. He didn't question things like that any more.

Charley was up there calling to Fork, asking whether or not he'd nailed the son-of-a-bitch, and Fork was yelling back as to how he wasn't sure if he'd gotten him or not, the two chattering like a pair of gossips at a church social. Cole gauged where Fork was from his mouth. The next time Charley called down to him about what was going on and Fork yelled back—"Nothing!"— Cole raised up and shot him with the Winchester.

Fork clutched his side and dropped over. He didn't say any-thing, didn't scream or call out for help. He just fell over into the snow. Either stone dead, Cole figured, or tired of answering Charley's questions while Charley was staying hidden up in the safety of those pines. For a long time, there was just the silence of the snow falling.

Then Charley called out: "You get him, Fork, or what?"

Cole called back: "It's just you and me now, Charley. You want to come down here and settle it?"

Charley must have run out of ideas because he didn't answer. A few seconds later, Cole heard crashing up in the trees and saw Charley spanking the rump of his pony with the barrel of his rifle as he charged over the top of the ridge and out of sight.

Cole found the buckskin still tied to the bough of the pines where there were a lot of cigarette butts stubbed out in the snow. The sun had suddenly appeared between a break in the clouds over the western horizon. It made Cole feel good to know that he was still alive and could still take notice of something like that, the sun breaking through the clouds. It would be dark by the time he got back to Deadwood.

* * * * *

By the time Cole rode up to the livery, the old man was properly drunk. He had a fat squaw sitting with him, warming her hands in front of the wood burner. She looked properly drunk as well.

"See what some of that coat money bought?" the old man said, holding the bottle out toward the squaw. "She's Crow Indian. Fat, ain't she?" he said happily.

Cole handed him the reins.

"I like 'em fat," he said, his lips spreading across his dark gums. "More to hold onto." His laughter was filled with phlegm. The squaw said something to him in her language. He looked at Cole and said: "I don't unnerstand a damn' word of Crow, do you?"

Cole's feet and hands were cold, stiff. They'd gotten wet from the snow, from falling in it and lying in it and waiting in it.

"Have a drink," the old man said, holding forth the bottle.

Cole didn't object. The whiskey put some of the fire back in his blood.

"Ya want," he said, "you can have her after I'm done."

Cole walked back toward the hotel. He'd been thinking about how close he'd come again to being killed, and he'd been thinking about Suzanne Logan and all the rest of what was waiting for him in Deadwood.

Chapter Twenty-Six

The child was asleep, the room quiet, peaceful. Suzanne sat in a chair, her gaze fixed on the window, staring out into the night, the sky red now from the storm, the snow collected against the sills. The glass windowpane had patterns of frost on it.

John Henry Cole removed the heavy coat, thankful once more that it had saved his life, and dropped it on the floor over his bedroll. In spite of the cold air outside, his shirt was soaked from sweat. Suzanne watched him in silence.

He sat down, cross-legged, on the floor and pulled off first one boot, then the other. Still she watched him. His chest was bruised from the slug that had never made it through the curly coat. He winced when he touched the spot.

"Are you all right?" she said at last as he rested his back against the wall.

"I've been better," he answered. He searched for his makings, but for some reason wasn't able to do much because of the cold stiffness of his fingers.

She moved from the bed, knelt beside him, looked into his face. The light in the room was soft yellow. The shadows played against her face as she took the tobacco and paper from his hands and began to roll the cigarette for him.

"How bad are you hurt?" she asked.

"Not very."

She wound the tobacco in the paper, licked the edges, sealing it, then twisted off the ends, and handed it to him. He struck a match off the floor and the flame from it danced in front of their eyes. She moved behind him, placed her hands on his shoulders, and began to knead the flesh there where his muscles were tight and aching. Her hands were cool, the fingers strong, knowing just where to squeeze. He closed his eyes and leaned into the pleasure of it.

"I worried about you today," she said, as her hands continued working at the knots in his shoulders and neck.

"Suzanne, there's something I need to tell you."

"Hush, don't talk, just let me do this, let me take away your pain."

The cigarette tasted good. He reached up with his right hand and placed it atop one of hers, stopping it for a moment

"Am I hurting you?" she asked

"Suzanne, Johnny's dead."

Something audible caught in her throat, but she didn't say anything. Her other hand ceased its movement, its cool strength resting just at the back of his neck.

"He was killed earlier today," Cole said.

She lay her head on his shoulder near the hand he was holding.

"Why?" she said. "Why was he killed?"

"It's complicated," he said. "Maybe we can talk about why in the morning. Right now, I just need to rest."

For a long time she left her head on his shoulder, her breath warm and soft and sweet against the side of his face. A single teardrop fell onto the back of his hand. It was warm as rain in summer.

"I'm sorry I had to be the one to tell you, Suzanne."

She swallowed. "I didn't love him any more," she murmured. "But I feel badly for him, and I feel sorry for myself for feeling that way."

He moved around, took her face in his hands. "Don't be," he said. "Don't be sorry because you feel bad for him, Suzanne."

"I'm sorry for Tessie," she said. "She will never know her father now."

"Only what you choose to tell her about him. Maybe she just needs to know the good parts, Suzanne."

For a long moment, she didn't speak except with her eyes, then she whispered: "Why do I feel so alone?"

"You're not alone," he said. "At least not tonight. Look at me, Suzanne. Tell me what you see." At first she avoided his gaze, but when he held her that way, she finally looked. "What you see, Suzanne, is a man who has spent most of his life drifting. What you see is a man who lost the only woman he ever learned to love and who has never quite drifted far enough or long enough to get over it. You had a man who hurt you, Suzanne. Maybe you'll be lucky and get over it. You deserve better."

"You don't know what I deserve," she said, her voice breaking, her tears spilling onto his hands. She wiped at her eyes. "Tell me something," she said, straightening, holding back her pain. "Are you afraid that you might meet someone that's worth falling in love with again? Or is it that you're afraid if you ever stop drifting, you'll learn the truth about yourself, that you don't deserve to be happy?"

"Maybe both, Suzanne. Maybe both."

"Our loneliness comes from the same place, John Henry Cole," she said. "Believe it or not."

He lay awake a long time that night, thinking about what Suzanne had said, about the loneliness coming from the same place. He thought of Liddy, of the passion between them, and wondered what it would be like with Liddy and him, once the passion burned itself out. Liddy was like a prairie fire burning across his soul, burning up his logic and reason, burning up all the will he had to resist her. But when the fire finally burned out, would there be anything left, he wondered. Was that where his loneliness had led him, in the path of a wildfire? And what of Suzanne and Tessie? What was he supposed to do about them?

His thoughts turned to another town and another woman. A woman he had killed a man over without meaning or intending to, a woman who in the end had seen him as just another sorrow for her to have to learn to live with—at least, until the next man in her life came along. Juanita Delgado—what had come of that? Lying there in the dark on the floor of a Deadwood hotel, Cole thought of how cruel life seemed to be sometimes, by giving us what we need, but seldom what we want.

Chapter Twenty-Seven

Cole awoke to find Suzanne packing clothes into the carpet-sided satchels. Tess sat on the side of the bed, watching her.

"I'll accept your offer of a pair of tickets to Denver," she said, seeing that Cole was awake.

"You've given up on the idea of staying here in Deadwood, then?" he said, not sure that he wanted her to go now.

"I've decided to take your advice and leave this unholy place," she said as she cast an eye toward Tess, who was holding a bisque doll dressed in a white linen dress.

"Just like that?"

She paused for a moment, the child's bonnet in her hands. "I finally realized that with Johnny Logan dead there really would be no point of our staying on."

He didn't really want to talk her into staying, but it did seem sudden, Suzanne's wanting to leave. But then, why not? He was doing all he could for them, and his life was complicated enough, what with Liddy and the ultimate reason he had come here in the first place. He had said he would be leaving himself in a few days. Why shouldn't Suzanne and Tess leave? What reason now was there for them to stay?

"We'll get some breakfast, and then I'll get you the tickets," he said.

"We're so grateful. I think you know that. I don't even know how we'll ever be able to repay you for all you've done for us." She looked at him with tears in her eyes. "It seems so inadequate, somehow, but . . . thank you."

The meal was somber, Suzanne speaking mostly to Tess, urging her to eat her flapjacks and not to dawdle. Cole rose and went over to check on the stage's departure. It was in less than an hour. He came back to the café and handed Suzanne the tickets, along with what money he'd gotten in an advance from Ike Kelly when he'd left Cheyenne. She was reluctant to take the money.

"Let's not have this conversation," he said.

Her lips were compressed, but she took the money.

They had finished the meal, so he carried their satchels over to the stage office and waited until the Concord was brought around. The weather had cleared, but the air was cold, and snow still covered the roofs of every building. Wisps of black smoke curled from every stovepipe. It was a dreary day.

He held the door open for Suzanne and Tess. Tess climbed in first and took a seat next to a man whose bulk took up the space of two. Then Suzanne climbed in and sat next to the door. The canvas curtain was drawn up to allow light; later, on the road, it would be rolled down to help against the cold.

Suzanne reached out and touched Cole's wrist. "Remember, you'll always be welcome if you come to Denver. We'll make out."

"I'll remember, Suzanne." Even as he said it, he felt they both knew that this was the last they would ever see of each other. "Good bye, Tess." She smiled and thanked him again for all the flapjacks. She was a sweet little girl. Cole couldn't fathom how Johnny Logan had been able to deny her.

Other passengers boarded, then the driver and the guard climbed up top. Cole heard the driver urge on the teams and snap the reins, and the Concord jolted, breaking free of the sucking mud. He watched as it rocked down the street, the wheels shattering plates of ice where the ruts and puddles were. Then they were gone, the stage and Suzanne and the little girl, Tess.

"You and that woman," a voice asked. "Something up between you?"

It was Miguel Torres, his usual stalking self, out of nowhere, suddenly there, having approached as silently as a cat.

"No. They needed help, that's all."

"How's the other one," he asked then, "the little gal that sent Johnny Logan to the happy hunting grounds?"

"I've got someone taking care of her, keeping her out of sight."

"That's good, because the way I hear it, some of that constable's friends are talking about revenge."

"They know who it was that killed him? They know it was Rose Pride?"

"They think they know." He snorted.

"Let them think what they want."

"You might not want that if you knew who it was they're saying killed him."

Cole was finding that Torres could sometimes be irritating. "You want to tell me who?"

"You. They think *you* killed Logan."

This was something Cole didn't need to hear.

"They think maybe you had a reason to kill him because of the way he opened your head with the butt of his shotgun. Not only that, but lots of folks saw that business between the two of you out on the street the other day when you shot King Fisher. They say you were ready to kill him then. They're pretty sure it was you who killed him."

"I guess you didn't bother to tell anyone it wasn't me."

Torres was doing his usual—scouting the street with his eyes as they talked. "You mean I should have told 'em it was the girl that did it, not you?"

"No, that's not what I meant."

"What, then?"

"Nothing."

"The other thing . . . they brought in two bodies this morning."

"Who did?"

"Fancy-talking Englishman, him and his ramrod, boy named Charley Coffey. You ever hear of Charley Coffey?"

"Yeah."

"Charley's made a name for himself." A wry smile played on Torres's lips. "If they had a contest for low-heeled assassins . . . men that'd shoot you in the spine . . . I imagine Charley would win hands down."

"I killed them," Cole said. "The two men they brought in."

Torres didn't act surprised. "You have any more tobacco?"

Cole watched as he rolled himself a cigarette with the tobacco and papers he gave him. He handed them back to Cole before striking a match with his thumbnail. "That's four," he said.

"What is?"

"The number of men you've killed since Cheyenne."

"I wasn't keeping count."

"Maybe you should." He blew out a stream of blue smoke.

"It's a violent world. What can I tell you?"

"More so in your case than in others. Why'd you kill them?"

Cole told him why, about his suspicions of Leo Loop, and of having followed him into the ambush. Torres nodded and smoked and kept his gaze scouting the street.

"So, you think it's this fellow, Loop, is it? You think he's behind the killings of those prostitutes you come up here to investigate?"

"I'd be damned surprised if he wasn't."

"How'd you come to figure it out?"

Cole told him the part about his visit with Leo Loop, about passing himself off as a new dealer in town, about asking Loop's permission to set up shop. He told him how Leo had wanted to shake him down.

"That it?" he asked. "You have a conversation with this man and you figure from that he's been killing whores? Why, because they're not paying for permits to operate?"

Cole figured Miguel was challenging what few investigative skills he had, that he was testing Cole to see how he matched up to a professional lawman, to himself.

"I think maybe the Englishman's in on it, too," Cole added.

Torres looked at Cole through the haze of blue smoke lifting upward from the cigarette that clung to his lips, his right eye squinting. "What makes you think so, that this Englishman's in on it, too?"

"My guts tell me."

"Guts," he said, then ground the spent shuck under his heel. Torres was a man Cole could easily dislike, but a man he had to respect. It was out of respect that he didn't tell him to go to hell. "There's also another consideration," Torres added.

"What's that?"

"Something that calls itself the town peace commission held an emergency meeting right after the Englishman and his gunner brought in those two corpses. They hired Charley Coffey as the new town constable. Your man, Loop, is he a big man, belly out to here?" Torres asked, holding his hands out in front of him.

Cole nodded.

"He's the one that suggested it, that they hire Charley. The Englishman backed him. Everyone else went along with it."

"Charley was the one that set up the ambush," Cole said. "Then, when it came to the real fight, he damned near beat his horse to death trying to get away."

"I'm not surprised," Torres said. "You want, you can go over to Nutall and Mann's and finish your business with him. He's over there now, having drinks bought for him by a grateful community of his peers."

"You've got to be joking."

Torres only offered that little smile that let Cole know he was enjoying the turn of events. "You think I am, go over and see."

"What are they claiming, the Englishman and Coffey, about the two men I shot?"

"Said you ambushed them. Charley said you were a professional assassin. Then the fat man said they should get a warrant for your arrest. But before they could do that, they needed someone to serve it on you. That's when the fat man nominated Charley, and Charley jumped to his feet like a schoolboy asking permission to go piss. They gave him Logan's badge and shook his hand and said go ahead, arrest you. But Charley said he needed deputies, in case you had friends about. You got any friends about, Cole?"

"Counting you, Miguel, or do you mean others?"

He gave Cole a look and said: "Charley and his would-be deputies are over there, getting themselves oiled to come looking for you. Because of Johnny Logan, and now those two dead cowboys. Thought maybe you'd want to know what they have in store for you."

"How far does your jurisdiction reach, Deputy?"

"However far I want it to reach," he said. "I'm an employee of the United States. The rest is my discretion."

"Does that include investigating the murder of innocent women?"

He shook his head. "Far as I'm concerned, John Henry, there's been no requests to the federal government to investigate the murders of whores."

"That's what you need," Cole asked, "an official request?"

Torres gave him a hard stare. "Don't push your luck with me, John Henry. I've got other things on my mind. This damn' gulch still belongs to the Indians as far as I know. I haven't heard differently."

"Here's what I know," Cole said, and told him of his suspicions that Johnny Logan had killed Flora, and maybe even the other two prostitutes. He told him about Flora's diary. He told him about why he didn't think that Leo Loop was a man to dirty his own hands. He told him about Calamity Jane and what she'd told him and that maybe there might even be a connection to Bill Hickok's murder.

Miguel Torres wasn't impressed. "You forget, I'm here looking for my brother and Shag Hargrove, or someone that knows where they're at. I didn't come here for any other reason. And until I find out about my brother, I'm not much interested in sticking my nose in business that has nothing to do with me."

"Let's go," Cole said.

"Where?"

"To see a friend of mine. Maybe she's heard of Robertito, or this Hargrove *hombre*."

He looked skeptical, but then, most lawmen do when it's not something they thought of themselves.

Jazzy Sue let them in, then, at Cole's request, brought Liddy to the parlor where Torres and Cole stood waiting. Cole made some quick, unadorned introductions between Miguel and Liddy.

"Mister Torres is here looking for his brother," Cole said. "Maybe you've heard of him. Robertito Torres is his name."

Cole could see Liddy running the name Robertito Torres through her mind. Finally she shrugged. "Sorry, I haven't."

"How about a man named Shag Hargrove?" Miguel interjected.

She thought again for a few moments, testing the name, then a light of recognition flared in her dark eyes. "The name's unusual enough," she said, "that I do remember it. He used the services of one of my girls at least once, maybe even twice."

Miguel shifted his gaze from Liddy to Cole, then back to Liddy. "I'd appreciate it if you could tell me which girl it was," he said.

"It would be Alice," she said. "Alice is the one who accompanied him on a picnic, I believe."

"Where might I find this Alice?" Miguel was eager, his hands opening and closing in anticipation that he'd finally gotten a break in his search.

"She and the others . . . the girls I had working for me until the killings . . . are all staying at Gertrude Franz's boarding house."

"Where does this Gertrude Franz live?" Torres wanted to know.

Liddy told him it was at the other end of the gulch, between Harris's Tent Manufactory and the Black Hills Brewery. "I can take you there, introduce you to her," Liddy volunteered.

"Not necessary," Miguel said in his usual loner fashion. "I can find her, this Alice . . ."

"Fournier," Liddy said. "Her name is Alice Fournier."

Miguel nodded. "Thanks," he said. Then, twisting the door handle, he turned halfway back to Cole. "Another thing, John Henry. Charley may be a back-shooter, but he's got plenty of drunken miners arming themselves, ready to get a little revenge. They're all bored and drunk, and that's the worst sort to deal with. You want my opinion, I don't think you're any match for that crowd."

"Thanks, Miguel."

"For what?"

"The vote of confidence."

He didn't smile. He just closed the door behind him.

Liddy asked Cole what was going on and he told her about the ambush the day before, about how it was Winston Stevens's men he'd shot. He told her about what Miguel Torres had told him about the town council appointing Charley Coffey constable.

"I think you should leave," she said. "Ride out and don't come back. They're going to kill you, John Henry."

He told her the rest of what Miguel had told him, the rumor about a hanging party for Johnny's killer. She swallowed hard.

"They wouldn't hang Rose," she said.

"It's not Rose they think did it," Cole said. "They're saying it was me. But if they get wind that it was Rose, who knows what they might do, especially if they're drunk and need to taste a little blood." She struggled with that. "You and Jazzy Sue and Rose," he said, "need to leave here tonight, find some place safe to stay for a few days until I can straighten this out."

"How will you do that?" she asked.

"Hell, Liddy, I don't know how."

"The old man," she said. "We can go to the old man's cabin."

"What old man?"

"Toole, he runs the livery stable."

Cole was skeptical. "He's a boozer," he said. "A gossip, to boot."

"No. He owes me," she insisted.

"Owes you?"

"I put him on the tab once when he was broke . . . with one of my girls. He wept like a child. He came here and wept, he was so grateful. I can trust him. He has a cabin up in the hills."

Cole had her draw him a map of the cabin's location and stayed with her the rest of that day until the sun went down. Then he walked her down the back way to the old man's livery.

The Indian squaw was gone, the fire in the wood stove now a smolder of embers. They found him inside, in one of the stalls, sleeping on his back. The barn was warm and sweet with the scent of horse and hay.

Cole shook him awake. He came up, swinging feebly, cursing, trying to grab Cole, trying to shake himself out of whatever nightmare he'd been having.

"Whoa," Cole said. "Slow down, dad."

Liddy held a bull's-eye lantern so the old man could see them. "What you want?" he rasped.

Liddy bent closer until he recognized her. "Toole, I need a favor."

He looked at her and some of the tightness went out of his leathery face. "Liddy . . . ?"

"Take it easy," she said.

Then he looked at Cole again, then back to her. "What kinda favor?" he asked.

"Two," she said. "Actually, I need two favors."

He shuffled in the straw.

"First, I need to use your cabin up in the hills," she said. "Is it still there, Toole?"

He nodded.

"The other thing is, I need you to keep this a secret, that I want to use the cabin. Can you do that, Toole? Can you keep it just between us?"

"Wall, I guess I could."

"No guess," Cole told him. "Either you can or can't."

He looked disappointed that Cole was there. "Yeah, sure I can," he said finally.

"Good," Liddy said.

"God damn . . ." the old man muttered, and lay back. "What day is it, anyhow?"

"It's Tuesday," Liddy said. "Only it's night, not day."

"Oh!" he gasped. "I've lost some more of my life somewheres. Oh!"

In seconds he was snoring again.

Cole saddled three of the old man's horses and put Liddy on one. He rode another and led the third back to her place. It was cold and snowing again, and no one was out on the streets that time of night because of the weather.

Jazzy Sue said she didn't know much about riding horses. Rose said she did and that she would help Jazzy Sue by taking hold of her reins for her and leading the pinto mare. Rose told Jazzy Sue that all she had to do was hold on to the saddle horn.

"Stay up at the cabin until I come for you," Cole told Liddy.

"And if you don't come?" she asked.

"If I don't, you're smart enough to know what to do. Just don't come back to Deadwood. Keep on going."

"Maybe when this is over . . ." she started to say.

Cole cut her off from the thought: "We'll talk about it when I get up to the cabin."

He slapped her horse on the rump, and waited there on the street until they disappeared into the blackness and the swirling snow.

He thought of his odds, standing there alone on a cold, dark night in a town full of men that wanted to see him dead—hanged, shot, or otherwise. He thought of the odds and how he might change them. There were few options, but there was one. The only man he knew in town who might have an interest in whether or not Leo Loop and Winston Stevens were involved in the murders of Liddy's girls was the man who'd come for the reward money Liddy had offered in the territorial newspapers—Kip Caine. Like old man Toole had told him that first day he'd talked with him, Kip Caine was a killing son-of-a-bitch. Right now, that's what John Henry Cole could use on his side—a killing son-of-a-bitch.

Chapter Twenty-Eight

That night in his search for Kip Caine, Cole kept to the shadows of Deadwood. Several times he passed the open doors of saloons where the talk was running high about the killings of Johnny Logan and the two cowboys, Tolbert and Fork. If Cole knew anything at all about Kip Caine, he knew he was in a saloon, a whorehouse, or an opium den. There were enough of all three in Deadwood. It was just a matter of finding out what his pleasure was that night: whiskey, women, or dope.

The first place he checked was the Number Ten. The crowd there was small, the place as somber as a wake. He slipped in the back door, stayed along the wall, out of the glare of light, scanned the room, saw Kip wasn't among the patrons, and slipped back out again. Then he did the same thing at the Black Hills Brewery and the Queen of Clubs and the General Custer. Kip wasn't in any of those places. Cole thought: *How hard can it be to find someone in a town three blocks long?* Finally he came to the Lucky Strike, Leo Loop's pleasure palace. He checked the loads in both of his pistols before going in the back door.

The place was crowded, mostly along the bar, where Charley Coffey was still holding court. They were drunk and they were loud, with Charley doing most of the talking. Charley was decked out in a long cowhide coat and that Montana Peak hat he wore with the four creases in it, his jug ears holding it up. Only now the peak hat was tilted back on his head and his face was flushed from drinking all day and he was barking threats and bragging how he was going to kill John Henry Cole personally.

He thought: *Yeah, Charley, here I am. All you got to do is look over to the back wall, if you want me that bad.* He scouted the rest of the place to see if Kip Caine was among those being mesmerized by Charley's tough talk. He wasn't. They were brave enough with the red liquor burning in their blood and carrying those long-barreled pistols down inside the waistbands of their pants. He thought: *If I stepped out of the shadows and yelled real loud, half of them would shoot their peckers off.* Sitting at a table listening to Charley boast were Leo Loop and Winston Stevens. They were sharing a bottle of expensive brandy, the stuff they keep for heroes and rich men, the stuff they keep hidden behind the bar. Cole saw Charley wasn't drinking any of it, the expensive brandy. Leo had a cigar clamped between his pudgy fingers and Winston Stevens wore a gray wool suit that wasn't made anywhere closer than St. Louis. They exchanged conversation now and then, their eyes darting toward Charley and his lynching party. Then Leo said something and Stevens smiled and nodded his head. Charley shouted something and the men hooted and slapped him on the back and waved their hats in the air. Cole thought that he'd seen enough to convince him that his decision to find Kip Caine was the right one in spite of the misgivings he had. Cole gave the crowd around Charley one last glance before departing the same way he'd come in, slipping out the back. The air was very cold and chilled the sweat that had collected inside his collar and along his ribs.

He started knocking on the doors of the bagnios and crib joints. He interrupted a lot of four-bit romancing but still didn't find Kip Caine. That left only one place for him to be: the underground opium dens. He made his way to that strange little section of Deadwood by taking to the back streets and alleyways. At first glance, the Chinese section was a small collection of shacks and tents. Most of the businesses were restaurants and laundries. But there was another business that went on in Chinatown, too. Opium.

He asked around and got a lot of inscrutable stares for his troubles. Finally he found one old fellow whose skin was the color of candle wax. He told him what he was looking for. At first, the old Chinaman said he didn't understand, asked Cole if he wanted to smoke some opium, or wanted to buy some opium pills. Cole explained it to him again, until he understood that he was looking for a white man and described Kip as best he could. The old Chinaman led him to an opening that led underground. He followed him down a flight of wooden steps that descended into what appeared to be a mine shaft. At the bottom of the stairs, there were several small rooms cut out of the rock and earth. The rooms went off in several different directions and there were lanterns lighting the way.

"Maybe the man you look for in there," the old Chinaman said. "You want, you can go lookee." He gave the old Chinaman a silver coin for his trouble, took one of the lamps, and started going from room to room.

The air in the underground apartments was cool, damp, but not unpleasant, unless one counted the sweet, heavy sent of the opium that was being smoked. Each of the earthen rooms had two or three cots, and on each cot a figure reclined, hidden mostly by the shadows, but visible enough to see. Cole approached each cot and held the lantern close in order to see the face of the person. Two or three were white women, probably prostitutes, their eyes half closed, their jaws slack, mouths open enough to show their teeth—like the dead, only not dead. Most were Chinese men and women, each one in a dream world that only he or she could know. The Army surgeon who had taken the Rebel lead out of Cole's back had given him laudanum so he wouldn't scream and fight the pain. Cole knew, looking into the eyes of these people, what they were feeling. He'd felt the same thing, and he knew how easy it was, once you were there, not to want to come back again.

When he found Kip, he had that peaceful smile on his face most of them had, like a man who'd seen something too beautiful to describe, like the face of God. His eyes were glazed, and, when Cole brought the lantern in close, they shrank, then jerked away from the light. They tried to hide themselves under his hooded eyelids, like night creatures scampering from the sun.

"Kip Caine," Cole said in a harsh whisper. He touched his shoulder.

The eyes crept out, like the way a turtle's head will come out of its shell after being scared—slowly, ready to hide again at the first challenging shadow. Cole spoke his name again in the same harsh whisper.

Caine lifted his head. "Whaa . . . ?" he muttered, his voice floating from somewhere down in the cavern of his being, the eyes edging more toward the center of their sockets.

Cole grabbed him by the lapels of his coat and pulled him up. That startled him, and he squeezed his eyes closed and his hands fluttered like wild birds trying to knock Cole away. "Come on," Cole said, pulling Kip Caine to his feet.

"No, no!" Caine hissed.

"Come on, god damn it!"

Cole pulled him outside, out into the cold. Kip stumbled, his limbs loose, unwilling or unable to stand. Cole half dragged, half carried him to a water trough. He stomped through the sheet of ice that had skimmed over the top. The ice shattered like cheap glass, much the same way the window at the café had shattered when King Fisher fired his pistols through it.

He pushed Caine's head through the jagged hole, held it under for half a minute, jerked it out again in a rooster spray of icy water. Caine coughed and sputtered and cursed. Cole had made sure to reach inside his coat and take out the gun he was carrying as he held him under the water. It was a .36-caliber Whitney Navy revolver, long and crooked as the hind leg of a dog. Caine's hands struggled for it. Cole shook him hard.

"Listen, Kip!"

"What? What the hell do you want?" Caine coughed, the wet hair hanging in his eyes.

"I want to make you a wealthy man," Cole said. "Two thousand dollars wealthy. That's why you came here, isn't it, to become wealthy, collect that reward money?"

Kip Caine shivered against the cold, his fingers pushing the hair out of his eyes, trying to get Cole to release his grip on him, but the opium had sucked all the strength out of him, had swallowed him whole. "What the hell you talkin' about?" he cried in full anguish.

Cole let him shake free of his grip. Kip rubbed his face with both hands, trying to rub away the freezing pain. "Je-Jesus!" he stammered at how cold the water felt, how it shocked him to have his head plunged into a trough like that. "You nuts or somethin'?"

Cole checked the street to make sure no one had been aroused by the ruckus of his pulling Kip out of the opium den and putting his head into the water. It was quiet—so far. He pulled Kip to his feet. Caine didn't like that, but Cole did it anyway.

"Take your damn hands off me!" Caine moaned. He didn't have any fight in him, much as he wanted to, the dope had cut his strings.

"We need to talk, and this isn't the place I want to do it," Cole said, pulling him along by his coat collar.

Kip slapped at Cole's hands, but Cole pulled him anyway—into the nearest alley. There he held him against a wall with one hand.

"What? What?" His cry more a squeal than a howl, shrill.

"Shut up!" Cole said.

Kip moaned, trapped by the dope and Cole, trapped in a place he didn't want to be. He offered a feeble struggle, then he finally settled down.

"If you can make out what I'm saying, Kip, just shake your head, OK?"

Caine looked at Cole, the eyes struggling to focus, his mind fighting the effects of the dope and the heart-stopping cold of the icy water. It was the look of something worse than fear, like he'd been caught in a nightmare he couldn't wake up from. Cole had been there himself.

"I've got a problem, Kip. And I need you, and this," Cole said, holding up Caine's Whitney. The eyes narrowed a little. Cole knew he understood. "You back me, I'll see you get the reward money Liddy Winslow was offering. How'll that be?"

He rubbed his cheek with the back of his hand. "I don't understand," he mumbled.

"You don't need to. You still know how to use this, don't you, when you're sober?"

Caine looked at the Navy. "That looks like the one I own."

Cole shoved it in Caine's pocket.

"You want me to kill somebody, that it?" His eyes crawled over Cole's face, looking for an answer, a solution to the night-mare he was having.

"I want you sober."

Caine tilted his head; his tongue lolled out of his mouth; he gave a deep sigh and moaned.

"Don't get melancholy on me, Kip."

Caine blinked several times, not understanding.

"It's the dope," Cole said. "It does that to some men, makes them melancholy."

Caine's head rolled back until it smacked the side of the wall he was leaning against. "Jesus!" he said again, a look of pain sliding behind his eyes. "Why you doing this?"

"I'll explain once I get you dry again."

"Well, that'll be a friggin' relief," he grumbled, then looked up at the red sky, the swirling flakes coming down. "Is that snow?"

"Come on," Cole said, shoving him along through the alley.

"Huh . . . ?"

"Just go."

Cole pushed him ahead of him until they reached Liddy's and went in the back way. It was dark and Caine stumbled around while Cole looked for a lamp.

"You gonna light a lamp," Caine demanded, "or are we just gonna stand around here in the dark like two old maids trying to save the fuel oil?"

"To tell the truth, Kip, I'm not sure I like you sober."

"Good! You think I give a damn what you think?"

Cole checked the street from the front windows, saw no one outside, pulled the curtains, struck a match to the wick in one of the lamps, and slid the chimney down over it. The light danced around inside like it was alive and trying to free itself.

Cole spent the next fifteen minutes making a pot of mean black coffee. "Drink that," he ordered.

Kip looked at it, sniffed it, screwed up his face.

"Drink it!"

Kip wasn't happy with the turn of events, but Cole kept reminding him of how much $2,000 was and what it looked like all together at one time—as if he really knew. Kip licked his lips when Cole talked about the money, and drank the coffee and gritted his teeth and drank some more of it.

The time dragged by, the opium clinging to his brain like ivy on a fence. Several times Cole checked the windows, and once or twice he saw men out on the street, but nearer to the main section of town. They carried torches. Cole could hear them shouting, their voices rising against the night. But it didn't last long, and after a while they disappeared inside one of the saloons. Cole guessed they weren't much for hunting down killers when it was cold the way it was and there was still more whiskey to be drunk. He thought: *So much for Charley Coffey's vigilantes. At least for tonight.*

"OK," Kip mumbled, after he had nearly finished the contents of the big pot of coffee. "Explain it to me once more, about the money, how I get to keep it all. My brain's starting to unfreeze from where you pushed it down in that god-damn horse trough!

Tell me again about the money. And don't ever do that shit again, huh?"

"I've gone through that part already," Cole said. "You want me to tell you again?"

"Yeah, god damn it, I want to hear about it one more time."

So Cole explained it to him, again; at least, as much as he thought necessary to explain. He told him the part about Charley and Stevens and Leo Loop wanting Cole put in a plain pine box and have him carried up to the boneyard on Mount Moriah, where Bill Hickok and a lot of other disappointed dreamers were sleeping the long sleep.

Kip listened and kept interrupting Cole about the money. Having a conversation with Kip Caine, Cole felt, was like trying to fast dance with a one-legged woman.

"I don't care nothin' about that shit," Kip said impatiently, "them wantin' to kill you. Just tell me how it is I can get that two thousand dollars."

"I'm coming to that," Cole told him again.

He nodded and shook his head irritably.

"All I want from you, Kip, is to back my play with that Navy of yours. I'm going after them full-bore. I need an extra gun. You back me up, you'll get the two thousand. Is that simple enough for you?"

"Yeah, that's what I like . . . simple."

"The other thing," Cole said.

"What's 'at?"

"You decide to switch horses in the middle of the stream, take up with the other side, it's you I'll kill first. We clear on that?"

Kip looked plainly disappointed Cole had brought it up, his allegiance. "What do I look like, John Henry, some damn' bushwhacker?"

"Those are the rules," Cole said. "Remember them."

"Rules . . ." Caine muttered.

Chapter Twenty-Nine

"When and how do you want to do this thing, John Henry?" Kip Caine moaned.

Cole had been staring out into the night, watching the snow falling from a sky that still glowed red over the shadowy outlines of the town. He turned to Caine who was holding his head in his hands, leaning forward, his wet hair hanging in loose strands. His muddy boots had soiled the carpet.

Kip looked up at Cole with reddened eyes when he didn't answer right away. "Well?"

"Not tonight," Cole said.

Kip looked relieved, dropped his head back into his hands. "Maybe I'll catch me a little sleep, then," he muttered. "'At's what I need, a little sleep."

Cole watched Kip stretch out on the divan he'd been sitting on. He walked into the bedroom where Flora's trunk was. He lifted the lid, took out the diary, and put it in the pocket of the curly coat. He wasn't exactly sure what he was going to do with the book, but it was all he had to try and tie Johnny Logan to Flora's murder. But proving that Johnny killed Flora didn't prove he killed the others, and it didn't prove Leo Loop was behind it, or anything else, and that was Cole's real problem. Johnny had already paid for whatever sins he might have committed. It wasn't he that Cole really wanted.

He walked back to the window. Kip Caine was snoring, his right arm flung across his eyes. Cole checked the street again.

It was still quiet, almost evilly quiet. He pulled his Ingersol and looked at the time. It was nearly 2:00 in the morning. *What now?*

He went over what few facts he already knew about the killings. Then he went over what he believed. Cole knew with all certainty that Leo was behind the murders, even though he had no proof. The reason was obvious. Liddy was hurting his business by running a first-class escort service and not the usual rough trade of a frontier town, the sort of trade Leo was good at running. But the question still persisted—why, if Leo wanted Liddy to fold her tent, didn't he just go after her directly? Why kill three of her young women instead?

Then there was Doc Holliday. How did he figure into the killings? The way Cole saw it, Doc could have prevented the murders, or he could have been in on them. Doc had had the opportunity for doing either. Doc was like a moving shadow against the night, a man one could easily forget about until the next time he ran into him—or until it was too late. But the questions remained why he would kill the women, what did he have to gain from it? Again Cole considered the possibilities. Doc could have done the killings for money. It takes a special kind of man to be a paid assassin, and Cole had little doubt that Doc possessed such a capability. Then, there was the possibility that he owed a debt to Leo—a gambling debt, perhaps—and Leo was willing to wipe the slate clean if Doc committed the murders. Doc was a notorious gambler, but the problem was Cole had never heard that he was a poor gambler. So it made the odds that Doc might have killed the women to erase a debt seem long. The only other connection between Doc and the killings was Liddy. Liddy had told Cole that first night they had talked that Doc had an interest in her. And he had more or less admitted the same thing himself to Cole. Maybe Liddy had rejected Doc's advances and it had made him angry, and he killed the girls to hurt her. But that sure seemed a long way around the barn.

Cole stood there, trying to piece the puzzle together. His reflection looked ghostly in the glass panes, and he wondered if he hadn't stepped into it, like Bill Hickok had done. According to Jane's version of the story, Bill had crossed someone in town and paid the ultimate price—a long, eternal sleep. Cole wondered if he might not wind up finding himself sleeping next to Wild Bill. All the odds were stacked against him ever leaving Deadwood alive. And what he had to fight with were only the diary of a dead prostitute and a dope-addicted gunfighter. Somehow, it didn't seem nearly enough.

Absently his hands rested in his pockets, the fingers of his right hand touching the grips of the self-cocker. His other hand felt the diary. Doc troubled him the most. And if any of them was going to kill him, Doc would be the one. At least that much Cole was sure of. As far as the others, Cole wasn't all that concerned. He figured he could kill Charley six days out of seven if it came to a face-to-face showdown. Watching him beat his horse over that ridge after the ambush had told him something about Charley's nerve. The posse of drunken miners would scatter like quail once Cole either dropped Charley or a couple of them. But Doc was another matter. Feeling Flora's diary in his pocket gave him an idea, perhaps a way to draw Doc out. Cole had to know the truth about Doc's involvement in the murders. And if the killing was going to begin, it might as well begin between Doc and himself. It was time he found out who had killed the fallen angels.

Chapter Thirty

John Henry Cole went out the back door, leaving Kip Caine stretched out on Liddy's divan. The snow was nearly knee-deep and crunched under his boots as he sloughed through it. He kept to the back streets and off the main drag as much as possible. With the snow, the night was nearly as light as day and the shadows were few. The sky was still glowing as red as old blood.

Cole slipped past the Number Ten and the Black Hills Brewery. The hour was late and the town was winding down from its nightly celebration. Miners were drifting back to their tents and lean-tos and boarding houses and flophouses, wherever they could lay their heads down for another night's rest before going back into the hills again. He crossed the street just before the Lucky Strike, and turned down an alley. He worked his way along a back street until he came to the narrow, raw lumber house Doc rented for himself and Kate. There was a light showing behind the frosted glass and tattered curtain of the single window in the front of the house.

He knocked on the door and waited, his hand resting on the butt of the pistol in his pocket. The knob turned, the door opened a crack.

"I've come to see Doc," he told Kate.

She was wearing a checked blanket robe, her right hand clutching the throat of it. She stared at him with unflinching eyes. "Doc's in bed," she said. "Who're you?"

"I need to see him," Cole said, ignoring her question.

She shook her head. "He ain't feeling well. Come back tomorrow, you want to see him."

She tried to close the door, but Cole put his hand on it. "Ask him to see me."

"Do I know you, mister? Have we met somewhere? I don't recall ever seeing you and Doc together."

"No, Kate, you and I haven't met, but Doc knows me."

She blinked, her face ruddy under the soft light. "It's still snowing," she said, looking past him, leaning a little way out to get a better look. That's when he could smell the liquor on her breath. It was a warm, sour smell.

"It's also cold," Cole said. "Can I come in while you ask Doc?"

"No," she said. "Doc don't like strangers in the house."

"Then I'll wait. You go ask him to see me."

"I don't know . . ." she said hesitantly. "Doc don't like being disturbed once he's gone to bed." She was trying her best to protect him, her man child.

"This is important, Kate," Cole said. "Otherwise, I wouldn't be coming around this time of night."

Still she hesitated.

"It could mean Doc's life," Cole said. And in an odd way, it could—except that, if it came to that, he would be the one trying to *take* Doc's life, not trying to save it. But it did the trick.

"Who should I say?" she asked.

"Tell him John Henry Cole. Tell him I've got a book I want to discuss with him. A book with names in it."

"Book?"

"Yeah."

"Just a minute," she said. "I'll go see if he's still awake."

Cole held the door ajar just so she couldn't close it and lock it. He wondered how Doc would take the news of his coming for a visit.

Cole heard Doc cough hard for several minutes. He heard Kate talking to him, saying something he couldn't make out because they were in another room, with the door closed. Then there was a silence, followed by the sounds of shuffling steps coming to the door. Cole's hand closed on the Remington. He feared Doc was coming better prepared than he'd been the last time they'd met.

Kate opened the inner door. "Come in, mister. Doc's getting something on." She entered, closing the door behind her.

Cole stepped into the room. It was a small, spare room without benefit of luxury or any sign of permanence—no pictures on the wall, no glass figurines on shelves, none of the things one would expect to see in a house that's been lived in for a time. It was the house of a temporary man. In the center of the room stood a table and two chairs, both plain and simply made. On the table a magazine lay open, and next to it a bottle and a half-filled glass of whiskey. An oil lamp gave the room its light. The ceiling was plaster, cracked in places. The dingy wallpaper was peeled loose where it met the wainscoting. It was not a room anyone would want to spend much time in. Doc's hat hung on the back of one of the chairs.

"You want to stand or sit?" Kate asked, coming closer.

"I'll stand."

She kept the robe clutched tightly around her throat; some of her nightdress showed below the hem of the robe. She went over and closed the magazine that was lying open on the table. "It's the latest issue of *Harper's Bazaar*," she said. "It's got all the latest fashions and the best stories. I can't sleep sometimes at nights. It's why I read, so's I can get sleepy. Always thought maybe someday I'd write a story about me and Doc, about our life together, and send it in to them. I bet it would make good reading." It was said in an attempt to be cheerful. "Doc says I'm just foolish. I don't know, maybe I am."

Cole heard something rattle behind the closed door, then watched as it opened and Doc appeared, wearing a long nightshirt, his thin legs exposed below the hem, his feet encased in a pair of carpet slippers. His hair was tousled from where he'd been lying in bed. His eyes darted from Cole to Kate then back to Cole. "Go on to bed, woman," he said to her.

"But Doc . . ." she started to protest.

He gave her a look of impatience. "This is private, Kate. Between men."

He hadn't put a hand on her, but Cole thought she looked as if he had. She went to the table, started to reach for the bottle and the partially filled glass.

"Leave it, Kate. Don't you think you've had enough . . . *reading* for one night?"

Something tugged at the corners of her mouth, some old wound, a hidden hurt or embarrassment. "Not enough, Doc. Not yet. I'm still not very sleepy."

"Leave it," he said, only this time without the same demand in his voice.

Her hand came away, and she picked up the magazine and carried it with her as though it was her only comfort as she slowly retreated to the bedroom from which Doc had just emerged.

Doc waited until she closed the door, waited until he heard the bedsprings squeak. Then he crossed the room, shuffling his feet so that the slippers whispered on the bare wood floor. He moved to the table, picked up the glass, and drank its contents.

"What is it you want, sir?" he said, pouring himself another glass from the bottle. He did not bother to turn his attention to Cole until he had completed the task. Wearing the nightshirt made him look small and old; his spine was curved and bony through the material. "Kate said you told her you had a book with names in it. What does that have to do with me, and at this hour of night?"

"Flora Pride, Doc. You remember Flora Pride?"

He raised the glass to his mouth, the heavy, well-trimmed mustaches parting, his eyes not inclined to meet Cole's as he drank. Then, when he finished, he lowered the glass and said: "What about her?"

The eyes had finally come to rest on Cole and they showed no sign they recognized anything he was talking about. "She left a diary, Doc. She talked about things, about Deadwood, its dirty secrets. She wrote down names in her diary."

It was a long shot, getting Doc to believe that Flora had written his name in her diary and that she had some dirty little secret on him. Cole was playing a weak hand against a man, who by profession, was a gambler.

"I am surprised she could write," Doc said. "She didn't strike me as the type who knew how."

"She did, Doc. She had a good hand, and she put down everything Johnny Logan whispered to her on those warm, tender nights when he wasn't with his wife or his chippy."

Doc pulled one of the chairs out and sat on it, the hand holding the glass as steady as a dentist holds his pliers. "Why trouble me with all this nonsense, sir?" His voice was weary but his gaze unflinching.

Cole was holding a handful of low cards and the stakes were high. It was too late to fold. "She mentions you in her diary, Doc." He pulled the book from his pocket and held it up for him to see.

Doc cocked his head slightly as though trying to gauge whether Cole was telling the truth about what was written in the diary. "Really?" he said, almost in a whisper, his voice weak. "What did Miss Pride have to say?"

Doc was calling Cole's bluff. He could either raise the ante or toss in his hand.

"She talks about you and Johnny Logan and Leo Loop and Winston Stevens," Cole said.

Doc snorted. "What about us?"

"I've got enough here to show it was Johnny that killed her," Cole said, avoiding a direct answer to Doc's question.

"Well, it's a little late for that," Doc said, reaching for the bottle again, pouring himself another round. "John Logan has met his fate It's either an early or late hour for me, depending on how you look at it."

"Maybe Johnny can't be hanged for the killings," Cole said, "but the others involved sure as hell can be."

Doc set the glass on the table gently, with great care and deliberation. "You mean the names you supposedly have in that book?"

"Yeah, those names."

"And I am reported to be one of those names?"

"She mentions you, Doc, there's no getting around that."

"She says that I was involved in killing those poor, sad women?"

"Tell me, Doc, were you?"

"What do you think, sir?" His gaze didn't waver. "Do I seem to you the sort that would murder women?" The forefinger of his left hand reached up and calmly smoothed the heavy mustache, swiped away the whiskey dew.

"You have a habit of answering my questions with those of your own, Doc. Why not just give me a straight answer?"

Kate called his name from the back room: "Doc!"

He half turned in his chair. Cole was distracted by the sudden plea of her voice. When Doc turned back around again, Cole saw a small double Derringer in his hand, aimed at Cole's chest. "You accuse me of something so heinous as the murder of prostitutes," he said, not raising his voice in spite of the anger that flared behind the eyes. "You come into my house, unwelcome, uninvited, disturb my privacy, and make accusations against me. What am I to do about that? What would you do, sir, given the same set of circumstances?"

Doc had proved himself a prophet. He had said when last they met that the next time the odds would be different. He had been right. There was no way Cole could get to the self-cocker before Doc fired off both loads of the Derringer, and at this short range, maybe eight feet, Cole knew that even the bulk of the curly coat wasn't going to save him this time. "Give me the courtesy of telling me the truth before you pull those triggers, Doc. Let's just say that, if I'm going to die, I'd like to think I learned the truth first."

"Truth," he said, spitting it out like a seed. "The truth is whatever most people want it to be. Lie becomes truth, truth becomes lie. Enough people hear a lie told often enough, they think it is the truth. The real truth becomes buried beneath the lies. That, sir, is what truth is."

"You mean like what they say about you, Doc?"

He nodded his head. "Yes, what they have said about me is an example of lie becoming truth, and truth being lost because the truth is not nearly as exciting as the lie. The truth is often too boring to repeat."

"Did you kill them, Doc? Did you have a hand in it?"

"Would you rather know the truth, or would you rather live?" he asked.

Cole thought it was a good question.

Doc coughed suddenly. Cole thought about going for the self-cocker in that fraction of a second—he probably could have, but he didn't. Doc stifled the cough, swallowed hard against it as it bloated his cheeks, the hand with the Derringer wavering slightly. Then he quickly tossed down the last of what was left in his whiskey glass to drown the sickness that had erupted from his lungs. He lowered the Derringer. "No," he said softly. "I didn't have anything to do with the death of those tragic women . . . it's not my style."

Cole believed him. "You were supposed to be watching them, though," Cole said, taking his chances that Doc had decided not to kill him there in the living room.

"I took the job as bodyguard for one reason, and one reason only," he said. "Liddy." This time his hands shook as he medicated himself with the liquor. The cough wracked him again; he gripped the edge of the table, fought it until it abated, then took a small linen handkerchief from his pocket and wiped his mouth. The red stain showed through as he balled it up in his fist. He drew breath before speaking again. "Like you, like every man who's ever met her, I was smitten by her the first time I saw her." The first sign of anything other than fierce intensity shone in his eyes. "She came to me, asked me if I would be a bodyguard for her and her girls. I didn't do it because I needed the money or had nothing better to do. I did it because she flattered me. She's very, very good at that, flattering a man." He seemed to be remembering it as though it had just happened. "Hell, what did I know about being a bodyguard? What did I want to know about it? Figure it out, man. Wouldn't you have done the same if she'd asked you? Look what you are doing for her as it is. You are risking your life much more than I ever did. And for what? Only one answer. You were as taken by her as I was, as any man is."

"You're overstating it, Doc."

"Am I? Tell me, sir, would you risk your life this much for a lesser woman, one without an ounce of charm or guile?"

"You're not going to believe me, Doc, but I'm doing this for a friend, not for Liddy."

He snorted his disbelief. "Tell yourself what you will, sir. We all like to tell ourselves whatever lie works. We choose to believe that we are too noble to risk our lives for something as simple and base as a beautiful woman. You see, truth becomes a lie, and a lie becomes the truth."

Cole wondered about that. "Tell me how it was I saw you and Johnny Logan and Irish Murphy talking privately outside the Number Ten the other night, if you and Johnny weren't involved in something."

"It was nothing, really," Doc said, his shoulders slumping visibly beneath the nightshirt. "Johnny heard I had paid you a visit. And Irish had also told him that you had been asking a lot of questions about the killings. They stopped me outside the Number Ten, and Johnny asked me what I knew about you . . . what my business with you was all about. I told them either to go to hell or buy me a drink . . . either way they wanted it. They chose to buy me a drink. I am not inclined to discuss my business with men such as Johnny Logan, not even on the best of days." A small, persistent cough nagged him and he coughed into the handkerchief again. Then, raising his gaze once more, he continued. "My visit with you was strictly of a personal nature. Even our enmity toward each other is strictly of a personal nature. Johnny wanted to know what it was about. I told him it was none of his concern. That was the end of it."

"One more thing I need to know, Doc. Did you take that shot at me outside on the street that night?"

He stared into his whiskey glass for a long moment, then said with almost mild amusement: "I thought I'd already clarified that point with you, sir. Had I wanted to kill you, I would have. Now, if you don't mind, I'd like to go back to bed. Kate and I are leaving first thing in the morning for Prescott, Arizona. I hear the climate is much better there, in more ways than one. I have lost my appetite for this town. It will come to nothing in the end. There is no promise here." He stood, but not quite straight, and concluded: "If you don't mind dropping the latch on the door on your way out . . ." Then he went into the bedroom and closed the door behind him. Cole could hear Kate say Doc's name.

Stepping back out into the cold, clear night that lay in ghostly whiteness, Cole was relieved to know that Doc hadn't been part of the murders. There were still plenty of folks in Deadwood that wanted to see Cole dead, but Doc wasn't one of them. And just knowing that was its own kind of relief. Cole was feeling better about the odds as he headed back to Liddy's house.

Chapter Thirty-One

In Deadwood, nothing good lasted long. The sound came out of the darkness, a long, punished wail of a sound, something John Henry Cole heard and recognized. He found her, lying in a snowbank behind the Black Hills Brewery. She was struggling to regain her feet, but she was as drunk as he'd ever seen her. A trickle of blood leaked from her nose and she smelled the way no woman should smell, worse than any muleskinner.

"God damn it!" she swore, struggling to climb out of the snowbank. "Jeezus and Mary!" She rose to one knee, tumbled backward before Cole could reach her.

Cole took hold of her, lifted her to her feet. She fought him for a little bit, trying to free herself. "Ya ain't molestin' me!" she shrieked. "I ain't no god-damn' crib tramp ya think ya can just haul off in the weeds and have at it with! Turn me loose, ya sons-a-bitches!"

Cole locked his arms around her until she became still. It was like holding onto a mustang that would try to kick you to death the minute it was let go.

"Jane, it's Jack," he said as reassuringly as he knew how. He didn't regard drunken wildcats a specialty, but with Jane he was getting used to it. For a few long minutes, she stayed stark still in his arms, just waiting for him to turn her loose so she could kick, bite, or generally lay him out. "You understand, Jane . . . it's me, Jack?"

He felt her give a little. "Jack?"

"Yeah, you remember Jack, don't you?"

"Jack?" She twisted her head around to get a look at him. Her breath was noxious. "Jack!" she exclaimed, the light of recognition invading her eyes.

"I'm going to turn you loose now, Jane. Don't do anything stupid, like try to bite me, OK?"

"Oh, no, Jack, why'd I bite ya?"

He let her go. She nearly fell over. He grabbed her again and held her steady.

"Oh, Lordy," she gurgled. "I must be a sight fer ya, huh?"

"You're drunk again, Jane."

"Oh, hell, don't I know it, Jack."

"If you had fallen asleep in that snowbank, they'd have laid you out in the morning, up there on Mount Moriah with Bill."

"Oh, Jeezus, Jack! What I wouldn't give to be buried alongside my Bill. It's what I want, what I pray fer ever night . . . to be with my Billy."

"Well, you keep drinking that paint thinner, you'll probably get your wish." Cole asked himself, as soon as he said it, why he was lecturing to Jane Canary on the evils of drink? Who was he to stop a body from going down the road they chose to go? Except he'd been there and knew there were demons waiting for those who went. And if they were the same demons he'd known, he didn't want anyone else to have to know them. He'd sort of taken a liking to her in a way he couldn't explain, even to himself.

"No! It's only right I join him," she declared. "Now that Bill's gone, there ain't no reason for me to live. What've I got to live fer, Jack? Tell me that."

"How about that daughter you mentioned, Jane? Isn't she worth living for?"

Her eyes teared over. The thought had stung her. "She knows how awful terrible I am," she bawled. "She wouldn't want a thing to do with me."

"Maybe you should let her be the judge of that."

"Oh, Jack, you say the damnedest things to make me feel bad."

"I wasn't trying to make you feel bad, Jane. I just don't think you ought to end it in some damn' snowbank."

Her eyes grew large, tears spilling out of them onto her smudged cheeks. "Ya don't, Jack?"

"No. No one should have to end up like that, not even the worst of us. And you're not in that crowd."

Strangely the words seemed to sober her more than if he'd poured a pot of coffee down her, or plunged her head into a horse trough. "Ya know, it ain't too late for me, Jack. I could start over. I could clean myself up and be a lady again, like the lady I was when me and Bill were an item. I could even go back East, see my baby girl. Did I tell you her name was Janey?"

"I believe you did."

She smiled sweetly. Cole hadn't known it was possible, but in that moment he felt some of her great loneliness.

"I'm a damn' mess, ain't I?"

"I reckon you are. Why don't you let me help you home so you don't freeze to death out here?"

She nodded.

She had a cot behind a lumberyard, a shack no bigger than the length of her bed and not much wider. But it had a small stove and Cole made a fire after he laid her on the bunk and pulled a blanket over her.

"Ya think it's too late, Jack, me gettin straightened out?"

"No, Jane, I don't. You're looking at living proof."

"Not ya, Jack. Hell, anybody but ya, I'd believe."

"I don't have a reason to lie to you, Jane."

She smiled that sweet smile again, her lids drooping. "Ever'body calls me Jane, but my real name's Martha. Don't nobody call me that, though. Just Jane, Calamity Jane, ya know. Sometimes I'd like it if someone would call me Martha."

"Martha."

She closed her eyes, the smile still on her lips. "It's nice to hear, Jack, a man saying my real name like that."

He waited until she'd fallen asleep, made sure there was enough wood shoved into the stove to last the rest of the night, then closed the door to that little shed she called her home. In a way, Cole reflected, she wasn't all that different from Rose or even beautiful Liddy, in that she was a woman who just wanted to be loved and cared about. In that way, she was no different from anyone.

He hoped, as he shuffled through the drifts of snow back to Liddy's house, that Jane *would* awaken with the same thought she'd gone to sleep with—a fresh start on life. But he'd been around long enough to know that just wanting something wasn't always enough, and that sometimes the demons are stronger. He hoped for her sake that wasn't the case.

Chapter Thirty-Two

John Henry Cole entered the house through the back door, the same way he had gone out earlier. It was quiet, dark, except for the ghostly light reflecting off the snow that had begun to pile up in huge drifts outside. He was tired and cold from his trek to Doc's house and from the day's events. He went to Liddy's room and stretched out across the bed without bothering to take off his clothes. In a few hours, it would be daylight again. Everything would start over, and he would confront the men who wanted to kill him. And they would confront him. He figured, if he was to stand a chance, he'd have to make the first move.

He lay there, thinking how he was going to prove that Leo Loop was behind the killings. He didn't know of any way, except to get him to confess. But getting a confession from him wasn't going to be as easy as waving Flora's diary in his face. It would have to be something more formidable, like waving the self-cocker in his face. A man like Leo would understand such directness. His thoughts turned to Suzanne Logan and he wondered if she and Tess had made it far enough south on the stage to have missed the storm. Another day of heavy snow and the gulch would be impassable; no one would get in or out. It was turning into that kind of week. He wondered how Liddy and Rose and Jazzy Sue were doing up in the old man's mountain cabin, whether they'd have enough supplies to last them through the storm. It didn't seem like anything came easy in Deadwood, least of all survival.

Somewhere in the night his thoughts turned into dreams as exhaustion closed in on him, only this time the dreams were different. He was in a mountain meadow, playing with a child, tossing him into the air and catching him and listening to his laughter, and it filled him with a great joy, a joy born of bone and flesh. The child's hair was golden, like the sun, and his eyes were bright blue and full of mischief and cleverness. He called Cole Daddy, and threw his arms around his neck and put his face to Cole's. Sitting on a blanket was a woman, a woman whose face Cole could not clearly see. She was wearing a white summer dress and a hat made of straw that shaded her eyes and a red ribbon was tied about her waist. He knew that he loved the woman, and that the little boy was their child, and that the world was a perfect place. Then the child began to call his name, only his voice had changed, had become deeper, like a man's voice.

"John Henry! John Henry Cole!"

Cole opened his eyes.

"Wake the hell up!"

When Cole's sight adjusted, he could see where the child's voice had been coming from.

"Don't even think about it," Kip Caine said. He had the barrel of the Whitney revolver pressed against Cole's forehead.

"What's going on, Kip?"

"Been thinking," he said.

"About what?"

"About money, what else?"

"I thought we already discussed that. Why the pistol?"

"Just don't get froggy and try jumping around," he warned.

"Two thousand isn't enough for you, Kip, is that it?"

"It might be, if I knew for sure you had it. But I got to asking myself, how do I know you got two thousand, other'n your word you got it?"

"My word's always been good enough, Kip."

"No, see, as much as you explained it to me, I still never did see no hard cash in your hand, or no place else, for that matter.

Now, was you to show me, say, even half the money, why, I'd put this old hog-leg away and apologize for disturbing your rest."

"And if I don't show you the money, what then?"

"Well, now, that's a good question. You see, one way or the other, I intend on leaving Deadwood with more than empty pockets. The plain truth is, I've never been a man to much care who was writing the check, if you know what I mean. So it don't make a rat's butt worth of difference to me whether it's you 'at pays me or someone else. Who do you suppose that someone else might be in this case?"

"You're thinking of giving me over to Leo and Charley, that it? You think maybe Leo would pay you good money for me?"

"I have to admit, it did cross my mind." Kip gave a twisted grin.

"You remember what I said about the rules, Kip?"

His grin increased until his teeth showed through the crack in his beard. "Yeah, that was the other thing, them damn' rules you kept telling me about. I ain't a man that likes living by no rules, John Henry." It wasn't exactly a laugh, the sound Kip made, more like a long grunt.

"I meant what I said, Kip."

He pressed the barrel a little harder into Cole's forehead. "Jaysus, John Henry, you forgetting I still owe you for pushing my head in that horse trough? That friggin' ice water liked to have stopped my heart!"

"Next time, I'll keep it there, Kip, till it does."

He thumbed back the hammer of the Navy. Cole heard the sound it made, the double click, metal against metal. It was the second time in a couple of nights he had heard that sound, and he hadn't liked it either time. And this time he couldn't expect Miguel Torres to come through the door, blazing away with his carbine.

"You pull that trigger, Kip, you'll get no money from either side. Or did you forget to think about that in all the other

267

thinking you were doing?" He could almost hear Kip's brain moving around, trying to understand it.

Kip eased the hammer down. "See, what I'm going to do is tie you up and leave you here while I go over and have a chat with that Loop fellow. I'm going to ask him how much he'd pay for you. That is, unless you can show me your end of the money now."

"You either take my word for it, or do what you will. Just remember what the rules were, Kip, what we agreed to."

He shoved a little harder with the cold steel. "Jaysus! Shut up about them god-damn' rules, will ya?"

"Tell you what I'm willing to do here, Kip. You slide that Whitney back in your pocket, tell me you're just having an off day, and you didn't mean anything by sticking your piece in my face, and maybe I'll see it as just that, you having an off day."

"You think I look that dumb?"

"This is a bad game you're playing, Kip."

"Get up!" he ordered. "Do it slow, or I might just pop you!"

Cole got up slow, like he wanted. Kip was nervous, operating on the edge. Cole figured it was the ill effects of the opium still worming through his mind.

"In there," he said, stepping around behind Cole and placing the muzzle of the Whitney against the back of his skull. "It won't take much, me pulling this trigger, you decide to try anything funny. Remember that. About a second is all it'll take to pop you."

Kip directed Cole into the kitchen, had him sit on a chair, and lit the lamp in the center of the table. There were several silk scarves lying next to the lamp.

"See, while you was gone and I was doing my thinking about all that money you promised but never showed me, I figured out how I was going to do this. I went into the ladies' rooms and found them silk scarves. You ever been tied up with silk scarves,

John Henry? I hear it's getting to be all the rage in the Denver whorehouses."

When he had finished tying Cole's hands behind his back and his legs to the chair rungs, he straightened and admired his handiwork. "There, you're all set for the ball," he said. "That ought to keep you until I get back from my negotiations."

"What if Leo decides to put a bullet in your brain instead of money in your pocket?"

Some of the grin fell away. "Why would he do that? It's you he wants. Most men are willing to pay for what they want."

"If you think Leo's the sort of man that would hand over two thousand dollars easily, you don't know Leo."

"He might with a little convincing," Caine said, spinning the cylinder of his Navy.

"And if he doesn't?"

"Well, if he don't, he don't. Then I guess I'll find that sweet woman you're so fond of, the one who owns this fancy house, and get her to pay for you. How's that sound . . . like a plan, or what?" He slid the pistol into his waistband. "I'll go over there soon's it gets daylight. As he spoke, he sat down opposite the table from Cole. "No sense waking Leo up and having him in a bad mood. I'll catch him at breakfast. A man don't mind talking when he's having his breakfast."

"All that money."

"What about it?"

"It's going to buy you misery."

He grunted again. "You think so?"

"You'll see."

"I've got to give it to you, John Henry, even trussed up like a hog waiting for the butcher, you've got *cojones*. Tell me how it was, shooting King Fisher like you done. Did it feel good to kill that son-of-a-bitch, or what? I bet when he felt that bullet going through his vitals he just about shit his pants."

"You know what I think it felt like?"

"What?"

"About the same way it's going to feel when I put a round through you, Kip. Only maybe a little better."

"Well, how do you think you're going to manage, all tied up like a hog the way you are?" He grunted in that strange way he had of laughing, half the sound coming through his nose.

The two didn't talk for a while after that, waiting for the sky to break dawn. A couple of times, Kip rose and walked to the window and looked out, rubbing the frost off the panes with the heel of his hand.

"Snowing like a son-of-a-bitch," he said every time he looked out. "Never seen so much god-damn' snow. Soon's I get my hands on that money, I'm heading south, far as I can get south. Maybe Mexico, some place like that."

Then he would sit back down across from Cole and smoke himself a cigarette and blow the smoke in Cole's direction. And sometimes he would take out the Whitney and rotate its cylinder between his thumb and forefinger, enjoying the clicking sounds it made. "Killed lots of men with this piece," he bragged at one point. "Killed Little Ray Barger over near Fargo on the Red River with it. You remember Little Ray?"

When Cole didn't answer, he continued as though Cole had asked him to tell all about it. "Little Ray was standing on the back porch, brushing his teeth. He was wanted for cattle rustling, stealing off the big bosses up that way. They put out a five-hundred-dollar reward on him." Kip aimed his pistol at some imaginary figure, squinted his eye, sighting down the barrel. "They say Little Ray had the best teeth of any outlaw that was ever killed in the territory. I imagine it was because he brushed 'em so regular, wouldn't you think?" He lowered the Whitney and looked at Cole, the side of his mouth turned up in a half grin. "Anyway, Little Ray wasn't the only man I ever shot with this. There's been others, and there'll be more, I reckon. Maybe even you, John Henry." He showed Cole the piece again by aiming it at him.

Then there was more silence, more trips to look out the window at the falling snow, searching the sky for the first sign of daybreak.

"What time you figure a man like Leo gets up in the morning?" Kip asked.

Cole didn't know and didn't care, so he let Kip draw his own conclusions.

"It's interesting how time can go so damn' slow when you got nothing to do, ain't it? But when you're having fun, like if you're with a good-looking woman or winning at cards, time goes by just like that." He snapped his fingers. "I don't suppose you ever thought about things like time, have you, John Henry?" When Cole didn't answer, he said: "Well, did you ever think about things like why time does what it does?"

"No." Cole thought Kip had the mind of a lunatic.

"Opium," Kip said. "Makes me think about things, like the way times passes. It's a whole different world, that opium world is. Damn' if it ain't. Could use me a smoke of it now. I ain't forgot you pulled me out of that Chinaman's last night and put my head in the water and messed with me. That's why it feels good, me going over to see Leo, sell you off like some butcher hog to the highest bidder. Leo don't buy you, I reckon maybe that pretty lady will."

"What if they don't, Kip, what then?"

"Oh, hell, let's worry about that when the time comes, all right?"

He paced over to the window again, looked out. The sky was growing lighter. Maybe an hour more before it was morning. He paced and he sat and drummed his fingers on the edge of the table, and he talked about some of the men he had killed with his Navy revolver. Finally the morning came.

"You got a watch?" Kip asked.

"In my pocket."

He retrieved it, snapped open the face, and said: "It's almost eight o'clock. I reckon it's time to go see Mister Leo. You think he likes bacon with his eggs for breakfast?" He snorted, then he jammed the Navy in his waistband, buttoned his coat, and pulled his hat down to the tops of his ears before walking to the door. "Now, don't go anywhere," he said. "You're like my new bank account. I wouldn't want to see you get lost." Then he closed the door behind him, and Cole sat there, wondering if he could have stepped in it any deeper.

Chapter Thirty-Three

John Henry Cole wondered if maybe Kip Caine had done some rope work in his time, because the knots he'd tied in the scarves were very good ones and he couldn't work his way loose. He felt like the biggest damned fool in the territory to have trusted a man like Kip Caine, then to have got caught by him with his guard down. Of all the glorious ways Cole had figured on dying, being tied to a chair and having a fat man like Leo Loop walk in and stick the barrel of his pocket pistol into his mouth and pull the trigger wasn't one of them. But that was the way it was going to end for him unless he could find a way out of the mess he'd fallen into.

He worked his wrists against the scarves until his flesh burned from trying. It was no use. He finally gave up the effort.

Funny, Cole reflected, what a man thinks of when he knows he's about to die. He was thinking about how good a smoke would taste, and a glass of good mash whiskey, and the company of a woman—Zee. He would have liked to take the opportunity to say some things to her that he had never got around to saying when he had had the chance. Then it dawned on him. Liddy wasn't the first woman to come to mind as someone with whom he would have liked to spend his last few minutes on earth. He figured it told him something he probably needed to know about himself, about Liddy. But in truth, none of it would matter in a few more minutes.

It felt like a long time had passed since Kip walked out into the cold snowy morning and bid him *adiós*, but he had left Cole's

Ingersol lying face-up on the table, and, when he checked the time, not more than a minute or two had passed. Suddenly the front door banged open, letting in a blast of cold snowy air. Something else entered the room besides the weather: Kip Caine and two Mexican *vaqueros*. The *vaqueros* wore big sombreros and heavy serapes and they were escorting Kip at the end of their pistols. One kicked the door closed behind him, and the other forced Kip to get down on his knees.

"Jaysus!" Kip shrieked. "Jaysus!"

"You be quiet, eh, meester?" ordered the Mexican who was holding his pistol to Kip's skull. "You be quiet or I'll have to shoot you. What do you theenk about that?"

Then the other Mexican came and stood in front of Cole, his pistol pointed at Cole's face. "You know who I am, Meester John Heenry Col'?"

"Yeah, I can guess. I never thought you'd ride this far north, though. You people must hold a real strong grudge."

"I am Julio Guzman, Francisco Guzman's cosin," the Mexican said. "You remember who Francisco Guzman was, don' you? You remember you shoot heem?"

"That's a hard thing to forget."

"We almost keeled you in the alley the other night, but then one of you frien's come by and shot Luis. You a very looky man, *señor*. Luis was not so looky."

"It's a long way to ride just to take a bullet," Cole said.

"So you see, Meester Col', now you responsible for the deaths of two of our cosins . . . Francisco, *and* Luis." Julio shook his head as if he was greatly saddened. "Me and Hijo discussed thees for a long time, what we going to do wit' you. You know, like a vote. Oh, we going to keel you, sure. Hijo, he'd like to keel you right now. But then I tell heem what I theenk, and he agrees with me. You want to know what I theenk, *Señor* Col'?"

Cole really didn't want to know, so he didn't ask.

"What? You hav' not'ing to say? It don' matter. I told Hijo, I theenk we should take you back across the Río Grande and keel you there, in our village, where everyon' can see. You know, like a beeg *fiesta*. Maybe put ropes around you and drag you behind our *caballos*. What you theenk of eet?"

"What the hell are they talking about, John Henry?" Kip cried. "I mean, Jaysus Christ, does everybody in the friggin' territories want to see you dead?"

"Shut up, meester!" Hijo ordered as he shoved the barrel of his pistol hard against Caine's bony skull.

"Hey, that hurts, god damn it!"

"Ees going to hurt more, you don' shut up," Julio warned him.

"You should have kept your end of the bargain, Kip," Cole said. "Now it's too late. You won't collect a damned cent. These two *vaqueros* are the cousins of Francisco Guzman, a Mexican bandit I shot and killed down in Del Río. Francisco was highly thought of by his people, as you can see. Not many Mexicans would ride this far north to avenge a death. They don't like the winters any better than you do."

Julio Guzman pulled a knife from under his serape and cut the silk scarves loose.

"What we do wit' heem?" Hijo asked, keeping his pistol pressed to the back of Kip's skull.

"Hee's your frien'?" Julio asked Cole.

Cole looked at Kip. "No, he's not my friend."

"Tha's verry bad," Julio pronounced. "Now we don' take no pleasure in keeling heem."

"Kill me?" Kip cried. "What the hell you going to kill me for? I didn't do anything! Fact is, I tied him up, made it easy for you to grab hold of him. Don't that count for nothing?"

"Face it, Kip, you've come down to bargaining with Mexicans, and you know how you always hated Mexicans."

Kip's mouth dropped open by several inches as the one behind him thumbed back the hammer of his pistol.

"I never said I hated Mexicans!" Kip squalled.

Hijo pulled the trigger, only the pistol didn't fire. The hammer fell on a dud. Kip screamed, lashed out, and struck the Mexican just below the belt, causing the *vaquero* to cry out in agony. This sudden act caused Julio to take his attention from Cole for just as long as it was needed, maybe two seconds, and Cole pulled his self-cocker and shot him. The round caved him in and he fell face forward with a groan.

Kip Caine was scrambling to his feet, trying to make the back door when Hijo pulled the trigger a second time, and this time the round went off, catching Caine in the middle of his spine and crashing him against the doorjamb. Maybe if Hijo hadn't been so upset with Kip for hitting him where a man least likes it, he might have thought things out and tried to shoot Cole first. It was a fatal mistake on Hijo's part. When Cole shot him, he toppled over and did not move.

For a few long seconds, there was a silence in the room that was greater than any other silence. Both of the Mexicans lay dead or dying. Kip was lying on his side, near the door, a moan escaping his lips as his hand still sought to reach up for the doorknob, trying to escape the house. Cole stepped over the body of Hijo, looked down into his youthful brown face. He was too young to die, but Cole opined he hadn't thought of that away back when he crossed the Río Grande with Julio and the other cousin, Luis. They were young hot bloods that had made a pact to avenge the death of Francisco Guzman. It was a matter of honor to them, and now they were dead. Francisco was still killing from his grave. Maybe now, this would be the end of it, maybe no more cousins would ride across the border when these three didn't return. Maybe Cole could finally put it to rest, the death of Francisco Guzman. He knelt beside Kip, looked into his troubled eyes.

"That Mexican got me good, di'nt he?" Cole looked at the spreading stain of blood on the back of his coat. "Can't god damn believe I ended up this way."

276

"How did you think it would end, Kip?"

"Wha . . . ?" His eyes searched Cole, trying to understand the question.

"I was just curious."

"I can't move my legs . . . Jaysus Christ!"

"You want a drink?" Cole asked.

"My hands are cold. . . ."

Cole went to search the cupboards until he found the decanter of cognac. He grabbed a couple of drinking glasses and returned to where Kip was lying. "I'll help you sit up," he said, reaching under Kip's arms and pulling him up so his back rested against the doorjamb.

"I don't feel nothing," Kip said. "Maybe it ain't so bad, after all."

Cole poured each of them a glass of the cognac. "Try this."

Kip drank it and said: "What is this?"

"Cognac."

Kip blew out air through his cheeks. "You were right," he said.

"About what?"

"About how that money was going to bring me misery."

"It usually does."

"Well, least you was wrong about them damn' rules."

"How so?"

"You said, if I broke the rules, it'd be *you* that killed me. Didn't prove out that way, did it?"

"No, Kip, it didn't."

His hand reached up and took hold of the front of Cole's coat; his knuckles turned white gripping it. Sweat was a sheen on his face. His eyes were beginning to lose their light. "Jaysus, but I'm afraid of what's on the other side, John Henry. . . ."

"Maybe it's not so bad."

"I always thought I'd live a long time. Most of the men in my family lived a long time. But then . . . they di'nt do the same kinda work as me." He coughed. The blood was spreading out on the floor below him. His hand, the one holding onto the front of Cole's coat, shook hard. "Jaysus! I'm afraid I'm going . . ." He gasped. "I'm so god damn' afraid . . . of dying."

"We all are, when it comes down to it, Kip. You're no different that way. I've got a feeling it's really a lot easier than it seems."

He stared at Cole in a strange way. "You mean maybe it's like . . . going . . . to sleep . . . somethin' like that?"

"Maybe like that."

"Oh, no!" he cried suddenly, then took a deep breath and let it out. "Oh, hell no!" His eyes moved upward until they showed white and his mouth opened and closed, and his hand yanked at Cole's coat. "No! No!" Then his lips moved like he was saying something to someone, only no words came out. He eyes were back with a look in them like they were seeing something only he could see. That went on for maybe a minute, then his face relaxed, and his hand fell away from the front of Cole's coat.

Cole eased him back down again. Kip Caine no longer had to worry about leaving Deadwood with empty pockets. He no longer had to worry about how cold the winters would get. Just like King Fisher and Johnny Logan and Bill Hickok and the three *vaqueros*, Kip Caine would be spending eternity in the shadows of the Black Hills.

The door opened slowly and Cole brought the self-cocker around.

"You can put that away," Miguel Torres said, looking around the room. "It looks like you've been busy."

Chapter Thirty-Four

Miguel Torres stepped around the bodies and helped himself to the cognac, then rolled a cigarette and claimed a chair to sit in.

"I lost count," he said.

"Of what?" Cole asked.

"The number of men you've killed since the trip up."

"What are you doing here, Miguel? I thought you were looking for Shag Hargrove."

"I found him."

Cole wanted to make a cigarette, but his tobacco pouch was empty. "Can you let me have the makings?"

Miguel pulled them his from his coat pocket and handed them to Cole. "Say, this is damn' interesting liquor, what is it?"

"Cognac."

The cigarette tasted good and it improved Cole's mood. "OK, Miguel, what did you find out from Shag Hargrove?"

"I found out he's dead, buried down near Lead."

"That's it?"

He looked suddenly old. "Didn't find Robertito." He scratched behind his ear, tipping his battered hat forward on his head. "That woman, Alice Fournier, the one I went to see over at that boarding house your lady told me about, she told me where I could find Shag. She said she knew Robertito because he and Shag were partners. She said she didn't know Robertito too well. She said Shag left for Lead after some trouble they had here. I asked her what kind of trouble and she said he and Robertito had found a small strike up north of here, but it was supposedly on some other man's claim and there had been a dispute. That's what she called it, a dispute."

"She say who the other man was?" Cole asked.

"That's the interesting part," he replied, staring at the amber liquid in his glass. "It was that Englishman, Stevens." Torres spoke around the cigarette hanging from his mouth, the smoke curling up into his eyes, and it caused him to squint.

"Well, now, that *is* a piece of interesting news. I think I know where they may have found their claim."

Miguel took the cigarette out of his mouth and flicked the ashes in the palm of his hand and then rubbed it against his pants leg, a habit some men had to avoid flicking their ashes on a woman's floor.

"What do you intend to do now?" Cole asked, but with only partial interest because of his own problems. His last hole card was lying dead, a victim of his own greed and the Guzman family.

"I think that one gal over at that cathouse knows something more than what she's saying," Miguel answered in a flat voice, as though talking more to himself than to Cole. "I think I need to go and question her again."

"The one you've been keeping tabs on?"

He nodded.

"What makes you think she'll tell you any more than what she already has?" Cole asked, wondering if Torres didn't have more interest in the woman than just asking her questions.

"I got a feeling?" he muttered around the shuck.

"I thought you weren't much for gut reactions."

He looked at Cole, his right hand wrapped around the same glass of cognac from which Kip Caine had taken his last drink. "I've been doing this a long time, John Henry. Some things you just know."

"Because you're a professional lawman, that it?"

Torres stared hard. "I didn't mean anything by what I said the other day, about the detective business. It's just my way."

"To hell with it. I'm too old to get my feelings hurt."

"How'd you wind up with Kip Caine and these Mexican boys?" he asked, surveying the destruction again.

"It's a long story," Cole said.

"You know, a Mexican by nature does not like the cold weather, and these are the first two I've seen this far north," Miguel observed. "Now, why would they come this far north?"

"Like I said, Miguel, it's a long story, and one I don't have time to sit around and tell you."

He drank the last of his cognac. "I think I could get used to this," he said, setting the glass down on the table. "It's got sort of a pleasant feel about it."

"Look, why don't we help each other here?"

"What makes you think I need help?"

"Maybe you don't, Deputy, but I do."

His gaze shifted to the winter scene outside the window. "You mean with Charley Coffey and his bunch?"

"Yeah, that's why Caine was here, to back me. Only he decided to change the rules after I'd laid them out for him."

"So you killed him because of it?"

"Not exactly, but it worked out that way."

"I could end up like that, John Henry," he said, pointing with his chin toward the dead gunfighter. "Or either one of them two."

"If you do, it won't be by my hand."

"I'm not so sure about that."

"Maybe I can work the girl for you, get her to tell me what she might not tell you."

"What makes you think so?"

"She sees you as trouble."

"I'm listening," he said, "but not real hard."

"I don't know what went on between the two of you, but something did, something that scared her enough that she's not going to tell you anything. Maybe she already knows you're the law, or maybe she thinks you're the one that killed those other women."

"How in the hell would you know how she sees me?"

"The other day, when I ran into you out in front of the bagnio, you remember?"

His nod was hesitant.

"I saw her looking down from the window up on the second floor. Dark, pretty, that her?"

"You saw her looking out a window, so what?" His irritation was evident by the way his eyes grew darker, more fixed.

"She looked like she was afraid you might come back."

"You're reading a lot into it, John Henry. Maybe she was afraid I wouldn't come back. You ever think of that?"

"I think maybe you went there to question her. I think you tried. But I think she got to you in a way you hadn't counted on. I think you paid her and she took you up to her room and, somewhere along the way, she became afraid of you."

His entire body stiffened like he had been struck a blow; his jaw muscles knotted and his hands clenched so hard the glass shattered in it. "You think I . . . ?" He started to say something more, then the words retreated into his throat. He had a lot of anger he was trying to keep in check. It took a couple of seconds for him to say what he wanted to say. "I didn't hurt her, if that's what you're thinking. It wasn't like what you think. If she's afraid of me, it's not because I hurt her or laid a hand to her." He grudgingly measured out his words like they were the last words he was ever going to speak. Droplets of blood fell from his cut hand.

"I'm not judging you," Cole said. "But what would it hurt for me to try talking to her this time?"

"What is it you want, exactly, John Henry?"

"I need you to back me up when I take on Charley and his bunch."

"I'm not a *pistolero*, or did you forget that?"

"I've seen your work, Torres, it'll do."

"I'm a federal lawman," he said.

"Then take off the badge and put it away for now, if it will make you feel any better."

"It won't."

"Do we have a deal?"

"I don't make deals, John Henry. You want to go ask that chippy what she knows, see if she'll talk to you, that's fine with me. I ain't asking you to."

"And if I run into Charley and his bunch on the way?"

"Then they better be armed and ready for a fight."

"That's all I needed to know. Let's go."

Miguel looked around the room once more. "At the rate you're going, John Henry, Deadwood's going to end up a ghost town."

"That might not be the worst thing that could happen to it, Miguel."

"Probably not," he said, and stepped past the dead men and out into the storm.

Chapter Thirty-Five

"Lucky for you," Miguel Torres said, as he and John Henry Cole trudged through the deep drifts on their way to the bagnio called The Miners' Retreat.

"How am I lucky?" Cole asked, glad to have the protection of the big curly coat. It was difficult to see more than ten feet in front of them, the way the wind was blowing snow.

"Lucky this storm came along when it did," Miguel added. "It's kept Charley and his crowd at bay, holed up over there in the Lucky Strike. I don't know what they'll do once they run out of whiskey and lies to tell each other. Die of boredom, I guess."

It was true, the storm had been a fortunate turn of events in Cole's favor. *About time*, he thought.

They walked with their heads bowed to the wind. The snow was drifted waist-deep in some places. For the second time since Cole had arrived, Deadwood appeared peaceful.

Miguel didn't bother to knock on the front door of the cat-house. He simply went inside. Cole kicked as much snow off his boots as was possible before following him in. They found themselves standing in a parlor. A mahogany settee with crushed red velvet upholstery stood against one wall. Against the facing wall there was a horsehair divan with a black fringe border wide enough for two people to sit on. There were glass lamps and blue drapes and a coat rack.

"It's where the women come to get selected," Torres stated matter-of-factly as they stood in the room.

"You seem to know a lot about it."

He tossed Cole a hard look. A little bell above the door had tinkled their arrival and a short, plump woman entered the room from behind a curtained archway. "Well, you boys must have a powerful itch, to hoof out on a day like this," she said. She had rouged cheeks and a mole near the side of her mouth. Her platinum hair was done in sausage curls and she wore a bone corset and pantaloons and long purple stockings. "They call me Big Annie." Then she stared at Miguel. "Ain't I seen you here before?"

"We come to see Josephine," Torres said without fanfare.

"Little Jo," the woman said. "Sorry, gents, she's laid up with the monthlies. I got other gals, though. And with it being a real slow day on account of this weather, why, you can take your pick. Let's see, there's Hettie, and Doreen, and Slo Foot Sue, except Sue's got a bad tooth that's been troubling her and ain't in the best of moods, if you know what I mean. Getting rode by a man when your wisdom tooth is aching ain't exactly something a girl looks forward to."

"We came to see Jo," Miguel repeated.

"Mister, I told you, Jo is out of commission for a few days." The woman half scolded, but Miguel was a single-minded man who didn't have much patience.

"We just want to talk to her, is all," Cole interjected.

She looked at Cole. "Talk to her?"

"Yeah."

"You trudged through them snowdrifts just to talk to a whore? You ain't even wanting to ride one?"

"You mind telling me which room she's in?" Cole asked.

"It'll cost you," the woman said, "talk will."

"How much?"

"Say, two dollars."

Cole was broke. He had given Suzanne Logan the last of his money. "Pay her, Miguel," he said.

Instead, Miguel showed her his badge. "You see this?" he said, stepping close to the madam. "I'm a federal lawman, and this is considered official business."

BILL BROOKS

"Mister, I don't care if you're the king of Siam and you're here to hunt turkeys, it'll still cost you two dollars, you want to talk to Jo."

"Pay her, Miguel. Let's get this over with," Cole said.

"I could arrest you and take you to Cheyenne," Miguel told the woman. "How would you like to ride all the way to Cheyenne chained to the floor of a stagecoach?"

She held out her hand. "You want to arrest me, go ahead. That, or pay the two dollars."

Miguel looked at Cole.

"It's why we came," Cole said, "to talk to her."

Miguel reached inside his shirt pocket and found the money and handed her $2.

"You both want to talk to her?" the woman asked.

"No, just me," Cole said.

"She's the third door down on your right, top of the stairs," the woman said. "I'd knock first."

"I'll wait here, if you don't mind," Miguel said, placing his flat stare on the woman. He was still a little put out by the demand of payment just to talk to a woman.

"No, hon, I don't mind at all. Fact is, you change your mind, I'll be right back there the other side of that curtain," she said, offering a wink that Miguel ignored. "Big Annie ain't too old nor too tired to go to the races." Miguel ignored the comment.

"I'll go up and talk to her and see what I can find out about Robertito," Cole said, ascending the stairs.

"Yeah, I'll just sit here and cool my heels," Miguel said, pulling his tobacco out to make himself a cigarette.

Cole knocked on the door and a soft voice on the other side asked who it was. Cole told her he wanted to talk to her. She said she wasn't feeling well and that Big Annie must have made a mistake, sending him up. "I ain't up to taking care of customers," she said.

"I'm not a customer."

She opened the door a crack and peered through it. "Then who are you?"

"Just someone that wants to ask you a few questions about a friend of mine." She was attractive with dark, alert eyes and dark skin. Young. Cole guessed her to be Indian, with maybe a little Mexican blood mixed in. "Big Annie said it was all right that we just talk."

She looked uncertain, but then opened the door wider and allowed Cole into the room. It was a small, spare room with a bed, a vanity, and an oval mirror framed in walnut. The mirror was cracked. There was the scent of crushed flowers in the air. She shuffled over and sat on the edge of the bed, and, when she did, the iron springs creaked. She was wearing a long cotton shift and her hair was black and straight and long. She had small brown feet showing below the hem of the shift. "What is it you want to ask me?"

Cole noticed the traces of blunted speech common to Indians when they spoke the white man's language. He figured maybe she was Sioux or Cheyenne. She looked a little hungry, thin, like lots of working girls he'd seen. Most of the time, it was the whiskey and hard life they led that kept them thin and hungry. For some, it was the opium they smoked in the Chinese dens that kept them emaciated. Then, when the whiskey and dope no longer worked, they turned to poison, and that always worked. She was young and pretty, but he could already see the slow death in her eyes. "I want to ask you about a man, an old friend of mine."

"Who?" She avoided his gaze, choosing instead to stare down at her bare feet.

"His name is Robertito Torres."

She looked up suddenly. Cole saw the light of recognition knot the edges of her mouth. "No, mister, I don't know any Robertito."

"I think you do."

She went back to staring at her feet, like a child that had just been scolded. "I'm not feeling too good," she whispered, holding herself with those thin arms. "It's that time, you know."

"Look," Cole said, standing by the door, not wanting to pose a threat to her, "I just want to know what happened to Robertito Torres, that's all. I'm not looking to hurt anybody or cause you any trouble."

She still didn't look up. Her black coarse hair fell straight down over her face. "I don't know this Robertito," she repeated.

"You sent his things home to his family. You took the trouble to do that much. I figure you must have cared about him to do that."

She swallowed back emotion that was trying to lose itself from some place deep within her. "So what if maybe I did?"

"It was a right thing to do. It was a kindness on your part." She rocked back and forth, holding herself. "The problem is, no one knows exactly what happened to him, because you didn't include a note. His mother is grieving for her youngest boy and she doesn't even know what became of him."

She bit her lower lip, trying hard to keep from saying more.

Cole went over and stood in front of her and waited until she looked up. "Josephine," he said, "you did a good thing, sending his belongings home to his mother. It just wasn't everything that needed to be done. You can understand that, can't you? You've gone this far. Why not just tell me the rest and put it behind you?"

"You don't understand," she said.

"What?"

"If they know I told you, I could end up like them other girls . . . the ones that got killed."

"No one has to know but me and you." Cole wanted to reassure her. "You loved Robertito, didn't you?"

Her chin trembled and she blinked several times, trying to hold back the tears. "He said he was going to marry me," she murmured. "He said soon's he could clear up his problems with his gold claim, we were going to get married and go away. . . ."

"How'd he die, Jo?" As he said it, Cole placed a hand on her shoulder.

"Them men . . . he had the trouble with . . . over his gold claim," she stammered. "They . . . killed him." She rocked back and forth, fighting the emotion of loss and fear. "I thought he was going to . . . take me away from here. I thought it was my chance to be something more than somebody's damn' whore. Robertito . . . I called him Bobby . . . he said he loved me. He said he didn't want me with other men no more. . . ."

"How did they kill him, Josephine?"

Her trembling hands came up to her face, the fingers trying desperately to wipe back the tears. Cole put her age at sixteen. "That man . . . that Johnny Logan." She was forcing the words out. "He came here one night and he said that he was arresting Bobby for trespassing. Him and Bobby got into an argument . . . that lawman hit Bobby with his pistol and knocked him down. I tried to get him off Bobby, but he hit me, too. Then Bobby tried to stop him from hitting me and Bobby's face was bleeding from where that lawman hit him. Bobby wasn't no match for that Johnny Logan. . . ."

"So Johnny arrested Bobby. Then what?"

She sniffed, her hand brushing under her nose. "Then I don't see Bobby no more, except the next day when I heard that someone had found him in an alley with his head broken in. By the time I could get down to see him, they already got him over at that man who fixes up dead people before they bury them. . . ." Her words broke under the sobs again.

Cole walked over to the water basin and poured some water over a small hand towel and wrung it out, went back, and wiped her face with it. She held his hands as he tried to ease her pain. "Take your time, Josephine."

She looked at Cole, really looked at him for the first time, and all the hurt trapped within those dark obsidian eyes penetrated his soul. "That man . . . the one who took care of Bobby . . . cleaned him up and put a clean shirt on him," she said, trembling. "He combed Bobby's hair wrong. Bobby never combed his hair like that man had it. I couldn't hardly believe it was even him when I saw him there in that box. He didn't even look real to me. I touched his hands and his face, and they didn't feel real to me, either. They were cold and hard, and it gave me a bad feeling, touching him like that, and I had to run away from there."

"Where did they bury him, Jo?" Cole asked as gently as he knew how.

"Up on that hill, with them other dead people," she replied. "I didn't go up there until later. One, two weeks, maybe. The grass was already beginning to grow again. I didn't even know if it was the right place."

"I'm sorry this had to happen to you."

She shook her head as though still not able to accept it. "I thought we was going to leave this place," she said, "Bobby and me. I don't know what I'm going to do now. Bobby, he didn't want me doing this. Most men don't care."

"Yeah."

"I guess they don't want someone to get something decent from life, they just kill them, that's all . . ." She broke off.

"Do you have people somewhere you could go live with?"

Her cheeks were stained with her sorrow and bitterness. "No, I don't have no one. My people are all gone from around here." She didn't elaborate where her people had gone, whether she meant they had died or simply left, or the circumstances of how she had come to prostitute herself in a Deadwood whorehouse at such a young age.

"I know it sounds a little late, but is there anything I can do?"

"No. There's nothing nobody can do. Just don't tell them men who killed Bobby what I said, OK? I don't want no more trouble. This ain't no kind of life, mister, but it's all the life I got."

"I won't tell them."

She nodded her head.

Cole turned to go, but there was one last thing he wanted to ask her. "Is Josephine your real name?"

She shook her head, a small light of something remembered coming into her eyes. "No, it's a name Big Annie gave me 'cause it sounded more like a white girl's name. Big Annie said some of the men wouldn't pay as much for an Indian as they would for a white girl. She made me change it to Josephine. She said it was a name that'd remind men of their sweethearts."

"What was it before?"

"Blue Water Dancing," she said.

"It's a nice name."

"My grandmother gave it to me."

"Maybe someday you will meet another man like Bobby."

"Maybe."

"And maybe he will call you by your real name."

She offered a weak smile. "I almost forgot my name," she said shyly. "Nobody ever calls me that any more."

"It's too pretty to forget," Cole said.

She shrugged. "Living like this, it don't give a girl much hope of having pretty things. Maybe, someday, I'll save a little money and go see my people. They went off to Canada. I'd like to see my grandmother again."

"Blue Water Dancing," Cole said.

She looked at him, her eyes full of curiosity now.

"You shouldn't forget."

Chapter Thirty-Six

Miguel Torres was checking the heel on his right boot when Cole came down the stairs from Josephine's room. The heel was run-down, as were the soles of his boots. He looked up.

"Well, did you do any good up there?" he asked, lowering his foot to the floor.

It struck Cole that, if Torres had paid for that child's services, he wasn't quite the man he'd thought him to be. "Tell me something, Miguel?"

His eyes narrowed. "You want to know did I buy her?"

"Yeah."

His nostrils flared. "No, I didn't buy her. I bought her some whiskey and we talked and she tried to get me to go upstairs with her and I did. But I didn't pay her for what you're thinking."

Cole didn't know whether to believe him or not. A man like Miguel, not accustomed to women, maybe he had paid her and just didn't want to admit to it. "I can see where a man might be tempted. Given the right circumstances, I can understand a man paying her."

He stood up, settled his battered sombrero on his head. "That what you think, that I went to bed with a child like that?"

Cole knew then he hadn't. "No, I just thought, if you had, it might have complicated things a little."

"You're a damn' suspicious man," he said, his jaw working into a knot.

"She told me some things about Robertito. But maybe we'd better take it outside." He wasn't sure who might be listening on the other side of the curtain where Big Annie had appeared from earlier.

They stepped back out into the storm that hadn't slowed at all. The winds whipped gusts of snow down the streets and plastered it to the sides of buildings and support posts and piled it deep in front of doorways.

"Where to?" Torres asked.

"Some place private."

Miguel scrunched his hat down a little more on his head to keep the wind from blowing it away. Cole did the same. "Some place private's going to be a little hard for you, isn't it?" he asked Cole as they trudged down the street. "What with half the town wanting to arrest you."

"I know a place that might work."

He was silent, just walking alongside Cole until they reached the old man's stable. "In here."

"You want to hold court in a barn?"

"Why not? It's at least out of the weather."

Toole was out cold, lying on a bed of straw, a bottle lying near his outstretched hand.

"Who's that?" Torres asked.

"Name's Toole. He owns the place."

"You reckon he'd mind if we shared his bottle?" Torres said, bending and picking up the liquor bottle. He held it up to check how much was remaining. "Two, three good swallows yet," he said, holding the bottle out to Cole.

"No, thanks."

Torres didn't bother to make a second offer but instead finished it off in one long pull, his Adam's apple bobbing up and down. "So, what'd she tell you?" he asked, when he had finished off the old man's liquor and tossed the bottle aside.

"She told me what happened to Robertito." Cole was careful to watch the reaction in Miguel's eyes while he repeated what he'd heard. Miguel already was sure that Robertito was dead, but hearing it said caused his eyes to narrow and his shoulders to slump.

"She say who it was killed him?"

"She didn't know for certain."

"Then you wasted your time."

Cole then told Miguel about Johnny Logan's arresting Robertito, and how the next day he was found in an alley with his skull caved in. He told him the part, too, about Josephine having gone to see him at the undertaker's, and that it was she who had sent his belongings home.

"Well, it was damn' civil of her, don't you think?" he said sarcastically.

"Hold on, Miguel. Robertito was going to marry her. She loved him."

He snorted his disgust. "I don't want to hear that shit. You seen what she was. My brother wasn't going to marry a damn' who- . . . !"

Cole came up close to him and put his hand on his chest. "Don't! Don't say it!"

Miguel jerked back, surprised that Cole had challenged him. "What the hell's got into you?"

"She's maybe all of sixteen years old and she fell in love with your brother, who had promised to marry her and take her out of the life she's living. She had the common decency to send his belongings home. She didn't have to take the trouble. So don't say what you were going to say about her, not in front of me, Miguel. Not in front of me."

It was a long moment of waiting. Finally he turned away and walked to the front of the barn, where the doors allowed a crack of dull light in from the outside. A long finger of snow lay along the hard-packed dirt floor. "She say where Robertito was buried?" he asked with his back to Cole.

"Up on Mount Moriah, at the little cemetery." Miguel's hands opened and closed several times. "She said Robertito had some troubles with his claim. The same thing you heard . . . he'd had some sort of dispute."

"You think it had something to do with the Englishman?"

"I can't say for certain, but if what I've heard is true, that he claims to own a good part of that country north of here and has several mining claims already up there, then it might be a place a man would want to look for gold. And maybe Robertito and his partner did just that."

"How could the Englishman own land that belongs to the Sioux?" Miguel asked.

"That's a good question, Deputy. But who's to stop him, who's to throw him off the land? Think about it."

"Those two you killed the other day, his men," Torres said, "maybe they were the ones, maybe they had a hand in killing Robertito."

"It's real possible, Miguel."

"Only one god-damn' way to find out."

"Yeah, I was thinking the same thing."

"You want to go take care of Charley Coffey and his bunch first?" Miguel asked, still with his back to Cole. He looked dark and menacing, standing there in the unlit building with the single blade of winter light knifing through the crack in the doors.

"Well, as much as we both want to head up there to Stevens's place, we wouldn't get far in this storm."

"No, we wouldn't get a mile," he agreed.

"Then let's walk down the street and see if we can find Charley."

"Yeah, let's."

Chapter Thirty-Seven

They pushed their way through the snowdrifts and the bone-chilling winds on a direct line to the Lucky Strike. There was something fearsome in it, the way they were going about taking on Charley and his bunch and whoever else decided to get in the way. It was a feeling Cole hadn't had in a long time. He didn't know exactly how to explain it, the coldness that took over his thinking, the little extra with which his heart was beating because he knew that he was walking into a fight. His mind was fixed on just that one event, the fight he knew was up ahead waiting for them, and everything else was forgotten. All he could think about was doing what he knew he had to do, and nothing else was of consequence. That was the way he was feeling, and, if he had to guess, he'd say that was the way Miguel Torres was feeling, too.

They didn't talk or discuss it beyond the decision they'd made before they left the old man's stable. Miguel had thumbed a fresh cartridge into his carbine and checked the loads in the Peacemaker Colt he had taken off the stage robber. Cole changed loads in both his pistols, then placed them in the pockets of the curly coat so he could reach them easily. The wind bit their faces and snapped at their clothes and tried to take their hats. But none of that seemed to matter, because as cold as the mind tends to become in a fighting situation, the blood feels like it's running hot in your veins. They reached the Lucky Strike, exchanged glances, and went in prepared to do what they had come for.

There were a few of the town's citizens, mostly miners, sitting around, but overall the place was quiet. Those sitting around looked up when Miguel and Cole stepped into the room. The small talk came to an end; someone coughed. "I'm looking for Charley Coffey," Cole said.

No one said anything for a moment. Then Harve, the barman, stepped out of the shadows from behind the bar. The swelling around his eyes from the fight he and Red had had gave him the look of an Oriental. "Coffey's gone," he said.

"Where?" Cole asked.

Harve placed the palms of his hands atop the bar, looked from Cole to Torres then back to Cole.

"Where?" Cole asked again.

Harve shrugged.

Miguel crossed the room and took hold of Harve's shirt front and nearly pulled him over the top of the bar. "He asked you a question, mister!" he growled.

"I don't . . . know," Harve stammered.

"God damn you don't!" Miguel said. "And you better be faster with an answer than I am with this Peacemaker." Miguel showed him just enough of the big pistol to get his attention. Cole kept an eye on the others in the room, in case there were any who thought they had a reason to get involved. No one moved. Miguel put his face up close to that of Harve's, and Harve tried to close his eyes, but was having difficulty because of the swelling. "I bet it'd hurt like hell I was to punch you in that face of yours," Miguel threatened.

"Please don't do . . . that," Harve begged.

Cole noticed Red, Harve's partner, standing there behind the bar, his hands hanging at his sides. He didn't seem to be in a fighting mood, watching the way Torres was handling Harve. Miguel looked like he was going to do it, hit Harve in his tender face, when Cole stopped him by asking Harve: "Then where's Leo?"

Harve shifted his swollen eyes toward the back, where Leo's office was.

"Keep him and these others out here while I pay Leo a visit," Cole told Torres. "I'll get Leo to tell me what Harve says he doesn't know. I come back without an answer, you can go ahead and bust him in the face."

Harve grunted, but Miguel held him in a bulldog grip, pulled halfway over the bar top, his toes barely touching the floor.

Cole didn't bother to knock on Leo's door before he went in. He had a chippy kneeling before him, his head back, his eyes closed against the pleasure she was giving him. "Leave off with that," Cole ordered. They both jumped.

"What the hell . . . ?" Leo started to protest, but Cole showed him the self-cocker.

"Go on, lady, find something else to do," Cole told her. She looked grateful and slid out of the room, closing the door behind her. Leo sat there, sputtering and trying to button up his front. "Leave it be," Cole said. Leo's hands stopped. "Time for the truth, Leo."

He looked at Cole, his piggish eyes full of anger and fear. "Truth about what?" he squealed, his face flushed.

"Everything, Leo. Start with the reasons you had those girls murdered, then go on to the part about where Charley Coffey is hiding."

"You don't know . . . what you're . . . saying," he stammered.

Cole thumbed back the hammer on the Remington. "Christ, Leo, it would be so damned easy to kill you, I have to fight the urge to keep from doing it." The piggish eyes shifted to the pistol in Cole's hand. "Only thing is, I want to do it slow, maybe shoot you in the legs first. What do you think that would be like, getting shot in the legs, Leo?"

Leo lost most of his color when Cole said the part about shooting him in the legs; the flesh around his neck and jowls was ashen gray as the winter sky; his face was a sheen of sweat, and the thin strands of his oily hair couldn't hide the glisten of his scalp. "You . . . can't do . . . this, Cole. It'd be murder."

"You think I give a damn what anyone in this town would call it, Leo? Do you want to know who's backing my play out there in your bar right now? A deputy U.S. marshal. Do I look like a man that's worried about being charged with murder?"

"You can't do this . . ."

Cole put the front blade of the self-cocker just under the sag of neck that spilled down from Leo's chin. "Go ahead, Leo, tell me again how I can't do this."

He swallowed hard enough that the flab of neck pushed against the barrel of Cole's pistol. "It wasn't just me . . ." he muttered.

"Go on."

"It was . . . Johnny who did it . . . he's the one that killed them."

"But you ordered it done."

He was trying to hold the bile down, choking on it, tasting it. He swallowed two or three times, and every time he did, the barrel of Cole's gun moved under the bobbing of his Adam's apple. "OK . . . all right!" he cried, throwing up his hands.

"You had Johnny kill those women because you didn't want the competition from Liddy's operation, is that it, Leo?" His eyes rolled until they showed white. "Wasn't there enough lonely miners to go around? You had to get all the trade, cut everyone else out?"

He snuffled, a thin line of mucous leaking from his right nostril. "She didn't . . . go along with the . . . operation. She wouldn't pay up . . . it was the principle of the . . . thing."

"Principle!" Cole was having a hard time holding in his anger. "You had those women killed for something as little as that?" Leo nodded again, unable to speak because the bile was right there in his throat, and, if he tried to say anything, it was all going to erupt out of him. "I don't get it, Leo. Why go after the women? Why not just kill Liddy instead? If you wanted her out of business, why not just take her out?"

He was shaking now, shaking and sweating and leaking through his nose. "He wouldn't let me . . ." he managed to mumble.

"Who wouldn't let you?"

"Stevens!" he blurted. "He wouldn't let me have Johnny . . . do her."

Cole felt he had finally got the truth. "Tell me exactly how he fits into this, Leo." He shoved the front sight of the self-cocker a little harder into the doughy flesh. Leo was clamping his jaws shut, trying to keep from losing his breakfast all over his gaiters. "We had a deal . . . I run things around here . . . he controls most of the big mining claims. He said between the two of us . . . we could control it all."

"He was already a rich man, Leo. Why bother?"

Leo swallowed again, like he couldn't get enough air. "It ain't . . . about money with him. It's the . . . power."

"So you supplied the guns and he supplied what, Leo, the brains?"

"Yeah . . . something . . . like that."

"Until Stevens came along with his schemes and money, you were just nickel-and-dimeing it, that the way it was, Leo?"

He nodded his head. "Nickel-and-dimeing it . . . that's right."

"I still don't get murdering the women. Why didn't Stevens just let you kill Liddy and be done with it? Why go to all that trouble to try to scare her off?" Leo was having a hard time coming up with enough words. "Let me guess." Cole was losing patience. "Stevens was in love with her, that's why he wouldn't let you kill her?"

"Not just . . . that." Leo groaned.

"What else?"

"She's his sis-sister, you know . . . they're related for Christ's sake. Jeezus . . . can you quit poking me in the neck with that?"

Cole held the barrel against his soft flesh while the revelation sank in. It was a big fact Liddy had forgotten to mention in their conversations both in and out of bed. The whole thought of it was doing a slow dance in Cole's head. "I should kill you for lying, Leo."

"Honest to Christ . . . Cole, it's the truth!"

Cole wanted to close his eyes and pull the trigger and feel Leo slide away from his gun. "I'm going out there, to Stevens's place, Leo. And when I've finished my business, I'm coming back here. You be ready to ride the stage with me back to Cheyenne to stand trial for the murders of those girls. You try running, I'll hunt you down and kill you myself. One way or the other, you're going to pay the check for this." Cole let down the hammer and took the pistol away from Leo's neck. A red mark showed against the doughy flesh where he had pressed it with the barrel. "Remember, Leo, what I said about trying to run."

As Cole turned toward the door, Leo was busy, bent over a spittoon. Cole stepped back out into the bar, where Miguel was still holding Harve by his shirt.

"What's up?" Miguel Torres asked.

"You can turn him loose now," Cole said.

Harve staggered backward after Miguel released him. As the two looked at each other, a sharp explosion sounded from behind the door to Leo's office. Miguel started to go back, but Cole stopped him. "What the hell's going on, John Henry?"

"I think Leo just paid his bill."

"For what?"

"His sins."

Miguel walked over to the front doors, looked out. "What's the next move?"

"Soon as this weather lets up, we pay a visit to Winston Stevens."

"Well, this must be your lucky day, then," Miguel said. "It just stopped snowing."

Chapter Thirty-Eight

They trudged back down to the livery. The old man was awake, repairing a harness with the help of a rusty awl and a bottle of whiskey. He looked up when he saw them walking through the shaft of gray light that filtered through the doors. Hay dust danced in the light.

"We need a couple of horses," Cole said.

Toole looked at Miguel, then at Cole. "You going up to see Liddy?" His eyes were rimmed red and his hands had been shaking as he tried to work an awl through the leather strapping of the harness.

"Not today, Toole."

"Who's 'at you got with you?" He switched his gaze from Cole to Miguel.

Before Cole could answer, Miguel told him who he was. Toole grunted the words—"Deputy U.S. marshal."—like they were bitter seeds in his mouth.

"How about getting our horses?" Cole suggested.

The old man coughed, laid the harness aside, and stood. "You want that same buckskin?"

Cole nodded.

Ten minutes later, Toole had both horses saddled.

"Eight dollars fer the pair, you don't mind," he said, holding the reins in one hand, extending his other.

"Miguel?" Cole said.

Torres looked unhappy at the request for more money but dug down deep into his pockets. "I'll want a receipt," he told Toole.

"Receipt?" the old man responded. "What the hell I look like, a bank?"

"I don't care how you do it," Miguel stated flatly, "but make me a receipt."

Toole grumbled, searched through an old wooden box he had in the corner, and found a pencil. He rummaged some more, then looked up. "I don't have a damn' piece of paper to write on. What the hell am I supposed to write you a receipt on?"

Cole took the diary out of his pocket, found a blank page, and tore it out. "Write it on this."

"Two horses, eight dollars . . ." Toole mumbled as he made the marks on the paper. When he finished, he handed it to Miguel. "There's your damn' receipt."

Miguel folded it and carefully placed it in his pocket. "The government is real particular about deputies keeping good books," he said. "A lawman that don't keep his books is just a man waiting to go to the poorhouse."

"Well, we wouldn't want that, now, would we?" Toole asked, taking a pull at his bottle, clearly put out for the extra effort he had had to make to rent the horses.

"Be glad, old man, that I didn't just confiscate these horses from you," Miguel said.

Toole spat. "That'd be the day."

"Let's go, Miguel," Cole said, walking the buckskin toward the doors.

"He's a feisty son-of-a-bitch," Miguel said as they started riding out of town.

"He's an old man with old memories," Cole said. "He probably got locked up a few times when he was a cowboy and never got over the experience."

Miguel didn't reply, but, instead, looped his reins over the horn of his saddle and made himself a smoke. "You want one?" he asked, holding out his makings when he had finished.

"No, I'd just as soon keep my fingers warm inside my pockets."

They took the north road that wound up through the hills that were now surrendered to the snow and boughs of trees that wore white blankets. The land looked clean and untouched. The heavy snow had given the Black Hills an endless beauty, vast and lonely, as if a man riding into it would be swallowed by it and never found again. The horses chuffed steam through their black, wet nostrils, and ice formed on Cole's mustaches.

Cole found that somehow he wasn't bothered by the weather. Maybe the reason was because he was still thinking about what Leo Loop had told him about Liddy and Winston Stevens. He couldn't stop wondering about the relationship between them. What was she hiding, and why hadn't she trusted him? It was disturbing in a way that seemed to ache down into his bones and forced him to fight the anger of being deceived. The truth, what was it? Maybe Doc had been right in his assessment of Liddy Winslow. She was a woman so alluring that she could get any man to do just about anything for her. Doc had nearly laughed at Cole's reasoning when it came to her. He was right that truth becomes lies, lies become the truth. Cold he could ignore, but not this.

"You look like you swallowed a nail," Miguel said. It was difficult to tell which was cigarette smoke and which vapor coming out of his mouth when he spoke.

"It sort of feels that way, too," Cole answered.

"Tell me . . . we heading into a big fight up there at Stevens's place?"

"It could be. It just depends on how much Charley Coffey wants to prove he's a real gunfighter, and how many others he convinced to throw in with him. Then there's Stevens to consider. I'd say of any of them, he's is the one I'd worry about."

Miguel nodded, smoking his shuck as if Cole was telling him about the new sport of baseball back East.

"Another thing you may want to keep in mind, Miguel. Stevens carries a sporting rifle. I've seen similar when Cody took the Grand Duke of Russia out to hunt buffalo. The damned thing could shoot a thousand yards accurately. My guess would be, Stevens sees it as sport, killing a man. It's another reason I figured he left England and came West. Out here, you can still shoot men for sport. You might want to keep that in mind when we get up there."

Torres grunted, flicked the shuck aside, and watched it sizzle in the snow. "Yeah, well, I've been shot at by some pretty fair men in my time. I reckon some toad from wherever the hell he's from don't worry me too much."

Miguel found a small flask inside his jacket pocket and brought it out. "To hold off the chill," he said, tipping it to his mouth. Then he handed it to Cole who took a small pull, just enough to feel the warmth course through his blood.

The heavy snow made traveling a slow process. The horses broke through chest-deep drifts in places. In other places, Torres and Cole dismounted and gave them a blow.

"Listen, Miguel," Cole said as they neared Stevens's place. "I'm sorry about Robertito."

"Me, too," he said.

"Maybe we'll get all of our questions answered once we have Stevens in hand."

He nodded but didn't say anything. A man that didn't say much when there was much to be said worried Cole. He didn't want Stevens to die the quick, easy death that Miguel probably had in mind for him. He wanted to see the son-of-a-bitch taken to the nearest circuit court and stand trial, then face a hangman. That seemed like a lot more pay back than a fast bullet to the brain. They rode the last mile in silence, Miguel with his thoughts, Cole with his.

"There," Miguel said, checking the reins on the steeldust he was riding.

Cole saw a strand of smoke rising in the distance against the white horizon.

"That must be his place there."

"Let's ride in slow until we get a better lay of the place," Cole said.

Miguel turned his flat gaze on him. "You think I've never done this sort of thing before, John Henry?"

"You want to spread out, or go in like we are?"

Miguel seemed satisfied that Cole had deferred to him on the matter. "Ride maybe fifty yards apart," he said.

Cole angled the buckskin off at a right angle to Miguel until he reached the distance Miguel had suggested. Cole saw Miguel shift the carbine from where he'd been carrying it in front of him. They got to within five hundred yards of the house when the first shots rang out from a stand of ponderosa pines off to their left. The first rounds blew up snow in front of their horses and caused them to buck and kick.

"Up there!" Cole shouted at Miguel, who jerked his mount's head around to face the trees. He charged without even bothering to wait. Cole kicked the flanks of the buckskin and chased after him, levering rounds and firing the Winchester rifle as rapidly as he could. It is hard to hit anything from a running horse, but then like the old Texas Ranger had once told Cole: *What the hell do you have to lose?*

They were perhaps twenty yards from the trees when Miguel's horse took a round in the chest that buckled its forelegs and sent Miguel sailing through the air. Cole pulled up hard on his reins, sliding the buckskin to a stop, and leaped from the saddle just as Miguel hit a snowbank.

Cole fired into the trees from a kneeling position while Miguel scrambled to recover his carbine. His horse kicked its legs and tried to get up, spraying a fountain of red blood across the white snow. Miguel took a hit that spun him around, but he quickly got back up and was firing the carbine, and Cole saw one man pitch forward from the line of trees. Then Cole heard a scream from the direction in which he'd been firing the

Winchester, and right after he saw three dark shapes darting away like frightened deer.

The sudden silence lay all around them, with not even an echo of a gunshot. It was like the earth itself was holding its breath. Miguel was fumbling with the breech of his carbine. He made sure there were no more shooters waiting in the trees before crossing the patch of snow that was now stained with the blood of Miguel's steeldust, and some of his own.

"You hit bad?" Cole asked.

Miguel looked down at the sleeve of his left arm. "Busted my arm," he said. "I can't close my hand and load this damn' Spencer."

"Leave it. Use the Peacemaker."

"Yeah. I hate to leave it, though. It's been a good gun."

"Christ, Miguel, it only shoots one round at a time," Cole said, not understanding why any man would want an old single-shot like that in the first place.

"Maybe so," he said. "But it gives me plenty of time to think what I'm aiming at before I pull the trigger. Not like what I seen you doing with that Winchester, shooting the bark off those trees. Did you even hit anybody?"

"You're a pisser, Miguel. You think you're up to more fight with that arm?"

He pulled back the sleeve and looked at it, then packed some snow around it. It was just a small purple pucker, but Cole could see where the bone had been broken underneath the skin, the way it bumped up at an odd angle. Cole pulled his bandanna off and tied it around Miguel's forearm in an attempt to keep the bone from shifting around too much. Miguel didn't say much while he did that, just looking off with a tensed jaw.

"I think we got one or two of them," Cole said, finishing his patchwork. Miguel looked at it. "The rest scattered up through those trees. I don't think they'll come back."

"Who's that leave, then?" Miguel asked.

"Just Stevens and Charley Coffey and whoever else might be up at the house, as far as I know."

"Their first line of defense," Miguel said, walking toward the trees until they found the man he'd shot, lying face down. He turned him over. The face was smallish, the eyes set close together, like a ferret's. There was black under his fingernails. Then they walked through the trees until they found the other one, the one Cole had hit. Cole found a bottle of whiskey in his coat and $20—probably more money than he had ever made mucking for gold. Well, he didn't have to muck gold any more.

"Miners!" Miguel concluded. "Charley threw up these half-wits as a first line of defense, hoping they'd get lucky and kill us before we ever reached the house."

"Well, now they know."

"What's that?"

"That they should have stayed miners."

"I guess the free drinks and a little cash money blinded their judgment," he said. "It don't take much to buy a man these days."

"It never has."

"You mind helping me make a smoke before we go up to the house?" Miguel asked.

They each had a cigarette. There was no point in hurrying now. It wouldn't help Stevens's and Charley Coffey's nerves any to have to sit up there waiting, wondering if their ambush had succeeded. Miguel glanced over at the downed steeldust. The horse had quit kicking.

"I reckon that old man back at the livery's going to be mad as hell because I got his horse shot," Miguel said.

"Maybe you can give him a government voucher for the animal."

Miguel snorted. "Yeah, right."

"How do you want to do this the rest of the way, Miguel?" Cole asked, remembering the last time he'd tried to give orders.

"Hell, what's wrong with just going up there and knocking on the door?"

"I don't think that's a good idea."

"You don't, huh?"

"You feel free to go ahead, though, if that's what you want to do."

"That sporting rifle," Miguel said, "how far you say that toad could hit a man with it?"

"I'd say four, five hundred yards easy. And if he's real good, maybe a thousand."

Miguel twisted his head in the direction of the house. "What would you say from here to the house? Maybe five hundred yards, maybe six? That'd mean he could kill us without us getting even a step closer than we are right now."

"If he was that good," Cole reminded him.

"Well, one of us has to circle around and go in the back way, then."

"You want to be the one?"

"It don't matter to me."

"No, I'll go, Miguel, you're liable to bleed to death going that far out of your way. Then where would I be?"

"I'm always pulling your shank out of the fire, John Henry," Miguel said with a shake of his head. "But just the same, it's probably a good idea you go this time."

"See you up to the house, Miguel."

"Yeah. Up to the house," he said as Cole broke for the trees.

Chapter Thirty-Nine

John Henry Cole cut through the stand of ponderosa pines, moving at a right angle in order to make an approach to the rear of the house. He saw tracks in the snow of the fleeing men who had tried to ambush them. They were going away from the house, probably toward a remuda of horses they'd kept stashed. Sun broke through the shifting clouds and splayed down through the tall, dark pines. Overhead Cole could see patches of blue sky. Where the sun hit it, the snow sparkled. A large snowshoe hare broke from the cover of a rock and darted away.

It took ten, maybe fifteen minutes for him to cut through the woods and come out the other side, where he could get a clear view of the house. It was a long, low building with a shake roof and a stone chimney. There were several outbuildings and a couple of corrals holding some blooded brood mares whose dark bodies stood in direct contrast to the snow. Their ears pricked up when they caught wind of Cole and they moved around in the corral, coming to stand at the rails nearest his position. He waited until they settled down before moving toward the house.

He let several more minutes pass in case anyone in the house had caught sight of the horses stirring in the corral. Finally the mares lost interest and went back to feeding on the bundles of hay that were scattered on the ground. There was a privy thirty yards from the house. Cole figured to make that his first stop when he left the woods. From the privy, he could make a dash to a small lean-to, and from there to the back wall of the house.

Anyone watching from inside would have a clear shot at him through the window. And if they were even half good . . . he didn't want to think about it.

He rested the Winchester against the trunk of a pine. There was no use carrying it, not if the fighting was going to be up close. He watched the rear windows of the house for another half minute, and, when he didn't see any movement, he broke for the privy. It seemed like it took him forever, crossing that patch of snowy ground. It was like one of the war dreams he'd sometimes have, the ones where he'd be in the middle of a battle and couldn't move, as if caught in quicksand. He ran and ran and finally dived behind the outhouse. No one had taken a shot at him. After a couple of deep breaths, he rubbed snow out of the workings of his self-cocker.

The only thing between him and the house now was the lean-to. He could see a bellows and an anvil and a rack of tools hanging from hooks. Snow was ledged up around the opening. If he could make the lean-to without taking a bullet, he could reach the back of the house. Carrying the self-cocker in his right hand, he reached in his pocket and took out the Colt Thunderer with the short barrel and held it in his left. He wanted all the hardware he could get in making that next run. A gunman in the window would have to be blind not to be able to drop him if he saw him coming.

Cole took a deep breath and broke for the lean-to. Suddenly the glass shattered out of one of the windows and a pistol shot rang out. A bullet whined off the anvil just as Cole dropped in behind the thin plank wall of the lean-to. He heard Charley Coffey's voice, yelling to someone inside the house that he thought he had got Cole. Cole was thinking: *Anybody but you, Charley, could have made a killing shot from that distance.* The problem was that he was trapped behind the plank wall. It was still a good ten, fifteen feet to the back wall of the house, and even Charley wasn't likely to miss a second shot.

Cole could hear Charley yelling for Stevens to come have a look, but there was no reply. Charley was saying how maybe he was already dead and that maybe Mr. Stevens ought to come have a look for himself. Then Cole heard the roar of the sporting rifle as it echoed out into the frozen silence and he knew then why Stevens hadn't come to the back of the house. He had been watching the front, waiting for Miguel to come from that direction.

Cole heard Charley shout: "What the hell!" His voice trailed away from the rear of the house. That's when Cole charged to the back wall and slammed hard against it, just below the window out of which Charley had shot when he'd tried to kill Cole.

"Your man . . ." Cole heard Stevens shout from inside. "Did you get him?"

Charley said: "Sure did. What'd you shoot at out there, Mister Stevens?"

"The ultimate game," Stevens said, his manner cool, assured. "There, can you see him lying in the snow, just about where we had those miners set up in the woods? I waited for just the right moment, Charles . . . that's quite important, waiting for just the right moment."

Cole didn't wait any longer. He crashed through the back door just as Charley was returning to check his own handiwork. He had a dumb, startled look on his face when he saw Cole. He was carrying his pistol down by his leg, not expecting company. He was way too late. The force of Cole's slug carried him halfway across the room and slammed him against the wall. He still had the dumb, startled look on his face when he slid to the floor, his legs out in front of him.

"Charles!" Cole heard Stevens call. "What's going on back there?"

Cole stepped into the main room just as Stevens was turning away from the open window. Smoke was still curling from the blued barrel of his sporting rifle. He turned his eyes down to the expensive gun in Cole's hands.

"Don't!" Cole said.

Some of Stevens's cool manner fell away and his teeth clenched.

"Lay it there on the floor and kick it away."

"It's a two-thousand-dollar custom-made weapon, sir," he protested.

"I don't care if Queen Victoria gave it to you in payment for stud services, lay it down and kick it away."

He did, a pained look on his face as his gaze followed it across the floor.

"Move away from the window."

As soon as he stepped aside, Cole went over and glanced out the shattered maw of glass. Lying there in the snow, at a distance of a hundred and fifty yards, was Miguel Torres, face down. He couldn't see any movement. "It's over, Stevens. Get your coat."

"Whatever are you talking about?"

Cole walked over and slapped him hard across the face with the back of his hand. He staggered back, then Cole slapped him again, and he fell to one knee. "It's not a debate," he said. "Get your coat!"

Stevens was bleeding from the lips and from the nostrils and his smoothly shaven flesh was scarlet where Cole had hit him. He struggled to stand, still wobbly from the blows. His hand reached up to his mouth and came away smeared with his blood. "You killed them?" he said. "All the men I'd posted in the woods?"

"Just the ones that needed it. The others got smart and ran."

Stevens walked in a slow, pained manner to the coat rack and took down a greatcoat and put it on. "What now?" he said.

"Out that way." Cole nodded toward the front door.

They walked the hundred and fifty yards to where Miguel was lying.

"Stand off a little," Cole told Stevens. He waited until Stevens walked off about twenty feet before he rolled Miguel onto his back. Miguel groaned when he did. The bullet had punched a fist-sized hole through him.

Miguel looked up at Cole, coughed. "Reach me my . . . flask . . . would . . . you?"

Cole reached inside his coat, pulled out the metal flask, smeared and sticky with his blood, unscrewed the cap, and handed it to him.

Miguel looked in Stevens's direction. "That the son-of-a-bitch that . . . shot me?"

"Yeah, that's the son-of-a-bitch."

Stevens flinched, but Cole didn't think it was from the cold or from having been slapped a couple of times.

"Ask him, will you?" Miguel said, then coughed.

Cole turned his full attention to Stevens. "He wants to hear you say it."

"What is that, may I ask?"

"He wants you to say that you had a hand in his brother's killing."

Stevens shrugged. "I don't even know this man," he said.

"His name is Miguel Torres and his brother was Robertito Torres and the other man's name was Shag Hargrove. You had Robertito killed because of a gold claim up around here somewhere."

Miguel was sipping the whiskey and coughing up blood and most of what life he had left was staining the snow beneath him. His eyes were a little glazed and he was slipping fast.

"Sorry," Stevens said. "I don't know the man of whom you're speaking." The sad truth for Cole was he believed Stevens probably had not known Robertito Torres, at least not by name. But the rest of it was true—that either he or Charley Coffey had killed Robertito and scared off Shag Hargrove. Cole was willing to bet the bank on that.

"What'd . . . he say?" Miguel sputtered.

Cole looked at Stevens, hard. "Go on, tell the deputy here that you had his brother killed over a claim." It wasn't a request but a flat-out threat on Cole's part.

"Maybe there was a man," Stevens said. "I believe I remember Charley saying something about it."

"There you go, Miguel. We got your man. Robertito's killer. You can rest now."

Miguel's eyes widened as though he'd suddenly thought of something, or seen something. He stiffened. "Killed us . . . both," he muttered. "God-damn toad like . . . that." Then Miguel Torres died much as he had lived, without fanfare. He simply closed his eyes.

Stevens was standing there, shivering, looking on. Cole stood up from the body of the lawman.

"I need to know something," Cole said.

"Well, I guess you are in the position to ask whatever questions you wish," Stevens said in that way that made Cole want to slap him again.

"You and Liddy Winslow," Cole said. "She's your sister?"

He nodded.

"Funny she would lie to me about it."

His right eyebrow arched. "Are you so certain that is what she did . . . lie to you, Mister Cole? Or was it more that she left out certain parts of her story when she was convincing you to do her bidding?"

"I'm not buying it, Stevens."

He smiled with his busted lips. "Well, I suppose a man of your low sensibilities would be blinded by a woman that was far beyond your station. I mean, look at you, a frontiersman!"

Cole didn't say anything. He just crossed the space between them and knocked him down, only this time he didn't slap him.

He hit him and felt his jaw snap. Then he dragged Stevens to his feet, put him on a horse, and prayed he would do something to make Cole kill him before they got back to Deadwood. *Go on, Stevens*, he kept thinking the whole ride back, *make this easy for all of us. Run!*

Chapter Forty

The old man was standing out in front of the livery, chewing his cud and spitting brown rings in the snow. His eyes fixed on Cole and Stevens and the body of Miguel Torres when they pulled up. He wiped a hand across his wet mouth and said: "You not only leave dead men out on the streets, now you're bringing 'em into town."

Toole looked at Stevens's busted lips and nose and saw how the blood had dried on the front of the expensive white shirt. Then he paid closer attention to Torres. "That the lawman?"

"It is."

The old man took notice of the stud. "Nice horse."

"You want to do me a favor?" Cole asked the old livery man.

"What's 'at?"

"Take Mister Stevens over and lock him up in that little log dungeon Johnny Logan kept out back of his office."

"You want me to lock up this rich man?" Toole asked, showing enough of a grin that some of his remaining teeth stuck out like old corn kernels.

"Yeah, that's what I'd like you to do."

"What about him?" Toole asked, pointing toward Miguel Torres.

"I'll take care of him myself."

"You leave anybody alive back up in them hills, Cole?"

"A few."

"I wisht I'd been there. Damned if I don't."

"How about it? You want to take Stevens over to the jail and lock him up?"

"Did somebody elect me to office?" he asked, scratching a face that hadn't seen a razor in a long time.

"You want, I'll vote for you."

He shrugged. "Might not hurt if I had some authority."

"Maybe if you were to take Johnny's job, become the new constable, how would that be?"

"I reckon that'd be all right," he said, his eyes glittering with the prospect.

"OK," Cole said. He searched through Miguel Torres's pockets until he found his badge. "I'm appointing you the new town constable."

Toole rolled his eyes. "Just like that? I don't have to apply or nothing?"

"Look around. You see anybody else rushing to take the job?"

"'At's about right," he said, swiping the badge alongside his pant leg to polish it. "Anybody that'd have the nerve or was crazy enough for the job is either dead, or has left town. The last of 'em left just this morning . . . Doc Holiday. Seen him and Kate boarding the stage just before the snow got really bad."

"Raise your right hand," Cole said. When Toole did, he said: "You're hired."

Toole jerked his head, took the badge, and pinned it to his frayed coat. "How's it look?" he asked, when he got it pinned on just right.

"Looks like they better get the women and children off the streets."

His grin touched both ears. "Come along, Mister Stevens," Toole said, taking the reins of the man's horse.

"Oh, another thing I forgot to mention!" Cole called after him.

He stopped, turned around, and said: "What's 'at?"

"As an officer of the court, you have the right to confiscate that horse as evidence. And if they hang Stevens here, you can make a claim to the horse and keep him."

Toole squinted. "You're tugging my peaches," he said.

"Look at it this way, Toole. Being the only damn' law there is around here, who's going to stop you from setting the rules?"

"'At's true." He nodded. "You're a pisser, John Henry Cole. I'll give you that."

Cole found the undertaker, a man named Clovemyer, and gave him instructions for Miguel's burial. He asked him to buy Miguel a new suit and a shirt.

"A man ought to look his best," Clovemyer agreed. "You want paid mourners?"

"No, I don't think Miguel cared much for strangers. But get him a headstone with his name marked on it."

Clovemyer said that, if the ground was frozen, he wouldn't be able to bury Miguel until the spring. "I might have to keep him in the icehouse till the ground thaws," he stated. "Winter's a bad time to die."

"I didn't know there was a good time."

"Huh?"

Cole turned to leave as Clovemyer began stripping the body.

"What about his personal effects, his money belt and rifle and pistol?" Clovemyer pointed at the belt tied around Miguel's waist.

Cole asked how much money was in the belt. Clovemyer opened it and counted out the money. "Nearly four hundred and eighty dollars. Should I take my fee out of this?"

"No. A man pays all his life for the living he does, he shouldn't have to pay for the dying. You take that money over to the Miners' Retreat . . . you know the place?" Clovemyer nodded. "You give the money to a girl name Josephine, tell her it's from Miguel Torres, Bobby's brother. She'll know. Tell her Miguel wanted her to go see her people up in Canada. Tell her that's what the money's for. That and whatever else she needs."

"And his weapons?"

"Sell them if you like, he won't be needing them."

Cole rode up into the hills, following the directions Toole had given him to the cabin. It looked peaceful the way it was nestled in a narrow valley. A curl of black smoke rose from the stone chimney and the long shadows of the pines stretched across the sparkling snow.

Jazzy Sue opened the door and offered Cole a warm greeting, saying how she was happy to see him as she let him into the cabin. Rose rushed to greet him like she was his daughter. "I was worried about you," she said. "I'm glad you came back."

Lydia Winslow sat in a high-backed rocker by the fireplace. She had not moved, but her gaze met Cole's. "John Henry," she said as she stood, smoothing her skirts, then the loose strands of hair around her face. She seemed slightly flushed.

"We need to talk, Liddy."

She blinked like she already knew what he had come for. She looked at the other two women. The room was small, not a place to hold a private conversation.

"I'll get my cloak," she said. "We'll go for a walk." She was wearing a checked shirt and breeches and boots that laced up. She put on a gray woolen capote that draped over her shoulders.

The clouds had lifted and been replaced by a dome of blue sky and a warming sun that seeped through their clothes. The weather had turned surprisingly mild, and it was a welcome relief. Maybe the worst of it really was over, Cole told himself.

They walked a short distance from the cabin. Cole was trying to figure out the best way to ask her about the truth and the lies.

"Tell me," she said, breaking the great silence that surrounded them in that place. "Is it finished?"

"All but one thing," Cole said.

She didn't say anything for a time and they walked in among some pines. The air was thick with their scent. "Winston told you about us," she said.

"Yes."

"Then you know my secrets."

"I know it's damn' confusing. And I sure as hell don't appreciate being lied to."

She turned and put her hand on Cole's wrist. "Don't. Don't accuse me of things you don't fully understand."

"Then explain it."

She sighed and removed her hand. "My mother was once an actress," she said. "In New York. She was quite beautiful, but not very talented. Her beauty earned her parts in plays that she might not otherwise have got. She was smart enough to know it wouldn't always be that way. One evening, a man came to see a play she was acting in. He immediately became smitten with her and began to pursue her. He was very wealthy, very charming, and very attentive to her, sending her rooms full of flowers after each performance. Mother found it impossible to resist him, and in short order he asked her to marry him and return with him to his home in England. She agreed because she'd fallen in love with him, and because she'd become pregnant with me."

The sun collected in her hair as she talked, and they weaved in and out of the light that splintered down through the pines.

"His name was Arthur and he had a small son waiting for him to return. The boy's mother had died giving birth to the boy. I was born shortly after Mother and Arthur arrived in England. So, you see, the timing was good." She had tried to make light of it, but the effort was painful. She moved among the trees, touching them as she talked, lost in a world of memory she had not visited in a long time, judging by the sound of her voice as she recalled the past. "For several years I lived a very charmed life as the daughter of a rich man. We lived in a large house on a bluff that overlooked the Thames. And in the summer we could see the young college men racing their boats through the green water. It was such a happy time for me."

Her voice broke slightly as she stopped long enough to turn and look at Cole. "As I grew into a young woman, my half-brother, Winston, began to prevail upon me for my affections. At first I thought very little of it. It started out as a game we played whenever no one was around. Winston said he was my handsome knight and I was his fair maiden. He would sometimes pretend to rescue me, and then kiss me. And the more we played the game, the more serious he became. After a time, I thought of myself as being in love with him." Her hands trembled as she averted her gaze. "As it turned out, on one occasion when everyone was gone from the house, I allowed myself to be taken by him. It was a house with such large rooms. I remember at one point hearing the hall clock sounding as if it were the heartbeat of an old man beating in the great silence. . . ." Her voice trailed off and a gust of wind swept over a ridge, lifting a tail of snow high in the air.

Cole wasn't sure he wanted to hear any more, but Liddy seemed compelled to tell him everything, as though she had to say the secrets she bore or they would suddenly kill her.

"He came into my room. I was watching the boats on the river. He came up behind me and touched me through the fabric of my dress. . . ." She raised her chin, her eyes staring into Cole's. "I won't say that I didn't like it, I did. I was fourteen, he was nearly twenty. I lived in a land of castles and tales of brave knights who slew dragons for the honor of maidens." She shook her head, biting down into her lower lip. "I had grown to believe that Winston really was my brave knight."

"You don't have to tell me any more," Cole said.

"No. You asked. I will tell you."

Cole found his makings and rolled a cigarette. His hands felt heavy and he seemed to have run out of words to say to her that would make a difference in her pain.

"As soon as it was over," she went on, "I knew what a terrible mistake it had been. The next time Winston approached me,

I tried to deny him. But by then he had already made up his mind that he was no longer going to be my knight. It happened several more times after that. Each time I tried to fight him. I begged mother to take me away, back to America, to New York, the place she'd told me so many wonderful stories about. I saw it as a way out of my situation. At first she refused. But then I told her what had happened. She went to Arthur and he sided with his son. He looked straight at me and said that I was tramping around with the local boys, that Winston was too well bred to have done such a thing. Then he accused Mother of having lied to him about her pregnancy. He said that I was not his child to begin with. . . ."

Cole wondered, as she told him these things, if he hadn't made a mistake in not finishing off Stevens when he'd had the opportunity.

"It broke my mother's heart to have Arthur turn on us, and she immediately left him and returned with me to New York. It ended up costing her life. She contracted tuberculosis from someone on the ship on the voyage over. She died within the year. I was then fifteen years old, alone in a city where orphans slept on the streets and ate other people's garbage to survive. I decided I would never eat garbage or depend on a man for my survival. Look what it had cost my mother. Shortly after, I saw an ad in the papers advertising for young women to go West with a local touring group of actors. At least, that was what the manager in charge called us at first. Later, in the cow towns of Kansas, he called us something else. The fact is, we were called lots of things other than what we were." She gave Cole a weak smile, the pain still there, buried deep, trying to rise to the surface. "The names men have for their whores," she said with a toss of her head. "Chippies, Cyprians, doxies, bawds, brides of the multitudes."

"And fallen angels," Cole said.

Her gaze revealed something tender. "Yes, and fallen angels, lest we forget. Clever names to hide the truth. Do you think it is easer, John Henry, that men call us those names in order to justify their own lust?"

"Maybe so, Liddy," Cole answered, remembering what Doc Holliday had said about truth. "How was he able to find you here?"

"Purely by accident, as far as I know. I had arrived in Deadwood only a few weeks before Winston. I couldn't believe it when I ran into him. He wanted to start up with me again. I told him I would die first." Liddy hesitated, the emotion of it cutting off her words.

"But still you saw him again," Cole said. "That's the part I don't understand."

She took a deep breath. "I have a daughter," she said. "She is back East, attending a Boston finishing school. She is Winston's daughter, a result of his raping me. I did everything within my power to keep her protected, to keep her from finding out the truth of her birthright." Her hair shone rich and red under the blades of sunlight piercing through the tops of the trees. "Winston somehow learned of her. He threatened that, if I did not see him again, he would go to her and tell her the truth about me. *His* version of the truth, whatever that was."

"Why would a man do that to his own daughter?" Cole asked.

"Because he enjoys his own madness."

"So you gave in to him?"

"What choice did I have? Even if I had left Deadwood, he could still find me, or find our daughter and tell her whatever lies he wanted to." Liddy paused. "Her name is Angelique."

"Like in angel."

"Yes, like in angel."

"So to hide the truth from me, you made it sound like he was just someone in your life when the subject came up between us that night?"

"Yes, and I would do it over again if it was to protect my daughter. I would tell whatever lies I had to, do whatever it took, to protect her."

"And you never suspected that Stevens might be behind the killings?"

"No. I knew he was after me, that he wanted me, to control me, to keep me for his own private sickness. But I never suspected he had anything to do with the murders. Did he confess them to you?"

"No, Leo did."

"You have them both?" she asked.

"Leo's dead. I'm taking Stevens back to Cheyenne to stand trial. If the law doesn't hang him, I will."

"Then that's the end of it," she said.

"Yes, I guess so."

"What about us? Have you thought about us, John Henry?"

"I have, Liddy. I've thought about us a lot."

"And what did you conclude?"

"I figure you knew from the beginning that Stevens was behind the killings, Stevens, Leo Loop, and Johnny Logan. You couldn't kill them yourself, so you did the next best thing. You wrote to Ike, asking for his help, and then, to hedge your bet, you offered a reward, enough money to attract men like King Fisher and Kip Caine. Ike, or all of them combined, would even the score and set you free. You never really cared about those murdered women. You wanted Stevens out of the way, and, if it meant that Ike or any of the others got killed, eventually one of them would get Stevens, no matter how many guns he had around him. It was a long-shot gamble, but it paid off for you. In that set-up, where do you figure I fit in? So, what about us? Nothing about us. The job's done and Stevens will no doubt be hanged, if not for killing the women, then for murdering a deputy U.S. marshal in the performance of his duty. I was there. I saw him do it. I heard Miguel Torres's last words. I even know why Miguel had to bring Stevens in. I have some memories I need to put to rest before I can move on. I'm afraid you're one of them."

"I see," she said. "But might there still be a chance for us later, when you've forgotten about those things?"

"Yeah, maybe, but why? I did the job you wanted done."

"I'd like to believe that there's some chance, John Henry."

"Well, I'm catching the morning stage to Cheyenne. Maybe you could lend me the money for a pair of tickets."

She nodded. "It's the least I could do."

"Another thing. You now know that Miguel Torres was murdered in the shoot-out we had with Stevens and Charley Coffey. I told the undertaker I'd come by before I left town and take care of Miguel's bill."

"I'll see to it," she said.

"You think you'll stay here in Deadwood now?"

"I'm not sure. I've been thinking of perhaps going to Boston and see Angelique and maybe find something there . . . teaching, maybe. I've always thought it would be a worthwhile vocation, teaching."

"The pay's not so good."

"Oh, I've a little saved," she said, a slight smile curving her mouth. "Which brings me to the matter of the reward money. You've earned it."

"Just the stage tickets," Cole said, "and Miguel's funeral expenses. The rest you can send to Ike directly."

"Can I ask a kiss of you one last time before you go?"

"I'd be damned disappointed if you didn't."

It was for Cole warm and gentle, the way she kissed him, but it was also a sad kiss as well, and it would stay with him for the entire ride back to Cheyenne and for a long time after that.

Before Cole left, he asked Rose what her plans were. She said Miss Lydia had asked her and Jazzy Sue to go to Boston with her.

"You ever been to Boston?" Cole asked.

"No, Mister Cole, I haven't," she replied. "Do you think I should go?"

"I think you'd like it," Cole said, "but I'm not sure Liddy would be a good influence on you, teach you what you will really need to know. If it doesn't work out for you, just you remember you can always get hold of me through the Ike Kelly Detective Agency in Cheyenne."

"Me and Jazzy Sue have become the best of friends," Rose said, "and, despite what you say, Liddy is nearly like a mother to me."

Cole kissed her on the top of the head. She said: "That ain't hardly a kiss at all." So he kissed her lightly on the lips, and said: "That's all the kiss you'll get from me." She smiled, and hugged him.

Chapter Forty-One

They all rode back to town together, and the three women left John Henry Cole at his hotel. The desk clerk was waiting for him.

"All the shooting going on," he said, "I nearly rented out your room, thinking maybe you'd fallen victim to the violence."

"Why didn't you?"

His mouth broke open until his purple gums showed above his stained teeth. "Hell, so many of my tenants have dropped like flies lately, I'm having trouble filling the vacancies as it is."

"Well, you'll have one more come the morning. I'm catching the stage out."

"Aw, hell," he said.

Cole decided that he would spend his last night in Deadwood in a tub of hot, clean water. He found a bathhouse three doors down from the hotel and ordered a bath. He sank down in the tub, remembering how good it felt and how long it seemed since he'd last had the pleasure of hot water and a bottle of mash whiskey and the peace of being alone.

In the morning, he would be taking Stevens back to Cheyenne. He'd told Toole to have him at the stage depot early and in chains. Cole didn't mind everyone seeing what a rich man looked like in chains. He was a murderer and all his money wasn't going to change that.

It felt good, the bath and whiskey and the rest of it, and knowing he'd survived and broken the case. "Here's to you, Francisco Guzman, wherever your damn' soul is hanging out these days!" he said, lifting a glass to an old friend and an old enemy who in spite of everything he missed just a little. Francisco had kept a little spice in things when he was alive. Men like Francisco Guzman were disappearing fast, and the frontier was going to be a lot less interesting without them. "And to your cousins, who honored you by following you to the grave," he added, taking another pull of the bottle. "Brave damn' men, and honorable ones . . ."

"Jesus, Jack, ya've gone to talkin' to yarself!"

Cole didn't want to believe it, but there she stood. "Calamity," he said. "How'd you find me here?"

"Aw, hell, hon, I'd be able to find ya in the middle of the Atlantic Ocean."

For once she wasn't drunk or indecent. She had on clean clothes, and Cole couldn't swear to it, but it looked like she'd taken some care in washing and fixing her hair as well. "If you came for a loan, Jane, you caught me at the wrong time."

She slid a chair over, turned it around, and sat down on it. "Didn't come fer no loan, Jack."

"A drink?"

She looked at the bottle. "Well, maybe just a little one," she said, holding her thumb and forefinger apart a couple of inches.

"Help yourself."

She took a swallow, then set the bottle back down again.

"You've changed," Cole observed.

She smiled. "Time to get on with my life, Jack. I've mourned Bill long enough. Let the dead rest in peace, that's what I say."

"Sounds like a good plan."

"Going to Denver," she said. "I met me a drummer and he wants to take me to Denver and asked me to be his loving wife."

"You agreed to that?"

"Not yet I ain't. I'll have to see how it washes out, me and him, first. Give it a few weeks, ya know."

"You look happy," Cole said. "Maybe it's the right thing, going to Denver with your drummer friend."

"Ya know the best thing about him, Jack?"

"No."

"He calls me Martha. Says it's a lot prettier than Jane. Ya know how I like to be called Martha."

"It suits you."

"Damned if it don't."

She sat there with a pleased look on her face and didn't say any more until Cole told her that the water was getting cold.

"Well, ya better get out of there before ya catch pneumonia, then," she said.

"What, with you in the room?"

She grinned sheepishly. "Don't hurt to try, does it?"

"Good luck with your drummer, Martha."

"See ya around, Jack." She stood and walked in that stiff way she had, closing the door behind her.

Cole hoped the drummer and Denver would be kind to her. He'd lied to her about the water growing cold. He had just wanted a little more time to himself and a chance to finish the bottle. He thought of the long ride back to Cheyenne and meeting Ike, and what he was going to tell him when he got back. He thought of Liddy, what they had shared with each other, and what they had talked about in their last conversation.

He felt he owed Ike his friendship, just as he owed Liddy her private pain. He thought about it for a long time, until the water did grow cold and the bottle rang on empty. Then he knew what he was going to tell Ike, next to nothing about Deadwood, but he would tell him why Frank Straw had been wearing a dress the day he'd brought him back to Cheyenne in the rain.

THE END

About the Author

Bill Brooks is the author of twenty-three novels of historical and frontier fiction. After a lifetime of working a variety of jobs, from shoe salesman to shipyard worker, Brooks entered the health-care profession where he was in management for sixteen years before turning to his first love—writing. Once he decided to turn his attention to becoming a published writer, Brooks worked several more odd jobs to sustain himself, including wildlife tour guide in Sedona, Arizona, where he lived and became even more enamored with the West of his childhood heroes, Roy Rogers and Gene Autry. Brooks wrote a string of frontier fiction novels, beginning with *The Badmen* (1992) and *Buscadero* (1993), before he attempted something more lyrical and literary in the critically acclaimed: *The Stone Garden: The Epic Life of Billy the Kid* (2002). This was followed in succession by *Pretty Boy: The Epic Life of Pretty Boy Floyd* (2003) and *Bonnie & Clyde: A Love Story* (2005). *The Stone Garden* was named by *Booklist* as one of the top ten Westerns of the decade. After that trio of novels, Brooks was asked to return to frontier fiction by an editor who had moved to a new publisher and he wrote in succession three series for them, beginning with *Law For Hire* (2003), then, *Dakota Lawman* (2005), and finishing up with *The Journey of Jim Glass* (2007). *The Messenger* (Five Star, 2009) was Brooks's twenty-second novel. He now lives in northeast Indiana.